Where Do I Go

Born in north Norfolk, India grew up along its picturesque coastline before leaving to study Cell Biology at Durham University and embark on a career in Marketing. Moving from the tiny towns of East Anglia to the hustle and bustle of the big city made her see the world for all its wonders and faults – it's a big place to try and change yourself, but India wants to give muted societal issues a voice and give scary topics a friendly face. She believes all good ideas come from a spicy Bloody Mary, a niche documentary and overhearing conversations in cafés.

India lives in south-west London with her husband and two young boys, Archie and Raffy. *Where Do I Go from Here?* is her second novel.

Also by India Rigg

Love, Loss and Little White Lies

Where Do I Go From Here?

India Rigg

HODDER

First published in Great Britain in 2023 by Hodder & Stoughton
An Hachette UK company

1

A CIP catalogue record for this title is available from the British Library

Paperback ISBN 978 1 529 38266 2
eBook ISBN 978 1 529 38268 6

Typeset in Plantin by Manipal Technologies Limited

Printed and bound in Great Britain by Clays Ltd, Elcograf S.p.A.

Hodder & Stoughton policy is to use papers that are natural, renewable
and recyclable products and made from wood grown in sustainable forests.
The logging and manufacturing processes are expected to conform to the
environmental regulations of the country of origin.

Hodder & Stoughton Ltd
Carmelite House
50 Victoria Embankment
London EC4Y 0DZ

www.hodder.co.uk

To my dad, thank you for always believing in me.

Before Age Mattered

I

Moira sits opposite me, transfixed to her screens.

I close my mouth, slightly breathless, having spoken my last word with what one can only describe as a little gusto.

It was the sort of speech where, in my mind, the audience is giving me a standing ovation, or at the very least a resounding clap. It's a sore reminder of how many times Luke and I practised this promotion speech together. He would whoop and cheer at me finally saying my piece to the rabid beast in the glass cage, and I would momentarily feel like I was part of a female powerhouse until I remembered that saying anything positive to Moira is like dressing up as a clown at a funeral.

But right now, I'm still basking in the thrill of a perfectly worded speech, clinging to the possibility I may have moved my boss to tears, perhaps wondering if she might even clutch me tight and weepily announce that of course I can have a promotion, I can have anything I want. That *hope* lasts all of two seconds.

'Can you repeat that?' Moira doesn't avert her eyes from the screen, a far cry from Luke's reaction, many moons ago. 'I saw your lips move but I wasn't listening, emails are firing in my inbox faster than you can swipe left at a wedding.' My efforts to capture Moira's attention have been about as successful as asking your partner to throw away the fifty empty loo roll tubes on the side in the bathroom or to put the seat down when he's finished or to stop shaving his balls over the toilet. *Aaah Luke, stop shaving your balls in my brain.*

I take a deep breath, ready to repeat the last five minutes of my Oscar-worthy promotion monologue.

Moira holds her hand up, my breath halting so abruptly it sort of expels itself anyway with a deflated rasp.

'One sec. I need to respond to this *urgent* email.' Moira pushes her glasses up the bridge of her nose and click-clacks furiously on her keyboard. Her nose scrunches and gives a little wiggle, like she's smelt something out of place – a child in the workplace or something equally as jarring to her, and her bottom lip moves fervently from left to right. Almost like she's eating a fantasy croissant on a no-carb day.

I close my mouth, cross my legs and make myself comfortable in the chair opposite. I smile to stop myself snarling.

Moira's teeth are bright white apart from a few flecks of her Sexy Sienna Charlotte Tilbury lipstick which she wears, without fail, every day. *I'll give you this little titbit Seff, you can thank me later. One of my proverbs to live by. Go bold or go home. You're a woman in a man's world – command and demand their attention. And nothing short-circuits a man's brain like lipstick. You want to be powerful in a boardroom? Wear something bold. Have you ever seen a woman of stature wearing some wishy-washy neutral?*

Only every single Kardashian but Moira always knows best.

Suddenly, out of nowhere, she screeches like a deranged banshee who hasn't eaten in, well, forever.

'Elliottttttt!' The tininess reverberates off the glass box we're confined in, and I close my eyes as if the room is about to shatter. Note to self – never shut yourself in a room with a starving, carnivorous creature; it simply cannot end well.

A timid knock at the door ceases the vibrations and brings my eardrums back to ground level.

'Don't fucking knock, I invited you in here. Idiot,' she barks, eyes still glued to the screen.

Elliott pushes the door open and walks in. Moira's office is soundproof, although, based on how much she shouts, she remains totally unaware. He must be as good at lip reading as I am.

'Hi. Erm . . .' *Don't stutter, she hates stuttering.*

'Where's that pitch deck I asked for? I told you it was urgent.' Elliott's doing his best to politely smile but he could be wearing a Ronald McDonald mask and Moira still wouldn't avert her glare from the bright lights of Excel and Outlook – it's like Vegas for workaholics.

'Do you mean the one you briefed in to me just before you met with Seffy? I don't mean to be . . .'

'Don't be belligerent, Elliott. What other one would I be talking about? Yes, that one. Get on with it. Chop-chop.'

She waves him out. Poor guy. This behaviour doesn't faze me. In the Moira-working-world, this is normal.

Moira's not the worst boss by any stretch. She seems to like me, kind of. Or I know how to manage her. I don't really like her, she's not the likeable type. She's crass, demanding and loud, but once you get used to that it's ok. *It's not personal, it's work,* she often says, although more often than not it is personal. Very personal.

I look out of the window into the grey abyss of Canary Wharf. Soulless. Tiny, male, obedient ants scurrying around below.

My eyes flick back to Moira's office. She's a career woman, like me, I guess. Her office is minimalistic at best. The only decoration other than a couple of pot plants (which the office horticultural team tend to) are her papers. Stacks of papers everywhere – it only adds to the busy/important ambience she likes to bathe in. Other managing directors have photos of their families on their desks, smiling gap-toothed children swimming with dolphins in Dubai or drawings of decapitated obese cats that say *Love you Daddy.* These smudged, artist interpretations of what a cat in hell looks like are never going to match Picasso's cubism but I guess you hang them on the wall to remember that you have a family at home that loves you.

'Right.' Moira stops typing and stares at me. 'Where were you?'

I take a deep breath, clasp my hands together and hope to dear God that this is the last time – I'm starting to bore myself. I speak as concisely and as quickly as I can. I don't want another email shot to be fired and distract Moira again.

'I was talking about the business I've won over the last year. The SIERRA capital account was worth three million pounds. I've been working with Matthew in FX sales, and we've nearly secured a new hedge fund mandate as well which is another potential two million in yearly revenue.'

'What you're saying, Seff, is that you deserve the promotion, am I correct? You want me to put you forward? Be your sponsor?'

No one calls me Seff apart from Moira – to mouth the extra syllable takes up too much time. To me, Seff sounds too much like Jeff, which is a name for middle-aged potatoes that walk around in suits from the 1980s.

I swallow.

'Well, yes. I think I deserve it.' *Own your words, Seffy.* This time Luke pops into my head saying something useful as opposed to shaving his balls.

'You know, you *do* deserve it. You work hard, late and you are always extremely busy, which I like.' The B word is like crack to Moira. 'There aren't many women in our line of work, are there? And do you know why that is?'

She pauses, but I know her question is rhetorical. Moira's questions are either commands in disguise or ones which she likes to answer for herself.

'They've got families. They prioritise family, kids over their own success. Subservient to men.'

I remain silent.

'I started to like you more, Seff, when you got divorced. Well, it's on the way. Have they come through yet, your papers?'

I stare at her, barely blinking. Flashes of my past exuberance come to the forefront of my mind – lazy sex in the afternoon, ceviche and white wine on the balcony. Luke. I open my eyes wider, hoping the whistling air con will dry them out.

She doesn't seem to care that boundaries are being crossed because Moira's a woman of no limits. She continues.

'It demonstrated to me that you have an opinion, and you won't let a man rule your life. I like that. Shows strength. I was worried you were going to tell me you were pregnant that day you came in crying. I must be honest: if you were going to start working four days a week, your career here would have been over. Obviously, I wouldn't be able to tell you that because of the legality of the whole thing but we both know that's what would happen. You would become more interested in nursery rhymes than the stock market. All that Hickory Dickory Dock garbage.'

Sometimes I wonder if Moira puts an act on at work to make herself seem tough, but other times, like now, I realise that no, she's just a total bitch. There's no escaping it.

She's really on one of her rants this morning. I wonder what happened in her past to make her so negative about EVERYTHING or if she simply enjoys this stale, corporate life so much she genuinely can't imagine anything that might derail her thrilling opportunities to work until midnight. She's got a thing about being pregnant too; she's never been the mumsy type, or even soft, caring; how most people imagine a mum to be. Moira's career is her baby. Whenever a 'congratulations' email comes through for one of the new dads, her ovaries coil in disgust, another knot in the fallopian tube for safety. Not that there's anything wrong with focusing on your career, believe me I know. It's just that Moira's so negative towards everything else that isn't career focused – holidays, friends, family. Any moment that you're not working is a moment wasted, in her opinion.

I hope I'm not like Moira. Replacing night-clubs with the bright lights of Microsoft 360, the shake of ice and cocktails with the dull whirrs of the community coffee machine and getting my monthly flirt-in by being nice to Tom in the IT department who seems to enjoy turning things off and on.

Moira hasn't finished.

'Anyway, I think we *will* promote you this year. Seff, you've assured me it won't be a wasted promotion. There's obviously no chance you'll be getting pregnant anytime soon – it's going to take you at least a couple of years to get back on your feet, then you'll have a wedding, the honeymoon period etc. By the time that's all over, it might even be too late.'

I sit in silence. I'm trying to ignore her words. She's trying to make herself feel better, that's all. That's what bullies do.

Moira is such a dick, but I need her to promote me. Unfortunately, she holds all the power, so I don't dare bite back. Not even a nibble at the end of her stiletto. I'm nearly thirty; I need some sort of medal to my name. Promotions are like a metaphorical trophy – although the only people that really care about them are the fifty leeching recruiters on LinkedIn. None of my friends seem to care about my career success. You don't get two hundred likes on Facebook if you post, 'I've got a promotion!'; people only care about buying a house, getting engaged, married and finally having children. People care more about smushed-up banana over darling Olivia's chubby cheeks than me working seven-fucking-years to make director. Olivia's been alive seven months. If I can't have children, I need to be a director by next year. I have to.

If I can finally tick off 'promotion' on my To Do list at least that will be some sort of achievement.

Suddenly, Moira lets loose another banshee wail. If I stay in her office long enough, she might go full attack mode. I don't think there's been a zombie investment bank movie yet.

'Fuck's sake, Elliott! Bloody wanker.' She slams her hand palm down on the desk. 'We'll have to continue this another day, fucking Elliott's sent the wrong cost to the client, what a twat. See yourself out.' She waves me away, droplets of spit furiously spraying as she types like a maniac, her hands flailing in the air between each hurling bang on the keyboard. I turn my head as if the keys might fling off in some sort of assassination attack.

I stand up, straighten my pencil skirt and click-clack in my heels out of Moira's office back to my desk.

I've done it. I've got my promotion before I'm thirty.

I'm successful.

Why do I feel so shit then?

Get eggs-ercising those muscles - only five days until you ovulate. Try to have sex in the next five days when you are most fertile for the highest chance of falling pregnant.

If only you could impregnate yourself from a dildo.

Not that it would make any difference. My fallopian tubes are about as knotty as Moira's. A big Double Carrick Bend in the middle of my chances of procreation.

If all else fails, maybe I could start selling my twisty old tubes as some sort of obscene macrame art.

2

And that's it, completed. Another day ticked off the list. Fabulous.

I twinge, thinking about what Luke would say at my ability to turn everything into a task, even the process of living life itself.

Why do I keep thinking about him? It's like he's a bad omen sitting on my shoulder, except he wasn't really awful, was he?

I close my eyes to cleanse Luke from my mind and get back to the safety net of my routine. I should be home about 8.30 p.m. Usual time.

My alarm electrocutes me into action around 5.00 a.m. Monday to Friday. I go to the gym before the office, usually for a spin class but sometimes I enjoy pulling weights to some thumping beat. Moira demands that we're on the desk no later than 7.30 a.m. and often it's a twelve-hour day so if I don't want to look like one of those city-slicker-potatoes-called-Jeff crunching numbers at his desk, it's crucial I do some sort of sweat-inducing activity prior to the start of the working day. I buy a flat white and fruit salad from Grind as soon as I exit the tube. Every day, without fail. A fruit salad – without apple in it, I really hate those. The apple always tastes sour and bitty, and it's only included because apples are cheaper than melons. Fact. Chocolate croissant on a Friday. For lunch I devour a boring chicken salad from 12-12.10 p.m. at my desk and have a protein bar to perk me up at 3.00 p.m. Most days I have three coffees, but I try to have the other two without milk because of calories. I'm not obsessed; I like routine, structure and rigidity. I'm all for pizzas, burgers, cocktails, you name it, at the weekend. Those days are planned in, that's why I eat chicken salad the other five.

Sometimes it feels more like existence than life but that's what happens when you work hard – you live for the weekends, the nights out, the holidays. Work hard, play hard.

I do have to keep reciting that motto. I love my job and I mean that. To be a director before I'm thirty is everything I ever dreamed of – well, nearly everything. It's just, sometimes. *Oh, I don't know.* I do wonder what comes next on the list. Managing Director? Do I re-add *Find a Man* and *Get Married*? I need to have something to work towards. I can't merely exist.

Would you be proud of me, Luke? Or are you happy to finally be free of Seffy and her ergophilia?

The tube pulls up, I sit down. I'm currently listening to a podcast about feminism. It's called 'Shut The Feminist Up'. It's ironic and I like that.

I always need to be educating my mind, to be doing something. Listening to a podcast about issues that affect the world is a sure-fire way to ensure that my forty-five-minute tube journey isn't wasted.

I shut my eyes and lose myself in Kat Clark's monologue, instead of memories of my soon-to-be-ex-husband. Win-win.

The sudden move above ground ignites my phone signal and I receive a flurry of erratic WhatsApps.

Gemma: What time shall we do drinks on Saturday?
Aurora: Are you wearing heels to the brunch? My order on ASOS STILL hasn't arrived. I'm getting angsty.
Harry: I'm thinking of quitting my job and becoming a gardener. I CANNOT take another picture of a Crunchy

Nut cluster. I'm having nightmares that I'm drowning in
bowls of Kellogg's helpppppp!

I cover my cackle with a cough as the other commuters
glare at me for interrupting the solemn vow of silence all
Londoners take as they enter the Underground.

Seffy: How many professions do you think you can try
out before you're thirty? Also, you would be the world's
worst gardener. You don't even have a garden.
Harry: I might become a patio-culturalist. It's like a horti-
culturalist only I would specialise in tiny metre-square
patios for people in London. That's if the Crunchy Nut
doesn't get me first. Is it even possible for a cluster to
have a good angle? I'm resigning.
Seffy: You fed that cactus I got for your birthday champagne! Stick to the clusters babe x

I smile and pop my phone back in my pocket.

Harry's my best friend. We met at school when we were
eleven. She drew all down my arm which made me mad but
then she smiled at me, held out her arm and said, *An arm for
an arm?* I angrily scribbled in biro all over her left arm and
we became pen-sisters. We're total opposites. I like to plan,
she's spontaneous. I care about work and money, Harry cares
about happiness. Harry's like a laxative for the anal in me. I
help bring her down to earth when she's about to catapult
herself into space.

I pour myself a Pinot Grigio and soda, my drink of choice.
Cheers to me. *Congrats on your promotion, Seffy.*

I sit for a while, lamenting the day. Listening to the gentle
chink of the two large ice cubes against the glass. Savouring

the acidic bitterness of the cold liquid, allowing the soft bubbles of soda water to sit on my tongue.

> *Sorry, I didn't see your message I was just putting the baby to bed. Congratulations! What happens now then? X*

Thanks, Maria.

My mum replies to a text I sent earlier: *Well done! You should be so proud of yourself my darling – a director before you're 30! You are still at that banking job, aren't you? Sometimes I lose track . . .*

Not that I actually have the promotion yet, but Moira basically said it was mine and I need something to celebrate.

I do want the promotion. I just wish I was sitting with Luke on the sofa celebrating with a Diet Coke in my hand and a baby in my belly.

He'd say something like, *I knew you'd get it. Now, let's take the money and run. I've always fancied bringing up a family somewhere hot, like Bali.*

Or maybe we would have gone out for dinner somewhere fancy to celebrate, for steak, our favourite. A magnum of champagne, crisp, cold and bubbly – we'd get drunk on happiness. I could do that now, with Harry if I wanted. A big 'show and tell' about my promotion. Or maybe that isn't what I want and really, I'm searching for a hug at home, a release, a warm embrace after the corporate struggle . . . I bet Luke and I would have had amazing sex that night, an orgasm of success, shared success, given he did help me get there. In his own way.

The divorce papers are on the side; they arrived a couple of days ago. It doesn't take very long to draw the curtains on a marriage when they were barely open. It's been four months since we decided to divorce. We don't have any shared assets, so it really is as simple as signing a couple of papers and clapping the dust from your hands.

I will sign them. I'm not going to make things difficult and there really is no point in trying to rectify anything. I can't get a new womb fitted so I'll never be right for Luke.

I will sign them because that's what I should do.

Sometimes I wonder what would happen if I didn't, though. Well, maybe not if I didn't sign them but if we'd never started trying. If we were just one of those couples who had decided children weren't for them.

At least I don't have to worry about losing the baby weight or having too many white wines on a Friday night or explaining to a child that cigarettes are very bad but sometimes Mummy needs them to calm down: *they're like dummies, but for adults*.

Eurgh. I don't need to stew over it anymore. I'm really not one to wallow in my self-pity. I move forward, strategise how to be better, make plans on plans on future plans. *Come on, Seffy, pull yourself together.* You've been *promoted* – that's basically cancelled out the divorce.

I switch on something mindless on Netflix, pour myself another Pinot and soda and do some scrolling.

Maddie Peters posted a new life update.

On the 16th of March we welcomed our gorgeous baby girl Emmy-Rose Peters into the world.

259 likes.

JamDodge1991 posted a new photo to the album Fam-a-lam.

A photo of Finian with his two-year-old, both dressed up as hula girls.

57 likes.

Carly Clay changed her name to Carly Macintyre.

Thank you to all my friends and family for the most incredible wedding, it really was the best day of my entire life. Now for the rest as Mrs Macintyre!

199 likes.

And that's my Facebook feed. No one uses it anymore other than to amplify the status of their stability. Births, weddings, engagements, photos of children, babies, partners. Love, love and more love.

If I posted: '*Just got that promotion! Huge pay-rise coming my way!*' people would call it gloating. Is it not gloating, showing me photos of your biological children when that can never be me?

No one cares about promotions or career success. It makes people jealous. They only care about: *when are you going to get married? Thought about having children yet? Are you pregnant, is that why you're not drinking?*

I have had a slight hiatus in that line of questioning, for a while at least. It wouldn't be very considerate to ask a recent divorcée when they were going to get married for the second time in two years. It would be verging on inconsiderate, rude even, but when it comes to your own body, your own womb, your own desires, other people don't seem to have any qualms in diving straight into the nitty gritty – as if you physically share a womb with your Great-Aunt Ida.

What the fuck is this Netflix show? I switch to *Sugar Rush*, my favourite baking show. The on-screen stress calms me.

At least Instagram is a bit more glamorous than Facebook. The photos of people's kids are edited with nice lighting and their faces are clean. The stream of smiling children is infiltrated with models in bikinis or meals at fancy restaurants – things that I can achieve – making it more bearable.

Where shall I go next on holiday? South Africa? Barbados? Los Angeles?

I'm my own person. No strings attached.

I could plan a route around America, cram everything into my two weeks core leave. It would be stressful, but I could manage it with careful consideration.

@Celine72 has changed her name to @ThirtyismyNumber.

A photo of her swinging her legs at the edge of the Grand Canyon, about to bungee.

Caption: I did it! Completed my 30 under 30 bucket list before my thirtieth birthday! It was magical, scary, myth-busting – follow my blog to see my crazy adventures and make sure to tag me in yours! #LifeIsForLiving #ThereIsNothingDirtyAboutThirty

I click on her blog and scroll through her posts, photos and videos. Wow. I pour myself another Pinot – *there's only ever three decent-sized glasses of wine in a bottle; if you can pour four, you're not doing it right.* Alarming to take your advice on this, Mum, but the wine has already been poured.

There are photos of Celine with tigers in Thailand, bungee-jumping off the Grand Canyon, white-water rafting, pythons around her neck, eating scorpions in Mexico.

Comment from A. Non: This looks great but who has the time OR MONEY to travel to thirty countries in a year?

True. How am I going to manage to take off enough days from work to travel to thirty different countries? That would be a country a day based on my annual leave. I don't think I could even plan for that.

I absorb myself in Celine's life for an hour or so.

Maybe that's what I should do. My own thirty under thirty bucket list. I love a list. I'm drooling just thinking about it. Something to keep me occupied, take my mind off the fact

I'm a young divorcée. In the 1950s it was all eligible bachelors, parties, cigarettes and whisky. Today it's Netflix, a family-pack of Wotsits and a scroll through the UK's most eligible fuckboys.

Sometimes, with Moira so close to my neck, it's like we share a lung; I feel like I never take time to focus on myself. I can make myself into a better, more rounded person. Stop worrying about parts of my body that I can't change, like the part that's supposed to be the beating heart of procreation but in my case, it might as well be made of stone.

Thirty is quite a lot of things to tick off on a list. Maybe I'll find some things that are easy to achieve and some that are a little more eccentric. #Balance.

I'm excited. My fingers feel electric.

I open up the notes section on my phone and type enthusiastically.

Thirty Under Thirty Bucket List

Hmmm. What's something I can start tomorrow? I need to start immediately. There's no point in having a list you can't action.

I should start doing my pelvic floors. *Gravity is a bitch when you get over thirty*, or so my mum says.

1 Do twenty pelvic floors a day – that's easy. They can't all be too adventurous, or I'll never complete any of them. I only have a year and I work full-time. And I'm not wild, or outdoorsy or spontaneous, I'm Seffy, the now nearly single banker from London.

I type some more out.

2 Read ten famous books – the novels you're supposed to read in English classes, *Lord of the Flies*, *The Catcher in the Rye* – those ones.

3 Watch ten cult movies – I'm not very good with those types of movies, I prefer chick-flicks or comedies, ones to unwind to. I need to buff up my movie knowledge – watch *The Godfather*. Some real grit.

4 Host a dinner party and make everything from scratch – I mean everything, even down to the bread or the little blinis which I'll serve the salmon on.

5 Go to an overnight festival – I've never been to a festival. The thought of not showering for days scares me.

6 Find a hobby – I swear at school everyone had a hobby. A sport they played at weekends or something they were really good at. I have zilch. What could mine be? Running? Flower arranging? What hobbies do thirty-year-olds have? Laundry? Botox?

7 Do something that scares me – sing in front of a crowd?

8 Do a dancing lesson – my dancing is as good as my singing. It's sexy being able to dance. I just need to learn one signature move.

9 Get on a TV show – even a game show? I think I'd be good at a game show.

10 Change a tyre – this is purely down for practical purposes. I can do what any man can do.

11 Learn how to start a fire in the wilderness – again, another life skill. What would happen if I got stuck in the woods on the common?

12 Do a community service project – I really should start giving back.

13 Complete in a running race – this goes alongside the hobby, but I would love to have a photo of me with a big badge.

14 Climb a mountain – now that would be an achievement.

15 See one of the seven wonders of the world – I really should aim to see all seven by the time I'm 100.

There're a few to get my teeth into. Things I've always wanted to do, skills that I should learn now I'm well into adulthood. I can always change them over time, and I need to leave gaps to add things in. Knowing me I'll probably hit fifty before I'm thirty.

This WILL be fun. A project. Lists make me happy; I can already feel my heart beating faster.

I need to leave my old aspirations behind me and set some new goals.

I walk over to the counter where the divorce papers are and sign. I almost sign *S Coates* before remembering she doesn't exist anymore.

I don't need Luke.

He's already left me.

I'm a strong, independent woman and I'll be fine on my own.

I reach for the corkscrew and pull another bottle of Pinot from the fridge just to make sure.

But I will be fine.

I'm ninety-nine-point-nine-nine-per cent sure of it.

3

Harry: *What's the plan for your bday then, babes?*
Me: *I don't know. You know I'm not big on birthdays. Maybe we can go for a few drinks or something?*
Harry: *Not big on birthdays? Don't make me laugh. Says the girl who drank turbo shots on the river ferry two years ago, dressed up as a football hooligan.*
Me: *That was a rogue year.*
Well, it is now. When will I ever wear Luke's Chelsea outfit again?
Me: *I guess we could go for a bottomless brunch.*
Me: *If you want.*
Harry: *It's YOUR birthday. It wasn't rogue, you're like that every year. If you don't have your one day letting off steam, you'll implode.*
She's right, but that was the old Seffy. The fun side that Luke brought out of me.
Harry: *Bottomless brunch? Unlimited alcohol, food, music, friends who want to celebrate with you? How utterly fucking BORING :D*
Me: *Sorry. Now you say it like that . . .*
Harry: *Please DON'T apologise Miss birthdays-are-sooooo-last-year, I'll count it as one of your Seffyisms. I'm writing them all down so I can reel them off in your eulogy – hates birthdays. Scroogier than Scrooge. I hate to say it, but clearly you'll die before me because of stress.*
Me: *Purlease, we all know that reckless behaviour leads to death, it's like Grim Reaper 101.*

Harry: *ANYWAY, there's a huge reason to celebrate this year.*
Me: *Why?*
Harry: *It's your last year of your twenties.*
Me: *Don't remind me.*
Harry: *AND . . .*
Harry: *You're divorced! So, it's a divorce and a birthday party. You've freed yourself from the shackles of a man. We should have been wearing black veils every day until you signed the papers then we could have ripped them off on your birthday and be like born-again-virgins. Some sort of feminist ritual. What do you call the opposite of a hen party? Get back in the egg? All cock no balls?*
Harry: *We could bring back the masks of Luke's face but this time, heavily vandalised?*
Me: *You get carried away sometimes, but ok let's do a brunch.*
Harry: *Great I'll organise. Bring your leftover dick straws and maybe I'll book a stripper.*
Me: *Who keeps leftover dick straws?*
Harry: *They're one of those items you never know when you might need. Always keep a dick straw handy my mum used to say.*

I cannot stare at Excel anymore. All I can see when I close my eyes are tiny little rectangles.

Briiiiiiing!

I can see Moira with the desk phone to her ear as I pick up.

'Seff. Where are you with that document?' Her voice quivers with unnecessary urgency.

'I'm about halfway.'

'Well, I need it.' *There are a lot of things you need more than a pointless Excel document, Moira, believe me. Happiness, something to turn you on other than work, food.*

'I'm still waiting for info from Mandy, Felix and Jose. I have info from the others, but I still need to input and format . . .'

'I needed it . . .' *Don't say it, don't say it.* 'Yesterday.' She spits the word as my insides coil.

To be clear, the brief was set less than twenty-four hours ago.

'I'll get back on it straight away.' I probably should stand to attention and give a salute.

Moira hangs up.

I look at her across the office, catch her eye and smile. Naturally, she doesn't respond but instead stands up and starts pacing around the room. She doesn't leave the office, so she needs to get her step count in one way or another.

Luke and I always made jokes about Moira and every time she hisses some stupid remark, it takes all my inner strength not to send it as a homemade meme to Luke. Mocking her made working with her more bearable. Now what am I supposed to do to cope?

I look back at my screen. Rectangle, rectangle, rectangle. Eurgh, Excel eyes.

You have one new email.

Dear all,
As you've probably noticed (!) Christine is pregnant and will be on maternity leave for nine months as of next week. Jane's organising a whip-round and we will be doing a cake in the floor two cafeteria at 12 p.m. on Wednesday. For anyone concerned about what will happen to Christine's position while she is on leave, speak to Martin.

Regards,
Stephen

Stephen's email could really have used someone checking it for misogynistic statements but as at least eighty per cent of the office are men, I'm sure they will go undetected.

I divert my stare to Moira who, if I'm not mistaken, appears to be rolling her eyes. She picks up her black virtual assassinator and holds it to her ear.

Briiiiiiiiing!

'Have you spoken to Elliot?'

'Erm, no?'

'Have you seen the email?'

'Is *he* pregnant?'

I can't resist.

'If people spent their time sending actual emails rather than telling each and every single one of their colleagues that they've had sex recently, we all might get better bonuses. Of course he's not fucking pregnant, Seff. He's pissing all over this mandate and I need you to step in. If we lose this client, then you'll both be to blame.' She hangs up before she's even taken another breath.

These pregnancy emails really rile her. It's as if a little bit of her happiness is sacrificed with every new life on earth. I'm sure I'll understand that feeling soon, too.

I decide to go to the toilet for a break. It's the only time when I don't feel like Moira's undressing me with her eyes, not in a good way, but as if she's preparing me for sacrifice.

I sit on the toilet, scrolling as an alert goes off on my phone.

Reminder: Pelvic Floors

I start squeezing. How do people do it without anyone noticing? It's hard to get the perfect squeeze from back to front. It's quite tiring. I'm not sure if I would be able to do this at my desk without someone thinking I'm masturbating.

I mean . . . desk masturbation? Totally not office appropriate – one of the bank's hard-boiled potatoes might convulse into mash.

Why do you get nine months leave only if you're pregnant? What if you can't have children or don't want to have children – are you not entitled to a career break? Each squeeze gets more vigorous and more intense, as I contemplate the injustice of it all.

I message Harry:

Me: *Why should you get nine months off just because you're pregnant?*

God, I sound like Moira. I can imagine the words coursing from her lips as she spits them in disgust. When on the flip side there'll be a tired mum sobbing that people think maternity leave is like some five-star holiday. I'm such a bitch.

Harry: *LOL #babyshamer. You don't. A guy at work last week left for a six-month sabbatical and I'm pretty sure he wasn't pregnant.*
Me: *I didn't realise people actually did those. Surely your whole career gets put on hold. You'd never be in the same position again. Like, who would promote you?*
Me: *And unlike maternity leave you DON'T GET PAID.*
Harry: *Life's not all about money you know. It's people like you that make having a LIFE more difficult for people like me. Life's not all about working, some people choose to do things for FUN – like drinking their morning coffee out of a dick straw – try it.*
Harry: *P.S you're starting to sound like a Jeff and they're reallllllly boring. They look like they could accidentally be buried alive and wouldn't even notice.*

I'm such a square. Why am I such a square?
I wish I could be a bit more rounded; I'm not asking to be a full circle; I'd be happy as a hexagon.

Could *I* take a sabbatical?

Is that something Seffy could do? I'm about to be promoted. My promotion. No, it's too risky.

But I have no husband.

No children.

No ties.

I have money.

And I do need a break.

I would like to have some enjoyment.

But my career? *Stop being such a square, Seffy.* Rounded people surely don't have these arrows of negativity continuously puncturing their thoughts of fun.

I feel an urge to message Luke and find out what he would do in my scenario before remembering that this whole situation is because of us no longer being together.

I sit at my desk, pondering. Basking in the sun on some luxurious career break or wallowing in Excel sheets. Where would I rather be right now?

I type in 'Sabbatical' on the HR portal.

Each employee who has five years of service with the bank is entitled to a nine-month sabbatical under PP LEWES Right To Leave initiative.

I've worked here for seven years, and I don't think I've known a single person to leave for a nine-month sabbatical and, more importantly, return.

If you are interested in the scheme, please speak to your Line Manager and the Human Resources Team. The amount of notice required is dependent on your workload and at the discretion of your Line Manager.

Moira's my line manager.

Decision made.

I close the HR portal and go back to militantly typing out sales figures in an eye-watering display of commitment and, perhaps, cowardice.

Normally, I watch Netflix while eating my dinner but tonight I'm reading a book. I often eat ready meals in the week because cooking eats into my relaxation time, scheduled from 8.00 p.m. till 10.00 p.m. Monday to Friday.

The first book on my top ten reading list is *Lord of the Flies*, so in my usual uniform fashion, that's exactly what I'll read first.

It's good, I'll give Golding that. Drilling down on civilisation and metaphorically symbolising the pulls on society through a few kids, a shell and a pig is genius.

I lose myself in Golding's descriptions and pour myself a wine.

I delve deeper into his words – civilisation versus savagery. Ralph's idealism, Piggy's naivety, and Jack's militant views.

The wine flows in my blood and Golding's ink imprints on my brain. Am I Ralph? Is PP Lewes my conch? Is Moira Jack? Then who is Piggy?

I've had too much wine.

I'm divorced. Drinking too much alone. I'm a carbon copy of my fucking mother.

My arm vibrates. I startle. My eyes feel sticky and dry at the same time. It's midnight. I must have fallen asleep on the sofa.

Harry: *I booked Biggy Smalls for your birthday brunch. I LITERALLY begged for a table. It's going to be fantastic. Call me ASAP tomorrow so we can discuss outfits.*

Thank God for friends. Thank God for Harry. I'd be so fucking boring otherwise.

I pour myself a glass of water and go to bed. I don't even remove my make-up.

One Month No Baby

Dear Aunty Aphrodite,

I'm not usually one for anything fluffy. You know, supernatural powers that transparent gems might hold or praying to superior beings.

I've seen people talk about it on Instagram. Well, mainly celebs. They manifest something, like being the most successful singer in the entire world and it just kind of happens.

It's not really me. Surely if it worked, we'd all be happy, successful, rich?

I like to be in control. Understand the cause and effect. Newton and Einstein are more my kind of guys.

I usually don't believe in all that stuff but sometimes you must think outside the box.

Things don't happen by dreaming; they happen because of hard work. I learnt that from my mother. She's one of those women who doesn't dress up a turd, she shoves it straight in your face. You have to be tough because the world isn't made of marshmallows and puppies.

My father got an A in Hollywood clichés when he had an affair with his secretary and my mother was left to look after me and my two younger brothers – Chris and Justin. My father came back begging my mother to forgive him (apparently – I was too young to observe) but she said – you've done it once, how do I know you won't do it again?

I say that as if I admire my mother. I don't. My admiration is whittled down to the single point in time when she didn't take my father back; that's where it begins and ends. Maybe if she had taken him back she wouldn't be so awful. But that goes against all my feminist views and puts power to the patriarchy, so I refuse to acknowledge that it was ever an option.

I didn't study Classics or Latin, so I don't really understand all the gods, goddesses or mythical creatures of the supernatural underworld. HOWEVER, I want a baby and I'm impatient.

Aphrodite, you're the goddess of fertility, please help me.

There's a clear science behind conceiving – you need to have sex. That's how I see it anyway. Sperm plus egg equals baby. A teeny, tiny foetus with miniscule fingers and toes, and let's not forget their delicate little nails and the rhythmic beat of their miniature heart. I'm doing all the practical things to make myself get pregnant, mainly having sex at every opportunity, but now, Aphrodite, I'm at my wits end – I need to be in bed with you as well as my husband.

I've had eight periods. EIGHT. That's eight eggs, eight chances of procreation down the toilet. That's why I've started this diary. As I'm starting it now, it begins at One Month No Baby. That's the title. We weren't trying, per se, just not not trying. If you get me. Well, Luke wasn't, and I was trying to take it easy, be relaxed, but that's just not me. I've been trying to get pregnant ever since the evening of the wedding. It's already becoming such a slog. So, this month, I ramped it up. Locked the accelerator into place, as it were.

Yes, I'm fully aware that eight months of unprotected sex is not very long; it can take years to create a human. I like things done when I want them done and it's eating away at me like a gnat, that I can't be standing on the other side of conception already. I dream about standing next to the toilet and looking down at that little white plastic stick with two blue lines on it. Having a feeling of overwhelming happiness seep from my brain down to my toes and a smile spread across my darn face. Messaging Luke a photo of the lines with a caption that I'll remember forever – There's three of us now, Baby Coates arriving down the fast lane.

Luke and I had the most glorious wedding in Tuscany, about eight months ago. Everything I'd always dreamed of. The heat from the Italian sun gleaming down on our guests as they sat in the vineyard waiting for my arrival. All my friends and family there. The dress of my ten-year-old dreams. Guests smiling, laughing, photos of us all living our best lives. The dancing, oh the dancing, into the early hours and finally, a pool party the next day where we lounged around reminiscing about the party of all parties. It felt like confirmation that I'm doing well in life. If you looked at me you probably wouldn't think I need confirmation (I'm not trying to be conceited), a twenty-seven-year-old, married, nice flat, good job, friends. I'm still insecure, like everyone is. You think you're doing well and then someone comes along and trumps you – sticks two fingers in your face and says, 'can't catch me now'. Well, I'll catch you.

I loved the wedding. Letting my hair down a bit. Sometimes I think I forget how to relax and be silly. But then I surprise myself. I was stressed of course; everything had to be perfect. I had quotes about love embroidered onto cotton napkins – I don't see the point in doing something half-heartedly. I know some people might think of me as stuck-up or at the very least a stickler for detail, but I work hard at everything I do and I deserve it. I want to be successful, so I guess it's like manifesting but less airy-fairy and more early mornings and late nights. Everything can be planned – a structured life is a perfect life. I try not to let Luke see quite how anal I am about planning but some of the anal-ness slipped out at the wedding. I couldn't help it – the way Lucia was folding the napkins was driving me insane. I wanted chic, not fucking toddlers practising origami. Swans, not geese, if you get my vibe.

I know I'm lucky. Fortunate, even. I spent YEARS looking after my brothers, with no father and a drunk mother. I'm not someone who doesn't recognise their own fortunes. See, told you I'm not arrogant, Aphrodite, I'm just being to the point, stating the obvious.

Luke looked gorgeous. He is gorgeous. He's the total opposite of me in terms of our character traits but cut from the same cloth in some ways – our ambitions, our love of good food and travel. If you could orgasm over list writing, I would. While Luke has never written a list in his life. I don't know why it doesn't bother me; I don't even want to 'fix' him like people probably think I do. I'm happy with him, and he makes me check myself, like an onsite therapist who you fuck and love all at the same time.

I thought the wedding was the crux of my happiness but then there was the honeymoon. Luke and I lounged around on Sugar Beach in St Lucia, drinking pina coladas and having sex in the afternoon. We read books that have been on our reading list for years, played cards on little wooden tables and chatted late into the night putting the world to rights. We'd wake up with the only worry on our minds being what time we should have breakfast, lunch and dinner as part of our all-inclusive deal. It was like planning in a world where no planning was needed – orgasmic.

People talk about the post-wedding blues, when you return to your day job, but I have a post-wedding ecstasy. I feel euphoric. Being invited to events as Mr and Mrs Coates, people finally taking me seriously as I introduce myself as a Mrs, having a life partner. I'm even enjoying the arduous process of removing my maiden name from every single document I've ever owned, and I've created a family email for us – hello@costadelcoates.com. I enjoy admin because it's structured. I can plan it; I know what's coming next.

I've always enjoyed lists; shopping lists, to-do lists, goal lists. I almost started salivating when I got to put a big green tick next to the 'Married before you're 30' line. The next one is 'Promoted to Director', closely followed by 'Get pregnant'. I'm hoping to move 'Get pregnant' to before my promotion and hide my ever-protruding stomach until I receive my cheque, that way I'll get more maternity pay. See? Everything can be planned.

I don't have any particular reason for wanting to achieve this set of things before I'm thirty, other than it being a milestone in my mind. It's just something I decided once. Maybe it's because when you're fifteen, being double your age sounds really old and it feels like the sort of age where you'd want your life to be in order. Luke thinks I'm silly for essentially putting a timer on my life, but we're different and that's ok.

And now I'm married, it seems stupid waiting around, or having a baby in a few years because I want one now. I'd already allocated a few months post-wedding to just enjoy being newlyweds but that time's drawing to a close.

What I've realised is that trying to get pregnant is the total opposite of enjoyable. Luke and I discussed trying for children post-wedding and it was agreed that we would just take it slow. Stop using protection and let it happen when it happens. But I can't. Taking things slow just isn't me, like trying to teach a fish to walk – it ain't gonna happen. Every time his penis enters my vagina, my mind screams 'BABY, BABY, BABY'. Images of tiny, screaming humans in nappies sit on my eyeline. I fake an orgasm and then desperately try to get him to come really hard, so it shoots up into my fallopian tubes like an arrow securing its target. I'm sure the speed of the ejaculation must make a difference. It's got to, hasn't it? Come on, Aphrodite, you'd tell me if I was doing the basics wrong, wouldn't you? Send me a sign or something?

I've been tracking my periods for eighteen months, ever since we got engaged, but I'm not sure how reliable it is. Instead, I've downloaded Eggly and synced it up to my Apple watch to find out when my basal temperature increases and the days on which I'm ovulating. We started having sex every three days because I wasn't sure just how much I trusted Eggly. It was every day at first but that got a bit much. I'd sort of lie there with my legs up (heard that's the best position for fertilisation) and wait for Luke to finish. I'd keep my legs up for a while to check his sperm knew the way to my golden nugget of an egg and then that was that until the next day. When Eggly sent me my first notification – Congratulations Seffy, you're ovulating! – I basically pulled Luke's pants down as soon as he opened the door. Luckily, he thought it was sexy.

I know the hormones won't show up for two weeks (I've done my reading) but I take a pregnancy test immediately just in case one of my previous eggs has decided to fertilise itself from last month's ejaculation.

Nothing.

I'm already bored of having sex. Luke's happy to oblige, for now. Maybe I should start upping the sex to every day again just in case? ANSWER ME, APHRODITE. It's not sexy anymore, it's a task that needs to be completed and ticked off my never-ending To Do list. I'm not even bothering to buy nice underwear; period pants will do. I wonder if Luke finds it monotonous too. I don't want to ask him in case I highlight how dull our sex life has become overnight. It's gone from horny newly-weds to a narcoleptic romp. I still do all the relevant actions and sound effects but the only thing I really want to say is – Did you come? And if so, how much? Do you think there's enough to fertilise an egg? Have you eaten enough protein today? Please to God say you've been taking your vitamins.

I don't even know when the shift happened. When I stopped wanting to be sexy, desirable and just wanted to be pregnant. It's all fine though, I know deep down everything will be ok, it's just that feeling of waiting. You know, when you want something so badly but you have no control over it.

We still go out for our weekly date night, which does help with the feeling sexy part but even then, instead of lustfully looking into Luke's eyes for pure love, a tiny part of my brain is whirring, working hard to ensure we don't get home too late so we can get back on the procreation train.

This morning, Luke asked me if I'd started my period. I had, two days ago, but I feel guilty admitting that one of my eggs has escaped his militant sperm. I just told him it was late and hid my tampons underneath mouldy bananas in the kitchen bin. I will have to admit that an unfertilised egg is slowly seeping from my womb at some point but maybe he'll just forget.

I know it will happen soon. My Facebook feed is full of pregnancy announcements; if everyone else can do it, surely, I can. I'm my mother's child so there's no reason why I can't bear my own. If she can get pregnant (while drinking herself into oblivion), then surely a respectful, law-abiding, well set-up woman in her late twenties with a good job and a loving husband can too?

I know if I said that out loud to anyone, they'd think I was a massive twat, but this is a private diary. People have children in all sorts of ways, under all sorts of circumstances but sometimes I wonder if my mother should have had us three at all. I mean, she really didn't do much in terms of raising us. We'd have been like three caged battery *hens destined for the slaughterhouse if it wasn't for me taking the reins.*

It's just the anxiety of it all and the waiting. I bought a cute outfit for baby Coates on the way home from work last week. Totally neutral as I don't know what the gender will be (obvs). A gorgeous oat-coloured knitted romper with a matching bonnet. It's the cutest thing I've ever seen. It makes my ovaries burst when I look at it.

I showed Luke when I got home but he didn't seem to have the same reaction. He told me to stop buying things for a human that doesn't exist yet. We had a bit of an argument after that because I told him that I didn't feel like he cared enough and he responded – You always do this Seffy, get obsessed about everything. I want a baby too, but you can't go out buying things for something that doesn't exist yet because then there's nothing to look forward to anymore. Baby Coates's outfit is stored away for safe keeping, unfortunately in the same drawer as my dildos but that's life!

I keep peeking in the window of Bibs & Bums – everything is so adorable. I have an argument with myself every day, but I can't, I just can't buy anything else yet. Luke's right. Maybe a pair of matching oatmeal booties but then I'll really have to stop.

Due to my menstruation cycle, Luke and I get a bit of respite from our three-daily romp schedule, which is great because I'm tired. I'm hoping our little five-day holiday will make it all the more exciting when we get back to it. Maybe that was the sign, hey Aphrodite, my period?

I'm going to cook us a nice dinner of roast pork and dauphinoise, maybe even have a Pinot and soda. It will be like old times. Luke and I will drink our way through a bottle, laugh over the chinks of ice cubes, he'll tell me I'm beautiful and I'll thank my lucky stars that he chose me when he could have his pick of the girls. Take a break from my sudden conception sobriety. I'm sure it will do us both good to relax. I'm more free-spirited when I take a break, I know that. And hotter. Luke said he gets a hard-on when my eyes sparkle.

Anyway . . . my dearest, DARLING Aphrodite, if you are the goddess of fertility, PURLEASE can you swing by my ovaries next month and make them pop? I'd be eternally grateful.

Hugs, kisses, a bowl of fruit for the gods etc etc.
Seffy xxx

Twelve Months Until Thirty

4

Bzzzzzzzzzzzz

   Bzzzzzzzzzzzzzzzzzzzzz

   Bzzzzzzzzzzzzzzzzzzzzzzzzzzzzz

I'm in a haze. Did I leave my vibrator on?

My eyes feel sticky, *wine conjunctivitis*, according to my mother, when I used to bring her a morning cup of tea. My mouth feels arid.

   BZZZZZZZZZZZZZZZZZZZZZZZZZZZZZZZZZZZ

My brain starts to come to. I was having one of those weird sex dreams again. It's my phone ringing. Since my vagina's stopped engaging in sexual activity my mind seems to be doing more of it. Metaphorical shagging. It's great.

I move my hand violently from left to right trying to find my phone from somewhere under my pillow.

My phone stops reminding me that the last penis I saw was fuchsia and made of silicone, and I see it was a call from Harry.

I gulp the remnants from the glass of water by my bed before my phone starts incessantly vibrating again.

'What have you been doing?'

'Sleeping,' I reply with that dry croak that always coincides with your first word of the day. That moment where you're not sure if you've actually woken up a mute.

'It's your bloody birthday – WAKE UP!' she screeches down the phone. 'Welcome to the last year of your twenties, my gorgeous, fabulous bestie.' Harry's definitely not become a mute; she's risen a decibel.

'Don't remind me.' I sigh.

'I'm stopping you right there. I'm having none of your negativity today. Every time you say something vaguely negative Nicholas, you're having a shot.' Harry and I decided to replace all the negative idioms, adjectives and nouns associated with women with men a few months ago and I'm all for it. Why should all negative people be called Nancy? Why not Nicholas, Nathaniel, Noah?

'Fine. Yipppeeeeee, my birthday, I can't wait to celebrate!' I shout down the line. 'That better?' I laugh – it does make me feel happy.

'You need to get up, have a coffee and some food and get ready for brunch. There'll be no skimping on the alcohol this year, so I'm advising you to have some carbs asap. A coffee and two croissants will be arriving on your doorstep in twenty minutes, and I've paid the driver extra to watch you eat one of the croissants.'

'You haven't? Don't they do that on TikTok?'

'Might do, I'm not sure. Anyway, get ready because brunch is at 11.30 in Soho. DO NOT BE LATE.'

'Harry, when have I ever been late for anything? You can't be late if you plan for traffic.' I dismiss the urge to roll my eyes seeing that I'm alone and they still feel heavy from the wine.

I hang up and stare at the ceiling. 364 days left to complete my bucket list, a year minus a day. I was born at one minute past midnight, prompt – you can't get any earlier.

The red book lies placidly on the bedside table – who spends their birthday-eve reading an allegorical novel?

A recent divorcée, that's who.

Happy Birthday.

That's the message Luke sent me. A full stop! There's nothing more passive aggressive than that. And no emojis. At least it was before 10.00 p.m. so it doesn't look totally thoughtless.

I try not to think about how I would normally spend today – lazy sex, breakfast in bed, presents still in the cardboard delivery box because Luke hated wrapping, but my throat tightens and suddenly I'm trying not to cry.

I blink back a lone tear as the doorbell rings and open the door to a young guy, looking awkward. He holds out a paper bag and doesn't leave when I say thank you.

'I have to film you eating one of the croissants or I won't get a tip.'

'Film me?' Fuck's sake, Harry. I thought she was joking.

'Can I not pay you the tip myself?'

'No, she said you'd say that. She'll leave me a negative review if you pay me and she doesn't get a video.'

'But I hate eating in front of people.'

'She said that too.' He passes me a blindfold. 'Wear this and then you can pretend I'm not watching.'

It's one hundred per cent a fetish, I know it. I guess I can swap out the 'Sing in front of a crowd' from my bucket list and replace it with 'Eating in front of a delivery driver blind-folded'.

I take the blindfold, start chowing down on the croissant and Papa Pastry starts filming.

'You wait, Harry,' I say, spraying flakes of pastry. 'Karma's going to get you.'

'You're a total twat sometimes,' I say, nudging Harry.

'You'll be thanking me later, I guarantee it.' She smiles. 'And it was bloody hilarious. I might send it to one of those Facebook forums and get three hundred pounds.'

'Don't you dare.' I eyeball her.

'Joking!' She loops her arm in mine. 'Aurora and Gemma are waiting – have you ever been to Biggy Smalls? I can't believe I got a spot at the Hip-Hop bottomless brunch – it's literally booked up for eternity.'

'Hip-hop – it's so me.' I roll my eyes.

'I know, that's why I booked it.' Harry smiles. 'It's nineties hip-hop – don't tell me you didn't spend years looking soulfully out the window in your bedroom, pretending you were in a music video with Kelly Rowland and her pals. You used to wear those skater jeans with the little chain . . . lame!'

I start telling Harry about my thirty under thirty bucket list.

'. . . things like how to change a tyre, learn how to iron, do my pelvic floors, cook etc.'

'Sounds like a 1950s housewife manual. Can't you do some more exciting things? What have you always really wanted to do?'

As if my phone can read my mind (thanks Mark Zuckerberg) it ignites like a fire in my palm.

Harry and I look down at the notification on my phone. A giant golden egg smiling with big googly eyes and an obnoxious musical fanfare – because who doesn't want to know your ovulation cycle?

Get egg-cited, you're ovulating! Have sex today for the highest chance of getting pregnant!

Harry looks up at me, and I already know what she's thinking.

She knows I'm divorced, she knows about the IVF, the sleepless nights, the arguments, the tears. She knows how much I yearn to have a little human growing inside me, and she knows as well as I do that it doesn't matter if I'm ovulating every day of the year, being pregnant is an impossibility. So why, Harry's thinking, does she still have that fucking annoying app?

'Birthday sex? What an egg-cellent idea!' She smiles, takes my phone and puts it in my handbag.

That's what friends are for – not calling you out on your birthday because they can already read the embarrassment spreading across your face and see the sadness in your eyes.

Birthdays are fun when you're in your twenties, early twenties, that is. They're fun when you wonder what the year has in store for you. They're fun when you feel like you have a lot of life to live. What presents will your loved ones buy you? What should you wear? Ensure you're wearing a balloon and a badge so that EVERYONE knows it's your birthday.

They're not fun when you get older. When life's aged you well beyond your years and the older you get the less chance you have of finding a partner, having children, achieving all the things on your to do list because you're running out of time. Birthdays only heighten anxiety with the sole purpose to act as an alarm clock you can never turn off.

I fully appreciate that twenty-nine isn't exactly old but the past two years have aged me – I feel like I'm about to turn sixty-five. I just saw thirty as this milestone in my head, the target for my life's to do list and now I'm so far from where I thought I'd be.

That's how I feel anyway. Harry would punch me if she could read my mind. *Stop being a negative Nicholas.*

Aurora and Gemma wave at Harry and me through the window. I see four espresso martinis on the table, and I can already hear Warren G's regulate blasting – liven up Seffy, it's your *birthday*. Not everyone can birth a child, it's an honour even being born.

'HAPPPPPPY BIRTHDAYYYYY!' Aurora and Gemma shout in my face as they hug me and shove an espresso martini in my hand. 'The last year of our twenties!'

'Do you think it's bad drinking espresso martinis and coffee? It's a lot of caffeine, isn't it?'

'Honestly, Rory, you worry too much.'

'Last weekend I couldn't get to sleep, my whole body was shaking. I just sat downstairs watching Disney+ until, like, 5.00 a.m. John kept asking me if I'd been taking drugs – does he not know me? As if I'd be up snorting cocaine or whatever it is.' She chugs with laughter.

'Cinderella on drugs must be crazzzzyyyy. Don't drink them then, or I'll give you a Valium – take the edge off.'

Aurora, or Rory as we call her, is a major worrier. She worries and overthinks everything. John, her husband of two years, doesn't seem to care he's married to a hypochondriac. Rory overthinks making a cup of tea; John would go out all day and leave the oven on. Frankly, I'm with Rory on this one.

Gemma, on the other hand, is a go-getter – she only thinks after doing something. She'll do anything. She's the type of person who goes out all night in Ibiza and returns to go for a run.

Then we have me: investment banker, list-maker, planner, recently divorced, and Harry: reckless, spontaneous, creative. On paper, we shouldn't be friends, but we've known each other since school, so it works. We'd started our periods together, had our first true loves together, lost our virginity together, cried together, laughed together; some of us have even wet ourselves together – it's hard not to be friends after all that.

Rory and I have watched each other get married and she's watched me get divorced. I wanted to be the first to have children, but the world had other plans for me. Luckily, I don't have to watch any of my friends give birth yet – too raw.

'Another round, please, sir!' Harry waves to a teenager with a large gold coin on a thick plastic chain around his neck and a cap on backwards. 'Actually, make it two and four shots.'

The bottomless brunch has well and truly begun. All the *crème de la crème* of nineties hip-hop is blasting through the dark den of a Soho club and the drinks are flowing.

Snoop Dogg's 'Gin & Juice' plays and a cake comes out covered with sparklers.

'Oh no, guys, you didn't have to!'

The whole restaurant sings 'Happy Birthday' and Harry stands on her chair, clapping and screaming the words.

'Remember how much we used to love layering our clothes?' Gemma roars with laughter. 'Seffy, I think you wore a dress, leggings and shorts all at the same time once!'

I cringe at my youth.

'I was such an ugly duckling.' I laugh and thankfully Harry finishes my sentence with, 'Who turned into a beautiful swan,' giving me a cheer with her drink.

Another round of drinks gets brought over and then exactly the sort of brunch you would expect for forty-five-pounds – a bun so white it could have been scrubbed with bleach filled with a fatty piece of bacon straight off the pig's back.

I silently thank Harry for forcing two croissants down me earlier, but even so I'm starting to feel the alcohol pulse through my veins. It's not that I don't enjoy being drunk – it's the lack of control I hate. The banging headache the next day as I reluctantly push myself through my list of tasks.

And the anxiety. It makes me miss Luke. And hate myself for what I did, what I became.

I blink away memories of how he would swing me round by my waist and do his silly little two-step dance, and look down at my own heeled feet which suddenly seem so isolated despite being surrounded by friends.

There's a group of guys who are dancing in a huddle nearby, peering over like a group of meerkats, or as the correct appellation ingeniously describes them, a mob. Harry's catching eyes with one of the blond-haired members and I just know any minute she's going to casually 'bump' into him because that's her 'revolutionary' pulling technique.

Rory's finally hit the amount of alcohol needed for her worry genes to magically disappear for a few hours and seems to have chucked half her drink over Gemma. It's the level of drunk that screams DMC time. The deep and meaningful. The chat you always have when you've had that one glass of wine too many. Where you tell someone you barely know your life story – what happened to your sister's hamster in 2006 and why you happen to still be sobbing about the furry little blighter.

'Want to sit down for a bit?' Harry asks me after scrawling her number on the blond-haired meerkat's arm in eyeliner. 'Can you believe it? I threw my drink on him on purpose and he bought me one to say sorry? You can't go wrong with the old bumper-to-bumper trick.'

We click-clack our feet across the sticky floor to the red velvet sofas. Sounds plush but the velvet's more like carpet that's turned into a brillo pad after being trampled on for fifty years.

Harry takes a selfie of us on my phone before inspecting it.

'I feel old.' Harry laughs. 'Look at my wrinkles.' She points to a few faint lines around her eyes. 'Obviously I've still got it though.' She winks at the blond-haired mob member again before inserting a finger into her mouth. I think it's supposed to be seductive, but she looks like she still has bacon between her incisors. It's not my style of flirting but I don't really know what that is anymore.

'Me too. One more year until I'm thirty. Then what? I'll be needing a Zimmer frame as a dancing partner.'

'What's the obsession with being thirty?' Harry eyeballs me. 'You'll be the same as you are now, just one year older. My mum says the thirties were the best years of her life.'

'Exactly. I'll be one year older. Another year further away from my prime.' I shake my head, thinking about that time when I didn't even moisturise.

'Prime? You're acting like one of the patriarchs. You do realise how sexist it is that women are defined as being ripe? It makes us sound like we'll become mouldy old apples that should be discarded in the bin.' Harry daggers me.

'All right, sorry, I won't use that word again.' I raise my eyebrows.

'Good, or you'll be joining the Jeffs in my metaphorical sexist prison. Anyway, I'm the same age as you. You're insulting me as well as yourself.'

'You know what I mean.' I look at her, silently trying to make her understand that being me is simply worse.

'If you're talking about being single and childless then no, I don't. Oh, whoops, a child just fell out of my birth canal as I was drowning myself in espresso martinis. Again, that's also me.'

'I'm not trying to insult you, Harry, I'm just telling you how I feel.' I'm not trying to make anyone else feel bad or judge them, I'm just explaining how shit my particular life is. Why do my feelings have to insult others?

'You think that I don't care about those things because I'm all reckless and don't have a job in a bank and go to the gym on a daily basis. Newsflash, Seffy, just because my life isn't as organised as yours, I still want those things. You think everyone exists in this binary of living an organised and regimented life and wanting a family or they live a wild life, longing to be forever childfree. We're allowed to be complex, Seffy. And just because I love the way my life is now doesn't mean I don't want that one day, so stop thinking I can't possibly relate or even get sad about where my life is sometimes.'

'I want those things now, that's all. I had those things.' I feel myself well up.

'Don't cry on your birthday!' Harry takes my hand. 'This is supposed to be a joyous occasion – we are celebrating the birth of the Seff-meister. You need to take this opportunity to start living your life – you've got your bucket list, you just need to up the game on that – I'll help you. And what happened to that sabbatical idea you were talking about?'

'Oh, nothing. It was a stupid idea. Moira would never let me do it.'

The blond-haired mob man starts walking over. Harry looks at him and pops the finger back in her mouth.

'Go on.' I nudge her. 'Go talk to him.'

'Do you want me to wing man you with his friends?'

'No, I'm going to go to the loo.'

I leave Harry and go and stand in the queue. Fuck. I've left my phone with Harry. Now I'll have to stand and stare, or worse, chat to someone I don't know.

'Here, you left your phone.' Harry smiles before handing it back to me.

'What have you done?'

'Nothing.' Her eyes light up mischievously.

Later, much later, I'm sitting in an Uber with Harry scrolling.

'Check your sent items.' She giggles drunkenly.

'Why?' I panic.

'Just do it.'

Dear Moira,
I would like to cordially request a six-month sabbatical; one year would be ideal, but I understand that in the banking world this may be impossible. Perhaps nine months; it would be like pregnancy leave but I'll never have to finish work early for the nursery pick-up once I return.

I think for my mental health, a sabbatical is a necessity.
I'll await your feedback with bated breath.

Kindest regards,
Seraphina

'What the fuck. Bated breath? Who says that?'

'I'm taking your life into my hands. You need to get a grip.'

'How are you going to look after me on a so-called "Crunchy Nut Cluster salary"?'

'You're not going to get fired, Seffy. Come on, don't be such a baby – you want to do it, I know you do. And change your password – everyone knows it's your birthday. You need to be more cyber-security-conscious, especially if you're going to be travelling round the world.'

'Well, just so you know, I'm really fucked off with you. You've probably ruined my whole career. But I'm not even going to bother talking to you until you're sober.'

'Harry?' I nudge her. 'Harry?' She lets out a large snore. 'Fuck's sake.'

5

I've been awake since 4.00 a.m. Nervous doesn't even describe it. I refreshed my emails all of Sunday. Nothing. What would Moira be doing on a Sunday? She basically lives and breathes through Outlook, why would that stop at the weekend?

Monday.

Came and went.

Moira was out with clients.

Still. Nothing.

Now it's Tuesday and I'm going to have to face the music.

I barely get a chance to sit down at my desk before . . .

'SEFFFFFFF!' Moira screeches from her office. She doesn't even bother to open the glass door, but I can feel her spittle on my cheek all the same.

This is it, I think to myself. No husband, no baby and no job. The power of three. My life list is well and truly in self-destruct mode.

I've barely pushed open the door before her words ring in my ears.

'Are you going through a breakdown? If you are, keep it out of work, Seff. It does nothing for your career. And don't say it's because I overwork you – you're a banker, it's part of the job description. It's why the salary's so good, so you can pay for counselling on the side.' *Clack, clack, clack.* Her witch's talons puncture the laptop keys. 'I'M JOKING, SEFF.' Her mouth's open so wide I can almost see what she's saying before I hear it. Saliva joining her top and bottom lip like strings of caramel.

'If you're talking about the email, well . . . ha . . . funny story . . .'

Moira cuts me off.

'The email?' She guffaws and a fleck of spit lands on her upper Sexy Sienna coated lip. Her eyes don't move a millimetre from the screen. 'Very clever, Seff.' She's never called me clever, so I assume it's meant in sarcasm. She continues. 'You're right, it is unfair that you don't get nine months off without having a child. I wouldn't give you nine even if you were pregnant. Well, I'd have to, but you know what I mean.' I hear a miniscule hiatus in the clacking, as if her fingers need a moment to draw breath. 'You can have seven and don't go getting yourself pregnant when you're away by some hessian-wearing, dreadlock-ridden hippy. It's uncouth.'

Sometimes I wonder if Moira's trying to mother me in her own weird way. I'm like a three-times removed work love child, except she can't remember giving birth and doesn't know why I exist.

'And I . . . still get my job back. You know, as a director?' The promotion. It's all I have right now.

'Who am I going to hire in seven months? It takes at least a year to get anyone decent. Elliott will cover you. This is very inconsiderate of you, Seff, I hope you know that. If you only want seven months off and I get to have you back to work at full capacity without a nervous breakdown hanging round your mind like an ugly dark cloud then yes, you can go. It's weak though, to need a career break. I thought you were stronger than this. Now get writing your handover and be bloody basic about it – Elliott *was born* fucking yesterday.'

She waves me out of the door. I am dismissed.

Fuck. I'm going on a seven-month vacayyyyy! Item four on the bucket list is now in action. I need to get planning. The ultimate list. I wipe away a droplet of drool and sit back at my desk.

But she did call me weak. Moira always has a way of making the positive tainted.

Weak.

Am I weak?

Is that why I ended it with Luke? Walking away from someone who loved me because I couldn't find the strength to build back our perfectly imperfect relationship.

It wasn't like when my mum and dad divorced; Luke didn't do anything so black-and-white wrong. I ended it between us but sometimes the reason why becomes all grey and fuzzy and I can't quite remember anymore. Maybe he didn't judge me as much as I made out he did, maybe it was all in my head and I wanted to hate him because I couldn't hate myself anymore.

My face illuminated by the light of my laptop, a fresh pad of paper and my Montblanc fountain pen in my right hand. It was a present from Luke; he was thoughtful like that. He'd celebrate every moment with me, making even the small things special. This was a gift when I won the Sierra Capital account – he said there was something original about owning your own fountain pen.

There's no point in getting all aggro and throwing out all the expensive gifts he bought me. The only person that will be missing out is myself. Lesson learnt from a traumatic he-said-she-said break-up when I was fourteen when I flushed away an extremely nice Tiffany necklace that Teddy's father had given me as a gift from America. *Don't be that girl,* my mum would say. *What's the jewellery done wrong? Clever people don't give diamonds away.*

I shake my head, trying to silence my mother's voice and return to blankly staring at a world map on Google.

There are so many countries and I've barely been to a handful. Do I do Asia, South America, Australia, Africa? It's not really feasible to travel the entire world in seven months, even with my military-level of strategic planning. I'm also a wuss. I'm not really the throw-caution-to-the-wind, jump-in-a-tuk-tuk-and-dance-on-the-beach-all-night kind of girl. My travelling involves staying in five-star hotels and sipping pina coladas on the beach. I pretend I'm cultured by booking boutique hotels and turning my nose up at any all-inclusive deal because it doesn't allow for that pied-à-terre feel. Luke was the one that forced the all-in-one honeymoon because he said I needed to relax and he was right, kind of. I'm the girl who types in *Is it safe to travel to the Maldives* and seriously considers the Foreign Office's advice on beach pickpocketing before I finally book my return British Airways seat to one of the most luxurious destinations in the world.

Usually, I'd go on holiday with Luke. We'd look at our list (standard) of places that we've always wanted to go; California, Tulum, Hong Kong, Essaouira, Zanzibar, and then I'd spend the next few days researching the hotels, activities, flight times before we'd finally click book, ready for our annual two-week vacay.

It's nerve-wracking going away alone.

Who will take photos of me? I'll have to make friends. It'll be like at nursery but worse. You can't give someone a half-eaten cheese sandwich when you're twenty-nine and expect a mouthful of Babybel in return.

I've always wanted to visit Asia; it's the classic gap yah that I never experienced. I want to see what all the fuss is about, why people suddenly find themselves and never want to come back to London to wear a suit.

Research.

Wine.

Plan.

Research.

More wine.

Plan.

My eyes are straining. My brain a whirl of train and plane timetables, hostels and hotels, local festivals, temples and the best eateries. But it's finished. My itinerary. I feel my heart jump with elation. My coloured Excel sheet with its multiple tabs makes me feel safe. I know what I'm doing, where I'm going. I feel secure again.

Dear Seraphina,

Please take this email as formal acceptance of your seven-month sabbatical. Your confirmed leave commences on May 30th, and you must return to work in January. Your salary and annual leave accrual will be frozen; company benefits such as travel insurance and private healthcare will continue as normal. Full details can be found in the attached PDF.

Please reply to this email to confirm that you have read the attached documents.

Best regards,
Sarah Cody
Director of Human Resources

Two weeks! I'm off in two weeks! It's only because Moira wants me back in time for the RJH CAPITAL mandate but who cares. I will be a woman of the world by the time I'm thirty.

I message Harry: *Want to come over and help me pack?*
Harry: *100%. How come Moira let you go so soon? Thought she'd have you chained to the desk.*
Me: *The quicker I go, the quicker I come back. Plus, the bank is dead over the summer.*
Harry: *Fair. Don't start packing without me – you can't wear a suit on the beach you know.*

'Oh my God, what is all that stuff?' I exclaim as Harry drags a huge bag through the door.

'It's your seven-month wardrobe plus survival pack. I already know that nothing you own will be suitable.'

'How do you know?'

'I've known you for nearly two decades – trust me.'

Harry starts pulling items out of her huge bag including a DISGUSTING navy and grey backpack.

'No way am I taking that.' I point to the bag. 'It's hideous – I'll be a target for crime. How will I fit everything I need for seven months in that tiny bag anyway? My cleansing routine alone needs a bigger bag.'

'I'm sorry, who gave you the right to be so judgemental? I'm helping *you* pack. Usually people say thank you.'

'You were the one that made me take this sabbatical in the first place!' I say, slightly dumbfounded.

'Yes, but you wanted to, you just needed a little push. Think of me as the best boyfriend you've never had.' She grins.

I grin. 'I'll miss you.' And I go to hug her.

'Stop being soppy.' She shrugs me off.

'Don't tell me I'm being too emotional for you.' I poke the bear.

'Emotional?' She smirks. 'That will be the day. The last time I saw you properly upset was when your rabbit got eaten by your neighbour's dog.'

'Anyway, this stuff . . .' I point around. 'It's just not very me, that's all.'

'None of this is very you, that's the point.' Harry starts taking brightly coloured garments out of the bag. 'This is why you need me. You can't take a suitcase travelling. End of. You'd be mugged before you got off the tarmac. And you won't be doing your ten-step cleansing routine – you'll be lucky if you have time to slap a wet wipe drunkenly round your grubby little face.' She rips out a wet wipe from the bag and targets my face.

'Get off!' I laugh, pushing her to the floor.

'Do you want a play-fight? You know I'd win,' Harry says, jumping on me.

'No wrestling! You're so weird.' Harry always used to wrestle me when we were younger, and I'd have to promise her a bar of Dairy Milk to stop.

'My gran used to watch *The World's Strongest Man* every Christmas, you know, and WWF.'

'You do know it's WWE if you mean wrestling? WWF is for animals,' I respond, laughing at her mistake.

'Yeah, the wrestling one. She was really into that,' Harry says, not batting an eyelid.

'Anyway, that's just not me, Harry. I need my things; I need to be prepared.'

'Seffy.' Harry grabs my arms. 'You need to listen to me. I know you don't regard my advice very highly but travelling – it's my thing. If you want to go on the road to enlightenment before you're thirty do exactly what I say and pack everything I tell you to. You've got money – if you hate it all when you get there, buy some more.'

Harry lays everything out on the floor.

'Why don't you take a flat lay of everything, document your journey? *Packing my things to unpack my emotions*.' Harry stands back, admiring her work – it's the creative in her.

'You love this, don't you?' I laugh. 'You always wanted to be the host on that makeover show *Ten Years Younger*. This is your dream, making me be more like you.'

'I mean, yes, I'm rather enjoying myself,' Harry says, smugly.

She starts handing me the essentials; mosquito net, mini first-aid kit, portable charger, condoms.

'Why do I need fifty condoms? I can't get pregnant.' I laugh – oh, the irony.

'INFECTIONS!' Harry screams. 'Seffy, you will be having sex and you can't focus only on the fact that you can't get pregnant. Travelling is a hot bed for STIs. Listen to me. I've had crabs and they are not pleasant. Imagine a guy going down on you and you're itching and . . .'

'STOP! Gross. I'm not going to be focusing on men or having sex. I'm focusing on myself.'

'I want you to have sex with the first person you meet. You need to be spontaneous. You're a hot, single woman, travelling around the world. You're going to have to bat away as many men as mosquitos. Add that to your thirty under thirty bucket list – be spontaneous and have sex with random men or women. I know you have frivolity in you – it's just got lost in the boring beige fabric of your suits.'

'I guess it would be cool, reinventing myself around the world. Like a sexier version of Travolta and Cage in *Face Off*.'

'What you find attractive is disgusting.' Harry puts a finger in her mouth. 'I also bought some clothes for your trip, but as you kindly pointed out I'm on a Crunchy Nut Cluster salary, so you'll need to transfer me.'

'What is this?' I say, confused as she hands me a pink nylon crop top and matching skirt.

'It's a co-ord.' She pushes her tongue into her right cheek, highlighting my ignorance. 'I went crazy on Pretty Little Thing, like I literally spent nearly two hundred pounds. I basically bought shares for you. Everything you own is too sensible or too expensive. Trust me, I'm a fashion doctor.'

Harry is anything but a fashion doctor in my eyes, but I don't want to upset her. I hold my breath and pack everything into my bag, grimacing at the amount of skin she wants me to have on show.

'Have you had any ideas about where you might go on your travels? I know you want to start with Hong Kong but after that?'

'Plans? Me? Are you joking?' I whip out my printed Excel documents with train timetables, flight times, and my exact itinerary for how each morning and afternoon will be spent over the next seven months.

Harry takes the sheets and looks through each one.

'So, I've planned everything for each day, where to stay; some I've pre-booked, some I'll book closer to the time. I've incorporated activities to complete my thirty bucket list too – like visiting the Taj Mahal in India, things like that.'

Harry laughs and then rips up all the sheets.

'Harry! What the fuck! That's hours of planning. I don't have a printer at home.' I feel my heart race with anger and anxiety. I have other copies, of course. But I printed a certain number of copies for a reason and now there's one copy less.

'I'm not letting you ruin this trip, Seffy. You need to be spontaneous. What if you meet someone? What if plans change? Your thirty under thirty list is total garbage too. What about all the things you've wanted to do, like join the mile-high club, not go on some lame ten-mile hike.' She stares at me, not blinking.

'What?'

'I'm not stupid, Seffy. Hand over the other copies of your itinerary. If you don't hand me at least three more, I'm going to ransack this flat.'

I know not to mess with her and retrieve the other five copies.

Sometimes I hate Harry and sometimes I love her. I know she is kind of right, but I was born with itineraries and plans in every single one of my chromosomes.

It should have been Harry and Luke, not me and Luke. He'd be on Harry's side right now, but then again, I wouldn't be going on this trip if I hadn't left him.

'If you're so het up about turning thirty and not having lived your life then listen – you need to be a bit more like me. I know the thought of rolling out of bed in the morning with no idea where you're going makes you feel sick and unclean but it's good for you. As soon as you come back, you'll be on the tube at six every morning, sitting at the same desk, eating the same salad, having the same boring conversations, and you'll hate yourself for not letting go a little bit. Promise me you'll do what I say. Here, I got you something.'

She hands me a little quartz bracelet with the words BE MORE HARRY on it.

'When you feel your anal sphincter muscles tighten at the thought of not setting an alarm or having a piece of bread on a no-carb day, think of me and let yourself go. If it doesn't make you happy, I'll wear a suit for a week and do everything you tell me to. That's how much I know you'll thank me.'

I smile.

'I'll miss you.'

'I'll miss you too. Now, show me your bucket list. I need to add a few things.'

Seffy's 30 under 30 Bucket List:
#1 Read ten good books
#2 Do 30 pelvic floors a day
#3 Eat in front of someone and be filmed
#4 Go on a seven-month sabbatical

Harry tuts and shakes her head.

'Just so you are aware – people won't write, "Oh Seffy was a great person, she read all of the GCSE syllabus books and had the tightest vagina we've ever seen" on your gravestone.' She adds two more to the list. 'Now, LIVE A LITTLE.'

#5 Be spontaneous EVERY DAY
#6 Sleep with random men and DON'T WORRY ABOUT ANYTHING OTHER THAN STIS!!!!!!!

6

I've sent my handover notes, put my out-of-office message on, and I'm standing in Heathrow Terminal 2 wearing a straw hat because Harry told me to. This is the day I start the reinvention of Seffy.

I look around the check-in desk – couples kissing, excited families ready for the annual vacation. I've never been at an airport alone. I'm not eighteen either, like the girl to my right with worried parents making her check her backpack for the tenth time, asking her to phone home every day, like a millennial version of E.T. I'm twenty-nine – is that tragic? Eleven years late to the gap year party.

A little boy wearing a bright green cap with a toucan embroidered on the front comes charging into me.

'WILFRED! WATCH WHERE YOU'RE GOING!'

A very stressed blonde lady who can't be much older than me marches over and grabs Wilfred by the arm.

'Apologise to this nice lady, please.'

'Honestly, it's fine.' I smile as I see the father of the small toucan frantically waving them both over to the check-in desk as he pushes one of those huge metal trollies overflowing with suitcases and two other pink and yellow toucans, kicking and screaming.

'Sorry,' Wilfred says with his head down before running over to the rest of his flock.

'Kids, hey?' She smiles, rolling her eyes. 'Who'd have'em.' She rushes off to join the rest of her loving, lucky family.

Me.

Me. I'd have them.

I blink back a few tears. My loving husband is about to officially be exiled and my chances of a family are already in the grave. I look down at my phone which used to have a photo from our wedding day as the screensaver but is now just a picture of a beach. I can see him now, the way his head turned as I walked down the aisle; his eyes lit up, and he gave me a little wink to make me laugh, relax me. When I reached the altar made of flowers and greenery he whispered, 'Beautiful as always, angel girl.' And now all the photos along with the memories are in the trash.

I'm sure the toucan matriarch didn't mean to be inconsiderate. How was she to know what she'd said and who she'd said it to? Almost boasting about her fertility, wearing it like a badge for the world to see. I'd do anything to be going on holiday with Luke and our children. Instead, I'm standing here alone on a version of maternity leave for the childless. Perhaps more relaxing but very short-lived.

People don't think about it. It's not like having cancer or a disease which you don't have to see every day or people do their best never to mention in front of you. People don't make jokes about a terminal illness. Everywhere I go I see babies, children, families and people make jokes about how difficult it is, how their life has changed, how they hate being pregnant. And I'm supposed to accept it, nod and agree because it's not a terminal illness. I'm alive. Infertility – it's not life-threatening, it's just threatening to the life I want to live. I can't procreate. Big deal.

I think now is the perfect time for some airport wine.

I feel very *Sex and the City*, propped up at the bar with a Pinot spritzer and a bowl of Nocellara olives. There's an extremely attractive man reading a copy of the *Evening Standard* to my right. He has the right amount of six o'clock shadow and a pair of tortoiseshell glasses that accentuates his eyes, rather than making him look like a Tarsier.

I might still miss Luke, but my libido hasn't completely changed course.

I send a selfie to Harry.

Me: *Do you olive my style?*

Harry: *Please stop being so lame.*

I see her typing again.

Harry: *You know if you have sex with a flight attendant you get bumped up to first class?*

Me: *Seems reasonable.*

Me: *Why don't you shag someone in a port-a-loo then you can fulfil your travelling-sex fantasy yourself?*

Harry: *You only live once babes! Anyway – port-a-loo? Completed it, mate.*

I see my flight change to boarding on the screen and my heart skips a beat. Eeek. Life begins at twenty-nine.

I sit in my window seat, having sorted everything out for the twelve-hour flight. I have my second book on the list – *The Catcher in the Rye* downloaded on my e-reader, headphones, sudoku book (I know it's lame but that's just me), some sweets, eye-mask and a huge bottle of water to ensure I don't start resembling a raisin. According to the time zone research I conducted pre-flight, I should really sleep for the majority of the journey, but I am someone who can survive on minimal sleep, so I'll have to weigh up how good the movies are.

After all, I am on holiday.

I love flying, especially long-haul. The movies, eating whatever you want – I always disregard the flight calories, even I can't foresee what they'll feed me, free drinks. It's the ultimate pig-out fest, and if there's a time difference it literally doesn't exist. Magic.

'Excuse me.' I look up and see Mr Dreamy Tortoiseshell. 'May you move your bag?' He smiles. I look at the hand tightly holding the leather handle of his holdall. It's strong, lightly tanned, and his fingernails look clean. Manly.

'Oh, of course,' I hurriedly answer, shoving it between my legs. The brush of my hand against my own skin is enough to arouse me and I flinch slightly with embarrassment as if he can mindread.

'A girl behind me spilt her juice box all over my seat so I got bumped up a class – win win!' He grins, showing me a set of perfect white teeth. Has Harry set me up? She knows I have a soft spot for someone with a straight set. I feel something inside me ignite, a buzz, a rush of blood. I really am desperate for some sort of sexual encounter with a hot-blooded male. I want to feel the passion again, feel the heavy warmth of a man on top of me, the clinging and clawing of hands on bare skin, hungry kissing. Satiation.

It's embarrassing that the simple act of some male attention is making my mind turn into PornHub.

Aaah fuck. I forgot to pack my vibrator.

We have a couple of minutes more idle chit-chat before we both sit back, our headphones firmly planted in our ears and the flight takes off. In the movies, a casual plane romance is about as easy as ordering a McDonalds. It's difficult to strike up a conversation when you've both got your ears plugged; maybe I could try at the next mealtime. Kiss over a microwaved tray of potatoes and a plastic cup of tea – classy.

My runaway script of a romantic sexual encounter with a warm, pulsing male has been shattered by the sterile conditions of my surroundings.

I sit back with a miniature bottle of Pinot and watch one of Hollywood's latest blockbuster comedy movies, where a group of pensioners have somehow been sent on an 18-30 club holiday in Cancun. If this movie's going to do anything for me, at least it's going to well and truly put the dampener on my erotic fantasy foreplay.

Dreamy Mr Tortoiseshell lets me out to use the bathroom and when he comes back, I notice he is without headphones.

'Have you been to Hong Kong before?' he asks as I settle myself awkwardly back into my seat. There're too many blankets, bags and human for such a small space even if this is Premium Economy. My mind immediately wanders to tangled sheets, the way Luke's hands used to hold the curves and arches of my back as if he was scared I'd disappear, the way he knew exactly where to kiss me and how each time felt as exciting as the first time even though it was impossible to count anymore.

'Never. Have you?'

'Yeah, a few times, it's really amazing. I'm actually going there on a stag. My friend has been working out in Hong Kong for a couple of years and we thought what a great excuse for a holiday and a party.'

'That sounds wild!' It's cringe. I know I'm cringe. I don't know how to be sexy anymore. 'I'm on a sabbatical and decided to do some travelling – see the world, you know.'

'That's cool. I've never heard of anyone actually doing a sabbatical.' Told you, Harry. But he does think I'm cool. No one has said that before either. 'I couldn't help noticing that you're reading *The Catcher in the Rye* – great book!' he exclaims, his eyes looking eager but it's probably my imagination.

'Oh.' I laugh. 'Well, I'm actually doing this . . .' I twiddle a piece of hair between my fingers, suddenly feeling coy, 'stupid thirty under thirty bucket list. Harry, my friend . . .' I caveat, realising that he knows nothing about me apart from my literary choice, 'told me I need to be more spontaneous, but one of my original things was to read ten good books – the ones that everyone says you should read but most people haven't.' I look at him, using the hood of my eyelids as a semi-shield, my lashes gentle fluttering, inviting him to really look at me. *Come on, flirt. You know how to flirt.*

'That's a great idea! Wish I'd thought of that a couple of years ago.' Ok, so he's thirty-two-ish – good age. 'What else is on the list?'

Fucking you. My brain urges my lips to say it, but my mind is still captivated by thoughts of Luke. The rhythmic feel of his body underneath mine, the hard waves in his chest, the grip of his hands around my waist.

I pull out my phone and open the notes section – where I have my original list and then my new one from Harry. Fuck.

'Ha ha.' I laugh awkwardly as *Sleep with random men and DON'T WORRY ABOUT ANYTHING OTHER THAN STIs* stares at back me. 'That's the new list, from my friend . . .'

'Harry,' he answers, smiling.

'Yes.' I smile back and hesitate. 'Want to get a drink?'

'Sure.' He presses the little air hostess button, and we sit in a slightly awkward silence. It's not the same as going to the hustle and bustle of a bar; sitting next to each other in a plane seat with other people's breath being circulated around you – they don't accurately represent that in Hollywood.

A few drinks later and I'm starting to feel drunk. Is this what travelling's like, having no inhibitions, meeting random men? It's so not me but I like it. Dreamy Mr Tortoiseshell is called Richard. Harry once told me that Richard was a pseudonym for Dick, after a fanciable Richard at Secondary School threw Quavers over her, which is both fact and fiction at the same time.

Richard asks me more about my bucket list and tells me all the hip places to go in Hong Kong and I eagerly scrawl them down in the notes section of my phone, imagining the look on people's faces when I upload my first selfie on Lan

Kwai Fong with a male model before he declares his love for me as we continue our travels and walk across the Great Wall of China.

It's not the steamy, romantic, flirtatious display that I'd imagined in my head because we're surrounded by the hum of the plane engine, nylon blankets, snores of aged men and plastic but not the fun kind.

We both laugh in response to a story about the stag who once got so high, he thought he was Batman, protecting all women in the hustle and bustle of Oxford Street at 3.00 p.m. Richard says, 'I've never met a woman as carefree as you are.' For obvious reasons, no one has ever said this to me before, so for the same reason, I lean in and kiss him.

It doesn't even seem to bother me that we are in the presence of hundreds of other people – they are as disengaged as they are on the work commute – and the air hostess has decided it should be night-time so we're all in the dark anyway.

I think about what Harry said, or the alcohol thinks for me. I should be spontaneous. I'm on holiday. And the last time I saw a penis was in my dreams, which is kind of gross.

I lean over and unbutton his jeans; he pulls the cheap nylon-dressed-as-wool blanket over as I slide my hand into his pants. Is this what frivolity feels like? I feel exhilarated and I'm not even receiving.

I start rubbing my left hand up and down his shaft as he grips my arm with pleasure to stop himself from groaning. I feel great. I feel wanted.

'Do you want to . . . ?' Richard gestures towards the toilet cubicle.

'No,' I respond quickly. 'Let's just stay here.' It's not that I don't want him to touch me, but I want to have my own fantasy thoughts of Luke, close my eyes and think only of him, when sex had meaning.

I suddenly start to panic that someone might see us, although everyone around us seems to have their eyes shut or is wearing an eye-mask.

'I'm about to come,' Richard whispers in my ear. Thankfully, the novelty of being wanked off by a stranger on a plane seems to fulfil a fantasy that's making him relatively quick to orgasm. Despite Richard describing me as carefree, the old, rulebook Seffy is really starting to panic that someone's going to come over and ask why she's wanking off the man next to her.

'Not in my jeans,' he continues. 'I've got to wear these to the stag.'

What am I supposed to do? Ping the little air hostess icon and ask her for some tissue because the stranger I'm tossing off doesn't want to muck up his jeans? Luke wouldn't have done this. I look around – Seffy, you should have planned for this.

'Here.' I put the plastic cup I had my gin in under his penis as he comes and releases a little groan.

I watch as the sticky white liquid slops down the side of the cup. Not very Hollywood. Richard goes to the bathroom to clean himself up. This really wasn't the sexual display my mind had taunted me with.

Now what do I do with it? I pour some leftover tonic in the cup to disguise what I've just done and shove it into the pocket on the back of the seat. It's not quite the coveted milehigh club but I think Harry would be proud.

We sit and chat some more and then get back to watching a movie. It's slightly awkward as we still have four hours to go and don't have much more to talk about.

'We'll be landing in Hong Kong airport in about forty-five minutes. It's 7.00 a.m. local time, with clear blue skies and a morning temperature of twenty-five degrees. If you could keep your seatbelts on and refrain from using the bathroom while the seatbelt sign is illuminated, that would be appreciated.'

'Rubbish please.' The air hostess holds a black bin-liner between her hands as she walks down the aisle collecting rubbish. I hesitate before leaning over Richard and plopping the cum-tonic mixture in the bag.

Richard looks at me, confusion and disgust wrapped into one emotion.

'Yes, that was yours,' I respond as I finish the last line in my sudoku puzzle. Men are the same wherever you go – never prepared to deal with the aftermath.

'Cabin crew prepare for landing.'

I lean back.

I've made it. Hong Kong, here I come.

Two Months No Baby

Dearest Queen Angel-face Aphrodite and her Loving Sister Vivacious Venus,

My period has been and gone and I'm onto my next cycle. Ten months of watching blood swirl in the toilet basin. Ten months is nothing in the grand scheme of things. It's just, I don't know. Well, Venus, you get me – I'm impatient. Impatience is a good thing, I think, in terms of drive and determination, but waiting to see if blood is going to seep into my knickers is not something I want to put a timer on. When I was younger, I'd pray for my period to arrive. I didn't want to have that conversation at sixteen with my mother. Asking for birth control was enough – *The pill, Seffy?* she'd screeched. *You're not even fifteen.* The only willy I knew was Mr Wonka. I smiled as I responded – *I always thought you'd make a glamorous grandmother.* Then she marched me straight down to the doctor's surgery and demanded I see Dr Faziar immediately. Being my mother, she also made me go to a family planning clinic and had explained to me, in detail, how your vagina expands to ten centimetres before a human rugby ball shoots out. I don't know if she was trying to push her own regrets about having children onto me or not, nothing about her surprised me anymore. She probably couldn't deal with the thought of a grandchild. Another being that has a bloodline link to my father.

It's hard not to be impatient when everyone's clicking their fingers and clacking their tongues waiting for the big baby announcement. I wouldn't be surprised if they've all put bets down at the local bookies like people do for the royal family. Can you imagine? People betting on your chance of procreation as if you were Prancer Dancer in the Grand National? Diane, the dreaded mother-in-law, is already doing my nut in. Luke tells his mother everything. I mean EVERYTHING. He told her that we were trying for a *baby, which is a cardinal sin in conceiving. You don't tell anyone until the seed is sown. What if something happens? It's bad luck. Just because you use the term 'trying for a baby', it doesn't make the reality any less clear. It's the same as 'making love' or 'shagging' – you're telling everyone in your address book, including your whole family and your partner's whole family, that you're actively having sex – would you do that normally? Why does all normal social etiquette go out the window as soon as the four-letter cannonball B-A-B-Y gets involved? Why can't they all be like you Aph – a silent witness?*

Diane kept asking, as a certain kind of woman over the thirty milestone does, when are you going to have children? Have you thought about starting a family? You only have so many years you know. As if my eggs were going to suddenly freeze up in an imminent womb ice-age. I could be lying in a pool of blood with a shot wound and she would still check if my womb was ok first. And that's when Luke said, we're already trying.

He was only trying to be nice, to please his mum, but still.

I mean? Do I want everyone knowing my sex cycle? I might as well send all my grandparents a home-porno; it would probably be more private.

Anyway, then darling Diane started WhatsApping me, sending me links to eat more bananas to improve my fertility and to stop drinking caffeine. She'd send them with a caption such as; Did you know that drinking caffeine every day can cause birth defects? I'm not trying to tell you what to do but it's known to cause infertility, premature labour and reproductive problems – I'd try to cut back if I were you. You're basically saying that if you see me drinking a Starbucks, I may as well take a dagger to your unborn grandchild. She crossed the line (even further) when she told me to make sure I had sex every day and, You know it's important to keep it exciting in the bedroom, even at my age. Have you tried role-play? What do you play? Pretend robbery at the Post Office on pension day? She once half-closed her eyes, put a hand on my shoulder and said, Seffy, it would be lovely if I could see at least one grandchild born before I die. As if I can pop out a fully-fledged human at the drop of a hat. Would you like a side of grandson with your dessert? I'll say casually as I whip up a homemade lemon meringue pie on a warm Sunday afternoon. I lost it at that.

It was funny that Diane was talking about dying as it was only the other week that she went to put some flowers on her father's grave and realised that someone had been buried in her pre-booked spot next to Luke's grandad. The next week when she returned to tidy up the dried blooms the spot had been emptied again – talk about jumping in your grave. Oh sorry, let me just dig up the body of this daughter/ mother/grandmother and chuck them in the empty patch of soil over by those trees. As if this poor DEAD soul had accidentally taken your room in a hotel. But that's the sort of woman Diane can be. She likes things done when she wants them done. Like me actually. I can't help it that I have no control over my eggs – trust me, I wish I had.

Is Diane the sign I asked for, Aphrodite? Because if she is (try and make the signs less irritating next time), I'll swallow all negative thoughts and bow down to her like the obliging daughter-in-law I am.

'She doesn't mean it,' Luke said, washing the pan he'd sautéed the onions in for the ratatouille, as I return from my own thoughts, leaning against the counter. 'It's just her way of being involved; she always wanted a daughter.' I can sense that slight exasperation in his voice as I explain again what he should be saying in response to his mother *as I read out yet another message, asking about the wellness of my internal fertility organs as if they control my mood.*

'I don't care, Luke! Don't you think it's slightly inconsiderate and rude? She's making me feel like I'm failing, that I'm not trying hard enough.'

'It's not an exam, babe.' He rinses the pan and places it upturned on the drying rack. 'It's procreation, it will happen. Just relax, ignore everyone else and let's just be us. I'm not asking you to agree with my mum, just placate her – she'll eventually get bored and move on.' He walks over and pulls me in for a hug. 'I love you, ok? Nothing else matters.'

It shouldn't matter. My husband's love should be enough for me. And it is. But I'd really like to be pregnant as well. We're going out on Saturday, to a friend's engagement drinks. I'll get to swan around with my gorgeous husband on my arm, tittering at people's jokes, have friends tell me how great our wedding was. It will be the confidence boost I need.

I think my period cycle is too long. I've been reading online, and I'm pretty sure I need some progesterone injections. If you have a long cycle, you need progesterone to keep the egg alive and I know that if I can just get this all sorted now, the whole pregnancy debacle will be over with. A couple of tiny jabs in the leg and that's it. Job done. Diane can get off my back.

Me: Do you think 42 days is a long menstruation period?
Harry: *I googled and it's the same length as a kangaroo.*
Harry: *Sorry. A kangaroo has three vaginas. THREE VAGINAS. Imagine a guy trying to find the g spot.*

I booked the doctor because I need some sanity back in my life. I feel like I can't talk to Luke about it anymore. We had a huge argument on Tuesday. We've been having sex every three days because I read that it was better for successful conception. Tuesday was sex day. I messaged him to see when he was getting home and he said I'm going out for a beer with Leo, won't be long. Two hours later, I messaged again. He said it's turned into a bit of a wild one and I'll be home later. I waited and I waited, and I waited. I must have fallen asleep because when I woke up it was 6.00 a.m. and Luke was fast asleep and stinking of whisky on the sofa. If it was a weekend, I'd be out with him, but I'm desperately trying to get promoted at work so I can't afford to greet Moira with furry teeth and a cloudy head. Anyway, I thought I'd be having a night in, fucking my husband – surely that's most men's fantasies?

'Do you know what yesterday was?' I say as I poke him. I hate arguing. We never argue but I can't help myself. I have a sudden need to release a wolf among the sheep.

'Erm?' He blinks gormlessly, his eyes red from a night of drinking, as if someone had farted on the sofa cushion. I wish I had. 'Tuesday?'

'Yes, Tuesday! We were supposed to be having sex! The whole cycle's messed up now. I can't believe you've been so inconsiderate!' I scream at him. I was trying to keep it calm but the air in my lungs has turned to steam. The wolf has been released. I can't take it back now.

'What the fuck, Seffy?' He sits up, looking at me as if trying to work out who's possessed his wife. 'You've gone crazy. We can have sex later. Big fucking deal.' He rolls over with his hands over his eyes.

'Why do men always think it's acceptable to call girls crazy or bossy or mardy? It's so misogynistic. I'll start using gendered descriptors to undermine your behaviour – authoritarian, bolshy, arrogant, irresponsible . . . twat. You don't understand, do you? It's fucking hard.' What's happening to me? I'd never say this. I know that it sounds

silly; Luke hasn't done anything 'wrong' really, but I want to be annoyed with him. I feel tears rolling down my face. I'm annoyed with myself. 'Everywhere I look people are falling pregnant as if you put your hands in the air and shout "me next"! All I want is to have a family and it's not happening. It doesn't matter how hard I work at trying to have a baby, nothing's working.' I start really crying. I can feel my nose fill with mucus, and I know my cheeks are red and blotchy.

'Seffy, chill out, you're making yourself stressed. I'm sorry, I didn't mean to call you crazy. I'm not thinking, I've just woken up, well, you've woken me up. Let's talk about it later. I'm super hungover and I need to go to work.' He slowly sits up on the sofa, and I smell a fresh waft of alcohol and stale smoke. He puts his hand out to me as he tries to make sense of the situation, but I can't. I suddenly feel distant from him. Why have I been shouting at my husband because he forgot to have sex with me?

I stand there, red-faced, tears dripping down my cheeks, in a self-induced rage, worrying about the state of my womb and future procreation. While Luke, not a care in the world, lies on the sofa pushing everything to the back of his mind for later or never. He should be feeling the same as me. Well, he can't procreate alone. Maybe I'll box off my womb as a no-go zone until I decide that I'm ready to procreate.

I went to the doctor's the next day and explained my predicament. He looked at me – you need to stop worrying. The more anxious you make yourself the harder this will be.

I asked him about my menstruation cycle and my imminent need for progesterone. The doctor advised me that I'm a woman in my twenties, who has regular periods and therefore I have nothing to worry about. The biggest hurdle in my pregnancy journey is putting too much pressure on myself. He prescribed me daily meditation and at least biweekly abstinence.

I thought about what the doctor said, and I guess he's probably right. As soon as I returned home, I went into my special box under the bed and collected all the used pregnancy tests, thoroughly scrubbed, and threw them in the bin. I don't want Luke to see them; he'll be mad. I do at least one test every day, sometimes two if I accidentally do my first wee straight into the toilet bowl and not on the stick when I wake up. You do the maths.

Is it weird to keep used pregnancy tests? It's like my training. I was keeping them to prove how hard I'd worked. Like some strange sort of medals.

I messaged Luke to apologise about the argument. He was fine about it. He said, I know it's frustrating Seffy but you really need to relax about it. I love you; everything will be ok. Don't listen to anyone else, just focus on us. There's no point getting stressed, it will happen when it happens – you can't mess with nature. He's going to come home tonight with my favourite sushi takeaway and a bottle of wine. And I'm sure that will lead to make-up sex which will be great and compensate for the lack on Tuesday. I want him to want me. I want that feeling of lust again. The grip of his hands on my inner thigh, holding handfuls of flesh, that raw, primal instinct I crave. His lips hanging on to mine, biting, touching, attached in ways that can't happen outside the ultimate urge of need. See Venus, I can be sexy.

A message from Ashleigh, the first one in the group of uni friends to get pregnant – Baby B is on the way! I replied, like everyone does, Congratulations! I'm so so happy for you! I'm not happy. I'm jealous. Why can't it be me? Why can't I be the first to have a baby? I want a mini-me to love, people to send me gifts of flowers, biscuits, cards and everyone to tell me how cute the mixture of Luke's and my genes are on a chubby little doll. It sounds superficial but it's really not. There are millions of reasons I want to have a baby but the main one is, to be a better mother than my own.

You know, Aphrodite, Venus, I don't even want a child for selfish reasons, like someone to look after me when I'm older. I want a child so I can give it the ULTIMATE childhood – I'm talking trips to buy pick 'n' mix on a Saturday, fast-track passes at Alton Towers, treasure hunts in the garden. The childhood I never had but always wanted. I can reinvent mine through the eyes of the child and they can live out their early years believing in love, fairy tales and Father Christmas. Surely that alone puts me at the top of the 'woman looking to bear child' wish list? If there is such a macabre thing.

I think I'll wear the lacy red set tonight to really get Luke's pulse going. Maybe if we go all out and have outrageous, raunchy sex, his sperm will swim faster and puncture my egg. You're right, Venus, I should try harder at being sexy. Maybe that's it. Maybe the boring, narcoleptic romps are not giving his sperm enough power.

Please PLEASE Aphrodite let this be the last period I have. I promise I won't even complain about cankles or insomnia, I'll welcome it with open arms.

All my love, kisses and hugs,

Seffy xxx

Eleven Months Until Thirty

7

It's humid in Hong Kong – my hair is in a constant state of flux. I've been living a life of luxury, staying in the Mandarin Oriental Hotel. I need to ease myself into travelling; I can't stay in a mite-infested room with three pubescents in my first week. *Fuck, Seffy you're such a snob sometimes.* I hear Luke saying it, the way he grounded me.

Hong Kong is an incredible place but it's hard when you're alone. I imagine myself wandering the streets with Luke, laughing, stopping for beers at hidden bars, smiling, kissing, simply being happy. I remember him now for who he actually was, not the monster I wanted him to be when I was hurting the most.

I peer through the window at girl gangs carelessly laughing at bottomless brunches or stand behind happy families waiting for my turn at attractions. It's a bit like London in that sense; people don't take pity on a lone ranger, or a ninja-turtle-impersonator with my backpack on, they look you up and down and then go through multiple scenarios in their head as to why you are alone. *Did she get stood up? Do you think he had an affair? Do you think she's a barren divorcee?* No one would guess that one; it's not socially acceptable. I've never been that good at making friends, that's why I stick with the ones I've got. I'm too awkward.

Thankfully, there's a trophy cabinet of solo exploring on offer. I've been doing a lot of walking, at least twenty-six thousand steps per day, and my calves have never been so toned. In the evening, when you're supposed to be out, drinking cold beers on sticky wooden lacquered tables, smoking Marlboros as if you were sucking sherbet lemons and becoming at one with your feral side, I've been inside watching Sky movies, which, I'm well aware, is on the lamer side of lame.

I have made one 'friend' – Mr Joseph Kwong as he introduced himself – the doorman. He's everything you'd want in a man, kind mainly – he asks me every day, *And where have you been today Miss Seffy?* He listens to everything I say and even laughs at my jokes. He always holds the door open and offers me a bottle of water when my make-up has melted off in the forty-degree heat (even Charlotte Tilbury hasn't made her foundation *that* waterproof) and my hair's standing on end looking cheaper than an IKEA toilet brush. I could be here on a business trip, but I think perhaps my Pretty Little Thing co-ords are giving it away slightly. I hope Joseph doesn't think I'm an escort, staying in a swanky hotel alone but even if he does, he hasn't let it tar our three-day friendship.

I took the Star Ferry yesterday across to Kowloon. I stood on the deck and watched as groups of expats partied on little yachts, drinking bottles of Asahi, diving like flexible bronzed statues into the gleaming sea. Richard and his stag were probably on one. If Harry were here, I'm sure we'd be joining in with some frat group, making our mark on the big HK. I walked along the Victoria Harbour waterfront to see the Avenue of Stars, and as if that wasn't cringe enough, I asked another unsuspecting tourist to take a photo of me with my hands in John Woo's prints for my Instagram. Harry laughed and commented, *John Who*? I licked a purple sweet potato ice-cream, the exact balance of sweet and savoury that I was searching for, creamy yet refreshing, and took in the salty smell of the sea. The infrastructure's incredible and everything's so clean – there's not so much as a wrapper on the MTR, and people didn't start tutting when I couldn't scan my Octopus card. In London I would have been slapped through the barrier faster than an Aldi cashier. Skyscrapers stretch as far as the eye can see, glinting in the sunlight like little stars. It's a magical place, like a theme park for the industrious. I can imagine myself living here, absorbed in my work in the day and partying with the other islanders at night. That would be if I could transport my friends here with me.

I've been trying not to think about Luke but sometimes, as I'm walking, I feel my hand stretch out, reaching for his. That close comfort, interlacing fingers, the way he'd gently rub my thumb with his, reassuring. Then my hand closes in on nothing but air and sharp nails, reminding me that I put the dagger in my own heart. My own stubbornness preventing it from being healed.

Joseph recommended that I head to Mong Kok for the street food, he said *There's no better place to eat Miss Seffy. You must try the pig intestines; they are a local delicacy.* He was right; for authentic Hong Kong, Mong Kok is the place. The heat, the smells, the noise, the culture – it's a party for the senses. I visited ten different stalls just to try as much as I could although I did give the pig intestines a miss. It would be entertaining to uncoil the fried offal, dangle it into each other's mouths and scream in a group, but not alone. The chitter-chatter between the stall owners, the friendly banter between owners and customers, that impossible heat beating off the griddle pans and the way you can taste the cacophony of sweet and savoury in the air. Salt of soy sauce and tang of rice vinegar cutting through the humidity, piercing your nostrils and making you want to go back for more. Clinking of pans, the noise of unfamiliar voices, your eyes darting from left to right transfixed by scenes you thought only existed in your guidebook.

It's not that I'm not enjoying myself, in my own way anyway. I'd rather be alone in Hong Kong than alone at my desk in London, being brutally attacked by a rabid banshee. I've been groomed by the world to become the working woman stereotype of my imagination. Long gone are the days when I would close my eyes and my brain would take me to far-flung galaxies where people lived on other planets, or I'd go hiking through the jungle looking for treasure. Figments of my imagination are overgrown with the treacherous tale of life.

I'm pondering all these thoughts while sipping a blueberry bubble tea on the wall near the harbour. That's all you can do when you're alone; think.

I check my emails because I can't help myself and hidden in the swathe of marketing spiel from companies I don't even remember giving my details to are two black and white daggers that make my heart skip a beat.

> *Dear Seraphina,*
> *Please find a certified copy of your divorce certificate attached to this email.*
> *There are no further fees to pay.*
> *I wish you the very best in your future endeavours.*
>
> *Regards,*
> *Rosie Landown*

I feel my anxiety rise and fall. My eyes water ever so slightly. Memories flash in front of my eyes before I swallow them away. I knew it was coming but it's just so final. That's it, the line in the sand. We are done.

I have this sudden urge to text him, to tell him I didn't mean it but it's too late. I want to hear from him, anything, so I send an unnecessary question instead. Just to be able to see his name pop up on my screen again feels like home.

Me: *Hey, did you get the papers?*

Do I put a kiss? Do divorced people put kisses? Probably not.
Luke: *Yes.*

I see the dots on the screen still whirring as if he has something else to say, before they stop and don't return.

Turns out divorced people don't put kisses or emojis, just
monosyllabic and passive aggressive punctuation. It's so not
Luke. It's so not me. It's so not us.

I feel a bubble rise in my throat, like a black hole, swal-
lowing all the oxygen that I need to breathe. A tear drips and
lands on the surface of my bubble tea. I need to stop thinking
about him. It's over. What's done is done.

I blink back the water that's slowly drowning my eyes and
go for the next dagger, although this one is surprisingly less
painful, almost an enjoyable stab compared to the first.

*Seff, as I KINDLY let you jaunt around the world, I need
you to go into the Hong Kong office tomorrow and meet
the team. They need you to sit in on a call with the PB
investors.*

Moira. I sigh.

I know that the Harry in me would tell her to fuck off. But
I already know what the Seffy in me is going to do.

I need it to take my mind off the fact that I am now officially a divorcée.

I reply: *No problem.*

I walk through the revolving doors and am immediately hit
by the cool breeze of the air conditioning. Due to Harry's
packing skills, I have nothing office appropriate, so I had to
pop to Central to pick up a pencil skirt and blouse. Joseph
took a step back when he saw me this morning – *Big day*

Miss Seffy! he squealed as my heels did the all-too-familiar click-clack across the hotel tiles.

I collect my visitor pass and go up to the fifth floor to meet Celine Chong, Head of Prime.

'*Néih hóu,*' I say as I see the petite lady with a perfectly trimmed short black bob of hair and a protruding belly. 'Congratulations,' I say, smiling.

'Hi Seraphina.' Celine responds in perfect English. 'Thank you, she is due in four weeks.'

'Please, call me Seffy.' I hold out my hand. 'Wow. It must be hard working so close to the due date.' Celine carries her baby girl well. She's still wearing a pair of black suede heels; the bump looks fake with her slender arms and legs, and she still only has one chin. That's what I hoped I'd be like, living my life until one day the baby would just pop out. Perfectly polished. People would say I was born to be pregnant which is totally against all my feminist views and only adds to the list of life expectancies us women are supposed to abide by, but I wanted to hear it.

'It is what it is.' She smiles. 'I'm grateful for every minute that I carry her. Shall we?'

Grateful.

That's what they all said – doctors, Luke. I should be *grateful.* Maybe if I'd listened it wouldn't have all unravelled like a loose ball of string being dropped from the top of Niagara Falls. I could have been like Celine, happy, having the child she always wanted, that I always wanted.

We walk through the office, people looking up and smiling at me as I walk. This is much more friendly than London. Celine is a breath of fresh air compared to Moira who doesn't let a breath slip about her personal life.

There are women.

Everywhere.

'So many women are working here,' I say before I can stop myself.

Celine laughs. 'Yes, I do notice that in our London correspondence it's always men. I've heard that, in our industry, many women leave work to have families – banking seems to be a bit of a boys' club.' I nod as if I understand that feeling. 'Women have families a lot later in Hong Kong.' Celine is so blasé, so open about something so personal. 'And you, Seffy? Do you have a family at home?'

No and I never will. In fact, the only person that I truly loved, well, we officially got divorced as of two hours ago. You're currently talking to the antithesis of family.

I check myself and respond with the more appropriate, 'Not yet.'

We stop outside a glass meeting room – four young women and one man sit inside around the table with a conference phone in the middle. This glass box resembles a serene terrarium instead of the animal cage back home. The only time I've ever seen this type of glorious gender imbalance is in a fashion house; I'd never have expected to see it in finance.

'Please go in and meet the team. I'll be back in a few minutes.'

Hi Moira,
You'll be pleased to hear the meeting went well. Please find the minutes below, any questions let me know.

Thanks,
Seffy

No response. I should have added in a YouTube link to a live birth to really make her head turn.

It's infuriating that she has this hold over me, but I do need my job back; I can't be dilly-dallying around the world forever.

'Seffy, this is Queenie, our desk assistant.' Celine introduces me to a glamorous lady, sitting behind the desk. Hair that Rapunzel would be jealous of and lashes even longer. White painted almond nails and fingers adorned with gold rings.

'Nice to meet you, Seffy.' She smiles confidently. 'You're from London, right?'

'Yes, I'm supposed to be having time off from work.' I roll my eyes and curl my lips upwards.

'Hmmm, I'm not sure PP Lewes understand the word "holiday". If you want to go for some drinks, meet some people, then let me know – I'm always up for fun.' She grins invitingly.

We exchange numbers, like we're going on a date, but it feels more rewarding than that. I've been missing that feeling of slight inebriation where your soul speaks before your brain, and everything is doused in a rosy hue.

I stop by a traditional Chinese medicine store on the way back to my extortionately overpriced duck down pillow and miniature selection of perfectly chilled Pinot Grigio – which I would like to drink my way through most evenings, but won't. My mum would basically have throttled me to the floor as a child if I had even sniffed the M&M packet in the mini bar. I'm also no alcoholic like my mother – I know my limits.

Rows upon rows of little packets, dried goods and information in traditional Chinese characters – I've always loved the way their language looks, like little pieces of art. I can't read it, but I can appreciate the way it looks. I pause by a sign that's written in English for the uneducated like myself; *Fertility Begins Here.*

I know I'm supposed to be out here enjoying myself, forgetting about the life I've left behind, but I can't stop. Today, I've got officially divorced and been back at work. Adding 'remembering I'm infertile' to the list really isn't going to make this day any worse.

I run my hands across the white information signs – *Adzuki beans, Lepidium Meyenii,Vitex.*

Vitex agnus-castus (Chaste tree berry) boosts fertility by increasing luteinising hormone and reduces symptoms of menopause.

Lepidium Meyenii (Maca root) can increase the chances of a healthy egg and sperm mobility.

Adzuki beans can promote healthy ovulation.

'May I help you?'

Her voice startles me.

'Oh. Erm, I'm just looking. Thank you.' I feel embarrassed. As if she's caught me stealing. It's like she's just found me out – a woman who can't perform the simple act of proving her fertility.

She has chestnut brown hair with rust-coloured highlights, scraped back into an immaculate bun. A white polo shirt tucked into a pair of forest-green chinos and white clumpy trainers.

'I can give you some information about some of the products?' It's as if she can sense my insecurities and knows if she doesn't speak first then nothing will be said.

I want to know. My heart is yearning to know about these products.

'Erm, yes that would be helpful.' I shouldn't feel embarrassed; these products exist for people like me. People who need help. It means it's not just me who feels like this. Sometimes knowing this makes me feel lonelier than ever.

She walks me over to a dark corner of the shop where some of the dry ingredients are laid out before me in little bowls.

'What are all these things?' I say, slightly astounded. It's like an incredible array of spices, as if she's about to whip up the most amazing culinary creation.

'These are medicines, vitamins and foods all known to boost your fertility. We have many women, here in Hong Kong, who swear about regulating and improving their Qi for successful conception.'

'What's Qi?' I ask, confused.

'Qi is vital energy, the ying and the yang that makes up and binds everything all around us. Your body has Qi and you need to regulate the flow in your body. Clear your systems and prepare your body, your blood supply, your ovaries to bear children.'

I never really thought about preparing your body. I sit still, intrigued by what she has to say.

She continues, 'We believe that you must think about cleaning your body and then nourishing it with good foods and vitamins, everything that you need for the baby. Many women come here.' She pulls out a little leaflet and points to it. 'These are all the bad things that your body doesn't need.' She gestures to a red circle which contains cigarettes, alcohol, coffee and crisps. Everything I read told me to avoid those things too. 'And then these are some foods that are really good.' She points to pomegranate, blackberries, purple sweet potato, shiitake mushrooms, some sort of bean. No one ever told me what I should be eating instead. 'There are also many vitamins and medicines that can help regulate you flow of Qi – Vitex, Maca, Carthamus Flower.'

I sit perplexed, 'And do these things work?'

'Yes.' She nods, enthusiastically. 'We have many women who swear by their Qi for fertility.'

I thought I'd tried everything. I know what the doctor said to me but there's still always that glimmer of hope even if I don't currently have anyone to procreate with. I can't help but always think about what could be; it's not like there's anything to take my mind off babies, however hard I try. I'm still not ready to totally erase having a family from my life. I want, more than anything, to be a good mother.

'What if you've been told that you won't be able to have children yourself?' I ask, feeling my throat close slightly.

'We think that sometimes people believe too much in modern-day medicine and don't open their hearts, minds and bodies to the possibilities of natural remedies.'

Is she right? I remember how I would sit and wish myself into the future, day after day after day, imagining myself sitting on the sofa, next to Luke, feeding our precious little one. Smiling at their chubby cheeks and squinty expression, cooing over the gurgles, stroking every tiny finger.

'I'll take the lot please.'

She clasps her hands together, bows her head and scurries off to the assistant who hurriedly packs up my bag.

8

Harry: *Did you know that a dolphin always sleeps with one eye open?*
Me: *No . . . why do they do that?*
Harry: *I dunno – they are really clever animals though; I might try it. See if it has any benefits.*
Me: *I don't think it's the sort of thing you can just 'try' – it's more something you'd see a therapist to stop doing.*
Harry: *I'd love it if I slept with one eye open, it would be hilarious when you had a one-night stand. Super creepy. I'll Sellotape my eye open tonight and report back any benefits.*

I'm laughing until the moment I screenshot the message, realising that I no longer have a husband to share it with. Luke would have laughed and made a silly quip involving cornea puns and horny dolphins and I would have laughed some more. I miss him.

It wasn't like any break-up I've ever been through before. He didn't have an affair; he still loved me, kind of. I can't help but wonder what would happen if I were like other women and my eggs had been waiting patiently in a line-up like the queue at the supermarket. Eventually, would we have divorced anyway? Would it all have got too much one day and he'd leave his washing-up on the side and that be the final straw? That's a reason people break up, isn't it, when they fall out of love? Except I didn't fall out of love, I momentarily forgot about it while I focused it all on an unborn child yet to be created. But he didn't ask me to come back. Or maybe it was all my fault. The hand I'd been dealt in the genetic pool was the catalyst, and always will be.

Queenie's arranged for us to go for some drinks tonight. I need a break from thinking, and I need to enjoy my life. *Be More Harry.*

I feel glamorous. I feel sexy. I feel like me. I plaited my hair in a French braid after my shower and now it's hanging loosely around my shoulders in soft waves, I've gone for a subtle, brown eyeshadow and even outlined my lips. I'm wearing a short black camisole dress with a slight cowl back to show off my figure.

I know I'm fuckable but without anyone to fuck.

'Wow, Miss Seffy,' Joseph exclaimed as he bows his head and opens the door.

'Thank you, Joseph.' I widen my eyes in slight flirtatious gratuity. 'I'm off to the Hong Kong Club to meet a friend.'

'Ah ha. Very fancy. I won't wait up.' He laughs and waves me on.

It's a short walk to the club to meet Queenie, over two zebra crossings – which I'm thankful for, given the heat. I can already feel beads of sweat on my brow and the slight cling of my dress.

The receptionist takes my name and escorts me to a dimly lit dining room. Polished walnut wood, racing green leather armchairs and the heavy smell of men's aftershave. It's like I've been given a secret key to where all the men do business at PP Lewes. It's a metaphor for a fancy crisp packet filled with deep-fat fried Jeffs. Moira would be quivering that I've been allowed access before her.

'Seffy! You look gorgeous!' Queenie gets up from the table and kisses each cheek. She's wearing a fuchsia pink bodycon dress, a dainty gold chain that sits perfectly on her collarbone and heels that I'm pretty sure are Dolce & Gabbana.

'So do you!' I return the compliment.

'Have you ever been to the club before?' Queenie asks, passing me a cut-glass tumbler of ice-cold water and popping an olive between her lips. 'Don't worry, drinks are on their way,' she says, the shape of the olive poised in her left cheek.

'No, it's a member's club, isn't it? I've heard there's a huge waitlist.' I've heard Jeffs talking about them in London. I silently wonder how the desk assistant can afford such luxury.

'Ya. My dad's a member and I thought it would be cool for you to see inside one of Hong Kong's most elite clubs!' She winks, laughing. 'Don't worry – it can be a bit stuffy.' She waves an arm round at Jeffs chatting, eating fried slices of their friends. 'I'll take you to some *real* bars after.'

Queenie names the hot places of Hong Kong which I eagerly write down in my notes section, pleased to have another list to rattle my way through. I tell her about my thirty under thirty bucket list to which she reacts with glee.

After the second mojito, Queenie checks her phone and announces that two of her friends are meeting us in Ozone and calls a cab.

'Wow,' I exclaim as we enter the blue lit bar on the 118th floor. The walls are made of refracted glass and the floor radiates light; everything is accentuated in gold. It's like a gaudy fish tank for a koi carp.

'Cool, hey? They do the best cocktails – the Ozone uses a creme de menthe and dry ice, kind of like the real ozone layer.' It's a questionable fact, but still I'll probably try it and give my usual Pinot Grigio a day off and my tastebuds a little zing.

As we clatter across the mirrored floor, we're greeted by a guy teetering over to us in his own set of heels. Hair swept over to one side, combed within an inch of its life and a bright, silk shirt covered in a sort of origami pattern that would appear crass on anyone else.

'Kit!' Queenie embraces him. 'This is Seffy, she's over from London.'

'London!' he squeals, pulling me in for a hug, almost toppling me over. 'I looooove London. Tell me alllll the hip places.' He links his arm in mine and drags me to the table. My face is plastered with a huge grin; this kind of friendliness I never get to see it. I love it. I could be like Kit if I removed my *Eau de Bitch*.

'And this is Ren.' Queenie introduces her Victoria's Secret model friend, whose smile makes her eyes dance. Her face is so elegant, it's as if Michelangelo carved it. Her hair cascades down in long black waves, filling out her slender frame. She looks how I wish I did.

'Lovely to meet you.' She holds out a delicately tanned arm, dressed in gold bangles.

Kit orders us a round of Ozones and some vodka shots and listens as he takes genuine interest in my life.

'Seffy's doing a thirty under thirty bucket list,' Queenie announces. 'Go on, tell them about it. I think it's so cool.' She nods her head and sips her drink.

'Yeah, erm, I'm doing this . . . bucket thing.' I suddenly feel all coy and shy. 'All the things I want to achieve before I'm thirty. I did make a list . . .' What am I saying? '. . . but it was a bit boring.' I laugh. 'My friend Harry told me it needs to be more spontaneous if I'm going to learn a few things from it, which she said I have to or it's just a set of tasks. So now it's more of an as-I-go-along-type thing.'

'I must see what you've done so far,' Ren says eagerly. 'What's made the cut?' She makes it sound like an exclusive club – a membership you'd die to get hold of. Being filmed stuffing your face with baked goods really lowers the tone.

'What are you supposed to be learning?' Kit asks, intrigued.

'Well . . .' I know it's the alcohol making my temporal lobe supercharged but it doesn't need to be a secret. 'I got married just over two years ago.' I watch all their eyes turn to my naked wedding finger and back up to my eyeline. 'And then I got divorced, officially last week, so I'm learning how to enjoy myself again.' I decide to skip out the whole baby part – I don't want to be a sob story.

'Oh darling!' Kit grabs my hands. 'In that case we need some more drinks!' He stands up and waves the waiter over.

'All the best people are divorced.' Queenie smiles. 'That's definitely something for the bucket list – surviving a marriage and a divorce.'

'We need to up our show and tell of Hong Kong in that case – this girl needs a party!' Ren giggles and orders a round of shots.

I show them all the list so far and recount in detail the whole tossing off into a cup story to which they throw their heads back in laughter. Seems like it doesn't lower the tone but adds another string of fun to my bow.

Maybe it's the six Ozones and the accumulation of dry ice freezing part of my cerebrum resulting in my impaired judgement, but I think Ren's flirting with me. I keep catching her staring. Every time I look up from my cocktail, she's studying me, her big brown eyes looking far deeper into my being than I would like. I would kill for her cheekbones and every time her hair brushes my shoulder I jolt, and she grins at my frigidity. I stare at Ren some more, trying to work out if I want to be her or if I genuinely might want to be with her. With another sip of Ozone, I come to the conclusion that I want to want her. If I fancy girls, I might finally stop loving Luke.

I excuse myself and go to the bathroom. I'm definitely starting to look drunk; my pupils are wide, and my spatial awareness is slightly awry.

I sit on the toilet, letting out a silent *ahhhh* as I pee. The bathroom's become a sort of sanctuary for me. I used to use the toilet like some sort of fortune teller, holding a little stick out to wee on every morning and wondering, hoping for two blue lines. Since the diagnosis, it's become a place where I often sit and think about what could have been – it's never just 'a wee' for me anymore.

Sometimes I find it hard to let go in a natural way. My mum was always such a powerful woman, and I never knew how she did it, not letting my dad's affair affect her until I heard the bins clinking on the way out. That's when I made sure I'd always be there to pick up the pieces, be organised for my brothers in case it was a day when my mum forgot to make breakfast or lunch or dinner. It's why I needed to ensure I had a successful career, one that paid for private health insurance, pensions, childcare. I needed to guarantee that I could stand on my own two feet, without a man. It was my own mother who made me determined to be a better parent, to prove that *fuck up* wasn't printed in my DNA. What a juxtaposition that is.

Anyway, this isn't a night for reminiscing. I pull up my thong, pull down my dress and flush the chain.

I look at my slightly bleary eyes in the mirror and retrieve my lipstick, ready to add a bit of class back to my look.

'Seffy.' I look away from my lips and see Ren behind me in the mirror.

'Oh, hey Ren,' I say, slightly flushed with embarrassment. Instantly feeling that electrical tingle from where her hair brushed my skin at the table.

'I've never been very good at doing lipstick, may you do mine for me?' she asks.

'Of course!' I reply, my hand feeling the butterflies, trembling slightly as I try not to give Ren an on-the-spot lip enhancement with my shakes.

She looks up to me, her eyes wide and then puts her hand on mine.

'I was thinking about your list, and you do really need to try new things.' She puts her hand on my chin and kisses me. I kiss her back. She tastes of creme de menthe and her perfume is sweet, tickling my nostrils. 'You're a great kisser.'

'Erm, thank you.' I feel myself blushing, not knowing what to say. 'So are you.'

'Ha! You British people are so polite, it's cute! Ready to join the others?' She kisses me on the cheek and leaves the bathroom while I compose myself.

I don't know what I was expecting, some sort of sexual exploration journey? But kissing Ren has not made me miraculously forget about Luke in five seconds. He'd probably never believe it – I'm not the kind of girl who kisses strangers in bathrooms, but then I would never have given a hand job on a plane either.

All it made me want to do is message Luke. He always used to ask me why girls spend so long in there. *What is so tantalising about bathrooms?* I'd tell him that all the best conversations happened in the toilet, ironic because we spent a great deal of our marriage talking, crying and fighting in the bathroom. It's come full circle for me now.

Seffy's 30 under 30 Bucket List:
#1 Read ten good books
#2 Do 30 pelvic floors a day
#3 Eat in front of someone and be filmed
#4 Go on a seven-month sabbatical
#5 Be spontaneous EVERY DAY
#6 Sleep with random men and DON'T WORRY ABOUT ANYTHING OTHER THAN STIS!!!!!!!
#7 Seffy's version of the mile-high club
#8 Stop restricting myself with my own sexuality

9

Justin: *Happy birthday sis! Hope you're having a good time in Hong Kong! Xx*
Me: *My birthday was over a month ago but thanks ;p xx*
Justin: *Fuck, sorry. It's the time difference and the beer. Mainly the beer Xx*

My youngest brother, Justin, has never been very good at remembering important dates. He's currently working on some renewable energy project in the Australian outback. He stays in touch when he's not trying to capture the sun to power people's nutribullets. He met someone six months ago called Carmella: *I've never met anyone like her, did you know she basically single-handedly saved the koalas?* It's hard to stay in touch because of the time difference, his job, my job and his lack of organisation. When I told him I was getting divorced, he arranged a huge card and bunch of flowers to be sent to my door and we had a *Get Fucked Luke* drinking marathon on Zoom.

My other brother, Chris, should suffer from classic middle-child syndrome and be an introvert according to many a famous child psychologist, but he's the ultimate gregarious type. He took it upon himself to be the older brother not only to Justin but also to me. Once he was old enough to feed himself, he saw himself as the leader of the pack – we were always trying to protect each other from the truth about our parents, to force each other to have a childhood.

It took a while for us to realise that our mother was an alcoholic because she didn't conform to the stereotypes they show on TV; she kept it together, for the most part anyway. It's just sometimes the lunchtime wine turned into afternoon wine and then late-night vodkas. She still managed to function and she didn't try to hide it; I don't think she thought she had a problem. When she met Adrian, she stopped drinking, and it was all holidays to St Tropez and mini breaks.

It's weird how it's not only your genes that make you who you are but all the little events that explode around you as you grow up. They teach you resilience, compassion, impatience – that the world can be broken down into tiny pockets of time and sequential events that if you habitually conform to, you can make it through to the next one.

I've been in Hong Kong for two weeks and what have I really achieved apart from going back to work again? I don't want to be work-obsessed, baby-obsessed Seffy – I want to be who I was when I was with Luke, even before I met Luke, before everything went wrong. I still conformed to structure, rigidity, lists, but I knew how to have fun, or Luke knew how to coax it out of me.

So, today, I'm checking out of the extortionate three-hundred-pound per night swanky king-sized bed with a bath fit for a miniature hippo and checking in to the Atlas Guest House at an eye-watering twenty-pound per night – cheaper than my daily subsistence back in London. Halla-fucking-lujah.

'Would you like a mixed or single-sex dorm?' the Australian on the front desk asks.

'Dorm? Like dormitory?'

'Yes.' She stares at me, deadpan.

'Any single rooms?' Harry would be kicking me in the shins right now.

'No, this is a hostel, not a hotel.' Touché.

'Then I'll go single-sex,' I reply quickly, not wanting to irritate her anymore and metaphorically rubbing away the bruise from imaginary Harry.

I pay upfront for two weeks and lug my ugly old backpack to my room. God, I miss Joseph.

You're such a princess. Luke's face flashes before me, laughing. *Go away,* I silently shout back.

I open the door to a pair of breasts in my face.

'Oh my God, I'm so sorry!' I exclaim, immediately shutting my eyes.

'It's ok, I'm no prude.' The skinny girl laughs. She's got dark brown hair with a couple of braids in the front, decorated with plastic beads. And she does have great tits. I think back to Ren. I know how to admire, but I also have a banging set of my own.

I laugh awkwardly, opening my eyes. 'Are you from the UK?' I'm ninety-nine per cent sure she has a Geordie accent, but geography's never been a strong point of mine.

'Way ay gyal! Yep, Newcastle born and bred. Tish – nice to meet you.' She holds out her hand, still topless.

'Seffy.' I smile. 'From London.' I dump my bag on my, thankfully, bottom bunk bed.

We have a brief chat before a girl with a short, wavy caramel bob storms in.

'And this is Margot.' Tish directs a hand towards the girl. 'Margot, we have a new friend – meet Seffy.'

'Hey, nice to meet you.' She smiles and waves.

'Margot's from Sydney.'

'I can speak for myself, Tish!' She grins. 'What about you?'

'London. Sydney's a great place, I went there once on holiday.' Remembering my night drinking cocktails with Luke overlooking the Sydney Harbour with all the lights twinkling, reflecting in his eyes, holding hands – safe.

'Yeah, it is nice, but you never think much about the place you grew up in, do you? Bet you don't go hailing down black cabs every weekend or doing open-top tours on red London buses?'

It's hard to tell people's ages when you get older, but Margot and Tish look on the right side of thirty. This is what I need, people who haven't felt the looming pressure of life's deadlines yet.

'Got any plans tonight, Seffy? We were going to hit Lang Kwai Fung and get druuuuunk.' Tish waves her hands chaotically in the air. 'We met some fit guys last night, out on a stag.' My heart skips a beat thinking about Richard, but who goes on a two-week stag? 'Margot pulled one of them.'

'Don't say it so crassly – more like, I relinquished my body to that of a man's.'

'Worse.' Tish looks solemn before continuing. 'Are you with anyone?' Tish asks me as she pulls out a strappy top from under her bed.

'No, very much single,' I reply, momentarily contemplating how you go from married to divorced to sharing a dormitory with two strangers.

'Great! That means more free drinks for us.' Margot laughs.

'Ugh. You know I hate it that men always think women need to buy them their drinks, as if we can't afford our own,' Tish says.

'Well, you can't! We'd never have got into that bar without those guys, not on our measly travelling budget. You should thank me for my kissing skills.'

'You win.' Tish slaps her own hand mockingly. 'Fuck it, if I want to use men for drinks I bloody well will.'

Margot and Tish continue with their friendly bickering, and I laugh along as I unpack my bag.

I pull out my e-reader, excited to finish the last few pages of *The Catcher in the Rye* and settle down on my bunk.

'What Wordsworth has you hooked then?' Tish asks.

'Salinger – *The Catcher in the Rye*,' I reply half-smugly as I thank my bucket list for not reading a steamy, smutty romp – I love them but it doesn't hold the same kudos.

'Great book,' Tish pointedly remarks.

'It is, isn't it. I'm trying to read ten famous novels before I'm thirty.' Do I look as lame as I sound?

'Thirty? You look *way* younger.' Tish says the compliment as if people who are thirty are about to collect their pension. If we believed everything the world told us, I think we'd all feel like that. Mortgage, married, kids, pension – life sign, sealed and delivered thanks very much. That's what I subscribed to, maybe my life path will be more exciting now.

I grimace slightly. I'm thankful that Tish doesn't think I look like I'm nearly thirty, but I know how old hitting that milestone seems when you're beneath the hump of twenty-five.

'How old are you?'

'Nineteen.'

If I had a drink, I would have spat it out.

'I'm almost old enough to be your mother.' I hate myself for saying it and oh, the irony.

'If you'd had me when you were eleven. Age is just a number; it's one of those milestones the world creates for us. I believe you can be however old you want to be. I feel more like twenty-five.'

'To be fair, you do seem closer to my age than nineteen.' I think about myself at nineteen, when I was counting bills and helping my mum's recovery – everyone else was out drinking slippery nipples in the local club. I've always felt old.

'You should read *The Handmaid's Tale* next.' Tish points to my book. 'Prepare ourselves for a male mutiny.'

'Tish!' Margot exclaims. 'Stop bestowing all your dystopian views on Seffy. Let her read her book and then we can get ready. It's your turn to do the snogging tonight so make sure you look hot.'

I can't tell if Margot's joking or not but Tish simply rolls her eyes and then gets back to whatever it is that she's doing on her phone – preparing for a male mutiny, perhaps.

We squeeze onto a high table outside Frank's. The three of us, it's like being out in London with my gal pals. A blanket of neon lights over our heads, each bar blaring its own music, hordes of people bustling through drinking, laughing, dancing. Some bars no bigger than one wooden table, but the atmosphere as great as all the others.

I'm wearing the pink nylon co-ord; I don't look like myself, but I feel like myself. Tish told me to wear it, she said I have a great body. It's the first time someone's said that to me in a long time. Luke used to compliment me on a daily basis but now everything about my ego is still bruised from the prodding, poking and analysing by a million-and-one doctors. I know, technically, I still look the same but I feel different.

'You look *très* fuckable.' Tish pretends to look me up and down, giving me the eye.

'Shut up,' I respond playfully, trying to pull the tight skirt down a millimetre more. I'm self-conscious but I know I should try and feel more liberated, like my new friends.

'I got us two beers each and then the barman gave me these shots for free,' Margot announces, pushing her way past a group of guys drinking from what looks like a shoe to get to us.

'It looks kind of gross,' I say, inspecting the fluorescent green liquid.

'It's probably just apple juice – ok ready, one, two, three, SHOTTTTTT!' Tish shouts, pushing the drink upwards in my mouth to ensure I don't miss a drop. It goes all over my chin and I wipe it away with my hand, grinning.

'Let's play a game. Let's each say why we're travelling, something crazy we've done and then what we want to do – I'll start.' Margot sips her beer. 'And by the time we're finished, both beers have to be drunk.' She takes a large swig.

'I'm from Sydney but you both know that. I left home when I was twenty because I felt like I wanted to see the world. Met this total dickhead guy called Brady who I fell head over heels in love with and we went to America then South-East Asia where he wanted to be a surf instructor in Bali. I did this all for him, ok?' She looks at us for reassurance while downing more beer. 'Then I found out he was fucking one of the girls at the bar! I thought we were gonna get married and have kids, ya know?' She shakes her head. 'OBVIOUSLY I left him, and I've been having the best time ever since. Doing what I want, sleeping with who I want, being a total free spirit.' She beams, slamming her glass down on the table. How she's already finished one beer I'll have no idea; I'm feeling gassy. 'What I want to do is be free. I'm sure I'll meet someone one day and settle down but for now, I'm happy just being me.' She pauses. 'Oh, and crazy thing?' She drums her fingers on the table. 'I got this stupid tattoo on my bum when I was pissed.' She pulls down her shorts and there, emblazoned in permanent black ink, is 'FUCK BRADY'.

Tish and I both spit out our beers in hysterics.

'Oh my God. That IS crazy. Ok my turn.' Tish taps her index finger on her chin. 'I'm from Newcastle, this little place called Tynemouth. I came travelling about four months ago, started in China. I've lived in Newcastle my whole life – I needed to see the world, think about my prospects, you know? I was working in this nightclub to save the money for it – taken me bloody ages! I don't know if I want to go back yet, I feel like I might end up travelling forever – there's so much of the world to see!' She looks up at the night sky animatedly. 'My crazy fact is . . . once I had a threesome . . . with twins.' She sits back, triumphant.

'Twins? Were they fit? Tell me more.' Margot leans forward. 'Ok, ok, after Seffy's turn.'

I sip my drink, slowly contemplating what to expose in my first show and tell since primary.

'I'm from London, been living there for about eight years. I was married to this guy, Luke, but we divorced, well, officially, a week ago.' I see Margot put a hand over Tish's mouth to allow me to finish speaking. 'I'm technically on a sabbatical from work – my friend Harry made me do it. I was too nervous. I decided to try and complete a bucket list before I'm thirty so here I am, having a blast, being spontaneous,' I say, glancing at my BE MORE HARRY bracelet. 'What I want to do, hmmm?' I pause. 'I want to have a life again, relive my twenties as I should have done in the first place. And my crazy thing? Oh, ha.' I laugh, remembering. 'I gave a guy a hand job on the plane here.' I need to remember the whole plane-Richard-cup scenario for all future drinking games, it's a good one.

'Your crazy thing is not gratifying some guy on the plane – it's having the strength to divorce and then come travelling alone!' Tish exclaims.

'What happened? Did he cheat on you?' Margot asks. 'Eurgh, men.' She shakes her head.

The barman comes over at exactly the right moment and Tish puts an order in for some technicolour fishbowl and three more fluro shots.

'No, he didn't cheat,' I say almost sorrowfully. It would have been easier if he had. 'We wanted different things.' I pause, not wanting to make Tish and Margot hate men any more than they currently seem to, and I don't even hate Luke, not really. It was my fault . . . I think. 'I can't even remember what happened now,' I say, not wanting to divulge every single part of my private life. 'It was just sad, really sad.' I sniff, feeling a tear trickle down my cheek.

Margot and Tish stand up from the table, rush to my sides and hug me.

'You're, like, the fittest cougar I've ever seen,' Tish exclaims and I know she means it as a compliment but surely twenty-nine doesn't count as a cougar?

I'm crying and they're hugging me just as the barman brings over a fishbowl that could fit an entire salmon in it. It appears that ordering a fishbowl also comes with sparklers and a lady who sings.

We all start laughing.

'Fucking great timing!' Tish screams.

'I think he sounds like a twat,' Margot says, taking a huge glug of the technicolour salmon water.

'Margot!' Tish gives her dagger eyes. 'Maybe he is a twat, but we can't judge as we've never met him. My boyfriend of two years left me because he cheated on me then tried to play it off as *me* judging polyamory – now *he* was a twat.'

'I don't even know anymore. All I know is I'm nearly thirty and I'm starting from scratch. It's great and everything, travelling around, but I feel like I should be at home with my husband thinking about having children. I have to find someone, date them, wait for them to propose, get married, buy a house – you know. I know that's not how you're supposed to think, you know putting it all on a man but I do still feel like that. I still feel beholden to a man.' Maybe I wouldn't feel like this if society didn't put so much pressure on it all. If from the moment I met Luke, people hadn't asked when we were going to get engaged, and from the moment we got married people hadn't asked when we were having children.

'Age is just a social construct. The world puts so much pressure on us, especially women.' Tish shakes her head angrily. 'Putting these pathetic, imaginary deadlines on us that we "have to" achieve in life.' She uses her fingers to create imaginary quotation marks, while rolling her eyes.

'Why should we be stressing about getting married or hurrying up having children? These are supposed to be enjoyable moments that happen, not things we wish away. And if you don't want to get married and have kids that's totally fine too. I don't think I do. I have a lot more in life I want to achieve for myself, I don't want to be tied down.' How is Tish so wise? She seems to understand her own wants, needs and desires, even her own body more than me.

'But I see all these happily married couples out with their two and a half kids,' I accidentally say out loud. But those deadlines do exist if you're a woman, don't they? How else do you explain being given the glamorous title of geriatric mother and the onset of the menopause?

Margot guffaws.

'Two and a half kids? Why do they always say that? What happens on the third child – you donate half their limbs to the midwife and say "sorry, but I've already reached my quota"?'

'I know it is stupid.' I laugh between my sniffs. 'I just feel that I'm at this point in my life where everything should be settled.' I think back to Luke, before we started trying. I like domesticity, that routine and structure, it made me happy. However dated my thoughts are, I liked being a homemaker. 'I want to know how the rest of my life will pan out. I hate the unknown, I'm not spontaneous like you girls. I worked hard for everything and now I should be rewarded but instead I'm starting again as if I'm eighteen – no offence,' I add, looking at my new two young pals.

'My mom always told me not to wish my life away. You might get sent down a path filled with dingoes, but you can survive it, learn from it and make good of it. You can make your life whatever you want it to be, master of your own destiny and all that. You need to work on you, and it seems like the best thing right now is to get drunk, lairy and dance.'

Margot gives me a last hug and pushes the fishbowl towards me. 'Drink up.'

Hours later, sweaty and four fishbowls down, we find ourselves in a brightly lit studio. I'm lying next to Tish, holding her hand.

'We all want a different one but in the same place.' Tish points to a laminated sign. 'You'll have to hold her down, she said she's squeamish.' The man says something and laughs. 'No, she said she really wants it.'

I nod back in agreement although my eyes are already watering.

I wince as the needle penetrates the top layer of my skin, short but sharp cat scratches.

Minutes later, I look down and see the symbol for 'spirit' on my groin. Terrible place to get a tattoo if you ever get pregnant, but I don't have to worry about that.

I smile at myself drunkenly in the mirror while Tish and Margot get their tattoos done.

I snap a picture of my now red and black imprint covered with clingfilm to Harry with the caption, 'BE MORE HARRY' and then pass out.

Three Months No Baby

Dear sweet, desirable, oh-so-mighty Aphrodite,

It's getting ridiculous now, I've spent close to half my rent on one-time use plastic sticks. I could build a fucking house with them. I feel like David Attenborough would take a gun to my head if he saw how I was single-handedly filling half the ocean with synthetic polymers and my own urine. I understand why they can't be reusable, but compostable at least?

A few months ago, I ordered a bulk buy of the pee sticks on Amazon, but they ran out weeks ago and now I can't reorder in case Luke sees how much I'm spending on our joint account. I can't go to any of the shops near work in case any of my colleagues see. I've been switching it up between the Sainsbury's, Tesco and Waitrose locals near home; it must be terrible for their supply chain management, they must assume someone's got pica and is physically eating packets of Clear Blue. I would go to self-checkout but some security fiend has decided that all pregnancy tests need to be encased in plastic cages so they can watch people squirm as they de-tag three boxes of multipacks. The lady at Tesco smiled the first time I came in with my warrant for all pregnancy tests to be immediately removed from the shelves; she touched me on the arm and said I hope it's everything you wish for. Now, when I see her, she sort of chews her lips together in anguish, so she resembles one of those cabbage patch dolls from the nineties. That's why I try and alternate between the local supermarkets and then the different checkouts to limit embarrassment for all parties.

I know I get obsessed with things. I have this desire to be successful and it's not limited to career progression. I want people to look at me and think, she's got it all. The total opposite of how people looked at my mother or our family when I was younger.

That look the cashier used to give my mum as she offloaded twenty bottles of white wine clinking down the checkout. Another party, Mrs Roberts? she'd ask as my mum slurred her response, What's life without a little pizzazzz? The look the cashiers give me now, it's the same they used to give me then, when I wasn't even old enough to wear a training bra. They feel sorry for me. I hate it.

Surely, beautiful Goddess of fertility, there must be a better way to find out you're pregnant? What did people do in ancient Greece? I guess they didn't know and then it just happened. I would hate that. It's the not knowing that's driving me balls to the wall or breasts to the floor if I'm going to go all feminist. If you could just tell me, Aph, that in one year, two years, or even THREE YEARS that I'll be pregnant, I can continue simply living my life not going insane. That's all I'm asking for.

My period was late this month. Eggly, this app that monitors your menstrual cycle, making you go on some sort of distressing Easter hunt every month only to find out that the older kids have eaten all your eggs, said I was due to start on the 5th. I did a pregnancy test, but I knew that it could be too early to read positive. The next day, still nothing. My boobs felt tender, and I felt absolutely knackered. Signs of pregnancy – major exhaustion, tick – breasts feeling like they've been pulverised with a meat hammer, tick; they were there. Honestly, the excitement building that there could be something so precious for me to cradle and care for was insurmountable. I didn't want to let on to Luke that I could be pregnant because I'd already planned the announcement and I knew it would be worth it. The next day – nothing, not even a pin prick of blood! I was almost salivating at the very thought of all the cell fission going on in my womb! Then on day four, I went for my first wee of the day on my not-so-trusty little stick of truth and it was pink. With blood. I burst into tears. Not just isolated droplets running elegantly down your face, but cascading waterfalls, volcanoes of snot, hiccups so violent I thought I might cough up my own lungs.

That's when Luke came running in. He obviously saw me sobbing into my hands on the toilet basin with a pregnancy test clutched between my mitts and assumed ...

'Seffy? What's the matter?' He crouched down by me. 'Are you? Are we ...?' I could sense the excitement in his voice; it was the same as mine a few days ago. So, he does want it all as much as me.

'No,' I snap back. He didn't know, but why does he always say the wrong thing? 'I thought I was, but my period's started.'

'It's ok.' He puts a hand on my knee, observing his wife hiccupping and spluttering like an angry hippo. 'It's just your hormones.'

'Hormones? HORMONES?!' I screech. 'I want a fucking baby, Luke, and instead of my egg being punctured with your sperm it's fallen out of my womb and is lying in this toilet. I'm fucking upset, not hormonal.' He doesn't think sometimes, he doesn't understand the consequences of using words in the wrong places.

He sits staring at me, astounded. I hate myself. This isn't what our relationship is. I wish I could rewind time when it really was all fancy dinners, surprise flowers, casual kisses on the sofa morphing into passionate coital displays. Ones where Luke wouldn't bother to take my dress off or remove my bra, not out of laziness but out of sexual urgency. Is the love spiralling down the sewer with my unfertilised eggs?

'I always seem to say the wrong fucking thing. I only said hormones because I thought you'd be pleased that I acknowledged there was other stuff going on for you.

Whenever you're on your period you always say it's your hormones, but now I say it, I'm in the wrong.' He purses his lips together in a tiresome smile and stands up. I don't even have the energy to explain myself.

I want to apologise for the outburst, grab his hand as he leaves the bathroom. But I don't. I let him leave, thinking I'm an angry psycho.

It must be my fault. It has to be. We never used to fight. I'm the one who has to carry the baby, nurture it and I'm not pregnant so it must be me. Luke's being supportive or trying to be. He can't help it if he doesn't understand every emotion I'm going through, particularly when I keep them inside. After these outbursts, I keep feeling like I'm twisting things Luke's said or imagining the way he looked at me. Is it in my head or is it real?

I feel like the whole world's out to get me, taunting me. Everywhere I look people are pregnant, their ballooning bumps staring me out as I try to ignore them.

Yesterday, on the tube, I was sitting minding my own business; well, actually I was reading this book about how to increase your chance of a successful conception which I inconspicuously masked with a book jacket about a couple who got murdered on their honeymoon, when I felt two eyes boring into my soul.

It was a lady with a 'Baby on Board' badge. It was as if, out of all the people on the tube at 7.00 a.m., she'd marked me out. Obviously, I gave her my seat and she was particularly gracious about it but why me? It's like an army of pregnant women are after me. Hunting me wherever I go. Parading around me in all their fertile glory. Why can't being pregnant be contagious? I'd have conceived by now.

Even having sex three days a week is becoming tiresome. My body feels lethargic. There's nothing exciting about having sex anymore because every time I open my legs, I wish and pray that this will be the time that Luke's sperm kicks into gear and zooms forward into my eagerly waiting egg.

When he's given me the final pump and lies back on the bed in that post-orgasm ecstasy, I lie there silently praying and wondering how long I should rest to give myself the best chance of impregnation. What's wrong with me? Is this how all women feel? Is getting pregnant really this hard? There must be something, Aphrodite? A pill I can take, an exercise regime? Is it like revision where you just have to put in the hours, the hard graft?

I crave the want we both used to have for each other. The urge to fuck, not to cement any feelings of love but because of innate attraction, primal instinct, raw sexuality. The way the orgasm came naturally, unexpected and felt like the first time every time.

Now it's boring, clinical, an unwanted task. I haven't even orgasmed for months. Do you have to orgasm to conceive, Aphrodite? If you do, I'm well and truly fucked right now.

Why do they even bother with sex education at school, pressurising all females to be on some form of contraception in case, God forbid, you bear a child before you're eighteen. If I'd known it was going to be this difficult, I would have started trying when I was fourteen.

I've decided to cut out alcohol and cigarettes. I never smoked every day, just the odd puff when I have a drink so it's easy now I'm on my journey to sobriety. It's kind of annoying and unfair that not only are you not allowed to drink or smoke for the whole nine months that you're pregnant, but you also must give it up while you're trying to.

Clearly, it's ridiculous that only the women need to remove all these 'toxic' temptresses from their life in order *to allow the egg to thrive but sperm (even if they contain an X chromosome too so are already basically female) are perfectly fine to douse themselves in nicotine and bathe in alcohol and still procreate like bunnies.*

Speculating on this 'theory', I dipped my toe in the gender discrimination water and asked Luke if he would consider also giving up alcohol and smoking the odd fag in order to increase OUR chances of successful conception.

'Darling.' I snuggle up to him on the sofa while we flick between movies on Netflix deciding what to watch. 'I've been reading about getting pregnant and I'm going to give up drinking for a while to see if that makes a difference.' The nights of us staying up late, sharing a bottle of wine and a few cigarettes out on the terrace are long gone.

'That's great,' he replies, transfixed to the trailer of Netflix's latest action blockbuster. 'That looks good, shall we watch it?'

'Yes, looks good to me.' He clicks Play, and as the introduction credits roll, I pipe up again. 'Would you do it with me? I think it would be good if we both gave it a try.'

He pauses the movie.

'Darling, I'm not giving up beer on the off chance. I've got a night out with the boys on Saturday, I can't exactly say I'm teetotal,' he scoffs. He thinks it's a joke.

'It's not teetotal, I just really want a baby. I want us to have a family and I know you do too. Please. . .?' I snuggle into him further. 'For me?'

Luke turns to look at me.

'I said I wanted to be casual, try but not try, see how things go. Our whole life will change when we have a baby but I'm not changing mine now.' I feel something in me begin to snap.

'But I already have to change mine, so why can't you help me out? It's your sperm and my egg – it's not all on me, you know. I also think you should stop smoking; I know you don't full-time but when you drink. Maybe you could do that instead.'

'You don't have to change your life – you're choosing too. You're the one that wants the baby immediately, part of your list. I'm happy to wait and let it happen when it happens. We've always been different like that. You like lists and order, I don't – we don't let it impact each other's lives. If you want to give up alcohol, that's your choice, not mine.' We've always been on the same page, what's happening?

I feel rage bubbling up inside me. Why can't he share my dream? Why can't he want it as much as me?

'Why can't it be like that time when we trained to run the marathon together? Treat it as a training exercise – we both work really hard at something and then we get to bask in all the glory when we succeed?'

'Aaah, Seffy, I just want to watch the bloody movie.'

'You do realise, Luke.' I almost spit his name like a curse from my lips. 'Male fertility issues have been on the up for decades now. It's probably because you allow your sperm to bathe in Neck Oil and stop to have a cheeky fag on the one marathon journey they ever have to do in their life. YOU should be trying as much as me.'

'I'm not going to even answer you right now. I don't like this side of you. You're making yourself annoyed, and me. Let's just have one nice night where we don't talk about babies or fertility or sex or pregnancy.' And he clicks play on the remote.

Me: *Why are men so fucking ignorant?*
Harry: *They can't help it; they were born without vital genes. That's what my mum said anyway. Yesterday,*

this guy at work told me you could wee into a tampon. Imagine?!

He doesn't even want to have sex with me anymore, he must find it as tiresome as I do.

I don't even watch the movie; I want to go to bed and cry, but I know that will start another argument. Instead, I sit next to Luke, not with my legs up on his or resting my head on his shoulder, just sitting there. Watching images move around on a screen, punctuated with gun shots that barely make me blink. I'm not present, just there.

Why can't I be a wasp or an ant, one of those animals that procreates through parthenogenesis? Then I wouldn't need Luke, I'd just need myself. Or Luke could at least take some advice from a Clown Fish where he'd do anything to enable our survival as a family – even change sex.

Just change me into a wasp and be done with me. Here is my sacrifice; Pinot Grigio, the odd Marlboro Light, seafood, whatever, I don't know– take it, Aphrodite, and replace it with an embryo in my caged womb.

HUGE love, Seffy xxx/

Ten Months Until Thirty

10

'Those photos you took the other night are really cool,' Margot says, pointedly looking at her phone.

'They're all blurry,' I respond, still reading my book. 'And we were so drunk.'

'We were, you're right but, no, I like the way you've captured the atmosphere; it's like you can really tell how much fun we're having from the picture,' Margot replies, still captivated by the photos. 'See, here, it's like you've caught the twinkle in Tish's eye.'

'My inner demons.' Tish raises her eyebrows, laughing. 'Don't give away my secrets, Seffy!' She waves her hands in the air like she's being hailed a witch.

'I thought you were a banker anyway, like, no creative bone in your body type of job,' Margot asks.

'I used to be really into art when I was younger but there's no money in that. It's not structured enough for me. Anyway, my mum used to paint, and she even managed to fuck that up.'

The next day, we stand in a line at Phoenix Fight Club, half-excited, half-nauseated. The instructor is small but scary. Her hair scraped back into a high pony, matching red and black crop top and leggings and some interesting-looking trainers – I'm sure they're fashionable somewhere. Her arms are taut, her thighs strong, and don't get me started on her eight-pack.

'Welcome!' She flashes a set of immaculate veneers which bear the same shiny, plastic look as her footwear. 'At Phoenix we do a mixture of HIIT and self-defence, focusing on Muay Thai. If you don't know, Muay Thai is often referred to as the art of eight limbs, as we use fists, elbows, knees and shins. Fighting is incredible for your fitness; I guarantee at the end of this session you will be drenched.' She grins again. 'Now, if I can get you all to pair up that would be great.'

I let Margot and Tish go together and find myself with a lady, mid-thirties (I'd guess) in a worn, grey-looking tank top and colourful mauve and pink leggings.

'Greet your partner and tell them why you're here today. Then we'll get started on the warm-up.' The instructor, Fay, takes a half-bow and then slides between the pairs, getting to know everyone.

Jenni and I bend our necks in a greeting.

'Hi, I'm Seffy.' I smile as I introduce myself. 'I wanted to learn some self-defence while on my travels.'

'Jenni.' It's like she's smiling but the way her lips curl upwards makes me stressed. 'I'm here to get a few minutes to myself . . .' She fumbles with her top, pulling the worn grey lycra over her tummy. 'And it's the best way to lose the baby weight.'

I smile at Jenni, trying to stop my eyes from immediately being drawn to her midriff. A flash goes through my mind: *at least I'll never have to lose the baby weight or have stretch marks.* I blink to stop myself being the person I hate. *You hate the thought of everyone judging you, so why do you do it to other people?* my brain says back.

'Must be nice to have a break although I'd probably find myself in the spa or eating croissants in a café!' *Make her feel good, Seffy, be nice.*

'You're telling me!' I can't help but notice the bags under her eyes and the spots on her chin. 'I'd love to be doing that, but I currently feel like a total slob. It's not fair that we have to carry the baby, birth the baby, feed the baby and then lose all the weight again after so our husband might want to make another baby with us, is it?' She rolls her eyes. 'And he gets to go out, drink, go out to work, sleep in the night and his body still looks the same.' That's me. I'm the 'husband' in the scenario, but I don't feel good about it. Jenni's anger, that's what I used to direct at Luke but without a baby.

She kicks into my right palm with a pounding force. 'Anyway, that's it, last one. I'm not having anymore.'

I stare at her blankly, wondering whether she's finished or not.

'Sorry.' Jenni shakes her head. 'When your husband's out all day and the only person you can speak to, however much you adore them, is an incoherent blob, you beg for adult conversation. Didn't mean to overshare.'

'No, don't worry I totally get it.' I smile as my left palm takes a kick and I realise I really don't understand an iota of child-rearing.

'Do you have children?' she asks as Fay instructs her to do a couple of punches, twisting her clenched fist to the left as she swings for maximum impact.

'Not yet,' I reply in that nonchalant tone that most women answer that question with. As if you have all the time in the world for procreation and it really is just down to you being ready for them.

'Lucky you.' She kicks again into my palm. 'I love them but fuck, they take up all my time. I barely get a minute to myself. I look back at the days where I'd spend three hours in the hairdressers, get my eyelashes done, get a massage, work out for leisure because I still had a waist and think why the FUCK was I so desperate to change my life. I was living in fucking luxury. It was like going from Paris Hilton to Cinderella – pre-prince, obviously.' She chuckles to herself. 'That wasn't even funny.' She laughs again. 'But I have to make myself laugh – I'm a stand-up comedian some days for myself and my little ones – Jack and Aurelia.'

Fay instructs us to swap over, now Jenni's taking a bruising.

'Is it really like that, though? Isn't it all about sacrificing your life for another? You know, one day, they'll be looking after you.'

Jenni laughs as I deliver two high-powered kicks. I'm not sure who they were aimed at, Jenni, myself, my parents, Luke?

'Ha. That's definitely something a non-parent would say.' I punch with power in her palm. *Bitch.* 'Sorry didn't mean to be patronising,' she quickly adds. 'That's what I thought. Like I said, I love my children, I would do anything for them, but it doesn't mean that most days they are really tough and monotonous. How many times can you watch *Cocomelon*?'

'You hate being a mum?' I look up at her, my fists ready to go, imagining this is the sort of thing my own mother would say. 'And what the fuck is *Cocomelon*?'

'It's such a weird emotion. I don't *hate* it. I love it when they laugh and cuddle you. And sometimes, I look down at all their tiny features in my arms and cry because I can't believe I made something so beautiful. I wouldn't change them for the world but yes, sometimes, I'll admit I hate it. When they're screaming in your face, you've had no sleep and you feel that you've given up your whole life and the little terrors don't even care that you exist. That's when I hate it. *Cocomelon*? Don't ask.'

'Hmm, interesting. I always thought I'd love being a mum.' *Grateful Celine, ungrateful Jenni.* Do people really take it that much for granted how lucky they are to be a parent?

'I'm not trying to put you off!' Jenni suddenly interjects. 'But it's a lot harder than people let on. If I had my time again, I'd make sure I had one hundred per cent done everything I wanted to do before I got myself pregnant. I'd have gone to more places, got drunker and taken waaaaay more drugs.'

I feel the slight itch of the tattoo in my groin. Is that the trade you'd make then, Jenni? A drawing in permanent ink, from a carefree night out, instead of caring for your own flesh and blood?

Fay shows us some techniques for self-defence and explains how we each need to knock our partner to the mat using a special six-point combat technique.

Jenni goes first and I succumb like a mouse to an eagle. I know that's what is supposed to happen but for some reason, it's really wound me up. Weak old Seffy, lying useless on the floor. Flailing around like a maggot.

My turn.

I do the six-point combat technique and with each strike I expel a tiny piece of life's irritations.

Strike 1.

'For not being grateful.'

Strike 2.

'For it not being me.'

Strike 3.

'For wishing it away.'

Strike 4.

'For thinking everyone has choices.'

Strike 5.

'For my body being broken.'

Strike 6.

'For just fucking me over. Continuously.'

'Argh. Just FUCKKKKKKKKKK!' I scream as Jenni lays dumbfounded on the floor and I sit across her chest.

Tish and Margot start awkwardly clapping and then the whole room brings their hands together, slowly, like the start of a percussion instrumental at a child's concert.

'Oh my God, I'm sorry. I'm sorry.' I jump up from Jenni and feel a sweat waterfall pour down my back, my eyes smarting from embarrassment.

'That's ok. I wish I could punch and scream every day.'

I take a little bow and leave the studio.

I swing my legs on the bench outside, looking up at the sky and taking in my surroundings.

I pull out my phone and capture the moment. The crisp, blue sky, not a cloud in sight. The humidity making my chest pound and the air feel sparse. The sharp lines of the buildings against the empty sky – cubism in all its glory.

My heart's beating fast, the blood rushing to my head, giving me a high.

There's no doubt about it, I feel good. Really good. The only person I've ever really told how I feel to is Luke. And even then, I lied. To take it out on someone, even if inappropriate, was exhilarating. No one even knew what I was on about. I was a Bridget Jones/Charlie's Angel hybrid. Electrifying.

I see Tish and Margot running towards me and I quickly scrawl on my phone:

#9 Get a tattoo (which I now can't remember the meaning of), while drunk and abroad
#10 Attend a self-defence class and for apparently no reason, verbally abuse a mother of two

11

'Come onnnnn!' I jump onto Tish who's lying in bed suffering with a hangover – their appetite for jollification is rubbing off on me.

'Are you sure we have to go on a hike today?' Tish sighs heavily. 'Can't we go tomorrow?' Pulling the pillow over her eyes.

'We're going,' I state firmly, grappling the pillow from her grip. 'I'll buy you a bowl of Singapore noodles from that stall you like and a coffee?' Tish releases the pillow slightly. 'And if you woman up a bit, I'll buy you a beer post-walk.' Tish also thinks that we should stop making women feel inferior with our words.

'And some crisps?' she pleads.

'Ok deal. It's like I'm a sugar mum.'

'At least that's better than a sugar daddy . . .' Nice to see she's back to her open-minded self. 'My friend had one once, and I was nearly sick in my mouth. Sugar daddy makes them sound like something you'd want to suck.'

'My friend Harry and I, we call those kind of men Jeffs.' I laugh thinking about it.

'I once knew a Jeff, he owned a corner shop near me and this one time . . .'

'Come on, Tish!' Margot stops doing her mascara and turns to her. 'We've got hours to listen to your rants on our hike – let's go!'

I send Harry a selfie of me with a Diet Coke and a portion of Chow Wan's signature Singapore noodles with extra soy and spice. You don't need to be hungover to have them, they are the perfect everyday breakfast food.

> **Harry:** *Carbs?! On a weekday? I LOVE THIS NEW SEFFY!*
> **Me:** *Routine isn't good on holidays. Anyway, calories only count in the country you were born in – fact.*
> **Harry:** *Then why on* You Are What You Eat *don't they just send people from Coventry to Calcutta? I'd like to see the average Brit being uphauled across the world overnight.*
> **Me:** *They'd have to change the title to* Brits Abroad *and ITV already have that show – they literally film British people complaining about the heat, food and people pushing in queues – we're not a very cultured nation.*
> **Harry:** *Hmmm, I feel a change of career coming along – Counting Calories – Brits Abroad Edition. We task the average Brit with cultured calorie swaps – digestives to dhal, chocolate to coconut and pancakes to Pad Thai.*
> **Me:** *OMG – don't give up the day job plez.*

'How beautiful is this, girls?' We pause, breathless, on the ridge. We're doing the popular dragon's back hike route, which follows the rugged coastline and beautiful beaches of Hong Kong before descending into some jungle and finally finishing up at the beach. The opportunity to have a cool dip and clink a couple of beers was the main persuasion for Tish and Margot.

'It's facking gorgeous! I feel like I'm in *The Famous Five!*' Tish smooshes her face against mine. 'The noodles and crisps really razzed me up!'

'What's *The Famous Five*?' Margot asks inquisitively while checking her make-up in her front selfie camera.

'Only one of the best childhood stories of all time!' Tish says, shocked. 'Don't tell me you haven't heard of *Just William*, *Tom's Midnight Garden*, or *Horrid Henry* either?'

Margot throws her head back laughing. 'Are they part of your man-hater books? *Horrid Henry*? *Just William*? What's next – Randy Ralph, Pornstar Peter? We read proper books in Oz, like *The Secret Garden*.'

'Look at all those yachts!' I exclaim, pointing at a quaint little bay over the ridge with tiny little boats bobbing on the water, taking some snaps with my iPhone. The sun glistening and gleaming, making the ocean sparkle like it's been taken straight from the pages of *Life of Pi*. One of my favourite books, Luke surprised me with a visit to watch the performance at the theatre. I clench my fist on itself, to bite away the want of sharing something so beautiful with him again.

'Oh, Seffy darling, take us on a yacht,' Margot pleads jokingly, hanging on my arm.

'I wish. I thought you'd have met someone by now who'd know someone who'd know someone.' I laugh, squeezing Margot's arm.

'Not staying in a five-pound a night hostel,' Margot scoffs. 'Maybe one day I'll meet a man who'll own a yacht and we'll go sailing out to sea, drink champagne and eat caviar.'

'Trust me, glamour isn't everything,' I reply, thinking back to the time when Luke and I would sit on beaches, sipping cocktails and eating fresh prawns and oysters and how I thought I was lucky. And then when things got really tough, like actual life for most people, not extravagant fairy tales, none of that materialistic stuff mattered anymore. I'd suddenly turned into Rumpelstiltskin, an ugly, malicious imp full of fabrication, spinning gold in return for your first child. 'I used to want people to look at me and think, she has it all, but when I was that *girl*, you know wearing the IT kaftan, eating oysters, drinking champagne, I don't think I felt as happy as

I am now.' *Woah, where did that come from*? 'Not that I'm like super-rich or anything like that,' I hastily caveat, not wanting to sound spoilt. 'I was just able to be comfortable, more than comfortable, buy nice things that I'd always wanted to.'

'You might be right, but I need to try it out first to know if I'd feel the same.' Margot grins and takes my iPhone from my hand. 'There's something so special about your photos and I can't put my finger on it. Why don't we go to Stanley market and get you one of those vintage Canons, then you'd really feel like a movie star, you know, silk scarf over the head, eye stuck in the lens?'

I flinch. Thinking about the time I told Luke that was my dream, and he was prepared to give up everything to come with me. I'd laughed it off like it was a joke. Has anyone ever really followed a dream when there were bills to pay and career ladders to climb? But what's stopping me? My mum? Luke? No one.

I look across from the ridge to the beaches, the sea gently lapping at the soft, white sand. I can see couples on loungers although they look like tiny, colourful ants. It's better looking at them from afar; this way I can make up stories about their lives, like Harry and I do and not hear their conversation in person.

Tish and Margot are taking photos of the scenery, laughing and joking while I sit and kick my legs back and forth on the ridge – freedom.

It's strange to think that a month ago I was doing the same thing every day. Then the divorce papers came through the post, and it was like they created some sort of domino effect of change. I was dreading that day, the official signature. I'd sign it and I'd be just like my mother – drunk and desperate for someone to love me. But I haven't been like that. I'm hiking in Hong Kong with two girls who are the polar opposite of me, and I'm totally and utterly exhilarated with life right now.

I twiddle my bracelet – BE MORE HARRY. I haven't thanked her enough; I'll plan some sort of surprise when I return, take her out pole dancing or something, she'd love that.

The world seems to be gradually aligning, but there's this little dark cloud hanging there with my future inside it and I'm not sure quite how to get rid of it.

'Seffy!' Margot calls, snapping me out of my daydream. 'Ready to go? Let's get one picture of us all first.' We push our heads in the shot. 'Say Lan Kwai Fong!' Margot takes the shot just as our mouths are poised in the 'Fong' position.

We walk together, mindlessly chatting as we descend the peak into the cooler forest. It's a welcome break from the humidity, even if a tad creepy.

'Seffy,' Tish says, elongating the syllables in the way people do when they are asking their parents for money.

'Yes?' I answer.

'You know you got divorced and then you came here?'

'Yeah . . .' Not really sure where this is going.

'What actually happened?'

'Errr.' I feel myself clam up.

'It's ok if you don't want to tell us,' Margot says hurriedly. 'But you were crying in your sleep the other night and saying something about a baby?'

My heart skips a beat, a ball of stomach acid rises into my throat and my fingers go all tingly.

'I was crying in my sleep?' Fuck, I still do that? I thought I'd stopped. I mean, how would I know I guess; my phone isn't a great conversationalist and I'm yet to have another bed partner. Harry was the kind soul who let me know that I divulged all my biggest secrets while subject to my own slumber.

'Err, yeah. Quite a bit,' Tish adds, biting her bottom lip in anguish.

Oh, fuck it. I have no idea what they heard and it's more embarrassing letting them in on my own undirected stream of consciousness than just telling them the truth. Maybe sharing my secrets will eventually blow away that dark cloud. There's no point in pretending anymore, I have nothing left to lose.

I take a deep breath.

'So . . . Luke and I met through a friend, we fell in love, got married. I thought everything was going to be perfect. We had the most incredible wedding in Tuscany, we both had good jobs, we rented a flat together but were thinking of buying a house – we just couldn't decide where and thought we should wait until we had a baby so we could choose the right area.' I pause and look at both of them walking slowly next to me. 'So then, we thought we'd start trying for a baby. Well, Luke wanted to keep it casual, just, you know, let nature take its course, but I'm not like that. Once I started researching and realising how actually hard it is to have a baby, I got a bit obsessed. We kept trying, I had a miscarriage, but the doctor said it was normal.' My eyes are wet. 'Then I discovered I couldn't have kids naturally. Luke and I split up and a few weeks later, we decided to divorce.' It's not totally the truth, but I'm not even sure why I left so I don't know how to explain it.

'What a twat!' Tish exclaims; she's obviously assumed that Luke pushed me into the divorce. 'Just leaving you in the lurch like that. It must have been heart-breaking. So, you found out you were infertile, and the dickhead decided to go and spread his seed somewhere else?'

'Hmmm, kind of. I mean it was a really difficult time, and sometimes I struggle to remember all the details. I didn't actually tell him I had a miscarriage at first, I was too distraught and I didn't want him to stop trying for a baby. I just don't think men understand how much pressure women put on themselves to be a mother. Like you know, you read about men who have a wank in a van, knock on the door and deliver their sperm and then off they trot to the next woman begging for a child. They're able to disassociate themselves from it.'

Margot looks at me.

'I watched them do it, in a documentary.' I add, in case Margot thinks I've been hitting up white van men in return for their sperm.

'God, I watched that documentary too – crazy!' Tish responds. 'I know what you mean about men. I never see my dad; he left my mum when I was only two – don't think he could deal with the tantrums.'

'Have you come to terms with it, you know, not being able to have kids? It must be really difficult – I'm so sorry.' Margot rushes to hug me. 'It's not something you ever think about, is it? You just assume that one day, if you want kids, you'll just have them, like grabbing a packet of sweets out of a vending machine.'

I laugh because it is kind of funny. Everyone just thinks that having kids is easy. We're sold the idea that having kids is simple, and we start periods as soon as we become teenagers.

'Not really,' I sigh, feeling a little tear trickle down my cheek. 'That's kind of why I'm here, travelling around. Completing a thirty under thirty bucket list and trying to have the best time of my fucking life. I was so set on doing everything by the rule book – you know, GCSEs, A-levels, university, decent job, married, house, promotion, kids, that I forgot to have a good time. To live my life. Now I know that I can't have children, maybe I should focus more on the things I can do. Well, that's what I'm trying to teach myself anyway.' And to get over Luke, I think to myself. Because it's so easy to hate someone, to blame them unnecessarily than to realise your own flaws and hate yourself.

'You can still have children you know though, if you want to. There's always adoption, surrogacy . . . you know. Only if you wanted to,' Tish rushes. 'You don't *have* to have children; like I said before, I don't think I will.'

'Yeah, I know there are options. It's just, it isn't my natural choice. I think I just had something to prove.' Like being a better mother than my own.

'It's really hard.' Margot sighs. 'I am just so, so sorry.'

'It's ok,' I respond. 'I have to come to terms with it at some point, I don't really have a choice. I found out about it ages ago so you don't need to be sorry, it's just life. Let's talk about something more serious, like what we're going to do this evening.' I turn to them both in turn, smiling, hoping the forced happiness will counteract the sadness.

We chat mindlessly for the next hour or so until we reach our final destination – the beach. I'm present in the conversation, but my brain is whirring in the background. I know there was a lot more I could say to Tish and Margot, a lot more opening-up I could do but emotions are not my forte. Just saying the words out loud helped me a bit, realising that I'm not alone, that the news I was given on that fateful day would be a lot for anyone to handle. I should think of myself as resilient for being here now. I am a strong, independent woman.

I want to be more like them, less fearful of emotions and what people think of me. Be honest.

We all strip down to our bikinis and run into the sea, laughing.

'Do you know what we should do?' Tish declares. 'Skinny dip!' She takes her bikini off in the sea and waves it above her head.

'No way am I doing that.' I laugh.

'You have to – for your bucket list.'

'Yes! For your bucket list,' Margot retorts, taking her bikini off too.

'Fine!' I undo my top and pull my bottoms off.

We stand in the sea waving our bikinis in the air, screaming and laughing.

'Shall we go get some beachside beers?'

'What about our bikinis?'

'For it to be classed as skinny dipping, we have to run back naked to our towels.'

I feel my body recoil with anxiety.

'One, two, three!' Margot screeches, and we run like children to our towels, giggling all the way.

#11 Skinny dipping with friends on a public beach in BROAD DAYLIGHT

12

Harry's eyes are wide and excited as she stares down her phone camera.

'Harry?'

'Yes, I can hear and SEE you, Grandma, it's like we're together again.' She smiles at me through the screen.

'Why are you wearing a wig?' It's the sort of thing Harry would do for a laugh; I don't know why I even asked.

'A wig?!' she scoffs. 'I dyed my hair pink! Do you like it?' I nod because I don't want to lie to my best friend. 'You're doing all this crazy stuff on the other side of the world, and I've basically turned into a more placid version of pre-travelling Seffy. I have to keep up somehow!' She fluffs her hair up and her eyebrows knit together as she peers into the camera using it as a mirror.

'I'm really not being that out there. It's just because I'm normally so strait-laced.'

'Purlease – you've tossed off a stranger on the plane, got a tattoo, skinny dipped . . . it's like you've realised you've only got six months left to live. You're not dying, are you?' Harry suddenly says, concerned.

'No!' I exclaim. 'It's nice to know that you only think I'm this free-spirited if I'm on death's door. Besides, it's how you live your life all the time.'

'Exactly, it's why I'll have no regrets when Jesus knocks on my door telling me my time's up. Anyway, I forgot I have something to tell you about your tattoo.'

'What? Don't tell me you got one too?'

Harry creases. 'Don't worry, I might get another tattoo but not one like yours. Yours means "sexual fantasy".'

'No, it doesn't.' I say it intuitively before realising I have no idea what it means because I'd drunk three fishbowls so I can't remember anything about the experience.

'Well, what do you think it means? Because I'm telling you, it means sexual fantasy.' She starts laughing so hard she's struggling to catch her breath. 'This guy at work told me – he did say you were fit though and probably most guys' sexual fantasy, if that makes you feel better?'

'Not really. Anyway, I can pretend it means spirit. Do we know anyone who speaks Cantonese?'

'Besides me? In our immediate circle of friends – zero. You can just pretend it means spirit and then when you're having rampant hot sex with a Leonardo DiCaprio lookalike you can tell him about being his sexual fantasy.'

'Great – deal.' I laugh. 'I might get more tattoos with hidden meanings now.'

'Please, it will give me great pleasure in guessing what they all mean.' Harry smirks. 'Anyway, where are you going next on your travels? Are you going with your new pals? It's like you're a cougar of friends.'

'Harry! That's rank, you make me sound like I'm grooming them. I love Tish and Margot. I've told them to come visit one day.'

'Nice!' Harry exclaims. 'I'll make sure I'm on my best behaviour.' She holds her hands under her chin angelically.

'Anyway, I'm off to India – in a few days actually. I'm a bit nervous – people say the food is, like, out of this world spicy.'

'Remember that guy I dated once, Rolo, the one who opened up my mind and body to the world's spirits? And he was a master of that sexual tantra stuff – still to this day, one of the best orgasms I've ever . . .'

'Yes.' I interrupt her – if I had a pound for every time I've heard about Rolo, I wouldn't be working in banking.

'Well, he said you HAVE TO eat vegetarian while you're there and always ask for a side of yoghurt.'

'Yeah, I get that.' Can't believe I agree with Rastafarian Rolo. 'Anyway, I have to go!'

'Good luck! Love you, miss you!'

We blow each other kisses and hang up.

I miss her.

I can't believe my tattoo means sexual fantasy.

For a moment, I feel myself tense up and then I start laughing, really laughing.

Because it's funny and what does it actually matter? Old me would have had a breakdown over something like that until Luke reassured me I was his sexual fantasy every day, but I don't need him – I'm my own sexual fantasy.

Maybe this tattoo can serve as a reminder of my weeks spent with Margot and Tish, teaching me I can be everything to myself.

We stand on the deck of the Star Ferry – Tish, Margot and I – crossing Victoria Harbour, from Hong Kong Island to Kowloon. I've already done the trip, but the first time was alone and not nearly as pleasant.

I click enthusiastically with my new Canon at the waves created from the junk boat, refracting light on glass, side profiles of my new friends.

'I can't believe you're leaving us so soon!' Margot cries as she switches out of the Titanic pose with Tish and pulls me in.

'I know, me neither – I've had the best time and I truly mean it!' I grin, my eyes squinting with happiness, putting all my crow's feet on display, but I don't mind. I was thinking about Botox before this trip, but I don't think I'll bother now. Tish and Margot don't seem to care; I don't really either.

'When I come back to the UK, IF I ever come back, I'm coming to visit you in your big swanky London pad. You're welcome to come up to the Toon to see me, but you'll probably hate it.' Tish is such a sweety.

'I won't! I'm dying to see that shot bar you used to work in. I'm not a millionaire – I think you'll be shocked at the size and state of my flat!' It's not just the appearance. Once the place I lived was filled with love, now it feels cold and lonely.

'What's the plan for when we arrive? Temple and then lunch? Then final temple, drinks and home? What time's the last ferry?' Margot loves a good plan – more than me sometimes.

'Not until 11.00 p.m. – so we literally have aaallll day.' Tish, on the other hand, is a bit more *laissez-faire*.

'I think temple first, then lunch – we might need refuelling,' I say, pondering what I might ask God for, if he can even help me.

'I can't believe you've been in Asia nearly a month and you still haven't been to a temple! Are you ok?' Margot puts her palm on my forehead. 'You should be bored at the site of another temple by now.'

'She's been too busy beating up mums, getting crude tattoos and snogging.' Tish sticks her pointy tongue out at me.

'Stop it. You're making me blush.'

'Wow. Wow. Wow,' Tish exclaims as we arrive outside Chi Lin Nunnery. The temple ahead of us is octagonal in shape and painted bright gold, with intricate carvings in the wooden walls. Against the backdrop of the grey sky-highs it looks like a mirage. Immaculately trimmed bonsai trees and lotus ponds in the garden at the front and a bright red bridge leads the way across a river, and in the background, I can hear the trickles of a waterfall. It's magical, serene, like taking a quick nap from the hustle and bustle outside.

'Why can't all churches be gold?' I ask no one.

'It's because in Christianity they don't want to look like they're ostracising people based on wealth. Or show off how rich the church is,' Tish explains – how does she have an answer to everything and HOW is she only nineteen?

'Is that true?' I love a good fact – Luke used to save one from every book he read on the commute to tell me every evening. I used to have a notes section on my phone, where I'd save all the facts I'd heard and was going to make a little book for Luke but trying for a baby got in the way.

'In my head it is, but I don't know.' She grins. 'Sounds about right though, ey?'

'Chi Lin Nunnery was founded in 1943. 1943! It is the world's largest handmade wooden building, built with a special interlocking system with no nails. All the Buddha statues are made from clay, wood and even gold. There's a total of sixteen halls.' Margot points to the gold building. 'This one I think is the Hall of Celestial Kings.' She continues, 'There's a picturesque garden out at the front called Nan Lian Garden – which we are standing in now,' Margot reads from an information plaque to our right.

We walk through the beautiful garden, the smell of blossoming flowers rich in the air, cutting through the pollution with sweet elegance, making your imagination believe you could be anywhere. Steam billows off the waterfall as the splashes of cold water meets with the humid air and my inner body immediate feels at peace with the world.

We stop and stand in the Hall of Celestial Kings; the smell of flowers is replaced with heavy incense lying thick at the base of your nostrils, and the sound of trickling water is replaced with a spiritual chanting. The bonsai trees and ponds are replaced with four gold statues of the celestial kings. We sit cross-legged and watch the chanting and drumming. There's something about it which is strangely therapeutic. The soft beats of the drum reaching a crescendo makes my heart beat faster but it's not putting me on edge and making my anxiety soar, it's soothing me. I feel in a trance, like they are gradually sapping the negativity from my body with each beat.

'Hey, Seffy,' Tish whispers, giving me a slight nudge. 'Shall we go?'

In my head, I feel like I could sit here all day. Sleep here, even, until I become at one with everything in my past, present and future.

There's a queue to a large Buddha statue in the main temple hall.

'Everyone is making a prayer and an offering,' Margot squeals as she makes us join the queue. 'We should too!'

I think about what I want my prayer to be – there are so many things. It's like when someone says if you had three wishes what would they be? And you always say, my first is to have more wishes. But how many wishes can you actually have before they stop meaning anything?

I think about all the things I could say but they'd be too long for a prayer.

'What did you wish for Margot?' Tish says excitedly.

'It's not a wish – it's a prayer. Some things should stay secret.'

'Same thing. You're still hoping for something that you haven't got.'

'Not really.' Margot shakes her head at Tish's incomprehension. 'People are waiting – your turn.'

Tish stands in front of the monumental statue for a very long two minutes.

'I had a lot to get off my chest,' she whispers to Margot and winks at me.

I don't know why I feel nervous; it's literally a private moment between me and Buddha. It's the embarrassment of speaking about my feelings.

I start speaking aloud, well, inside my head – something which I used to do a lot at home when I was younger, when I even judged myself.

Dear Buddha,

Sorry, I didn't really know how to start that. It's not really a letter. Do I say Hi or Greetings? Or do you just know because you're already in my head?

Maybe I shouldn't even say a prayer, I don't even know enough about this. But aren't religious spaces supposed to be welcoming, forgiving, and if I can't say what I want here, then where can I?

Sorry Buddha, my internal monologue is overcrowding what I want to say to you.

I've never prayed that much, maybe that's why I'm in the position I'm in. I should have given some more time, thoughts to you and stopped being so lost in my own selfish world.

Anyway, I want to say thank you, for watching over me in Hong Kong. I've only been here a month and I already feel like I'm starting to find myself in ways I never thought were possible. Everyone I know who follows Buddhism seems to be very at one with themselves, that's just my observation anyway. Sorry, I'm babbling, it's just nice to be able to speak, not be judged and have all the time in the world to say my part, despite there being a queue behind me.

I guess that's what I want, to be at peace with myself. Stop comparing myself to others and wishing I were different. Learn that I am who I am, and I should be thankful for that.

So, yeah, thank you and if you can lead me on a path to self-discovery, I mean, I guess you kind of have already, I'd be really grateful.

Thank you again.

I look up from the floor and see a little old lady, hunched over, grinning at me with only half her teeth. She touches my hands, bows her head and says something to me which I can't understand before giving me a bunch of flowers.

'If I've ever seen a sign, that was one of them,' Margot says wisely, raising her eyebrows.

'What did you wish for, Seffy?' Tish asks eagerly.

'It's not a wish! It's not a genie, it's a prayer to Buddha,' Margot says, exasperated.

'I had a little chat with him, said thank you and that I wanted to be led on a path of self-discovery.'

'Well, I think it's a sign. Make of it what you want. But if it was me, I'd be thinking my life was about to turn upside down – in a good way, of course.'

'I guess that's number twelve on my bucket list then!'

#12 Find yourself with Buddha

Four Months No Baby

Dear Admirable Aphrodite, goddess of love, fertility, beauty and all things great and good and her valiant Roman sister, Venus,

Oh my-bleeping-God, I'm fucking pregnant. I'm fucking PREGNANT!!!!! Thank you, Aphrodite, Venus – you're bloody ('scuse the pun) heroines!

My menstrual month started as usual – late. It's always late, I've never had regular periods, but they always come in the end. I think it's because my body operates at a high stress rate. I push it to full capacity every day and sometimes, it must think 'God I can't be bothered with womb-shed and bloating this month' so procrastinates until the last minute.

I was waiting, waiting for it to come. Doing my usual sashaying around Tesco, Waitrose and Sainsbury's in a mixture of hair-up, hair-down and Luke's caps to purchase my daily supply of the old pee tests. And I got the symptoms that I always get, the tingle in the nipples where I need to slap Luke's hands away faster than a flasher on the Northern line, the bloat where people embarrassingly give up their seats on the tube for you and the Mount Everest size spot that even a Tik-Tokker can't cover up. But as we know, we've been here before. The signs for period and pregnancy are the SAME. I mean, who even designed that? Major flaw I say.

I did the test. Nothing. The usual anxiety set in. Will I ever get pregnant? What's wrong with me? I really want someone to inherit my love for organisation and my grandpa's lighter from the war. I desperately want to be a mother, to prove to myself and everyone around me that terrible parenting is not genetic, a mini-me to have everything I never had. I want to spoil them with love. I want my child to feel as if I can't give them any more, it's how I used to feel with Luke, before we started on this dreaded baby train.

I felt really tired, like exhausted. I fell asleep on the toilet at work for two minutes, and I only woke up because some-one used the hand-dryer.

Luke came home from work one night to find me lying on the sofa which is totally unlike me. I didn't even work out that morning.

'Do you want stir fry tonight?' he asked, putting his bag down.

'Yeah, ok. I'll help.' I jumped up from the sofa – pleased that Luke offered to cook, as I really couldn't muster the energy.

We went into the kitchen together where he started abhorrently chopping up the chicken into little squares.

'Don't cut it like that, I want it in strips.' It was such an intense thought; I didn't even have time to retract it.

'It doesn't really matter, does it?' He laughed and car-ried on mutilating the meat further.

'It does. I don't want mine in squares.' I remember my mum trying to carve the chicken for the roast, swigging from the bottle, cutting her hand and the blood seeping into the moist, steaming white flesh. 'It's making me feel sick.'

'Come on, Seffy.' He guffawed. 'It's chicken. It all gets turned into mush once you eat it anyway.' He goes to put his arms round my waist, mocking me. 'Would you like it cut into stars, little princess? Raw, meaty, pink chicken stars?' He was just messing around, we always mess around, banter. But I could see it now, me screaming, my mum just staring at her hand, wine still in the other. I couldn't take it.

'Stop it! You're making me feel sick.' I felt tears in my eyes. 'I don't even want stir fry. And I'm starving. You've ruined my dinner.' I was annoyed, sick, upset.

'What the fuck, Seffy?' He looked like he was about to perform some stupid magic trick, holding his chicken hands

out like a budget Charlie Chaplin. His eyes were confused, his mouth in an awkward equivalent of a half-up, half-down hair do.

It wasn't his fault, I was acting out. Was I actively trying to make Luke hate me?

I left the room and cried alone in the bathroom, my stomach rumbling.

Ten minutes later . . .

'I'm sorry, it's my period.' I snuggled into Luke's chest. It's not his fault my mum was like a toddler raising a family.

'It's ok.' Immediately accepting of my apology. 'I thought that might be it. You always go a bit nuts around this time.' He'd obviously forgotten about the whole hormones argument we had last month.

It's always ok for a woman to be called 'crazy' or 'nuts' but if you even mock the red eyes and sniffly nose with 'man-flu' they get in a 'strop'. I want to say fuck you but I realise I'm slightly on the back foot after my chicken outburst.

And it's just a word Seffy, you've called him worse than nuts.

The next day, I woke up and still felt tired. I check my app and by that point I was eight days late. EIGHT DAYS.

I did a test and . . .

Two lines.

Two mother-fucking lines.

But the main fortune teller is faint, like you can barely see it. I held it under the light at different angles and one hundred per cent it was there. I know a thing or two about pregnancy tests and in all my experience of angling my urine stream onto a tiny bit of absorbent paper, I'd never seen this.

I rushed into Tesco – no disguise needed – and purchased an ultra-early digital Clear Blue.

And what did it say?

PREGNANT!

I couldn't concentrate at work all day. I let Moira's comments about my Excel inefficiency wash over my head. Nothing could dampen my mood. In nine months, I thought to myself, nine months and I'll be out of here. I'll be lazing around on the bed with my gorgeous little new-born. I'll be having coffees in idyllic London cafés with all my fancy friends from my antenatal class, and I won't even feel embarrassed about breast-feeding in public. I will want everyone to know that I nourish this child that I have grown!

But what to tell Luke? I wanted my announcement to him to be perfect. I was going to film it so that once the twelve weeks passed I could show all my friends. Will he cry? Will he swing me round?

I didn't have time to go to the baby shop on my way home. I'd go tomorrow and maybe I'd do a little treasure hunt around the flat for Luke. Or send him on a hunt to find me. It was too early to show him a scan but maybe I could save the test.

Luke started nuzzling my neck when we got into bed, rubbing his hand on my thigh. I was pregnant and he seemed to find me even more attractive. Pheromones. I declined his offer and blamed it on my period while secretly grinning to myself. At last, sex wouldn't feel like such a chore anymore. I'd be able to enjoy it again. Maybe I'd become one of those sexually rampant pregnant women that you read about in Cosmopolitan.

Today, I've woken up with stomach cramps, feeling a bit sick. I've heard that it can be part of the implantation process, but nevertheless, I'm a bit worried. I go to work as normal, sit at my desk, crunching numbers in a never-ending sheet while googling pregnancy announcements. I really want it to be perfect for Luke. It's been four long, hard months for him, even longer for me. He will be so excited. We'll stay up late discussing how we'll raise little baby Coates and even pre-organise our Mamas & Papas private shopping experience to get the best for our little one. And the babymoon, where shall we go – Mauritius?

Thank you my gracious, sexy, gorgeous Aphrodite xxxxxx

Dear Aphrodite, fuck you.

Things were too good to be true.

You've ruined me. Taken me to hell and back.

This is what happened – post-stomach cramps that you led me to believe were normal.

It feels a bit like I've wet myself. I touch my hand on my leg. Blood. Oh my God.

I rush to the toilet and find more blood. My period?

The baby.

I quickly google nearby prenatal units and message Moira to tell her I've got a sickness bug. She has a phobia of catching illnesses from people, so as expected, she tells me to leave immediately.

I fast-track through the queue at St Thomas'. The nurse asks me if I have anyone who could be with me, but I reply no.

She makes me pee into a little pot, where she dips some sort of litmus paper before sitting down next to me and telling me I've had a miscarriage.

She tells me it was really early on, it's quite common and not to worry about future procreation despite giving me a leaflet on nearby counsellors and family planning clinics.

I leave wearing a nappy, tears streaming down my face. Like a giant baby, which is morbidly ironic.

I sit outside on a little bench surveying the river. The sun's shining and there's a cool breeze; it should be a relatively pleasant day. But it's not. It's the worst fucking day of my fucking life.

I think back to that fleeting happiness I had over the last twenty-four hours. How much of a good mum I would have been? I would give anything, ANYTHING, to be a mother. What's wrong with me? Fresh tears build before flooding down my face in mini rivers.

Aphrodite, you know me by now. I've spent months writing to you, praising you – how could you do this to me?

I'd do anything to be pregnant, literally anything. Is there a science to it? More than sperm meets egg? How can people get accidentally pregnant when it's this hard if you're physically trying?

I don't want to tell Luke. I don't want to tell anyone. I know you shouldn't have secrets if you're married but I can't tell him. He'll feel sad for me, check I'm ok, say we should give this whole trying for a baby malarkey a break. I just want to get back on it, I want to be pregnant, so I forget the loss.

It's crazy how I hadn't even met the ball of cells in my womb, but it still feels so devastating. I'm supposed to bear children, it's what I want, and I can't do it. I know this isn't how everyone feels, but I do, there's nothing I want more. I want to have it all, the husband, the career, the friends, the money, the life, the baby. I don't want to share the roles; I want them all. To be the husband and the wife, the caregiver and the breadwinner. I want to be strong, independent, successful, but I'm not. My body isn't able to keep an embryo alive while some people can have ten kids.

What if I can't have children? I know it's an irrational thought. As I've said before, I'm my mother's child. The doctor said I'm young, fit, healthy. There's no reason why I wouldn't be able to have them. I don't want to be one of those women who doesn't understand what it's like to have sleepless nights or change a nappy. I want to teach my own flesh and blood how to read and write, I want them to ask me why the sky's blue and the grass is green. I want to see their faces light up when I make footprints out of washing powder on Christmas Day or tell them we've booked a holiday near a waterpark.

*What's the point in me working so hard, earning all this
money, if I have no one to give it to?*

I'm going out with the boys for a few drinks after work,
is that ok?
Perfect. I can sit at home and cry alone.
No problem, see you later x

> *Fucking Diane.*
>
> *I've just seen this incredible documentary on how the
> Japanese use purple sweet potato to improve their fertil-
> ity. Not sure if they sell that in Tesco but I'll keep my eyes
> peeled. Hope you're well X*
>
> *ARGHHHHHHHHHHHHHH!*
>
> *I swing my right arm in the perfect overarm throw and
> listen for the resounding splash.*
>
> *Fuck.*
>
> *My phone.*
>
> *Fuck, fuck, fuck.*
>
> *Did she literally sit at home and concoct the most incon-
> siderate message she could think of?*
>
> *Why does everyone seem to think that my having a
> baby is any of their business? It's making me feel more pres-
> sure. More, even, than the amount I'm putting on myself.
> Which is essentially impossible.*
>
> *When I started this month's letter to you, I thought
> this would be a letter of utmost gratitude. One I'd frame
> and keep in a special memory box alongside the pregnancy
> test and my first scan. It's not. It's a letter where I say,
> 'what the fuck'? How can someone who is trying this hard
> to conceive have this much bad luck? It's like when your
> parents would tell you if you revised really hard for your
> GCSEs you couldn't possibly fail.*

I'm essentially revising every second of my existence and I'm still failing. What else can I do? I'll never ask for anything again. Apart from maybe a new phone and not quite as painful periods.

Have I done something wrong in a past life? Am I not grateful enough? Am I really my mother's child and you won't let me ruin another life on earth?

FUCKING TELL ME APHRODITE SO I KNOW.

I just need to know.

Please.

Seffy.

Nine Months Until Thirty

13

I cry when I say bye to Tish and Margot. It's very unlike me to get so close to people in just a few weeks.

'Don't goooooo,' Tish says as she hugs me tight.

'You always meet the best people travelling.' Margot runs to join us for the hug.

'Look at us, the perfect throuple.' Tish grins, giving us both a kiss on the cheek.

'Maybe that can be next on my bucket list, throupling and threesomes,' I joke back, feeling a tiny lump in my throat.

'You're a free, sexually liberated woman – do whatever sets your pulse racing. But I'd advise girl and guy, not twin men,' Tish replies, cocking her head to one side.

'Amen, Tish,' Margot says, squeezing my hand. 'You're a sexy, independent powerhouse – you don't need no man.' She wags her finger sassily.

'I don't want you to think that when you turn thirty, you're in for some horrible surprise – it's not all bad. You've given me my mojo back.'

'Stop acting like you're sixty-five, girl – mojo, no one says that anymore FYI! If I'm half the woman you are, Seffy, I'll be fucking proud.' Tish pulls both my cheeks together and kisses me on the lips. 'When I first found out your age, it was like spying on your schoolteacher shopping in the local Tesco . . .'

'Shut up!' I give Tish a friendly shove. 'What and releasing the tap on her extremely dissatisfying personal life while purchasing potato smileys?'

'Ha, no. Then I realised you're probably one of the coolest people I've ever met – if I were Luke, I'd never have let you go.'

As I'm packing for the next leg of my trip, I find the brown bag of fertility foods from what seems an age ago. I can't believe I forgot about them. Shows how much having fun can change your outlook and make you forget what your whole focus was only a few months ago.

I don't need them. All they are doing is making me remember how hard I tried and how hard I failed. It's not that I'm at the end of my journey with my questions and answers but there must be another way than eating beans and sprinkling powder in my tea. Plus, I can't test the theory anyway because I have no one to conceive with. I'm sure if I wanted to impregnate myself with a stranger's sperm, all I'd need to do is ask, but I'm not quite at that level yet. It's too out of control for me, and after the tattoo incident, I could be sold anything – dog sperm or something.

Harry: *Hello?*
Harry: *Your phone's off. No one under sixty switches their phone off. EVER. You know that right?*
Harry: *Hellloooooooooooooooo*
Harry: *I'm really fucking bored. We should swap lives like that movie* Freaky Friday *– like I'd have your money but be travelling and you'd be working because you are one of those weird people that enjoy it.*
Harry: *Is this the day you fly to Delhi?*
Harry: *Purleaaaseeee tell me you met some incredibly wealthy guy at the airport who whisked you off your feet and you're now travelling on his private jet, taking the mile-high club to new levels and eating sushi off each other's nipples. I'd really be jealous then.*
Harry: *REPLY!*
Me: *Sorry, sorry sorry!*

Me: *Yes, I'm here, just arrived. Sorry to disappoint you but my journey was incredibly boring. It's not my trademark trait you know, having sexual encounters on planes, like serial killers in movies who leave trinkets on their victims.*
Harry: *It should be.*

As Harry ripped up my itinerary before I'd even boarded my first flight, I don't have any pre-booked accommodation. Luckily, I still remembered some of the names of hotels in central Delhi from my extensive research. What do you do otherwise? Do you just turn up on whatever the main street is, knock on the door and ask if there's any room at the inn? It didn't work out very well for Mary and Joseph, so I doubt I'd have much more luck. Although she was told she was pregnant by an angel.

Delhi, like Hong Kong, is humid and polluted. If you were ever looking for the ideal combination for breakouts and major frizz, this is it. My skin is wet and sticky, attracting dust, general debris and the odd fly, which is really doing wonders for my complexion, and Harry made me leave half my skincare routine in London.

'Taxi?' A man hangs his head out of the window. 'Where are you going?'

'Yes please.' I smile thankfully and heave my backpack off my left shoulder onto the pavement. 'Claridge's?'

'Yes ma'am.' The little man dressed head to toe in white does a bow and then chucks my heavy backpack in the boot.

'Sorry.' I shake my head, correcting myself. Why would I leave the Mandarin Oriental just to go back to the old Seffy before I found my mojo (sorry Tish, pizzazz, zest – do they work?) again? But I don't know any hostels because all I researched before I left for my travels were fancy hotels. 'Do you know any nice hostels?'

'I have just been to one with a very nice man – Amigos, I think it was called. Shall I take you there?'

'That would be lovely, thank you so much.'

'Where are you from?' The man asks me as I recline in the plastic seats. The cab smells of incense and the seats are covered in those plastic slipcovers – I've seen them on sofas in American movies – a feeble attempt to keep something looking nice while ensuring it doesn't look nice. I never understand why they do that; surely, it's way more gross. Are they expecting a murder scene? Do they literally think they are in *Taxi Driver*? I'm all for pre-empting but it does seem a bit much. Think how much skin must be stuck to it when you peel your thighs away at the end of the trip.

'London,' I reply.

'London!' he exclaims. 'I went there once. Camden Market, do you know it?'

'Camden? Why did you go there?'

'It was a trip . . .' He slams on the brakes, beeps his horn furiously and shouts something out of the window. I smash into the front seat, leaving a sticky plastic imprint on my forehead – attractive. 'Stupid man. Not looking where he's going. You know Indian drivers are the best in the world, very safe.'

'Yes.' I nod, smiling, while gripping the back of the front seat with both hands. There are so many cars on the road; I thought London rush-hour was bad, but this is another level. A cacophony of different horns beep in the air. It's not just vehicles on the road; goats, even a cow walks between the cars. There don't seem to be any rules or awareness of danger when it comes to crossing the road as people flit between the cars selling sweet treats, stopping dead in their tracks as cars zoom past them.

I snap away on my camera, the ultimate tourist, but I really don't want to miss a beat. I want to remember everything, everyone.

A young girl knocks on the window, smiling, holding out her hands for money. She can't be any older than six, but the driver bats her away.

We sit, stop, start, stop, start in the immense traffic – five, maybe six lanes of cars piled up as far as the eye can see. I shut my eyes for a bit, I didn't sleep very well on the plane, but the jolting of the car, beeps and shouting from my driver is not exactly relaxing.

'The Delhi Gate!' I exclaim, pointing to the decadent architecture. I've done my research of course, and it's the first image that pops up on Google when you type in 'Things to see in Delhi'. Luke would have laughed and told me to get a job as a tour guide.

He makes a sudden swerve towards the attraction and then comes to an abrupt stop.

'May I have a look round? I'll only be five minutes.'

'It's ok, ma'am, I'll wait. You can trust Abhay.'

I step out of the car and walk towards the incredible feat of architectural ingenuity. It towers above everything around it, and I have this strange mirage that the new me could be standing the other side. Like a future deja-vu, that one day I'll come back here and think about who I once was. Before I can shake the thought, I see a little girl lying on a mound of clothes and rubbish. She looks about five; she has a grubby T-shirt on and no bottoms. Her hair is matted and scruffy, her delicate facial features covered in dirt. I feel my eyes water.

I walk towards her, she looks up at me, her eyes big, round and hopeful. Not expectant, just hopeful. I hand her a two thousand rupee note and she puts her arms round my shins tight. I know it's nothing. I know my face is wet, I can feel it. I cast my stare further afield and see more children, more poverty.

I feel guilty. Guilt that I was born into a home with warmth, running water and sanitation. Guilt that I feel upset about the hand I've been dealt in life when these children would give anything to be as fortunate as I am. Guilt that I throw away food or eat myself into a glutinous state after a few wines too many and these children might not even eat for days.

There are so many children here in need, so many children who need homes and families. Guilty. Guilty. Guilty.

I feel this pang that I want to help, however small that may be. Abhay sees my tears when I sit back down in the cab.

'You ok, ma'am?'

'Yes, the children, it's so sad,' I half-stutter, my voice breaking.

'Very sad.' He looks down in agreement. 'You must be grateful for life.'

It's that word again. Grateful. But for some reason, it means so much more now. I should stop feeling guilty and start feeling grateful for all that I do have.

#13 Stop feeling guilty and be grateful

We pull up outside Zostel Hostel, and it's as if someone's fired a technicolour paintball gun at the exterior. That slightly unkempt look, clashing colours, remarkably feels like home to me now – dense orchid perfume hanging heavy in the air and the tinkle of jazz on a grand piano – that's very much the old Seffy. I didn't feel grateful then, and I didn't appreciate those things.

I lug my backpack, which I'm getting rather fond of, into my dorm, say hello to my roomies and lie spread-eagled on the bed. I'm wearing one of the nylon tops Harry packed for me, but I think it's starting to give me a rash. I take it off and lie in my bra. *Aaah, freedom.*

'Hey, excuse me?'

I open my eyes and see a timid young girl looking down at me. Her hair is henna red, seeping slightly onto her forehead, signalling that she must have just had it dyed.

'Hey.' I open my eyes and smile up at her. I feel a brush of cold air and remember I'm lying half-naked. *Fuck.* I hear Tish in my ear – *It's a bra Seffy, it covers your breasts, which are the most natural food source on planet earth, come on.* 'You ok?'

'We're going on a wander, and I thought you might like to join us?' Her eyes are eager; it's nice that people want to hang out with me. 'It's hard knowing what to do when you're alone.'

'Sure, thanks so much!' I grin back. 'Let me find a top that's not giving me hives and I'll be with you.'

I grab my camera and one of the only tops made from cotton that I can find and catch up with the group.

I've been capturing Delhi in any way I can, the distribution of light and shadow falling between the delicate architecture of the buildings, street sellers, people smiling, waving, music from taxis, vendors – the way cultures, demographics, species intertwine seamlessly. It's more than beautiful.

Photography was always a childhood dream, but I've never had the time or inclination to chase it. I've never really had hobbies either unless you count work or the gym but they're basically necessities.

#14 Start a hobby – I think mine's photography?

We stop by a sign, text written in Hindi and decorated with yellow, orange and red flames. The red-haired girl, Jade, peeks her head round the corner and a tall, spindly man beckons the group inside.

The people in the hall sitting cross-legged on the floor turn to look at us, smile, nod, clasp their hands together and turn back to the gentleman on stage, who continues to speak enthusiastically.

I look at Jade who turns to me; she doesn't seem to know what's going on either.

Suddenly, drums start to play, shakers are being rattled and coloured plumes of powder are released into the air.

An older man with greying hair and a white linen shirt walks over to us, holding several garlands.

'Thank you,' I say as he hangs the colourful, perfumed flowers around my neck.

He nods back in acknowledgement.

'Is this a party?' I ask him. He looks at me and shakes his head in confusion.

'No? A service?' I ask again. He shakes his head again, still looking puzzled and walks away.

Hmmm, none the wiser, I think to myself, although it doesn't matter.

I feel a tap on my shoulder and turn around. It's the old man with a young boy, wearing a linen shirt and a stream of thick, black hair swept over to one side.

'Hello.' The boy smiles. 'My grandfather said you have a question? He doesn't speak American, but I learn it at school.'

'Nice to meet you.' I smile broadly. 'Ha ha, I'm not actually American, I'm English, from the UK.'

'Oh, you look like you're famous, big . . .' He points to my head.

'Sunglasses,' I reply.

'Yes, sunglasses. And very nice clothes, it's how the Americans dress.'

'Thank you.' I grin back, accepting the compliment and wondering what they teach him about English dress-sense in school. 'I was just wondering why you're celebrating.'

'It's a party for God; we do it every week, to celebrate and be thankful.' He smiles again, it taking over his whole face. 'You must stay, it's a party for everyone, we love guests, my grandfather is very happy.' He turns to his grandfather and

says something in Hindi to which the old man smiles enthusiastically and grabs my hand.

'Thank you, it's so kind of you. Is everyone here your
family?'

'Family, friends, neighbours – anyone who wants to join
us!' A little girl starts pulling on the bottom of his shirt. 'Sorry,
my sister, she wants me to dance.'

'It's ok, you go and thank you again for letting us join in
and being so welcoming.'

'Welcome to India – one big, happy family!' He laughs,
raising his hands in the air as he bends down and scoops his
little sister up while she squeals.

A group of children rush towards me, holding more garlands, grabbing my hands and swinging them in theirs. I
smile, laugh, feeling free. I feel loved even though I've met
them for less than five seconds. I've never met a community
so welcoming, so loving, so desperate for others to feel their
love.

We dance, shake bracelets laden with beads, run outside
with the children, share delicious hot pastries and the sickliest
sweets I've ever tasted, and I feel almost at one with the world
again.

I silently click my camera, focusing in on a baby and realise that I'm not overcome with jealousy at the young woman
holding her or sadness that it's not me on the other side of
the camera. I click again, watching the baby girl play with
her mum's hair, tangling her podgy fingers in her thick, black
curls. My thoughts aren't negative or judgemental, they are
simply taking life in for what it is – beautiful.

If I spend my whole time wishing I were someone else,
somewhere else, then I'll never appreciate what's on my
doorstep. Then I'll have no enjoyment of life at all.

I do feel grateful.

14

Delhi was an implosion of the senses. A cornucopia of history, culture, cuisine, street life. One of those cities that managed to dazzle me beyond the bright lights of Lang Kwai Fong, even in the dark. I stayed at the Amigos Hostel for about a week and a half, tagging on to different groups exploring the Red Fort, Mughal Gardens and Khari Baoli – the largest spice bazaar in Asia, munching through stuffed parathas and jalebis dripping treacle to keep me energised. My film reels are starting to look like they're straight out of a *Lonely Planet* guide.

I lost myself there, feeling all footloose and fancy-free – grateful that I get to experience this magical world in all its colourful glory.

There's a lot of time to sit and put the world to rights on a three-and-a-half-hour train journey to Jaipur with no internet. I demolished my dinner of spiced chickpea curry and saffron-infused rice in under five minutes. Getting dinner was a pleasant surprise. At home, it's usually a Pret salad I've picked up at the train station or if I'm feeling really boujee, one of those overpriced snack pots like calamari or tiger prawns steeped in olive oil. Luke used to say they were a waste of money and to be honest, he was right. Once he bought some griddled prawns in a pot as a surprise for a train journey to a friend's wedding; they stank the whole carriage out and he hadn't thought through peeling the shells off. We laughed the whole way there.

I settle back into my book. Oh Atticus Finch, if only my own father's behaviour were as exemplary as yours. Wouldn't it be amazing to have someone like that to look up to, when faced with such adversity your honour just shines through? Instead, my father, when faced with some young girl showing him a bit of attention at work, needed to massage his ego and forget for a moment that he was in his fifties with a WIFE AND FAMILY, and go and make himself feel young again.

I made a mistake too; maybe I'm more like my father than I think. *If only I wasn't so stubborn, hey Luke.*

'Chai. Chai. Chai,' a young boy, maybe fifteen, calls as he walks between the aisles of the train compartment with his little tea trolley. He stops and fills up my plastic cup from the silver flask.

I allow the sweet scents of cinnamon and black tea to waft around my nostrils before taking a sip of the comforting brown liquid. I shut my eyes. How does this taste like home when I've never tasted it before? I've tried a chai latte before, a sip of Harry's, but it's nothing like this. The one I had was all sugar, no spice and had whipped cream on top – it's how us Brits like to butcher culture. In this one, I can feel the spices partying on my tongue, balanced out by a delicately sweet richness that ties it all together.

Luke made me a chai latte once when he was treating us to an Indian fakeaway. He'd seen how to do it on some cooking show, and he'd gone out to buy all the ingredients and then set aside a Saturday afternoon to prepare it all. It was when we were trying for a baby; he wanted to treat me as I was feeling down. He put on my favourite movie – *Pride and Prejudice* – and told me to relax. I'd forgotten about that moment until now. It can't have all been sour.

I know why I came on this journey; I say it was to give myself something to do, feel like I've achieved something before I'm thirty, but it's also to get over Luke. I know it's stupid, but the whole time I was tossing Richard off on the plane, I thought about Luke. I thought about how funny and ridiculous the situation was and how much I wanted to joke about it to Luke. I know it's weird. Wanting to tell your ex about your new sexual experiences, but sometimes it's like that. Your body's somewhere new but your heart's still in the old place.

The thing is, it's not just about not being able to have a baby, it's about losing the love of my life at the same time. I lost my past, present and future all in one swoop. I need to get over Luke, and he seemed all too happy to say goodbye to me. Well, he didn't even really say anything, it was me who did all the talking. I can't remember between fact and fiction anymore, what actually was said and what I said in my head.

Sometimes I feel like I'm grieving. I sit and remember us laughing and joking at stupid TV shows and YouTube videos, or the way he knew my coffee order and order of my milk preference or to ask for the dressing on the side. The way that, when we went on holiday, he'd go swimming in the sea and I'd read my book on the beach, scared of what might be hidden beneath the seaweed and the sand and eventually he'd manage to entice me in, at least for a paddle. Luke wasn't scared of anything. He liked exploring, trying new foods, going on adventures. He was like Harry in that way, he made me more exciting.

I'm building a new version of myself, with tattoos and aeroplane flings, one who eats carbs for breakfast. I'm gradually pulling myself away from everyone who tells me to be a certain way and learning how to be whoever I want, but I still miss him. I still love him.

I look at my phone, desperate to stalk his social media profiles, to see his smile, to imagine the warmth of him next to me now. Looking out at the scenery, mindless conversation that you have with someone you've known forever, completing sudoku together.

I keep having these urges to text him. I think I'll have to block him as there is nothing I can do now.

I count to ten, breathing slowly, and go back to the comfort of kind, genuine Atticus and my chai.

This is the life. Thirty-five-degree heat, gleaming pool to cool off in, good book, cocktail in hand – bliss. I lie back on my sun-lounger and close my eyes. I can feel beads of sweat starting to form on my forehead and chest. I love that feeling; uncomfortably hot. It's totally bearable when there's a body of water nearby. Normally, I might have felt a bit body-conscious, getting into my skimpy bikini in front of strangers when I've been eating well over my weekly allowance of carbs and my spin classes have been replaced by late-night dancing and sugary shots. But I'm here on a journey of the mind, not the body. Anyway, I'm having the time of my twenty-nine-year-old-life so who cares if I'm leaning towards the relationship fifteen with no relationship? That's the fifteen pounds you put on when you're in a relationship. I read it in a magazine.

Eurgh, Seffy! Why do I relate everything to relationships, babies, family? Why can't I just make it about me? I'm enjoying myself, I've put on a few pounds, there's nothing more or less to it than that.

Splash!

What the fuck?

I sit bolt upright and remove my glasses. I'm drenched.

'Sophie! What did I tell you about jumping in the pool?' A drowned rat in child form bobs up in the middle of the pool, pulls her goggles off her head, sticks out her tongue, laughs and jumps out the other side.

'Oh my God, I am so sorry. She's turning into such a little madam. I feel so embarrassed. I really am sorry.' The lady, wearing a wide-brimmed ivory straw hat and black sun-glasses sounds apologetic but she looks almost too glamorous to have ever said sorry before.

'Oh, don't worry,' I reply, but my internal monologue is saying all sort of unpleasant things to Sophie the splasher. *Seffy, don't let your Eau de Bitch come back*. 'I was about to get in anyway.'

She takes a spot on the lounger next to me. 'Do you have kids?'

'No,' I respond, in this moment happy to be alone.

'Don't think I'm presumptuous but I thought not – you look way too relaxed and way too good. What I would do to be reading by the pool for a few minutes, not having to pretend to be a shark or watch some badly acted performance of *Peppa Pig*.'

'Ha. Why do all parents seem to say that?' I laugh off the comment, but I am interested to know the answer.

'Children – you love to hate them. You love them but fuck, they are annoying.' She takes a sip of the drink in her left hand. 'Imagine all the annoying traits from you and your partner mixed in a pot and then churned out as a smaller, more annoying version but one that also has no idea of danger, or manners, or sleep, or when to be quiet.' She takes a much longer sip this time.

I tense, ready for that familiar rage, like I experienced at the boxing club with Jenni, but it doesn't come. I feel like I can appreciate the annoyance and the stress.

'Hmmm. That does sound quite irritating.' I ponder on a miniature being who's obsessed with order, stubborn, impatient – sounds like a mini dictator. Do I have any nice attributes?

'Quite irritating?' she questions. 'Imagine telling this mirror image of all your personality traits off and realising how annoying all your friends must have been finding you for the past thirty-odd years. The realisation, it's embarrassing.'

I laugh. She's right. I used to have Luke and Harry telling me when I was being snobby or judgemental or whatever else they used to say, now I only have my own consciousness.

'I feel like I already know how infuriating everyone finds me – one of my friends tells me to take laxatives because I'm so anal.' I can acknowledge my own flaws.

'Lucky you – I've had to wait until now to realise. I'm lucky someone even wanted to procreate with me.' She chuckles to herself. 'I'm Belle by the way, short for Mirabelle. It sounds like the wine, I know.' It's surprising I wasn't christened a similar name – Grigio, Sauvignon, Riesling.

'At least you're not called Whispering Angel – I always think that sounds like a nickname for your vagina.'

Belle throws her head back laughing.

'I'm Seffy.' I hold out a hand – I like Belle, she seems more like me. Poor Jenni, I was such a bitch to her and I don't really know why. 'Do you want another drink?'

I come back with two gin slings.

'The barman made them for me – I asked for something strong and refreshing,' I say as I hand her the fizzy, pale green liquid. 'I'm normally a wine drinker but today feels like a cocktail day.'

'Mummy, can I have a coshtail?' Sophie asks.

'No, this is a special drink for Mummy. Go and ask Daddy to take you for a drink and snack at the bar.'

'Mummy's special alcoool,' she says, grinning, showing a black hole where her two front teeth should be. It's like someone's trying to teach you very early on how important it is to look after your teeth – how hideous you'd look if you only had half a set. Sophie splashes off to find her daddy. Belle doesn't strike me as an alcoholic, but Sophie's comment hits a chord, reminding me of my younger self. *Mummy's special drink*. Special enough to make you lie in a dark room until midday, forget to wash yourself or us and make us stale bread sandwiches that I pretended to enjoy to be polite.

'So . . .' Belle takes a sip of her drink. 'By what fate of the stars do you find yourself by the pool, free?'

'I'm divorced, on a secondment, completing a thirty under thirty bucket list because I can.' I grin back although I can feel my heart beating in my chest. I'm not cool and confident, I'm anxious and hot. *Own it. You're hot,* Tish said to me when I put on my pink PLT co-ord – *stop judging yourself, no one else is.*

'Amen, sister.' Belle doesn't even seem to blink; maybe she didn't hear me. 'You do you. Never take life for granted.' She takes another sip of her drink.

We pause for a minute.

'How did you meet . . . ?' I gesticulate towards the guy throwing Sophie up in the air in the pool.

'Simon. Ha, well that's a story. I was dating this utter wanker, Ashley. I'd trapped myself. I felt like I couldn't leave him, I don't know why. My life was boring. He wanted me to be the off-the-shelf 1950s housewife and I wanted to be young and free. But I was too scared to leave. One night, I met Simon, and he was everything I wanted. It all happened so fast. I left Ashley. But then, a few months later, I found out I was pregnant. Don't ask me how I didn't know, I was the first to think people were stupid for not realising they'd at least missed a period or something. Simon's a bit older than me and he'd said he didn't want kids and after the whole housewife scenario, I thought maybe I didn't either. But I couldn't get rid of it, something just wouldn't let me. Ashley didn't want anything to do with her. To be honest, I feel sad he's her dad, but she's better off without him.'

'Gosh, that sounds . . .' I don't know. Is it bad? Is it good? She had a child.

'It's a weird one, hey? Sophie was a mistake but not a bad one. Simon loves her like she's his own. It changed everything. Instead of romantic dates, holidays and sex it was all nappies, sick and haemorrhoids. If it wasn't for that mistake, I don't think I'd have children. I love her but sometimes I wonder what life would be like if she wasn't here.' I think how lucky I'd think myself if I just randomly had a child. Belle unknowingly interjects my thoughts. 'That's awful, isn't it? To think that.'

'No. It's the same when you don't have children, you always wonder what if.' *What if* are two words that constantly float around my subconscious.

'It's nice to have a choice though, isn't it?' I had a choice and I still have a choice. I've been living my life as if choice has been removed, like I'm a robot and my path of existence has been programmed in.

Belle and I are the same. Neither of us chose our fate but it's almost as if our lives should be swapped.

'It's funny, isn't it?' Belle says.

'What is?' I ask.

'When you meet people on holiday, you chat to each other like you've known each other for years. We've met all but five minutes ago and I've just reeled off my entire life story. Sorry,' she quickly adds. 'Telling a complete stranger how I sometimes feel about my child is so cathartic.'

'No, I like it. A special bond that exists between women around the world, it makes you feel part of something.'

'Mummy, Mummy.' Sophie comes running up to Belle. 'Elephants. Daddy says I can ride one like a pony. Can I? Can I?' she shrieks, waving her chubby arms in the air.

'Well, let Daddy go on with you. I hate heights and animals.'

'He won't, he said you have to,' she says pulling at Belle's arms, splashing the remnants of her drink around in her glass.

'I've always wanted to ride an elephant, so I can go with you, Sophie, if you like?'

#15 Ride an elephant (with non-blood child)

The Jai Mahal Palace feels even more glamorous when you are viewing the spectacle riding a two-and-a-half metre high elephant.

I'm riding an elephant! Mummy! Can you see me? Take a photo! And then the other things kids say such as, *Do you think he minds? Is it a girl or a boy elephant? Can I feed him after? Can I take lessons like I do at Pony Club?*

I hope Sophie appreciated it. We had a photo together and she gave me a hug. Belle said thank you, as did Simon. I don't really do selfless things for other people; I do things for me. I appreciated sharing my first ride on an elephant with Sophie; in fact, I was more grateful than she could ever imagine.

I stand by what I said about feeling more at home in hostels than hotels now. But this hotel holds something special for me. Something I needed to experience to let go of. Luke and I were watching a series of *The World's Hidden Gems* and this hotel made an appearance.

He said, *that's my dream place to get married.*

But it didn't fit into my idyllic image of a white wedding against neutral stone and regional wine.

Maybe if I'd thought more about the person as opposed to the portrayal our marriage would have got off to a better start.

It's my favourite and worst picture I've taken so far – it's a photo of memories that haven't even been created.

15

Belle and I are going out for a curry. She said it's to say thank you, and I'm sure it is, but she also caveated that it's not often she gets to go out alone and talk about things that don't involve the care of a four-limbed being, one without fur.

As we step out of the hotel, we're greeted by a procession of colour, noise and people.

'What the . . . ?'

'THIS is why I LOVE India!' Belle exclaims, clasping her hands together. 'You never know what you're going to get.'

'It's . . . incredible,' I exclaim, taking in a breath of hot air, tasting the joy. A procession of coloured saris, swaying, clapping, moving at one with each other. Rich pinks, reds, oranges and yellows as if someone's dipped their finger in a paint pot and swirled them all together. The beat of drums, punctuated with human voices and the jingle of bells. It's a positive cacophony for the senses. My brain remembers how my five senses were ignited on my first London tube ride, but I bash it away. I don't need reminding of the life I've momentarily left behind.

An euphoric man, riding on the back of an elephant wearing gold chains and beads, eagerly encourages us to join the procession, wildly gesticulating with his arms in the air.

The sun's starting to set, the blue haze of the sky is turning to darkness and the party of people is giving the city its own bright, disco ball. I don't feel like I've ever been part of the light of the world.

'Come on . . .' Belle grabs my hand.

'I thought we were going for curry. There's this incredible rooftop restaurant that specialises in Rajasthani Thali?' Why am I always so rational, so boring, so unable to grab life by its big, bright, sparkly disco balls?

'Seffy! We can't pass up an opportunity like this!' Belle shakes her head in disbelief. 'You don't have kids, no ties, you don't have to be up at 6.00 a.m. tomorrow – I WANT your life. We can grab some food en route – let's see where the night takes us.'

We jump into the procession, being moved forward by the heaving crowd, and other tourists are being pulled in as we drive through the city, like a colossal, flamboyant centipede. Cars beep in appreciation, people stand on their balconies clapping, waving, blaring their own music from little radios like a million different choruses from the world's choir.

'What's going on?' I ask a guy in a forest-green linen shirt hopping from one foot to the other near us – blatantly a tourist.

'KAJLI TEEJ!' he shouts over the banging of a drum by a teenage boy with a mop of dark-black hair.

'WHAT'S KAJLI TEEJ?' I shout back, trying to let the drum loosen up my tight shoulders through some sort of musical massage.

He points to a young couple sitting cross-legged on a gold, throne-like structure, being held up by four young boys. The girl is dressed in red and gold, her face made up like a serene doll, waving like a queen.

'It's to strengthen marriage.' He adjusts his shirt which has ridden up. 'Apparently. I googled it! But it seems like a massive party, a celebration of life from what I can see!' He shakes his head from side to side. 'Enjoy it, you don't see this stuff every day.' And he runs off, bouncing from left to right, like a deranged rabbit.

Belle is waving her arms in the air, while a lady in the most gorgeous deep-purple sari looks adoringly at her and gives her a handful of gold bangles.

I'm staying at the hotel where Luke wanted to get married and I'm now being sucked into a festival that celebrates marriage. Is the universe trying to tell me something?

What is wrong with me – do I have an innate ability to see the negative in everything? *Be positive.*

'Seffy, look! Oh my God, they look beautiful. Their dresses, their moves.'

Belle points to three young girls dancing in the centre of the crowd. Bright, cobalt blue dresses with a crimson red underlay, fanning out with every twirl. The cloth decorated with intricate gold thread, bringing out the gold of their spectacular head-dresses. The clinking of bangles accentuating every clap.

'Come on!' Belle grabs my hands, and we try, failing miserably to copy their moves. Belle tries to encourage her own bangles to clink like her own bejewelled percussion, but they simply slide up and down her wrist with barely a clang.

'How do they make it look so easy!' I laugh. 'I haven't danced like this in forever!' No alcohol needed to lubricate my moves, just pure joy. The temporary absorption into the moment. I'm dancing in the street with a lady I met hours ago, I don't need to be negative.

A group of ladies next to us, dressed in saris in the same crimson red, gold bracelets up to their elbows and the swirls of fresh henna on their hands start to do their own dance. Shaking their hips and alternating arms with the dainty forward, backward step of their feet. They look me in the eye, beckoning us to join them.

'I feel like I'm on *Britain's Got Talent* or something!' Belle exclaims.

'We would be bottom for everything.' I chortle. 'I never realised I was this bad at dancing,' I say, slightly breathless.

'Who cares? Live your life like nobody's watching!' Belle swings herself forward, pronouncing every step like a baby giraffe walking for the first time.

I take a step back and let Belle continue practising her moves. I lift my trusty camera to my right eye and try to live in the moment while preserving it for eternity.

#16 Dance and don't be afraid to be part of something

We fall out of the procession, laughing, sweating, tripping up on our own feet.

I feel drunk, that feeling of slight inebriation, toxicity but without ingesting anything other than people's happiness.

'*Now* I'm starving,' Belle says, licking her bottom lip. 'Shall we get something from one of these stalls? Ooh look parathas. I LOVE parathas.'

When we were in the swathes of the procession, I could only smell the thick perfume of heavy incense but now we've left it, the aromas of warm spices, sweet dried coconut and freshly baked naan and parathas fill my nostrils, my stomach rumbling.

My thoughts fling to how proud I used to be, planning every single restaurant on Luke's and my latest holiday. I'd spend hours researching the reviews, scouring Trip Advisor, desperate to surprise him with something off the beaten track. Desperate to be cool, original, different.

This is everything I ever wanted to be, without even trying.

We sit down at a dark, wooden table next to a man who can't be much younger than seventy, mixing a giant cauldron of chestnut brown liquid. I can smell cinnamon, coconut and a familiar spice but I can't put my finger on it.

We sip on cold Tiger beers as the old man pops two stone bowls with fragrant curry, fluffy rice and a chapati on the side in front of us. I pop a pepper in my mouth and continue the conversation.

'. . . and did you see the camel . . .' Oh my God, my mouth. Is. On. Fire. 'Fuck! Something's burning in my . . .' I go to take a sip of my beer.

'Don't!' Belle takes my bottle away. 'It will only make it worse, trust me. You need milk but when I was in this Ayurvedic clinic, they taught me that it's all in your mind. Think cooling, calming, happy thoughts and the burn will just slip away,' she says, closing her eyes serenely while I sit there thinking someone's singeing my tongue off with a hot poker.

The old man sees my face and passes me the carton of coconut milk, making little to no effort to disguise his laughter. So much so, some of the other stall owners have come over to witness the spectacle.

I'm still sweating, like one of the Jeff potatoes from my past London-life, fresh off the tube in August.

I manage to catch my breath between gulps of warm coconut milk. It's not refreshing but my mouth is extremely thankful, and my tongue starts to return to life from its paralytic state.

'I've heard of Ayurvedic clinics before – is that what they teach you?' I choke. 'To impress people with your ability to eat hot curries?' I can even manage a joke now I can feel my tongue again.

'Be a pretty extortionately priced party trick,' she scoffs. 'No, it's holistic healing – wellness is a delicate balance between mind, body and spirit. They teach you to look at things differently. I started hypnobirthing when I was pregnant with Sophie.' She sips her drink, looking at me. 'I've never believed in all that crap either to be honest, but when my mum told me about the pain of birth, I thought I'd try anything. It still hurt, obviously.' She looks up to her forehead and holds her palm outwards to demonstrate that she's not some witch who likens shooting rugby balls out of your bits to having cocktails with friends. 'But I did the breathing and it helped so much. If you panic, you make the pain worse by sending too much adrenaline round your body.'

'Hmm, interesting.' I like that it has science to back it up.

'And then I was reading about the rise in Ayurvedic clinics in London in *Stylist* magazine, and I decided to give it a try. It transformed me, honestly. I can't recommend it more. You should do one here. It started in India, over three thousand years ago, and it's likely to be a hell of a lot cheaper and more authentic than in Central London. Do you want another drink? You still look a bit hot. You should add eating hot chillies to your bucket list – you probably won't be doing it again.' She titters and orders two more Tiger beers.

'I should head back to the hotel, got to be up at 6.00 a.m. remember?' Belle says, purchasing the beers while rolling her eyes. 'Let's drink and walk, I feel like taking in more of the atmosphere.'

We walk in silence for a minute or two, admiring the happiness that this tiny corner of the world has to offer.

Groups of people are gathering round stalls, playing their own music, doing their own dances, sharing sweet and savoury treats. Everyone we pass gives us large, welcoming smiles and encourages us to join them.

It's contagious. I feel totally at home here, more than I have done in months, possibly even years.

Belle breaks the silence with a lurid comment, but one I have no option but to laugh at.

'I know I shouldn't say it, Simon's an incredible guy and he does have a great cock,' Belle slurs and giggles, obviously suddenly feeling the effects of alcohol. 'I've aways wanted to have sex on a plane, all that, having to be quick, doing it in secret turns me on. Surely, it's loads of women's sexual fantasy?'

'No, you wouldn't!' I exclaim as Belle shrugs. 'It's really not that glamorous. Too small a space to do anything really wild.' I chortle. 'Anyway, this guy Richard, who I met on the plane to Hong Kong, he didn't give anything back and he had to come in a plastic pot like it needed inspecting. It was gross actually, funny but gross.'

Belle lets out a loud laugh.

'Yeah, maybe it would be hotter if you were given some amazing orgasm by a Jude Law lookalike. Well, that's my fantasy anyway.'

'We can all dream – I'll let you know if it happens on the way back.' I snort.

'I know this is going to come out the wrong way, and I don't mean to sound patronising.' Belle turns to look me in the eye. 'But is that what it's like being single? I dated Ashley for ten years then went straight from him to Simon. Is it all master of your own destiny – feeling sexually liberated?'

I don't even need to think about my answer.

'Ha! I wish.' I spit out my beer, thinking about how much of an oxymoron my life is. 'That's what I've wanted my life to be like, in well, forever. All I've been doing is following a structured path of rigidity, that I've totally made up. I don't think I've ever allowed myself to enjoy the present. Tonight is the first time I think I've ever let myself go, like really go.' I think about the way I moved in the procession, flinging my own stereotypes off my body with every flick of my hand, jerk of my leg. All the stereotypes that I've given myself around that feeling of sterility and being a perpetual patient.

'I don't know anything about you really, but from what I can see, you have a fire inside you that's getting ready to be released. You know, people mature and learn at all stages of their life, there really is no rush to grow up – it's as boring as they say, I assure you.'

'Ha – I'm nearly thirty!'

'Thirty?' Belle shakes her head, smirking. 'That's so young, you're about to enter your good years, I assure you! Anyway.' We stop outside the gate to the hotel. 'Back to Mum duties – I want to stay out partying all night!' She opens the gate and steps through.

'Do you know what?' I suddenly say, thinking about our conversation. 'I'm going to stay out for a bit, I saw some people at that bar round the corner, I think that green linen shirt guy from the procession.'

'That's exactly what I would do if I were you.' Belle grins. 'See you tomorrow.'

Five Months No Baby

Dearest angelic, altruistic, auspicious Aphrodite and Venus, please, oh please get in my ovaries and make something happen up there – cell fission or whatever,

It's been a horrible month. I told myself at the time that the miscarriage was nothing. I needed to pick myself up and get on with it. How I used to do at home when things went wrong, like the time my mother wet herself on the sofa and I spent the night cleaning up her vomit and urine before my Physics exam. Everyone experiences hardship, it's how you deal with it that makes you great. Well, that's what my mother says anyway. She slurred it over some wine which was slightly hypocritical, to say the least.

But there's this fear inside me. I'm scared. And fear makes me feel embarrassment. I always felt inferior to everyone when I was younger. I'd look around at the smiling, loved-up couples at parents' evening while I stood alone, checking my watch in a foolish attempt to look like someone was eventually arriving. I'd wish that everything was perfect like in everyone else's life. I wanted people to stop feeling sorry for me and start feeling jealous of me.

Everything about this miscarriage brings all those feelings to the forefront, feelings that I thought I'd left behind when I started university.

That hope I had that I was growing and nurturing a tiny human. Something that didn't even know who I was, but I was so ready to love has died.

Harry messaged me: *You've been cordially invited to Thirsty Thursday – Abacus has its red carpet out for you – meet me there tomorrow 7.00 p.m.*
Me: *Sorry, got a big day Friday. Maybe next week?*
Harry: *But you always want your hangover on a Friday, so it doesn't ruin your weekend. What's wrong with you?*

I tried to push it to the back of my mind. I got home before Luke and cooked a dinner of roast chicken and vegetables so that he would think everything was normal. It's a weekday, no carbs, just the usual meat and two veg. When he walked in the door, I gave him a big kiss and asked how his day was. He did his usual, fine thanks, and yours? Then switched on the sport. I can't remember what the game was because I find physically exercising myself tiring enough and it only makes me feel inadequate. I am a fast runner, and I should have been in the first set for P.E. at school, but I have a higher chance of knocking myself out with a tennis ball than managing the timely coordination of hitting it to my opponent.

It was a standard Mr and Mrs Coates weekday evening. Apart from the fact that I was still bleeding and therefore hidden beneath the fabric of my trackies was a glamorous incontinence pad that the nurse had told me to wear.

I don't know why I feel like I can't tell Luke. I know he'll be nothing but supportive, he'll be sad. Oh, he'll be so sad. I don't want him to feel sorry for me, for us, for him to go through the sadness and the worry. I want to give him what we both want, a baby. He doesn't need to experience all the other aches, pains and ailments – he just needs to see the end result.

I tried to deny myself all sadness in the hope that my mind would just forget that the whole miscarriage ordeal even happened. I stared at the blood lying on top of my padded nappy and told myself it's just a period, you get one every month. Tricking my brain. It's what happens sometimes when people experience intense trauma, they literally believe what they tell themselves, even if it isn't true.

When we were lying in bed, I tried to keep my distance from Luke because, obviously, I didn't want to have sex but also, I didn't want him to know what fluids were being leaked underneath my black silk negligee. My sexiness is a façade so deep that it is my entire being.

He pulls me in for a hug.

'I love you.' He nuzzles my neck.

'Love you too.' I kiss him back. 'I'm so tired,' I reply, trying to put a nail in the let's have sex coffin.

'You're so sexy, you know that. My wife.' He puts his hand in between my legs only to be greeted by my adult-sized nappy, sending all his mental images and my work in the gym down the pan of female reality. I don't know if he even believes I poo or grow bodily hair – I'm happy portraying the robotic wife.

I grab his hand.

'What's that?' He laughs, jolting his head and neck back like he's just touched an electric fence. 'Feels like a nappy!' Irony, irony, irony.

'Oh.' I let out a high-pitched laugh like a hyena on helium. 'I started my period and there seems to be a short-age of tampons in Boots,' I exclaim, grinning like a maniac. 'I had to get these gross pads instead.'

'Shortage of tampons?' He questions my point which is perfectly normal because I'm pretty sure if there was a shortage of tampons it would be a national outrage and the Daily Mail would be having a field day with all the sensationalist puns – WOMEN LOSE THEIR RAG AS UK HIT BY TAMPON SHORTAGE – IT'S A CODE RED SAID 33-YEAR-OLD WOMAN FROM CROYDON EXPECTING MONTHLY VISITOR.

'Yeah, something about the ports being held up.' I try to mentally trick Luke's brain into thinking he is at some sort of educational pub quiz. 'Did you know we get the majority of our sanitary wear imported?'

'Well, I don't care what you wear. I love you anyway.' He kisses me again. I feel my face go all hot and my eyes *start to sting. I know he loves me, so why I can't I share my secret? 'I'm sorry that, you know, your period's started and you're not pregnant. It will happen you know.'*

'I know.' I smile back before turning over and silently crying into my pillow.

I'm lying to my husband. And I don't know why.

I turned up to my emergency doctor's appointment, agitated and angry.

'So, you are worried about lumps in your breasts?' she says, eyeballing the notes on her computer screen.

'No. It seems that I can only get a doctor's appointment if it is deemed an emergency. I contemplated what constituted an emergency and I thought suspected cancer sounded about right. I'm not trying to be a dick or take up valuable NHS time, but I really feel that my mental health is taking a beating and unfortunately, however twenty-first century the world pretends to be, health problems that you can't feel or see are still thought of as ridiculous.'

Dr Crawley stares at me, her hands poised over her keyboard. She tries to look expressionless as I'm sure that's what they teach you at patient-liaison school, but I can see her eyes blinking in that we've-got-a-nutcase-on-our-hands-here way behind her black frames. It's ironic that she's already degrading my mental health and making it into a mockery purely by blinking but whatever, I'm not here to make friends.

'Seraphina? Am I ok to call you that?' I nod. 'I'm sorry you feel that way about making an appointment with us. We take mental health extremely seriously here, and we even have dedicated GPs who have specialised in certain areas such as anxiety and depression.'

'My problem is unique! I'm not depressed really, well, I don't know, maybe I am. I am anxious – you should

prescribe Xanax here. When I went to America, I slept like a dream for two weeks. It's honestly a miracle drug. If it were legal here, you'd have no problem, it would be as if everyone was watching, I dunno, Great British Bake Off on repeat. Anyway . . .' I change the subject, aware that I've gone off on a bit of a tangent. 'I've been trying to have a baby for five months now, well "officially" five months but I stopped using protection months before that, and nothing's happening. I had a miscarriage last month and I just don't know how long I can go on for. Everyone's telling me not to worry because I'm young, but I'm worried.' The words rattle off my tongue quicker than I can release them from my chest.

'Miscarriage is extremely hard. Have you spoken to someone about coming to terms with the loss? I can put you in touch with a wonderful lady called Ruby who specialises in that area.' She starts typing on her computer.

'I don't need to speak to someone. I mean, it has hit me harder than I thought but I know if I could just get pregnant, I wouldn't be feeling like this anymore. I just don't know what I'm doing wrong. It can't be this difficult. Having sex is supposed to be the most natural thing on earth. It's making me go mad. All I can think about is having babies. What my life will be like when I have one. I test and test and test and every month my fucking period arrives like a very unwanted guest, like my dad turning up at my graduation.'

She stares back at me, trying to be as consoling as possible.

'The biggest obstacle in successful conception is stress. You need to try and relax, take the pressure off yourself. As you said before, you're young, fit and healthy, and you have regular periods. I'm sure everything is fine, you purely need to relax. Have you tried the app Headspace?'

I nod.

'Great, well I think some meditation would be really good for you. Try and do some different things with your partner, take your mind off the focus of conception and I'm sure it will all happen very naturally.' She pauses and jots a few things down. 'Can you clarify exactly how many months you've been trying?'

'Officially, five,' I reply immediately.

'I'm afraid we don't offer fertility treatment until after one full year of trying.' Fuck, I should have lied. 'It can take couples up to a year to conceive which is perfectly normal.'

I leave the doctor's surgery feeling slightly aggravated. I wanted Dr Crawley to help me. I wanted her to tell me that there was a one-hundred per cent chance I would be pregnant next month. That's the acknowledgment I need, Aphrodite, I need reassurance.

I don't think Dr Crawley understands what this is doing to me, mentally. Every time I go to the toilet, I get heart palpitations wondering what colour the bowl will be. I'm spending hundreds of pounds on pregnancy tests and vitamins and everywhere I look in the real and online world, I see people growing humans like they're planting grass seed and think how unfair it all is.

I contemplate what Dr Crawley said to me, we don't do anything until a year. That's on the NHS obviously, but I have private healthcare. I shouldn't have said the five-month thing, I'm so annoyed with myself. She agreed I was young, fit, healthy and had regular periods – I am probably stressed. I know I'm stressed. Maybe it's not even me, maybe it's Luke. It does take two to tango.

Are you trying to tell me something Aph? That it's my husband, not me?

'Would you be open to going to a fertility clinic with me?' I ask Luke over dinner. He's still wearing his apron. I'm glad he does most of the cooking, I find it tedious.

He tilts his head backwards, places his teeth over his bottom lip and lets out a sigh.

'Seffy?' *He holds his knife and fork in such a way I think he might lunge at me.*

'What?'

'How many times have we had this conversation about pregnancy?'

I shake my head, confused.

'Never!'

'I love you, I really do, and I want a baby with you but all we ever speak about now are babies and we don't even have one yet.' *He takes a lingering look at his plate as if hoping the lasagne could eat him instead.*

'I'm asking if you'd go to a fertility clinic with me. I don't think we've ever had this conversation before.'

'Don't be facetious. We haven't had this exact conversation before, but we've had many similar ones. We're in our twenties, we don't need to go to a fertility clinic.' *He shoves a forkful of butternut squash lasagne into his mouth and chews furiously. A bit of squash sits on his chin. I would tell him, but he's annoyed me.*

'I'm just saying I think it would be good to check. Don't you think we should have been pregnant by now? It's been five months.' *I brush away the memory of the miscarriage, knowing we have been pregnant but for some reason it didn't survive.*

'It's because you're too stressed. You're making having a baby one of your little projects and you're getting frustrated that it's not happening quick enough for you. It's nature, you can't work hard at something natural, it just happens when it happens.'

'That's stupid. Do you even understand a woman's menstruation cycle? If we have sex when I'm ovulating, which is exactly two days a month, I should get pregnant.

Your sperm should swim into my womb and puncture a little egg – it's science. But for some reason your sperm seems to be getting distracted and even though I'm ovulating, nothing's happening. I didn't think sperm had a personality, but clearly it has the same ability to get as distracted by a fly on the wall as you.' I know I'm being spiteful but I'm angry. This is why I didn't tell him about the miscarriage – he doesn't understand.

'Oh Seffy, give it a fucking REST! I don't want to ruin all the time we have of just us by talking about something that doesn't exist yet. Everything has to be on a timeline for you – what about my timeline?'

'You don't have a timeline! Men can make babies until they're eighty – I can't. I have regular periods.' *Slight lie, I do have a period every month but it's not exactly clockwork.* 'How do you know it's not you? How do you know what's going on with your sperm?'

'My sperm? There's nothing wrong with my sperm. You've seen it with your own eyes.' *He laughs, thinking it's a joke again.* 'What about your eggs, I've never seen those.' *He laughs again, going to put his hand on mine, like this is all a game.*

It's like he's flicked a switch.

'You are so FUCKING STUPID!' *I scream.* 'Do you know what your sperm count is? No. You have no idea, it's not always on the girl. Men can be infertile. Think about that. Imagine if there was nothing in your balls other than air, no chance of you passing your genetics on to anyone ever. Does that not worry you? Think for a second how that might make you feel and then maybe you'll understand.'

'Honestly, Seffy, fuck you.' *He stands and leaves the room. I hear the clink of his keys and then the door shut.*

Silence.

This is what you've led me to Aphrodite – I've become a total fucking menace. In what kind of world do you play a top trumps game with your husband about who could be carrying the dud genes. It's psychotic. It's abhorrent. It's criminal. But I just did it.

Luke did come back, and we did kind of make up again, but it's not been quite the same. We kiss but it's more of a marriage protocol than a feeling. I still stand by what I said, it could be him just as much as it could be me, but I said sorry, just because.

There's something to be said though about feeling stressed and not conceiving.

Was stress a problem in ancient Greece, Aphrodite? I'd be interested to know.

Maybe I need to get in the mindset of being pregnant. You know, fully live and breathe the life of a pregnant woman. You know, if I manifest being pregnant, maybe it will just happen, and I won't even notice. Be one of those women who goes to the toilet after a night of cocktails in Coyote and a baby falls out.

Love Seffy (In case you haven't noticed, I'm getting quite desperate now) xxx

Eight Months Until Thirty

16

That night in Jaipur with Belle goes down as one of the best nights of my life. It felt like the crunch point for me, the hotel, the festival, the freedom. Everything boiling down to the point where I, Seraphina Roberts, either sink or swim.

I made the decision to take Luke's name when we were married, to become Seraphina Coates. It wasn't as fun, changing my whole identity back to Seraphina Roberts. That's the fourth time my name's been changed. I was born Seraphina Lowe, and once the divorce was finalised, my mother made us all change our name back to her maiden name. I was so proud to finally be released from the shackles of my dysfunctional family and start my own thing – The Coates. Now I'm back to being a Roberts. It's not just the diagnosis of infertility, the divorce, losing the love of my life – I lost my identity. I want to be proud of who I am.

The night of the festival is the first time I've ever felt how I think I should feel. I've always been Seffy, but I've felt like the world's been stopping me from being who I really am. I moved out of the hotel the next day and haven't looked back since.

I'm finally embarking on my journey. I can't change the past. I loved Luke, I loved what we had but it's gone. There's so much life to enjoy and it's everywhere; I don't even need to go out searching for it.

That's how I felt and for the last week, I've been doing exactly that. I've not let an opportunity pass me by. I've been to the monkey temple in some of the old city ruins, a night trail at Nahargarh Fort, helped some friends I met at the local tea palace at the elephant sanctuary, went to some insane night-club on top of a glass building that I still can't remember getting home from.

I've got rolls of film hidden in my backpack for safe-keeping, desperate to develop them, but I feel like that will be a nice surprise when I get back to reality. Something to keep the fun alive.

The only niggle I have is the infertility. Divorcing Luke and my love for him is something I can get over, eventually. But the functioning of my organs is ingrained in me, and I would love a final shot at seeing if there is a miracle cure.

The Ayurvedic clinic I chose was supposed to be one of the best and an absolute bargain because it's not been advertised in some hip magazine and there to entice people who've bled the Botox needle dry and are looking for their next wellness fix. My driver, Jay-Jay, drove me through a canopy of jungle foliage, monkeys playing in the vines, birds chirping in the trees. I hung my head out of the window like a dog so I could take it all in. India is such a country of colour; we need the artist who created this to visit London and paint over the grey. Everywhere you look, everything you taste, everything you smell is a cacophony for the senses, taking your mind to places you could only ever dream of. It brings back that never-ending childhood imagination that you thought was lost under spreadsheets and bills. Whereas Jaipur was doused in a warming pink, Jodhpur is a cool blue that makes the buildings blend into the bright horizon, so it really is like a floating city.

The clinic itself is white but with an intricate pattern of pale blue circles all over the right-hand side. There is a water trough out at the front, decorated with fragrant flowers which guests are encouraged to wash away the day with and a hessian mat where we are to leave our shoes, and we are met with the smiling faces of the clinicians dressed in floaty white trousers and jackets. It's immediately peaceful. Not only are you away from the hustle and bustle – India is beautiful but it's not peaceful – your mind switches off too. It concentrates the brain on releasing built-up tension, something I wish I was able to do more often. The inner workings of an organisation fiend are anything but relaxed, there's always a list that needs writing.

Darling Seffy, how are you? I need to speak to you. Nothing urgent, just a catch-up with my girl. But please do call? I tried but I got that funny dial-out tone – where are you again? So much going on I can't remember. Love you XXX

My mother. What does she want? She never asks me to call her, allowing my brothers and me to do it on our own terms. Oh well, it's probably something stupid like she met a lady in the florist's who knew me when I was two and what a surprise it was. I get that often. Messages about people with names I've never heard of. She acts as if Beyoncé was buying sausages in the local butcher's. Her contact is usually through WhatsApp though, never really a phone call. Odd.

'Miss Seraphina?' I raise a hand to signify to the young man that I am her. 'Please follow me for your dosha assessment.'

'May I take your phone?' a smiling Indian girl asks, holding out a white basket. 'Being without technology enhances the experience.'

'Of course!' I smile back, turning my phone off and popping it in the basket. My mum can wait.

I look round the room from the soft couch. It's not like London, where everything is bright white in an effort to be neutral, but unless you're paying the designer homeware price tag, it comes across as sterile and uninviting. It's colourful. Prints on the wall of gods and goddesses, a large rug in the middle of the room in pale pink and with large, bright blue elephants, like a mixture of Jaipur and Jodhpur. Plants on the floor, hanging from the ceiling, on the desk, making the room feel oxygenated and fresh. A little stove with a pot of boiling water bubbling away and a bright-red basket filled with gold trinkets and bells.

The door opens and a petite lady walks in, dressed in white robes. Her hair is hanging loosely around her shoulders apart from a black headband, and her skin is perfect; it enhances the glow of her smile.

'Hello, Seraphina. Welcome.' She clasps her hands together. 'My name is Dr Amrita and I'll be your prescriber during your time here. I can see from your notes . . .' She looks down at her notepad. 'You're here for one of our taster sessions, is that correct?'

'Yes,' I respond. 'I believe it's a five-day course?'

'That's correct. Do you have any allergies?' I shake my head. 'We will now take your dosha assessment and then I will offer you a bespoke detox tonic in line with your physical make-up. How does that sound?' She smiles. Her voice is serene, calm, woozy, but I trust her instantly.

'I mean, I don't really understand anything you just said but you're the expert!' My voice goes high-pitched, the way it does when I don't want to admit I'm afraid or that my knowledge of a subject is sub-par. 'May I ask what a dosha assessment is?' I am nervous.

'Of course.' Her eyes crinkle in an inviting way. 'I was getting to that part. Dosha is the basis of Ayurvedic medicine. We use the three elements, vata, pitta and kapha and see how they fluctuate in the body according to a variety of factors such as the seasons, time of day, digestion and how this can change the process of growth, ageing, disease. If we take care of our vata, this will in turn regulate the other two.'

I look back at Dr Amrita, still none the wiser.

'I mean, I am going to have to trust you because the only pitta I know is one you eat with hummus.' My voice breaks into a nervous 'ha' which lines up with the embarrassment of my dad joke – ironic as he was never around to mortify me with his quips.

Her mouth stays poised in the upright position.

'Are you happy for me to begin?'

I nod, not trusting myself to speak.

'Firstly, I need to ask you what brought you to our clinic? What are you hoping we can help with? General health and well-being, does your life need rebalancing? Or something deeper that maybe we can begin to address?'

'Er.' My voice cracks. I really wasn't expecting a therapy session. More of a yoga, acai bowl, lifestyle retreat. Couple of downward dogs and sun salutations kind of thing and we're all on our merry way.

'It's ok, we don't judge here. This is a safe space.'

'I met a lady, made a friend actually, while I was in Jaipur, and she recommended I try Ayurvedic therapy. She went through quite a messy break-up and said it really transformed her life. I actually . . .' I swallow. 'Just got divorced. My husband and I wanted children, but I couldn't have them.' I can feel tears trickling down my face as I speak. It's like my body doesn't even have the energy to stop and allow myself time to cry.

I've been a different person these last few weeks, but it doesn't change how I really feel. What I feel like mother nature intended for me to do. I need to get it all off my chest to start afresh.

Dr Amrita sits opposite me, her hands clasped, her head tilted to one side. The lips are only curled upwards on one side now and slightly sucked in.

'I don't know what I'm expecting really,' I continue, suddenly thinking more realistically about the whole situation. 'I'm not expecting someone to give me a magic pill and I'll be able to bear children, although, if that's possible it would be great,' I add, back in straight-talking Seffy mode. 'I don't want to be so negative all the time. Stuck in this vicious cycle where I hate everyone who has children and wish beyond heaven and earth that I could have my own.' The casual tears stop, and I start hiccupping before a fresh flood pours down my cheeks.

Dr Amrita sits beside me and hands me some tissue. She doesn't rush my outburst or even console me, she waits patiently, allowing me to release.

'Sorry, sorry. I'm ok. That's why I don't talk about it. I'm an ugly crier, people don't need to see this.' I motion with my hand towards my assumingly blotchy pig face.

'One should never apologise for their feelings. If we can't release it, how can we let go? I'm afraid we can't offer a cure for infertility. We always offer hope with our practices, you never know, stranger things can happen. But especially not in five days – we are not magicians!' She lets out a little tinkle of laughter. 'I'm sorry.' She shakes her head. 'I said cure infertility. I shouldn't have said that. It's not a disease. I have met women who say it feels like that but it's not. It's an underlying condition that can be overcome. It doesn't need to be something that you feel you live with and are reminded of every day, something that impacts your day-to-day well-being. It can be expelled from your life in a way that you think differently, you change your objectives, your purpose. We can help with that. I feel that it's a happiness you're searching for, a balance in your mental well-being and perhaps your physical too. Maybe you need to let go a bit.'

'Thank you,' I say. 'For not treating me like a patient. I want to go back to being Seffy again. The person I was before

I knew about my infertility. I am still exactly the same person, just now I know. Knowledge isn't always power.'

'I will ask you a series of questions and I need you to answer me honestly. Then I will take your pulse and examine your body type. I need stool and urine samples, then we will create your five-day plan. Please, drink this detox tonic and relax through the next process.'

Once the inner workings of my mind have been prodded far more than any doctor ever has before, Dr Amrita is finished.

The lady who took my phone earlier is back to take me to my room and explains that there will be yoga in half an hour, followed by lunch – which kind of sounds like what I originally signed up for.

A painted sign hangs above the bedroom:

It's all about balance and living a good, wholesome, complete life where the mind, body and spirit work together to serve you and those around you.

I already feel more open to new relationships, less rigid, less snobby. I feel like the girl I was before I knew my mum was an alcoholic. Young, carefree and able to have fun. The girl who played with 'Polly Pockets' and 'My Little Pony' before real life took over my imaginary play.

Finally, I feel like I'm breaking down the walls to Seffy 3.0. I managed to climb the hill to get here and now the glass box which encases her is cracking.

I can see her.

17

'Do you have a family?' I ask Dr Amrita, while lying on the crinkled linen sheets of the bed, staring at the whirring of the fan, and watching a family of flies and mosquitoes mate with each other.

'What do you mean by family? I have parents, a husband, my sister and her children.' She answers in her floaty, sincere manner.

'Children.' I always mean that, why don't I just say that? Do your own offspring define your family? Why have I forgotten about all the other pieces that make up your unit?

'No, sadly, not.' The tone of her voice doesn't change. No break, no abrupt pause, no croak.

'Oh.' I feel my neck tense. 'Is it a . . . choice?'

'No, I think we're very similar, my dear.'

'You mean, you can't have children either?' My heart's pounding. I've never spoken to anyone who suffers like I do. I've always felt the outsider.

'Well, no, I couldn't have children. My husband and I tried for many years, but I think the world had other plans for us. I'm much too old now; those years are behind me.'

'You don't look too old to have children.'

'That's very kind of you.' Her laugh tinkles like the keys on a piano.

'Why didn't you tell me when I told you about me?' I ask, slightly confused. My diagnosis is such an important part of who I am, if I met someone else like me, I'd be falling over to tell them.

'You think your lack of children defines you, but for me, it's not part of my identity. I have so much more to me. It does make me feel sad sometimes, of course. But I treat my sister's children like they are my own; my whole family raise them. I couldn't work here at the clinic if I had my own family, not in the same way anyway.' Dr Amrita pauses. 'Would you like to meet them, Seffy?'

I've had my twice-daily yoga and meditation with the Guru Pema. I've had my daily detox tonics; I've read in the garden and allowed my mind to become one with the gentle breeze in the trees and the tuneful chorus from the peacocks. Oh and of course, I've had my Panchakarma treatments. The Purvakarma is much more relaxing; an oil massage to remove my toxins followed by a strong herbal tea. Dr Amrita prescribed me with a course of Nasya to help regulate my breathing and emotions. It involved her massaging the inside of my nose. The inside of my fucking nose! If someone told me they were going to slowly penetrate my nose I would have thought it was some sort of sick sex act that you might sell videos of on Only Fans. It was not that comfortable and super weird; I wanted my back massaged to release tension, not the inside of my nose. I haven't been able to wax my nasal passage for weeks either and I have a thing about being totally hair-free apart from on my head, obviously. That's for the Jeff potatoes back in London.

After the official treatments, it's time for me to meet Dr Amrita's family.

We drive a few miles to get to her home on the outskirts of Jodhpur. Her house is painted in that mystical sea blue. On the exterior, the place itself is nothing spectacular, no grandiose design to behold. A concrete grey box with the bottom half of the building painted in blue, two windows and a doorway but without a door.

'Why are the houses here blue?' I ask Dr Amrita as we pull up outside.

'Everyone thinks it's paint but it's not. It's a mixture of copper sulphate and limestone which looks blue in the light. It repels insects but I think it's quite relaxing too, don't you?'

'Yes, very serene. Makes me think of seaside holidays.'

'I've read about the love of a British seaside holiday – fish and chips, bumper cars and candy floss. I think in an Enid Blyton one they went on a trip to the seaside once, by train.'

'Enid Blyton! I can't believe you read those too.'

Before Dr Amrita's even switched the engine off, two young girls in floral dresses, one emerald and one saffron and a young boy with his top off and scruffy denim jeans, run out of the house screeching.

Dr Amrita speaks to them in Hindi, and they grab me by the hands and rush me inside. A young lady stands at the kitchen table making chapatis; Dr Amrita's sister. The little girls place some of the flour mixture in my hands and show me how to make the flat structure by turning my palms and pressing on the dough mixture, while the little boy runs around throwing flour in the air and his sisters shake their head at him.

We don't speak much because of the language barrier but speech isn't needed. We bond over cooking, play and laughter. Their husbands arrive home, kiss their wives and shake my hand. We eat homemade dahl, chapatis and a deep-red curry filled with the intense flavours of chilli and garlic. Dr Amrita, who I now call Rita by her invitation, translates some of her family's questions, my favourite being, *Do you see the King every day?* From little Saffron.

Rita drives me back to the clinic after dinner. After a moment or two of reflecting, Rita speaks.

'You see, Seffy, that's why I don't crave anything else, I feel like they are my children. Why do they need to be biological?'

'No, I can see why.' It's the home set-up I thought only existed in fairy tales. A home built with happiness, not bricks and mortar.

Before I step out of the car, Rita takes my hands in hers.

'Remember, deep realisations happen daily if you continue to strip away those layers of your emotions. We do not want you to sacrifice anything when you go back to the real world. It's about balance and living a wholesome and complete life – mind, body, spirit work together to serve you and others around you. The more you participate in the Ayurvedic practice, the deeper we can take you. Most of all, be happy.' Her eyes crinkle in that familiar way and she gently lets go of my hands.

#17 Embrace your own life through learning from others

I'm at one of those internet cafés. The ones you see on sitcoms, seedy places where old men go to sign up to freaky porn fetish sites so that their wives can't find out. The computers are boxy, yellowing monitors with grubby fingerprints over the screens with a whirring pattern of primary colours as the screensaver to remind all users of the pleasantries of Windows 99.

If these boxy contraptions connect me to the world, I'm not one to complain.

'Skype?' Harry guffaws. 'Skype? Who uses that anymore? It took me ten years to find my log-in details – dancing-catqueen – that's what I chose to call myself. Can you imagine people saying that on Zoom with the clusters? Hello, dancing cat queen, can we have your presentation please, or would you like to perform Mr Mistoffelees with your other famous feline friends?' She laughs loudly. I've missed that sunny expression.

'Can you see where I am?' I gesture to the ten yellowing monitors and keyboards around me. 'Skype is advanced. The

WiFi is shite everywhere else; I can barely get a connection long enough to send a WhatsApp.'

'Are you wearing make-up?'

'No, well not really. A bit of mascara. Why?'

'God, I'm jealous of your tan. It's been raining nearly every day here for a week. I had to dry my tights on the radiator at work yesterday – England in the rain really is the pits.'

'I don't want you to hate me but it's like thirty-five degrees here and I haven't even been sunbathing.'

'What have you been up to then? Tell me more about your travel tales – any hot Indian hunks? I bet you could practise the Kama Sutra out there with some guru, that's one for your bucket list.'

'As tempting as that sounds . . . I've been at an Ayurvedic retreat.'

'What's an . . .' Harry says something incomprehensible, but it starts with A.

'Ay-ur-ve-da. It's a special type of mind, body and spirit therapy – to be honest I thought you'd know all about it.'

'No,' Harry says abruptly. 'Is it one of those super-hippy affairs where you all sit around taking hallucinogens, shitting and puking and then waxing lyrical about how much you've changed?' Harry's sarcasm is unwavering.

'Ooooh, someone's got a thing against finding yourself. No, it was more massages, positive vibes and disconnect. A lady I met recommended it and I do feel really good.'

'I don't have a thing against finding yourself. I just feel that you're constantly looking for something that's not there.'

'That's what therapy is for, duh. It's about moving on. Anyway, I really have moved on, I have so much to tell you, but it really is for in person.'

'You need to look forward, stop victimising yourself,' Harry continues, obviously not listening to what I said – or maybe the internet is worse than I thought and I'm not coming through properly. 'There's nothing you could have done which would have changed the outcome. Luke was a dick, a total fat chode. But how are you going to change the fact that you can't have children? Rewind twenty-nine years, back to the genetics between your mum and dad's sperm and egg? You need to embrace the present.'

I sit, staring through the screen.

'You'll see I'm a different person.' I think about Rita and her gorgeous family.

'Anyway,' Harry carries on. 'I'm not saying this to upset you and I would tell you in person but clearly I can't, and I feel like there's no better place to hear this.' She coughs nervously. 'You've got the whole rest of your travels to come to terms with it, get over it, you know.'

'Get over what?' I ask, but I feel ready for a gut punch.

'Luke's got a girlfriend.'

The words hit me like four bullets to the chest.

A girlfriend.

A fucking GIRLFRIEND.

How does he get to walk out on me, divorce me and meet someone else? It's barely been six months. Not just meet someone else, start a life of new beginnings. Because that's what it is. A relationship. More than my fleeting Freudian slip with Richard. It'll be girlfriend, engagement, marriage, kids. And I'll just be watching from the social media sidelines as all these pressing announcements get plastered for the world to see. I might as well be posting photos of me standing alone in an empty carpark with the caption – still nothing to announce yet. Still meaningless.

It feels like the last few weeks of growth haven't happened. Rita's family are immediately a figment of my imagination.

'Seffy? SEFFY!'

My eyes blink my mind out of this new whirlwind of emotions.

'Are you ok? I'm sorry. I just had to tell you before you found out. She's not fit, I promise. A poor man's Seffy.' She makes a sick face. 'He'll be single again soon, I'm sure of it.'

It doesn't matter what she's like. It means he's onto the next chapter. Our book, our story has been closed and he's onto the better-written sequel.

'How do you know?' I whisper, the words cutting through my throat like shards of glass.

'Rory told me. She saw it on Instagram. Like I said, she looks like a total lemon, can't imagine she has much of a personality.' I know Harry is trying to make me feel better but it's not really working.

'I feel a bit sick.'

'Oh God, Seffy, I'm sorry. I just knew it would be the worst thing if you saw it on your own and then had to tell me.'

I feel my eyes prickle.

'It's not fair, is it!' My eyes boiling over with rage and upset. 'I get lumped with the dud genes; my husband doesn't want me. He doesn't have to deal with the lifetime of upset. He gets to find someone else to love and have children with. I have to sit here . . .' My voice tapers off into a cry before I find breath. 'And think about my whole life and how if I ever meet someone again, I'll have to go through the whole do you want children chat over and over, reliving every moment, until I find someone who is ready to settle with me. And that's what it is, settle. Because most people dream of having a family and even if I find someone that's happy with just the two of us, I'll still be dreaming of it and everything I once had. Because I'm not over it. There I said it. I'm not FUCKING OVER HIM.'

The man behind the reception desk stands up, looking over to my station. I give him the look of a deranged girl shouting at a screen.

'It's not fair. I'm sorry. I know it doesn't matter what I say about her, it will still be horrible. I thought there was a high chance that you'd be upset, and I've already spoken to Janine – she says I can come out for my annual leave. I was thinking Thailand? We can party, let loose, forget about everything at home.'

I nod.

'I've missed you. Please come, I need you.'

'Love you. I'll sort out the arrangements and let you know, ok? We'll be the terrible twosome again in the blink of an eye.'

18

As expected, it was a horrible night after the Skype with Harry. One of those nights where your imagination runs wild, to the point of feral, like dreaming of birthing your ex-husband in front of your whole family.

I left the internet café, my face all blotchy like raw sausage meat straight from the fridge and tears streaming down my face. The owner of the café came up to me as I was leaving, held his arms in the air and shouted, 'Don't worry, be happy!' before bursting into a very well-practised, but badly out of tune interpretation of Bob Marley. I smiled because he was only trying to be nice, but it wasn't exactly a game-changer for my mood.

Finding out your ex-husband, who you're still blatantly in love with, has a new girlfriend (serious enough to plaster all over Instagram) is a time when you want to run home, hide under the cover of your duvet, pull out your matted and chewed one-eared rabbit that you've had since you were two – Bun-Bun – order a pizza and sob, uncontrollably, in front of some melodramatic movie. Until you feel like it's physically impossible for your body to release any more water, like your body is drought stricken. Your head's gone all fuzzy and you call upon a friend to take you on some tragic night-out – sticky floors, greasy men and tunes cheesier than Gouda – snogging a plethora of guys' faces off like you're the last person left on earth with oxygen still in your lungs. That's what I want to be doing. Not lying in a bunk bed in some grotty hostel, wiping snot onto a pillow made of sandpaper and screaming out my ex's name in the night when I'm supposed to be making friends – not alienating myself from the other two girls in the room who now think they've been flung into an episode of *American Horror Story* written by the cast of *Mean Girls*.

I'm pleased Harry's coming out. I'm a tragic mess right now and I need some of her electricity to charge me up again.

I was doing well, so well, but I guess I hadn't planned for my ex to have a new girlfriend. I hadn't prepared myself for that. I was only ready to move on from Luke because I thought I was doing well, that I was better than him, in one twisted way or another.

After Harry told me about the new woman in Luke's life, I did what any sane ex would do. I unblocked him on Instagram, saw the photo of the 'announcement', screenshotted it (so as not to do any accidental liking or unliking), and spent the evening zooming in on her face. Deciding that she must be boring, all rebounds are. But maybe that's what Luke wants? Stability. She obviously loves kids; she's got fertility written all over her eager face. Maybe that's what he thought. I need to find someone the total antithesis of Seffy – will it make him happy though? Probably.

I'd been off social media due to the Ayurvedic retreat, but I swear once one bad thing happens it's like some sadistic game of dominoes. There was the usual sludge of obnoxious boastfulness slithering down my Instagram feed; beetroot lattes at Elan Café, Pudsey's first dip in the sea – yes that's a child's name, not a dog – and then there it was. I scrolled up and down a few times to check that the username and image hadn't got mixed up. Another gut punch as if Luke hadn't twisted the knife in enough.

I can't believe it! Our miracle baby, coming to a borough near you - @RoarALion

Rory.

Bloody Rory.

RORY IS PREGNANT.

That image. She's done the announcement, well, exactly how I would have done it. A little black and white scan with some white baby's breath stems and a cute pair of knitted booties. Twelve weeks? She must have been pregnant at my birthday brunch. Does she not know alcohol is bad for the baby?

Was she even trying?

I'm not spiteful. I don't want to be spiteful. I should be happy that my friend is pregnant.

Congratulations! Can't wait to meet him/her <3 <3 <3

It's not that I don't mean it. I do, kind of. Luckily, for me, your body doesn't change colour with your emotions, like a mood ring, otherwise I'd be the Grinch of pregnancy announcements.

Following the double gut punch, when I thought I was doing ok, I decided to delete my social media for at least a month. It's like Marie Kondo – If it doesn't bring you joy, get rid. It applies to a lot more than several pairs of bootcut jeans from Topshop's renaissance years that you couldn't bear to part with.

#18 Clear out digital wardrobe through major social media detox

I'm taking myself on a pilgrimage to Agra to visit the Taj Mahal on the way back to Delhi. It's one of the wonders of the world, so definitely worth a place on the bucket list, and I'm kind of hoping that all the serenity and being at one in a building so grandiose will only do wonders for my morale.

Agra itself is nowhere on the beauty scale of Jaipur and Jodhpur. It's all dusty roads, commercialisation and money-driven locals trying to take advantage of tourists' naiveite. I managed to stay in one of the hotels nearby to the Taj Mahal and for some reason or another, I was upgraded to the presidential suite; I can only assume that they took pity on me. It usually makes you feel good getting an upgrade; it's like you've won a fluffy toy out of those machines at the arcade. It's not so great when you're knocking about in a family suite – where everything from the four sets of robes to the double and twin bed serve as a sore reminder of why you're here alone.

It should have been a room service sort of night, but I feel that would put me well into the throws of the definition of tragic. So I put my face on, or at least a meagre interpretation of what my face should be and traipsed down the corridor for dinner in the only restaurant.

I order myself a salad and a pizza for my main – everything is catered for westerners, and through total legitimate reasoning it has been decided that we only eat beige, packaged food. That was what I felt like, anyway. I look around the restaurant, finding myself watching a group of young girls and guys drinking and laughing on the table nearby. I'm off social media, I've never been into gaming on my phone apart from a brief fascination with Candy Crush, and I can't be bothered to read. Tonight, I'm the observer. I don't even want to think. That evening with Rita and her family, the festival with Belle, all seem a world away.

'Oh, God, sorry.' One of the girls laughs apologetically as she bumps into my table, knocking my water glass. 'Can I buy you another?' She's drunk; I can hear the air of jovial confidence on her tongue that comes hand in hand with a few wines.

'No, it's fine. Honestly, it was only water.' No, please don't sit down. Please don't sit down, my mind utters as she pulls out the chair opposite. Fuck's sake.

'Are you here alone?' the girl asks.

'Did you not feel him when you sat down? You're sitting on my imaginary boyfriend.' It's a shit joke but it just came to me, and I could do with having a laugh, even if it's from myself.

'Does he still count as imaginary if he's a total arse?' she responds questioningly.

'I think then he goes from imaginary to non-existent.'

She goes to cheers me but looks at my water.

'You know if you cheer with water, it's bad sex for life?' Her face is screwed with anguish.

'That's where I've been going wrong then. If it's vodka, does it dramatically improve?'

'Yes, if you drink enough.' She grins from ear to ear and orders a bottle of wine for us. 'Come and meet my friends – it's terrible drinking alone.'

'. . . and this is Lolly.' Dre introduces me to her other five friends round the table. The group seems nice enough; they're here on a two-week holiday – friends from school, all at a loose end this summer. I remember that time, when you'd go on holiday with friends, drink ice-cold wine in fancy bars and stay out all night. I'd kind of forgotten about friends, if that doesn't sound too weird. I associated everything with a partner or a family and forgot that the real jackpot of life is having a strong cohort that you love and trust.

'You know, you have to leave here about 5.00 a.m. to see the Taj at sunrise, before it gets crowded,' Leah says, eyeballing the empty glasses scattering the table.

'It's one day, we'll be finnnnneee,' Dre slurs. 'Anyway, I might not even go to bed, I'm frivolous like that.' She shimmies her shoulders provocatively.

'I've still got some of that stuff from the gardener at that hotel.' Lolly winks at the group.

'You cannot take mushrooms at a sacred place!' Leah scoffs disapprovingly.

'Why not, it'll be way more magical.' Lolly looks cheekily at the group. 'Who's in? Seffy, you want some?'

'Ermmmm . . .' I really don't know how to react. I'm not the best in social situations, I don't really know how to please a crowd. Being offered drugs, which I don't take anyway, by strangers, is a total shock to my well-oiled system. But I have an urge to be reckless. To do something I couldn't do if I were pregnant like Rory or trying to impress a new version of Luke. 'Ok, yeah I will.' I *force* an instant smile to mask any anxiety creeping in.

'Great!' Dre says grinning, holding my hand. 'Honestly, they're fine. I took some a few days ago, had the best time,' she whispers in my ear, already seemingly on that buzz. 'You look like you could step out of yourself for a bit anyway.' She squeezes my hand. 'That's two takers, well and Lolly. Leah, Maxy, George, Meems?'

Leah and George refrain but the others are all in.

'Ok, let's wait a bit. We want to feel the up just by the time we leave.'

I've never taken mushrooms before; I've already made a mental note to add it to my list:

#19 Get high with strangers – mushrooms at the Mahal

I ate five as Lolly said they were quite strong. It was not enjoyable at all. No garlicky portobellos on toast as I'd imagined. It was like eating pieces of dirt. The sort of thing you see kids doing in the park and you wonder why no one stops them. They tasted of soil, mushing around your mouth, getting stuck on your tongue and round the back of your teeth. I gagged a few times, but we all did.

'Here, drink this, it will take the taste away.' Dre gives me some wine to swig from the bottle.

'Now we wait. Don't take more, you'll start to feel them kick in probs in about forty-five minutes to an hour.'

When our taxi arrives, we're all feeling a bit giddy. My head's starting to sway in and out of itself; it could be the erratic driving but it's more likely the mushrooms. I can feel the soil curdling with my stomach acid and sitting on the top waiting for a particularly big bump in the road.

'The Taj Mahal!' The driver expels the words like he's about to conjure it out of thin air.

I look round at the others; their pupils are the size of saucers so I can only assume mine are the same.

'Did you go through the sick bit?' Lolly asks me as I nod. 'You're about to come up; it only gets good from here.'

We stand with the crowds of people looking ahead at the monumental feat of architectural design before us. The grounds are designed in long rectangles, with boxed trees in uniform straight lines, reminding me of toy soldiers, and monkeys scrabbling round the forecourt.

The sky is the perfect colour of bubble gum and the Taj Mahal the white of marshmallows. I can taste the sweetness, fond memories of my dad taking me to the sweetshop on Saturdays before he got bored of us. My tongue starts to salivate, and I have the urge to take a huge bite out of the roof.

Dre holds my hand. 'Isn't this just so . . . magical?' She looks ahead, her eyes filled with awe.

My marshmallow home is floating ahead of me, in the clouds, like the beginning of the Disney movies, the blue castle logo. I feel like I can write my own story here; my mind's taking me on a magical journey that I can write myself.

I feel invincible as I skip down the path with Dre and Lolly for a closer observation of this structure carved out of marshmallow dreams. I can taste the sickly sweet Flumps on my tongue, how I used to pull them apart, getting them stuck on my fingers, in the grooves of my nails.

'We have to pray,' Lolly says. 'Maybe that we never leave.' She laughs, spinning herself round on the steps.

'Hasn't this been delightful?' Dre says to me. 'I knew you'd have a great time. Everything's better with friends.' She puts her hands on the stone wall, kissing it. I want to laugh but I also want to kiss it myself. Taste the sweetness. It looks so delicious.

After a bit of dancing to the bemused look of other travellers, we all sit cross-legged on the steps.

I stop thinking about gorging myself and satisfying my sugar cravings by eating one of the seven wonders of the world, as a face hovers in my eyeline.

Luke. He's all fuzzy like he's on one of those old school projectors.

'Fuck off.' I stretch out a hand to bat him away, but his face stays there. His eyes penetrating mine, wide and big. His lips slightly parted.

I hear something far away; it sounds like girls' voices. My new friends must also be wondering why my ex-husband is here.

'I want you to leave me alone. I don't want to think about you anymore.'

His face stays fuzzy, out of focus. Zooming in and out, like he's attached to a bungee cord.

'Please, Luke.' I want to cry but my eyes are too wide. 'Nothing's changed for you, go and live your life – be happy. It obviously wasn't meant to be.'

I know that face. It's the face he made when I said I wanted a divorce.

'Get out of my head! If you can be happy then so can I.'

Six Months No Baby

Dear Arrogant Aphrodite,

Why, oh, why can't you see that I desperately want to get pregnant? Do you like me begging every month? Do you like watching me squirm in anguish as my period edges nearer?

It's not fair. The whole thing isn't fair. I'm at that age where everyone suddenly got married and now everyone's having children. It didn't happen gradually either. It was all bottomless brunches, girls' holidays and dates from hell until suddenly it wasn't. It's like a mass invitation got sent out but I was missed off the invite list. All the influencers I follow online are sharing little black and white photos with streams of Congratulations, so well deserved, you'll have such an attractive baby. Then there's the gender reveals; that's a whole announcement in itself. Cakes filled with blue M&Ms, colourful cannons, balloons filled with pink heart confetti. I look at it with distaste, but I know I'd do the exact same thing. It's basically a rite of passage in the twenty-first century. The midwife adds it to her list of checks: Have you been taking folic acid? Avoiding soft cheese and cured meats? Filmed yourself shooting a cannon filled with coloured smoke because you think everyone else cares as much about your offspring as you? It's a bit gender discriminatory, categorising blue for boys and pink for girls before they've even set foot on earth, but it wouldn't have the same effect if you popped red or green smoke; people might think you're about to birth a dragon.

Anyway, it's irritating that I'm at that stage in life where I can't ignore the fact that people are mating like rabbits and miniature versions of everyone I know are popping up in every corner of the world.

No one in my immediate friendship group has got pregnant yet, thank God. When I say immediate, I mean in my four – Harry, Rory, Gem and I. Obviously, other friends

from university have done their little announcements. I've
even met some of the new generation. And they are cute. I
do everything I can to ooze maternal instinct. That's what
you want ey, Aphrodite? Proof that I want to be a mother.
I hope that holding the little helpless blob, breathing in that
glorious new-born smell, stroking their minuscule fingers
and 'oohing' over the speck that is supposedly a nail will
allow some sort of intense cell fission up in my fallopian
tubes. My insides will go all gooey and mushy and be
primed for pregnancy. It hasn't happened yet.

It was Maria who made me think of 'being in the
mindset'. She gave birth to a little boy called Rupert and
she told me:

'It's so weird, if I hear Rupert cry my boobs start imme-
diately leaking.'

'Why's that?'

'Because your body just knows stuff. If you go out and
you're breastfeeding, and you encounter a bug ...'

'What kind of bug? Like a spider?'

'No! Like a cold virus or norovirus, you know.'

'Yeah.'

'Well, your body will already start producing anti-
bodies, so by the time I go to feed Rupert he'll already be
protected. How insane is that?'

'Insane.'

It made me think that maybe it is the same about get-
ting pregnant, your body might just know. I'm trying to
justify the miscarriage to myself; maybe my mind wasn't
truly ready in the way that I thought it was. It would be a
pretty morbid sacrificial sign, Aphrodite, if that is the case.
Maybe I haven't been around enough babies to really fire
up the maternal drive in me. I watched a bit of One Born
Every Minute *but it made me cry and be sick at the same*
time.

Maria also said some things that really annoyed me. Clearly, I had to ask her about the birth because I swear that's woman-to-woman etiquette. She seemed happy that she only had one rip penetrating out of her vagina and close to but not quite in her butt hole, when I still worry about bleaching mine.

Me: *Would you rather be childless and still have a butt hole or have twins but you're not sure where your vagina starts, and butt hole ends?*

Harry: *What the fuck is wrong with you? Butt hole for sure it's got the best G spot. But that can't be a choice? Midwives don't say – are you sure you want to go ahead with the pregnancy because there's a chance you'll lose your anus.*

Harry: *Are you saying most women now have no butt hole?*

Harry: *Please answer you're scaring me.*

My eardrums had to endure the graphic description of Rupert's head coming down the birth canal and bobbing between her labia, so much so she couldn't tell where his head began and her vagina ended. Which she then went on to liken to that pushing and squeezing of the last bit of toothpaste in the tube. I'm not sure Colgate Marketing would appreciate that. So, I thought, why not ask a couple of questions for myself?

'How did you find the whole conception thing? It must have been really stressful.'

'Honestly, it's crazy but when we went to my antenatal classes nearly everyone else had been trying for at least a year or had IVF. We just decided we wanted a baby and next month I was pregnant. I swear Joe's sperm must have

superpowers; it's like he just looked at me and I got impregnated.'

'*That's really lucky,' I reply with the enthusiasm of one of those goats in Morocco that's been told to stand in the tree again as another batch of tourists arrive.*

'*Yeah, I guess. I mean I have other friends who it's happened to as well. One of my friends did a test when she was away from her boyfriend for two weeks and it was positive. I mean that's like some biblical shit.' I'll caveat this with the fact that Maria is not that smart.*

'*Doesn't that mean that they had sex before she went away or was pregnant and she didn't know? Sperm can live for five days in the womb.' Obviously, I've done my research.*

'*I mean, yeah, but it sounds more dramatic the way I said it. When are you and Luke thinking about having a baby?' Why does everyone think it's ok to ask that question? I don't tell them any of my other thoughts or which nights I give Luke a blowjob so why should this be common knowledge to every woman and her dog?*

'*I mean, we've discussed it, and I think we want another year of just being us, you know,' I lie. Maria has the mouth of a foghorn, so whatever I say will be front page of the* Mail *tomorrow.*

'*I mean, you're young, healthy. I'm sure it will just happen. I'll get Joe to give Luke some tips on superhero sperm.' She cackles as if it must be some sort of witchcraft to be getting pregnant that quick.*

My brain purely does not have the capacity to hold the rest of Maria's drivel.

Things have been slightly off since I had that argument with Luke. It's like we've realised how horrible we can be to each other and we're walking on eggshells waiting to find further cracks. I feel bad so I keep buying him treats on the way back from the office, like double chocolate chip cookies from Sainsburys', and making sure I say 'I love you'. I am still annoyed but I don't want him to stop loving me.

All our plans involve us having a family. We used to have conversations on long car journeys about our future. Discussing potential holidays with the future Coates, where we might all want to live in our 'forever home', mock arguments over our baby name list. We'd talk about how fulfilling our lives would be, how Luke wants to take them to rugby and football tots. He'd be the perfect father too, much better than mine ever was. He wants to read them bedtime stories, change their nappy and cuddle them on the sofa until they fall asleep. I'm excited to be a good mother and make our home a safe haven for our little ones.

There isn't a snapshot into my future that involves simply Luke and me growing old together. Everything involves my future children, although at the moment in my dreams their faces are blurred out. I don't envision going on Caribbean cruises solely with my husband or driving round in a fast car with only two seats. I want to be doing the nursery school pick-up with my other mum friends, rushing from work to nursery to after-school clubs with bits of porridge on my suit and a lonely crayon in my hair. It's unorganised, unlike me, it's everything that's not me, but it is me all at once. I'll save up and take the kids to Disneyland on my compulsory two-week annual leave because that's what I do. And I'll have the odd drink, but I won't turn into my mother.

As much as the internet can make you think that your common cold is in fact a rare form of cancer and can have you sobbing on your bed within two fatal clicks, it's also a great community.

It was on one of my conception blogs that I found Tiana. She runs an ovulation party every month for ten women at a time. It's all part of that being in the mindset of getting pregnant.

It's only fifty pounds, less than five Clear Blue tests. Why not?

'Welcome. Welcome!' Tiana raises her hands in the air as if she is making a calling and air kisses each one of us. She's wearing some sort of emerald-green kaftan which flows around her and is a stark contrast to her rich, auburn hair. She looks like a character from Game of Thrones, *not that I've watched it, but I see snippets over Luke's shoulder.*

She encourages us to sit down in a circle on some flat cushion pads covered in navy and red diamonds. They look handmade. Not that I have a problem with sewing your own cushions; it just helps to accurately describe the ambience.

There are ten women including Tiana and myself. I would say I'm the youngest here by at least seven years. One of the women has grey hair! And I'm worried about conceiving!

'Look around.' Tiana gestures with both arms around the circle. 'These women are your menstrual sisters. I want you to breathe in the aromas from the tea in front of you, take a sip and think long and hard about why you're here today.'

The tea is hot, and the herbs are strong, making my nostrils twitch. I'm here, I think to myself, because I'm running out of options. I'm impatient and I'll do anything; surely that's the biggest sacrifice I can make?

'Most of you don't even know why you're here, do you?' she asks the group rhetorically. Some women twitch on their cushion pads. 'Do you know what an ovulation ceremony is? Sometimes we call it a party because it IS a

party of the inner workings of the body. It's a celebration of hormones, jubilant festivity of the release of one of your sacred eggs. A commemoration of the egg in the womb.'

I know I paid to be here, but my mind can't help but hurry her on to the part where she encourages successful ovulation.

'We are all sisters of nature,' Tiana continues. 'We were all created the same way, from one sperm and one egg. The inner workings of the human body are complex; however, they are the same. We all need food, water and air to survive. My eggs are no different to yours, to yours . . .' She points round the circle. 'They all need the same ingredients to survive and prosper.' Some of the women nod in agreement. 'This session is about knowing your body, knowing within yourself that when you ovulate, your skin will get pinker, you will release pheromones, you will become more sexually attractive to your partner. Ovulation is a process of life. You have all been put in this session because you have similar menstruation dates and therefore similar ovulation cycles. You've heard of best friends starting their period at the same time and encouraging each other? We are going to embody the same approach with ovulation. The next few exercises are going to encourage a closeness between you and the women around you and hopefully stimulate that all important release of the egg.' She stands up excitedly and clasps her hands together. 'Let's begin!'

Tiana comes round and helps us with our exercises, mainly holding each other and breathing. I was put in an ovulation couple with Brenda who seemed to enjoy me holding her, shown by raspy breathing down my neck.

At the end of the session, some of the women were opening their eyes like they'd just seen the world for the first time. They couldn't compliment Tiana enough: That was *incredible! How you can make me feel that way with your voice, I'll never know. See you again next week.*

Turns out some of these women are here to try and prevent the onset of menopause. I'll have to hope that if it's this hard to get pregnant, my starting of the menopause will be tricky too.

This is me going the extra mile, Aph, I hope you've taken this on board.

I didn't feel thankful. I felt nothing apart from stupid. I've never been into all this mystical stuff anyway so I don't know why I thought hugging a woman called Brenda for an hour would make me get pregnant.

It's like I feel guilty. Oh, so guilty about the miscarriage. Like I could have done something different. The quicker I get pregnant, the quicker the pain of loss will go away.

I told Luke I had a late gym session.

'You smell funny,' he laughs, cuddling me. He doesn't. He smells of comfort, warmth, safety. I wish I could share what I've been doing, what I'm going through because I know it isn't all about me, but at the same time I feel so alone in it all.

'Do I? Like what?' My voice suddenly on edge.

'I dunno, like the contents of my grandma's tea cupboard. It's kind of nice though.'

I wonder if this is the pheromones Tiana was talking about. We have sex just in case, although I'm pretty sure the smell was just that horrible tea.

Oh Aphrodite, I'm not going to start begging again. I bet no one else does this every month.

I hate to say it Aph, but you should be thankful you're still seen as relevant in the 21st century – you don't even have an Instagram profile.

Seffy xxx

Seven Months Until Thirty

I don't know what happened at the Taj. Lolly and Dre said it appeared I was shouting at someone even though it was just us.

The comedown was out of this world. I spent most of the day throwing up in my presidential suite, which, luckily, was large enough that I didn't have to smell the stench of stomach acid from my bed. I couldn't eat anything all day but when the evening arrived, I decided to go all out and rent a movie on Sky and order every single type of beige food they had on offer to my room. I even ordered ice-cream, which I used to call liquid fat.

Like I said, my memory is more than hazy, but I feel like I got something off my chest. I'm about to meet my best friend in Thailand and have a fucking-fantastic-time, I don't need to face the reality of work, or Moira or new boring-straight-off-the-shelf-girlfriends. I'm free.

Harry: *Arghfkkkk! I can't believe we're going travelling together. FINALLY.*
Me: *Please hurry. I miss you.*
Harry: *I've packed everything. Like my entire flat. I hope you haven't ruined the wardrobe I packed for you, I'm dying to wear that pink co-ord and the glittery halter neck, did I buy that for you in the end? Dancing on the sand, drinking fishbowls. I've heard in Thailand, they even have this red bull stuff that has cocaine in it?! Like totally legal, don't sweat ;p*

Me: *Ha you're talking to a seasoned shroom taker – dw I'll hold your hand.*
Harry: *Fuck off. I need this plane to hurry the fuck up. I don't want to miss a second of my friend having a midlife crisis – it's the best fucking thing ever to have happened to you.*

There's a hot guy on the plane, but my moment with Richard was all luck. Turns out not all fit men serendipitously sit next to you on the flight and allow under cloth finger play. I could even be imagining his good looks, but since the news about Luke's new girlfriend I feel compelled for someone to find me attractive so I can feel good about myself again.

Instead, I sit back and listen to an audiobook while the perfectly preened ladies with tight chignons, dressed in white shirts and dark-green neckerchiefs come and serve me a lunch of Thai green curry and rice. I have a couple of Bloody Marys complete with a side of peanuts to take the edge off. Then I sleep like a log – no night terrors, just peaceful. Least I hope not. When I wake, I feel rested and happy. Like I've forgotten all that is wrong in the world.

I wait for two hours at Bangkok airport for Harry's flight from Heathrow to land. It's ok, I'm used to doing my own thing now – being the master of my own watch. Besides, this is the last alone time I'll have for three weeks.

I've been rattling my way through my reading list and I'm currently on book number five – *I Capture The Castle*. I like Cassandra, I see a lot of myself in her. It reminds me of my own childhood, although far more glamorous than mine, even if she does write sitting in a kitchen sink, selling off furniture to buy food.

Airports, I've come to realise, are a hotbed for families. Children everywhere, screeching, running round and desperate parents wringing their hands, trying to keep their animal pack in check. I watch a husband and wife darting round with a huge silver trolley filled with four suitcases, the woman pushing a double buggy, the man holding a little boy's hand who keeps trying to make a dash for it. The mum looks exhausted, and she's got another one on the way too. Four? *Save some for the rest of us* comes to mind before I swallow the comment.

Don't be bitter, think about Rita.

I hear the tired mum, *Ben, I'm going to sit down for a bit.*

She comes and sits on the row of metal chairs a few down from me, releasing a huge sigh of exasperation or maybe exhaustion. The two children in the pram start kicking their legs and crying, and she tries to placate them with some snacks from her bag. Ben comes over. 'Come on Sal, let's go get a drink or summat, we're on holiday. I've got work tomorrow.'

He sees me looking at them as I try to look away.

He rolls his eyes. 'Just have to look at her to get pregnant these days.' He snorts as 'Sal' throws him a couple of daggers. I mock a fake laugh and go back to staring at nothing.

Think about the positives. Think about the positives.

If Luke had made me pregnant, then I would never have known that there was a fun, frivolous, flirtatious side of me that existed. Because I'd never be sitting at this airport on a sabbatical. When you're stuck in the train of life it's very hard to take a different direction – the tracks can move but quite often they get jammed.

Think about what I can bring to the table now I've been travelling, the stories I could tell my children. Maybe it's all about being a mother when you're truly ready and not because it's another thing to tick off life's list. What's the hurry to complete all the things that you're supposed to look forward to? I'm enough by myself. Some people might even say too much.

I used to love the airport; I liked the thrill of going away. The smells, the noises, the people, the airport breakfast, buying your last-minute holiday reads at Waterstones. Watching the groups of lads drinking beer at 7.00 a.m. because at the airport, time doesn't really exist.

I keep getting distracted between the words on the page, my own thoughts and the airport activity. The feelings of guilt between Cassandra and Simon; Rose and Neil disguising their love with hate is taking my mind back to Luke. Are we just pretending not to love each other?

We used to go on holiday a lot, Luke and I. Well, still dictated by our annual leave, but usually three a year. It probably sounds excessive, and now I have no partner to do things on a whim with, it seems even more out of the realm. We both loved travelling, so it seemed a usual pastime. I know it makes me sound spoilt, but that life was a far cry from my childhood, believe me. Surely, we all deserve to douse ourselves in gold from time to time?

The airport used to seem like Luke's and my special place. Sacred. Which I know seems odd for a place with such a high footfall, but it did. It's not like those years we spent together were a waste of time. I'm sure if we had divorced for another reason, like adultery, I'd have been annoyed that he'd wasted some of my fertile years, but for me it's made absolutely no difference.

He was a good partner, maybe that's what makes it so hard.

One of my favourite holidays was to Essaouira.

We stayed in this magnificent five-star hotel, with a gleaming infinity pool that had an unspoilt view onto a private beach.

The first few days we swam, we ate, we fucked. Like all young couples.

'An omelette bar, Seffy, my favourite!' His cheeks wide with glee as he placed his order with the chef. 'You can't just have fruit on holiday, darling.'

'But I love fruit.'

'But look at everything else. Pancakes, eggs, turkey, bacon, waffles, fresh yoghurt, honey.' He points to the buffet; I know it's what we signed up for at an all-inclusive, but it feels like a display of gluttony.

'I don't even know what to get; I've never really been to a place like this before.' I suddenly feel small, not confident, not sexy.

'I'll get some things for us. Enjoy yourself; this is luxury, this is what we work for.' He squeezes my shoulders as he gets another plate.

I must have been to hotels like this when my parents were together; in fact, I know I did. I've seen pictures. Justin, Chris and I grinning by the pancake bar, eyes wide with glee, Nutella spread over our chubby faces. But when Dad left and Mum took up her new hobby, we stopped. We didn't even go caravanning like normal families. Turns out you can't drive when you're drunk. Well, you can try, but then they take away your licence.

That's why I loved going on holiday with Luke. It made me think back to the time when I was part of a family unit, when we did normal things, and it makes me feel giddy imagining my three offspring grinning by the pancake bar.

The next few days were much the same. We went to rooftop bars and drank mojitos, dancing in the medina in the early hours and then laughing down the streets home. We spoke about our future, our friends, how lucky we were to have each other.

I'd get out of the pool, squeezing the water out of my hair, Luke would grab me by the waist and say how beautiful I was. I would look at him, sun-kissed and happy and think how lucky I was to have met him. My perfect, unperfect, match.

Then it started raining, turns out for the rest of the holiday. A freak storm, aftermath from the east coast of America. I was upset that our ultimate holiday was ruined. How can the weather dictate happiness?

The first day of the rain, we stayed in our room, ordering room service, snuggling up and watching films. The second day, Luke went to the shop and bought a pack of cards.

'My dad always used to play games with us on holiday, do you know any?' he asked me, dealing me seven cards.

'No, my dad wasn't really like that. Nor my mum.' We played hide the bottle, the lady from child service is on her way.

'Well, my darling, future Mrs Coates.' Because we kind of knew even before the engagement. 'I will teach you every game I know, starting with Seven Card Rummy.'

We played three games; Luke won two.

Over the next few days, we played Slaps, Crazy Eight, Go Fish.

I didn't mind the rain. I almost secretly hoped it would rain more, confining us to our cosy days of room service, cuddles and cards.

It was then I knew that he was the perfect man for me. There were no spoils.

I bite a huge chunk out of my baguette, sighing. Maybe it is all a game. The giant charade of life, ey?

I can hardly imagine a holiday like that now, eating mainly in hotel bars, private beaches – only seeing catches of the city on the one day we designated for exploring. It's not that there's anything wrong with that, relaxing beach holidays are great, but there it is, another thing I've discovered about myself – I like to explore new places as much as recline in them.

Suddenly, I see her. My gorgeous friend. Her backpack slung across one shoulder, slightly too heavy for her to carry, so she's almost walking with a limp. Her hair brown – she must have washed the pink dye out – tangled slightly round her shoulders as she tries to run a hand through it, in that all-too-familiar Harry motion. She does it when she's looking for someone, or waiting, or thinking. She's wearing a pale pink cropped T-shirt that's stretched across her large breasts and a pair of navy blue harem pants with little white stars on them. It's so Harry. She looks like a seasoned traveller before she's even arrived. I see her, we clock eyes and I wave, smiling. She throws her bag down and starts running towards me.

I click the button on my camera because who wouldn't want to remember the moment their best friend came to rescue them?

20

'This is the fucking life,' Harry says kicking off her flip-flops and lying back on the lounger. We're staying at the Chang hotel on Koh San road; it's the only place with a rooftop pool, which Harry and I decided was a necessity.

I murmur in agreement.

I sit up on my lounger and take a few snaps of the skyline.

'I've never known you to have a hobby, you know like normal people do,' Harry taunts, watching me with the camera.

'I used to like art when I was younger,' I answer her, but even I thought I'd grown out of it.

'I thought it was just you trying to be alternative.'

'Am I that obvious?'

'Yes, obviously you are. Anyway, I'm not talking about massaging bits of charcoal over leaves when you were fourteen, I'm talking about now!'

'Shame, leaf rubbing was a particular favourite of mine.'

Harry sticks out a pointy, pink tongue at me.

'You go to the gym and stuff but it's not really a hobby because who actually likes rubbing themselves on objects covered in other people's stale sweat and being so out of breath you think you've punctured a lung.'

'Some people do like going to the gym you know. It can be a hobby. I love spinning.'

'People who call the gym a hobby are people who don't have any hobbies,' Harry snorts. 'In that case I've got tons of hobbies – typing out emails to cereal enthusiasts, eating three meals a day, having sex. Well, that would be a hobby if it was more regular, it's probably more like a . . . a sick bug, but one you want to have a day off work for.'

'Who likens sex to a sick bug?' I choke on my drink. 'Anyway, I have a hobby now, officially. You don't have any, they change every week. Your hobby is thinking of hobbies that never come to fruition.'

'So,' Harry says, slurping on her Pina Colada in her right hand and finishing it off with a chaser of beer from her left, ignoring my comment. 'How are you feeling now?'

'Me?' I ask as if Harry might have a sudden urge to know how the man dressed in the full waterproof Nike bodysuit next to her is.

Harry looks around astounded and shouts out, 'Everyone ok?' to which Mr Nike jumps, looks around the pool and gives a hesitant thumbs up. 'Yes, you!' she directs at me.

'I'm fine!' I answer in that super upbeat tone that no one answers anything truthfully with. 'I've been having such a great time, I really feel like I'm a new person, I mean I've been . . .'

'Seffy!' Harry practically slams her Pina Colada on the plastic table and pulls her sunglasses down to the bridge of her nose. 'I've known you for nearing on two decades, I can sniff out your lies like a Jack Russell searching for cocaine at Heathrow.'

'They mainly use spaniels.'

'Whatever! Tell me how you're feeling about Luke. I bet that bell end hasn't even had the decency to message you after plastering his new girlfriend over social media. What a twat.'

'Luke?' I use the same quizzical response to her earlier question, as if I have no idea who my ex-husband is. 'Yeah, you know, it was a shock, but I am fine . . .' I remember Lolly and Dre telling me what happened at the Taj Mahal and push it to the back of my mind.

'There's fine and there's fine. I hate that word, it means nothing, yet everyone uses it as a way to describe complex emotions which a simple four-letter word simply does not have the capacity to do. I'm not going to stop asking about it until you give me an adequate response. Then we won't speak of him again. So, tell me.' She sips her beer, still dangling from her left hand. 'How you're ACTUALLY feeling.'

I swallow. I hate talking about my feelings, I always have, and I always will. Especially at 2.00 p.m., one drink in. I feel like if I use the real words to describe what I've been through, what I'm going through, everyone will walk away from me.

But I know Harry and she's persistent.

'I, errr, it really hurt me.' I bite my bottom lip. 'Even though I know we're not together, I always wanted him to want me. I know it's selfish,' I add quickly, even though Harry doesn't blink. 'I felt like I had everything with Luke, he was almost like the male version of you.'

'I mean there's only one Harry LeQuinn but I know what you mean.' She grins.

'Then I lost everything, more than everything. It's not just our relationship, it's all my childhood dreams crushed. I have to get over Luke and all my ideas of what I thought my life might hold. He knows everything about me, I don't need to explain my moods to him, he understands my obsession with order – he gets me. He knows I'm infertile. If I meet anyone else, I'll have to go through that whole conversation again; why I can't have children, what the options are. They might decide not to pursue anything with me because they want children naturally and I can't, and that's fine!' I exclaim, wondering what I'd do if I met someone like me. 'Sometimes . . .' I swallow again, feeling mucus slide down the back of my throat. 'I wonder why I let him go when he was so willing to stay with me. Why I walk away when things aren't perfect. Why I obsess over having this perfect, ideal-istic life when in reality I'm the problem; my life can never be that image of perfect that I once had. I'm the one that should be judged.'

'But you didn't let him go, darling, he was the one that left you! Like I said, total twat.'

I close my eyes, remembering those words.

'He didn't. He wasn't. Our relationship was so broken it felt like it could have been either of us. That the moment had already happened before someone said the words. But I requested the divorce. It was me. I regretted it almost instantly, but Luke didn't say anything, so I felt like I'd done him a favour and then I never looked back.' I wipe away tears on the back of my hand.

I choke on the memory of his brown eyes slowly drowning themselves. The way he looked crushed, broken, in the same way I felt.

'Oh, Seffy. Darling, I'm so sorry.' Harry puts her glass down and lies next to me on my lounger, stroking my hair like Luke used to do. 'I know you feel like you still love Luke and maybe you do and it's still so raw for a relationship that was so deep. Sometimes when things break down so much there really is no coming back from it, however much you want it; maybe it was too broken. We need to get you back out there, let our hair down and you can see that there's so much more to life than Luke and marriage and babies. Nothing, absolutely NOTHING in life is perfect and what one person thinks is perfect is different to the next. You are perfect to me, you just need to find your own, new version of it.'

Five hours later and we're on the strip.

Harry made me feel better. We ordered multiple poolside cocktails and then danced to Miley Cyrus and Taylor Swift because Harry said nothing gets you out of a slump more than a wrecking ball and a bit of Tay-Tay.

'We need to sober up a bit,' Harry slurs. 'That's why the beer's good, it's like, you know, not as strong as cocktails but a bit stronger than water.'

'What about some Pad Thai.' I point to a small Thai lady crushing peanuts and adding them to a bowl made from a palm leaf. 'I'm feeling a bit hungry.' That's a lie; I'm at the stage of drunk where I could eat ten family-sized KFC buckets and still have room for more.

We stand on the street slurping our noodles. It's not elegant; they're hanging out of our mouths as we suck them up. Our lips covered in the sticky sweet and sour sauce. They're delicious, we already had them when we arrived in Bangkok. Hot noodles, with the tangy tamarind and lime, salty soy and the sweetness of brown sugar. Hot, meaty pieces of chicken, succulent and juicy, all contained in a palm leaf.

'I could eat another,' I say greedily.

'So could I.' Harry nods in agreement. 'But we can't! We mustn't be sick, and we need to get drunk – this is a Harry and Seffy special. A night to remember.'

We walk towards this underground club on the main strip. It looks like the entrance to a cave with giant neon parrots surrounding the door. I get out my purse to get us in.

'Seffy, over here!' Harry shouts.

I walk towards her, a little way back from me, standing by a stall filled with dead bugs. My skin crawls.

'Eurgh, what is that?' I point to one of the boxes.

'Dried crickets I think.' The lady behind the stall nods, smiling and holds out one in her hand to try, making a 'mmmm' sound with her lips.

'That is disgusting! Rank, come on let's go.' I try to drag Harry's arm away.

'No, we're eating one, for the bucket list. We're stepping it up a gear.'

'Please Harry, no, no, noooo,' I beg, dragging her arm as she shrugs me off and pays the lady for a bag of dried crickets.

She pops one in her mouth and swallows. 'Delicious.' She smacks her lips provocatively. 'Your turn.' Harry holds out the paper bag.

'I can't.' I shudder.

'You've got to. It's a dare. Pretend it's Luke's dick or something, but don't spit it out though.' She chortles.

'Fine, whatever.' I snatch the bag and shove a cricket in my mouth. I don't chew, just swallow. 'There.' I open my mouth and waggle my tongue. 'All gone; can we get on with our night now?'

#20 Eat crickets for a midnight snack

'You're getting good at eating in front of people.' She grins. 'First croissants, now crickets, whatever next?'

'Girls, girls you wanna go to a show?' A tiny Thai man, dressed in a fluorescent white T-shirt and matching trainers with blue flashing lights at the bottom stops us on our way into the club.

'What kind of show?'

'Ping pong. It's very good. Thai speciality, everyone must go. Special price tonight only one thousand baht per ticket.' He waves the paper tickets in our faces. 'With drink!' he adds, smiling, all his teeth on show. I've never seen a mouth quite like it.

'What do you think it's like?' I ask Harry eagerly. 'Like one of those insane table tennis tournaments but instead of a bat, they use their vagina?'

'How do you even find out you have a talent for something like that?' She sips her free strawberry daquiri. 'We'll find out soon, look.' She points to the black box in the middle of the room which resembles a stage. 'Someone's coming on.'

It's blindingly obvious that most of the people in this room are men, apart from a couple of rows at the back, filled with tourists, including myself and Harry.

The men at the front cheer and say something in Thai when a goddess of a woman wearing a red satin bra and thong waltzes onto the stage.

I don't know quite what I was expecting, maybe a little introduction, some sort of hilarious compere that you get at shows in the West End. Not here.

Some seedy club music blares out of the speakers dotted around the room, and the dancer takes off her bra.

Underneath are two ruby nipple tassels which she spins round to the glory of the drooling crowd at the front.

'Oh, I think it's like cabaret,' Harry whispers in my ear knowledgeably.

I nod in agreement; it must be. A sexually liberating experience for all involved.

The dancer whips back her thick, jet-black hair, lies on the ground in a scissor position and out of her thong pulls a string of razor blades attached to a red ribbon.

'Are they razors?' I ask Harry, concerned.

'No, they can't be, it's just an act. Like a magic show but with extra sexiness.'

The dancer starts shredding some paper with the razors and the crowd start whooping. Well, that's the crowd at the front. Everyone in the two rows we're in seems slightly worried.

She takes a little bow and walks off the stage. A new dancer comes on, this time in a blue velvet lingerie set. They're all stunning. I wonder why they are doing this show when they could easily be models.

This dancer gets full naked and pulls out ten, YES, TEN, silk scarves from her vagina.

'Where are they coming from? What the fuck is this? I was expecting a tennis tournament with a seductive underbelly of cabaret.'

The first dancer, although at this point, 'dancer' doesn't seem quite appropriate as she seems to have a lot more skills, comes back on stage and pulls out a bottle of 7UP from inside her.

'What the fuck? Now this is getting really weird,' Harry says in my ear. I can hear whispers among the other tourists.

She then proceeds to put the 7UP back inside her and pulls out a bottle of Coke.

'Tell me this isn't real?' I wince to Harry. 'I think we should go, it's really seedy and I don't feel like we should be supporting whoever is in charge of these women.'

'Let's just watch the actual ping pong part and then I agree we should go.'

The two women come back on stage and sit at either end with their legs wide open, vagina on full show. The men at the front look like their eyes are going to pop out of their heads – it's disgusting.

And then we all get what we paid for. They are popping ping pong balls out of their vaginas, like they're at some sort of open-minded tennis match.

We all clap wildly; I mean it *is* skilful. I don't think I've met anyone who can do that before. It's still kind of gross though. I've never really believed in all the strip club culture. Why don't they have clubs full of men dancing for women to put their hands down their pants and watch? Why does everything revolve around gratifying men?

We get up to leave just as the extra dingy music comes on and the lights turn down even lower. There are some loud cat calls and wolf whistles coming from the front of the stage. We turn to look and there in front of us is a live sex show.

The girl in the red lingerie is now having full-on sex with a guy on stage. He made a great show of pulling the condom out of the packet and then inserting his latex clad penis into her vagina. Now, they are performing some 'Cirque du Soleil' type of sex performance in front of at least fifty people.

I look at the dancer in red; she doesn't look very happy. She's standing on her hands while the guy fucks her from some sort of weird behind/on top position. She should be having a great time. I'm sure we've all imagined a man taking us on like that. It's basically what Harry said I need.

'I'm going to ask for my money back!' Harry says assertively.

'No, don't cause a scene. Let's just go and we can tell people not to come here. I feel like we're going to get in trouble,' I beg.

Harry has made her decision though and when she's made her decision, that's it. She starts walking over to the Thai guy that sold us the tickets, the one with too many teeth for his mouth – like a baby wearing a set of dentures.

'Excuse me?' She starts shouting as soon as he's in her vision, but he ignores her. 'Hello?' she shouts again. 'Oi you, I'm talking to you!' She taps him on the shoulder and stands there with her hands on her hips.

'Hello pretty lady.' He grins, showing his garish gnashers.

'HA.' Harry lets out a fake laugh. 'No respect.' The man looks confused. 'This,' she points around the room, 'is disgusting. Look at that poor woman, on stage doing-I-don't-even-know-what to put food on the table at home.'

'Ha.' His lips curl up into a snarling smile. 'You chose to be here, you paid me. Like all the tourists, you think it's funny. Whatever. Go home.' He turns his back on Harry.

I can see rage boiling inside her.

'If we'd known what it was, we would never have come! False advertising. I thought it was going to be a sexually liberating version of Wimbledon, not seedy porn. I want my money back.' She stands her ground. I plead at her with my eyes to forget it and just go home. The tooth monster doesn't even turn back round but carries on talking to his friend.

Harry takes her drink and pours it down the back of his neck.

What happened next was a blur. Some disproportionately large, muscly men came out of nowhere. Lifted us over their shoulders and then chucked us outside, literally threw us onto the street and shut the door.

We look at each other, lying in the gutter and start laughing.

'Never do that again,' I say to Harry. 'We could have died.'

'Let's get a drink and then let's leave Bangkok. It's put a bad taste in my mouth. I want beaches, drugs and parties. Fit guys and glowsticks. Ok? And I'm not settling.'

'Deal.'

#21 Get kicked out of a live sex show while sticking up for women's rights

'I've never been to a full moon party before,' Harry says excitedly. 'I've heard such good things, like, you know, as if Gatsby was organising a party in the 1920s.'

'What time should we go down?'

'I dunno, maybe like nine? We can drink a bit before, some of those buckets on the beach so we're not too sober. What were we doing, staying in Bangkok, when this is the fucking life.'

We've been in Ko Pha-Ngan a few days now, allowing the sun to beat down on our faces, lying spreadeagled by the pool, playing UNO. Since I got everything off my chest to Harry, I've been feeling more like I did in India again. It probably was, in the end, too broken with Luke and if I hadn't said the word, he would have done it for me. Divorce. It's just sad, irrevocably sad. But I can get over sad things; they take time, but I have time and friends. Really good friends, like Harry.

Friends that play UNO properly, unlike Luke – somehow he always made me pick up four cards. It was so unfair.

'What do you think of those guys we met earlier?' I ask her.

'The Australians? I mean one was slightly red-neck – he told me he put an iguana on a spit-roast and ate it, but I thought Finn was fit, and Jack.'

'I thought Jack seemed a bit like a bad boy,' I reply as if that's not the kind of guy we all dream about.

'What are you planning to do, marry him on the beach?' Harry chucks her head back, laughing. 'That's what you want, Seffy. Bad boys for fantastic sex and then settle for the good guys later.'

Harry jumps up from her bed. 'Jack says let's meet them on the beach in half an hour.' She says it excitedly, her eyes flickering.

'But it's hours until nine,' I reply. I kind of wanted to relax in the room a bit, psych myself up for the full moon.

'He says we have to go to magic mushroom mountain with them, get some of the good stuff before the party starts.'

'Ok,' I jump up, 'let's go.'

'I thought you'd be putting up more of a fight,' Harry laughs.

'You're talking to an experienced shroom taker.' I hope supposedly shouting at a mental image of my ex-husband doesn't repeat itself and this time I just stay in a world made of marshmallows.

'Don't forget your ticket!' Harry points at the black slip of paper with neon yellow bold writing, KO PHA-NGAN FULL MOON PARTY, and I pop it into the pocket of my shorts.

'Are you ready then girls?' Jack revs the engine on his scooter and Harry lets out a little shriek as she grips his waist tighter.

Harry said she'd go with Jack as his bad boy vibes were making me feel slightly unsafe and I'm clinging on to Finn for dear life.

'Yesss we're ready!' we scream. They do a final rev for good luck, and we're off up the mountain.

It's exhilarating and terrifying at the same time. Speeding down the winding tracks is a far cry from my previous holidays with Luke. That was for the old Seffy.

As Finn turns into the corners, shouting at me to lean into the bends, I feel good. Normally I'd be too scared to do something like this, with or without Harry. But now, it's just something I do – new experiences, it's all part of the re-born Seffy.

I know it's too early, but I'm already thinking about sleeping with Finn. As I cling round his waist I can feel the shapes of his ab muscles, the slight dampness of his shirt from the humidity and the spicy scent of his aftershave. I hope he can't smell my pheromones because they are going wild.

I hate the thought of Luke sleeping with another girl but she's his girlfriend so I can no longer pretend that he's been living a life of abstinence since me. It's partly down to the fact that I am ridiculously horny due to my lack of sex that I'm desperate to jump into bed with Finn and partly because, even though Luke will have no idea what I'm doing or WHO I'm doing, I want to make him jealous from afar.

When we finally reach the mountain and the guys turn off the engines, Harry and I remove our helmets, Harry doing the full Bond girl display, hair flying in the non-existent breeze. Mine kind of stays stuck to the nape of my neck tangled in sweat and dirt.

Harry turns and whispers to me, 'I'm going to fuck Jack tonight, I can tell.' Before making eyes at him again.

'What do you want, girls?' Finn asks, passing us the menu as if we are about to order brunch.

Harry and I look at the laminated paper uneasily. Neither of us really know what to choose.

'Want me to help you? I've had them before.' Jack thankfully cuts the awkward silence. 'We don't want anything too strong; we want a good time, not passed out on the beach.' Surprisingly sensible from a *bad boy*.

In the end we go for one Flying High shake and one Shroom Smiles, both, Little Mr (yes that's what he called himself) said are perfect for a full moon party.

He hands over the two shakes, one a light lilac and the other a grey sludge. I didn't see what he mixed the mushrooms with but when I take my first slurp, I'm reminded of that horrible soil taste that coated my teeth and tongue, making me gag.

'Let's get some beers to wash this down,' Finn says, chuckling slightly as I hide away another appearance from my gag reflex. This is not in the dating-how-to-impress-someone 101.

We sit on the edge of the road, taking tiny slurps of the thick, bitty shakes and washing them down with beers before getting back on the bikes to the beach. I know there's no way the shrooms' magical power has taken over my mind yet, but I feel great. It's like I can feel the process taking over my body, ever so slightly. The loosening of my limbs, a smile being gradually etched across my face, the gentle widening of my pupils. All my irksome inhibitions floating away.

I don't know what happened to time after our trip to the mountains but suddenly I find myself on the beach, surrounded by people, eyes wide, dancing like I've never heard music before.

'Here we go, girls!' Jack pushes his way back to us from one of the drinks cabins on the beach offering plastic buckets that you used to build sandcastles with when you were a child but now are filled with ninety-per cent proof alcohol with ridiculous, highly offensive names like Cunty McCunt Face, Shut Up You Beach and Fuck a Duck. I don't think the name corresponds to the contents.

Everything is simply beautiful. The contrast of the pearly white moon against the black sky, it reminds me of popcorn in the cinema and I don't know why. The way the ripples in the sea catch the light from the moon and the light from the beach swallow it and then bring it back to life again. The stars glinting in the sky like little diamonds.

The beat from the music engulfs my whole body, my whole being. I don't even need to try to dance because it's like the rhythm is now inside me. Glowsticks everywhere; around people's necks, wrists and bodies, colourful paint streaked over their faces, in their hair, like we are all part of some special, secret tribe. A peaceful group where we just dance, every second of every day.

'Seffy, I FUCKING LOVE YOU,' Harry bellows in my ear. 'Isn't this beautiful, it's so FUCKING BEAUTIFUL.'

'I love you too!' I kiss her on the lips and then continue dancing with my hands in the air and the sand between my toes.

'He's fit, isn't he?' Harry points at Jack.

'Yeah, he's gorgeous,' I say looking at the way his eyes are now sparkling, his glowsticks setting them off. '*And* he's a bad boy.' I wink.

'I'm going to snog his face off; you should do the same with Finn.' She encourages me to finish the rest of the bucket with her. 'On three, let's go snog our men and then meet back here.' Suddenly childlike.

I watch her walking over to Jack, pushing her hair back behind her ears as I walk over to Finn. I see her look at me and mouth, *one, two, three* and then she pulls Jack's face into hers.

I see Finn and I can tell by the way he's looking at me that he sees me.

I stand on my tiptoes and pull his face towards mine, ready to push my way into his mouth but he's already accepted, his tongue dancing with mine.

I can taste the faint metallic soil of the mushrooms, followed by the sickly-sweet orange and strawberry of the drinks but it's delicious. He grabs the nape of my neck and gives my hair a little tug. I like it.

'Eurgh, get a room you two.' Harry's voice carries before she jumps up behind me, grinning.

'More drinks?' Finn asks, his eyes wide and smiling and he walks off towards the wooden shack.

I look out at the revellers on the beach, transfixed by their seamlessly moving limbs and the colours drifting into one bright rainbow. When I turn back, Finn's waiting with a pink bucket and Harry's nowhere to be seen.

'Shall we go find the others?' I say, looking into those soulful brown eyes of his – they remind me of Bambi.

'What about we sit for a bit? We can catch up with them later,' Finn says taking my hand. We walk a little away from the party and sit on a fraction of beach where we can watch the edge of the ocean kiss the sand in a familiar greeting.

I feel my heart beating unnecessarily fast from all the drink and drugs, and we take a sip of the bucket in silence for a minute.

'What's your story then, Seffy?' He breaks the gentle sound of the lapping of the sea and the distant beat of the music.

'My what?'

'Your story, everyone has one. I don't really know much about you.'

'Oh, well my name is Seraphina, I live in London and I'm travelling on a sabbatical.' I answer as if I'm introducing myself at my first job, not to a hot guy I've been drooling over all day. One I've just made out with on the beach.

'And my name's Finn, I work on the oil rigs, I drink and barbecue at the weekend. Could we be more stereotypical? And boring!' He releases a laugh which makes me fancy him more. 'Tell me who the *real* Seffy is. I feel like there's something you're hiding.'

'And what makes you say that?' I ask, intrigued.

'The drugs mainly,' he replies and we both laugh. 'Your friend Harry is an open book, but there's something subdued about you. I might be wrong, but I feel there's something in your past that you don't tell many people. Like maybe someone hurt you? I dunno. I've had too many mushrooms, sorry.' He shakes his head, and we laugh again.

'And what about you?' I ask him, trying to deflect the fact that he's the first person in forever to see past my exterior, regardless of drugs. I was right, he did *see* me.

'I was engaged, thought she was the love of my life, she broke it off, said we didn't share the same goals.' He takes a glug of the bucket. 'One of those things, I guess. I had six months on the rig, working, drinking. You know they fly girls in?' I shake my head. 'Every so often they fly girls in and you can, you know.' I nod. 'I didn't. I never did when I was with Elodie either. I worked, I cried. And then I thought, fuck it, stop moping around, and I've been out here for four months.'

'Oh God, I'm sorry, I didn't know.' I feel like I want to cry in solidarity but the shrooms have made my eyes too wide and tears a distant memory.

'I didn't expect you to know!' He grabs my hand and chuckles. 'I'm sharing so you can share too. If you can't have the classic deep and meaningful when you're on drugs, when can you?'

'Well, I can trump you on the engagement. I was married and now I'm divorced.' Finn gives me a high-five.

'You've won, I'll go home.' I'm sitting on the beach with a hot guy, high as a kite, and opening up about our emotions was the last thing I thought we'd be doing but it's giving me more pleasure than I anticipated.

'He was called Luke. I thought he was the one, then I realised he wasn't. We wanted children, tried and tried, thought it would just happen, like it does for everyone, but it didn't. I took a test, and it was me, I couldn't have them.' I look out at the dark sea wondering what secrets it harbours. God, I told Harry my true feelings and now I can't stop. Someone muzzle me.

'I'm sorry.' Finn passes me the bucket. 'That's why we come away isn't it, why we chat to strangers, to forget our troubles. I know I'm soppy, I've been told it before.'

'You're not soppy, you're nice.' And I kiss him, really kiss him. It feels passionate, seductive, meaningful even if I don't really know him.

We stop kissing and get back to our DMC. Social etiquette and passion isn't really on the agenda. The mushrooms have taken over our tongues and made them desperate to waggle at all costs – no holds barred.

'You know I got really into Buddhism at a point in my life, and I don't know how you feel, but they believe that you shouldn't put more pressure on yourself to have a family if you can't and cause undue suffering. You should accept and move forward. I started reading more when Elodie and I broke up, and it's really helped. They don't believe in dwelling on the past but thinking about the future.'

'That's a nice message. I've been trying to only think forwards, but it's hard isn't it?'

'Anyway, enough of the sombre chats. Do you want to dance for a bit? Cheer us lost souls up.'

He takes my hand, helping me to my feet.

As we walk along the beach, I see something lying on the sand, moving around on the floor.

'Do you think it's a dog or something?'

'I dunno.'

We walk slightly closer and what I thought was a lame dog turns out to be Harry and Jack having sex on the beach.

'Come on.' Finn pulls me away. 'Let's go make our own memories.'

Seven Months No Baby

Dear vicious, vicious Venus and your more spiteful, malicious bitch of a sister, Aphrodite,

   Thank you for making it come to this.

   My body feels like a fucking pill jar. You shake me, I rattle. I take more medicine than someone with a terminal illness. Folic acid, collagen, extract of green tea, cod liver oil. You name it, I take it. Anything to make my body seem more fertile, munching on B12 like it's about to become extinct. Anything to try and prevent me losing another baby.

   The truth is, I'm scared.

   I'm terrified.

   Even if I do see the two blue lines of my dreams, how do I know it won't be lost? Do I wait for the worst to happen, or just try and assume it was a one-off? How can you prepare for both life and death at the same time?

   I probably should have spoken to Luke about the miscarriage at the time but now it's too late. I'd say it wrong; he'd feel bad that he didn't notice.

   I lost a baby. I know I never met them. Never knew if it was a boy or a girl. What colour hair he or she would have. Which part of my genes and which part of Luke's made that perfect ball of cells. It was a total stranger yet part of me all at the same time.

   I've seen women on Instagram who've had miscarriages and they seem to have a baby a few months later. Maybe that's the key, to get straight back on the procreation train. I think about that little life all the time though and I feel so lonely from it. People say that miscarriage is common, like that stops it from hurting. It doesn't.

   I've been trying to live my life like normal, to stop my brain trudging through the what ifs.

   When Luke comes home, I force myself upon him, trying to make myself look sexy so he doesn't coil back inside himself. But it's not the same. I spend all day at work, doing tasks for other people, I go to the shops on the way home to conjure up something for dinner in an effort to be the perfect housewife, as well as contributing to my share of the bills. I cook, clean, do the laundry, sort Luke's dry-cleaning and then in the two hours I get to relax, eat my dinner and watch TV. I now have to make sure that every other day I schedule in time to conceive. I'm exhausted, both mentally and physically.

I know it's only been seven months since I started this diary, but seven months is a fucking long time when you're tired. It's 213 days, 5,112 hours of worrying.

I look round the school gym hall. The worn-out white netball pitch on the floor, the scruffy jungle gym against the wall. And the smell. That stale stench of perspiration and sweaty socks. Not pungent enough to be overwhelming but lingering, like an unwanted ex, in the base of your nostrils. This is supposed to be one of London's best schools. That's what it says on the mud-brown and navy sign outside the entrance. Well, best state schools, in the five-mile area. A claim riddled with caveats.

I'm accompanied by nine other women – Naomi, Camille and Rosalin, to name three.

We sit in a circle and tell stories to each other. It's like a precursor to an AA group as after the birth, the sleepless nights, the days-after-days playing Baby Shark, it's hard to see why you wouldn't become an alcoholic. They make it sound like that anyway and I just repeated what Maria said. They make it sound like they didn't even want a baby, how is that fair? I wouldn't complain.

Rosalin finished telling the group about her privileged life in west London and how she'd heard that the Nightingale Wing was the best in London, that's what her friend Maggie had told her anyway and she'd know, she gave birth there three times – a real super-mum, no one knows how she does it. Three under three? Without a nanny, it's unheard of this side of the river.

Emily, the midwife, and mum herself to 'two little terrors' makes a gesture in my direction.

I smile, look down at my protruding belly and tap it gently. Mimicking everyone else. None of the other mums seem to be able to keep their hands off their own bumps.

'Hi. I'm Seraphina but most people call me Seffy. My husband, Luke, and I are expecting in September. A little girl and we're having her in Chelsea and Westminster. This is my first, so I don't really know what to expect. I'm a little nervous actually.' Understatement, I'm sweating buckets – it's seeping into the cotton. I'm encased in a cheap cocoon from some dodgy Amazon seller. I think about the baby that could have been growing inside me and hope that if I pray hard enough, he or she will come back. I smile to signal that my spiel is over. The rest of the mums-to-be smile back politely and clap.

I don't know why everyone keeps clapping when you're pregnant. People clap when you win an award, when you're at the theatre or when the pilot lands a Ryanair flight without crashing. Does being pregnant warrant a self-gratuitous clap? We're all sitting round applauding our own fertility and ability to fuck. ROFL. Thank you, ovaries, bless you Mrs fallopian tube, bloody military salute to my husband's sperm for being an Olympic swimmer and finally I'd like to clap myself on the back for being attractive and quite fuckable, despite not having the boobs of a Porn Hub's college girl.

The conversation moves to more serious matters.

'Everyone says that the clothes you dress your baby in are an extension of your own personality. So, it really does matter you know. I've already started collating her *wardrobe. I've even got some amazing, unique vintage pieces from this cute little shop in Notting Hill.' Baby vintage? Am I missing something? I wore my cousin's clothes when I was younger, we called them hand-me-downs.*

'I've told my parents not to buy anything colourful because it will be going straight in the bin. I don't want people thinking that Raef is a spawn of the Chuckle brothers. We're going for a grey, neutral palette. Babies get quite red skin and I think grey will complement his complexion.'

'Snap! We're going for that kitsch scandi-vibe. Think a Dutch-Yeezy collab. I just hate all that colourful stuff, dino prints for boys, flowers for girls. It's so nineties and not what I would want my baby or MY style defined as.'

One of the more opinionated mums takes it upon herself to go round the group and describe the style of our unborn children.

'My mum loves to knit and I ABSOLUTELY ADORE that vintage baby look. I'd probably describe it as a Charles Dickens baby vibe. Naomi, you'd probably be scandi-baby; Camille, I think award-winner baby – like the baby version of Crufts, not offensive, I just mean you look pristine. And you.' She points to me in my leopard print dress and trainers. 'ASOS-baby.' My whole personality and future child's have been funnelled into the descriptor of an online fashion outlet. Fantastic. It's clearly a Zara dress I'm wearing but whatever.

Me: *Would you ever use ASOS as an adjective to describe someone?*
Harry: *Not unless that was the only thing exciting about them. Like their whole existence was ASOS. Have to be a bit of a loser to be described as an online shop-*

ping outlet. I wouldn't even describe a shopping bag like that . . .

After a couple of other discussion points including the four levels of vagina to butt-hole tear that happen while giving birth to your precious bundle of joy and the imperative topic of do you or don't you wax before? I've always had a thing for my obstetrician and is anal bleaching safe? it's time to depart from my fellow pregnanties until next week.

I smile, wave bye, and knowing full well that the lining of a pregnant woman's bladder is on par with a muslin sack, I make my way to the toilet.

I sit on the toilet and close my eyes. Reach round to my back and unclip the elastic bands. The padded cotton bump parts from my sweaty stomach a couple of centimetres. Aaah, bliss.

I don't know why I hate all these women so much. I wish, wish, wish I could be applauding my own fertility and deciding whether or not to bleach my arsehole before I give birth.

An alert on my phone goes off.

Happy Tuesday Seffy, you're ovulating. Today you have a 70% chance of getting pregnant.

I check my temperature on my Apple watch. I do feel warmer. Must be my hormones. I need to get home to Luke.

I google '15-minute aphrodisiac meals' and clip my bump back on so no one sees me for what I am.

Fake.

Obviously going to an antenatal class when you're not pregnant is totally crazy. Nuttier than a fucking granola bar. I'm sorry, Aphrodite, I don't know what got into me. I just needed to know what it's like. What if I never get to go to one?

I thought if I went, I'd hear stories about the struggles of being pregnant, conception and other people that maybe went through what I went through. You know – baby loss. I thought it might make me feel more positive, see other people like me but who now have their beloved predecessor on the way.

My reasoning is normal though, Aph, I promise. I wanted to imagine myself with the pregnancy glow, a protruding bump that people look at and touch adoringly while I plan the colour scheme for the nursery. I want to think about my life and how I will nurture this gorgeous future being, ensure I never leave it to look after siblings – prove everything about my past wrong and build my own perfect family.

But it wasn't like that at all.

Due to the realisation that normal people don't attend antenatal classes on a whim, I decided to bite the bullet and pay the extortionate amount for a private fertility test. And I asked Harry if she thought it was a good idea and she said whatever makes me feel more comfortable.

I can't go on the way I am; it's an insurmountable pressure, the not knowing what's going on inside me. I simply must know that everything's in order. It will make me more relaxed, remove my anxiety, probably more likely to conceive.

It's all a journey ey, Aprhodite? It must be or it's all a fucking waste of time.

'Hello, Mrs Coates, lovely to meet you. May I call you Seraphina?'

'Please call me Seffy.' I gingerly smile back. I'm twitching nervously on my seat.

'I understand you've come here today for some fertility tests, is that correct?' I nod.

'And may I ask what's led you here?'

I suddenly feel stupid, like I'm wasting her time. Luke's words flash in my mind – *Just be patient. It will happen, everything will be ok, I promise.*

'My husband and I have been trying to conceive for seven months now, which I know is not a long time in the grand scheme of things,' I hastily caveat, not wanting to look naïve and remembering Dr Crawley's words. 'I really want a baby.' I feel my voice quaver. 'I'm impatient, I know that. My husband tells me it all the time but I'm really struggling. I had a miscarriage a couple of months ago and you're the first person other than the midwife and another doctor I've told.'

'I'm so sorry.' Dr Cartwright looks down at her notepad.

'I know I'm a healthy woman in her twenties, I have a monthly period and I ovulate. I know I probably have nothing to worry about but the whole conception thing, it's weighing on my mind. I can't sleep, I feel anxious, I feel stressed. I just know if I can be sure that I can have children and it's just a case of time, then I'll be much more relaxed. And you can't put a price on that, can you?' I look at Dr Cartwright, smiling, waiting for her confirmation that I'm not totally deluded.

'We get this all the time; I'll perform the routine tests but I'm sure there's nothing to worry about.' She makes some notes on her computer and then asks me some questions. 'Can you tell me the last few dates of your periods and your ovulation, if you know them? Don't worry if you don't.'

'No, it's ok. I have this app Eggly, I can tell you exactly.' I go to my phone and recite the dates to her.

Dr Cartwright asks me if I smoke, drink, the vitamins I'm taking, and takes my weight and height. 'Wonderful, thank you, Seffy. Now we'll move on to the physical examination. It's a bit like a cervical screening. Lie back on the bed and I'll gently insert this spectrum and have a little feel around. I'm looking for fibroids, any signs of endometriosis, pelvic inflammatory disease, that sort of thing.'

Sounds lovely, I say to myself.

After a quick rummage around my insides, Dr Cartwright sits back and removes her gloves.

'Everything looks to be in order physically. I'd just like to do a transvaginal ultrasound and take a couple of pictures to send off for observation. Then we will follow this up with a blood test to check your progesterone levels for ovulation and finally, we'll do a full STI test.'

'And when will I get the results?'

'You should get them in a couple of weeks, all being well.'

Dr Cartwright finishes all the tests and then sits back at her computer screen, typing her notes.

'Have you seen anything of concern?' I ask her anxiously.

'Not today, but as I said, we do need to wait for the results to come back. I wouldn't like to get your hopes up, but you seem to be a healthy lady in her late twenties, who just has a case of anxiety. But if we can ensure that is all it is from today's tests then that is extremely important.' She smiles at me. 'I'll be in touch in a couple of weeks. Take care.'

I felt slightly better after seeing Dr. Cartwright. At least, once the results are in, that's it. Luke resisted the chance to get a fertility test so once again it fell to me to take the hit. Whatever; if I'm in the clear, then I'm in the clear, there'll no longer be ambiguity around my eggs.

This. THIS is what you've driven me to, Aphrodite. Well, I've gone totally crazy. I went to an NCT class wearing a fake bump and then to a fertility clinic. Well, soon I'll know for sure, and I may even stop writing to you. It seems like you throw my letters in the bin every month anyway.

Seffy.

Six Months Until Thirty

22

I wake up with a jerk. I was dreaming, but my fantasy world's just been shattered by someone smashing my head open, sending soaring pain across my temples. I move my hand wildly, checking my forehead to ensure someone hasn't left an axe hanging out of my skull.

Those Shut Up You Beach buckets. Paint stripper. Eurgh. It's making me gag. Fuck, I feel terrible. I'm so dehydrated I think my tongue has finally had enough, dried up and vanished.

I manage to turn my head to the left and see Harry sprawled on top of the duvet. Her body slightly pulsating with the last remnants of fluorescent paint, like a dying glow-worm.

She's fully dressed, and so am I.

I try to take my mind off my broken body and go back to my dream. Except it wasn't the result of an overactive REM cycle, it was real.

The way Finn pulled me close to him on the beach. Both hands meeting round the back of my waist, riding up my top. Droplets of perspiration sitting on my lower back, where his palms gripped me. Feeling the warmth of his body against mine.

It was like we were having our own full-moon party. The music pulsating in our ears, blood pulsating through our body. Adrenaline, lust, animal instinct.

He pushed his tongue into me, making me feel wanted, sexy, desirable. All the other thoughts I had dissolved away into nothingness.

Every so often, we'd push away into the folds of the other dancers but then come back to each other like lustful boomerangs, interlocking on the beach.

'Seffy?' Harry croaks.

I think about Finn. I can taste him again, the force of his lips on mine.

'Seffy?' She croaks again, with a light urgency in her voice.

'Uh huh,' I groan. Finn's vanished into thin air and I'm back to lying in bed with an axe hanging out of my skull.

'God, I thought you were dead for a second. Don't ever do that to me again.'

'Do what?' My head pounding with every syllable.

'Not answer me when I'm in this state. I feel like someone forgot to check the bedding for a person and accidentally threw me in a washing machine with the sheets. I feel all bashed and bruised.'

'That's probably from having that big Australian dickkkk inside of you.' I laugh, emphasising the word in a cross between an Australian accent and Donald Duck.

'He had a glorious penis, like probably in my top five penises. Wait.' She pauses, her drunk brain slowly catching up. 'How do you know I had sex with Jack, I barely saw you after?'

'Finn and I walked past your sexual display on the beach – front row seat. I thought it was one of those stray dogs at first. You sounded a bit like one as well.' I'm winding her up.

'Shut up!' She throws a pillow at me. 'Don't compare me to a dog again. Probably better than that ping pong show we went to, like I said, top five penises. I might go back for seconds. Did you sleep with Finn?'

'No, but he is fit. We snogged a lot and chatted. He was a good kisser. Not too wet you know.'

'I don't go out snogging fish that often so I'm not an expert on the wet kiss. Maybe you should find out if he's also in your top five penises.'

'I don't really keep track of penises in the same way you do. I don't know if I really even look at them. How could you look at it in the dark anyway?'

'It's not just the look, stupid, it's the feel of it too. Like not too big, not too small, not too wide.'

'You sound like you're reading porn's version of *Goldilocks and the Three Bears*.' I chuckle.

'That's what it was, Goldicock.'

'That is actually fucking terrible.' I guffaw.

'I did kind of see it anyway because it seemed to have some sort of glow paint on it; maybe it was on purpose or maybe it was the shrooms, but I kept sort of seeing this thing lunge forward at me like I was duelling a knight.'

'Surely it was the shrooms; who paints their own penis?'

We managed to make it out of our hungover sweat box for some noodles at a beachside café, remnants of glowsticks and buckets scattering the beach. Jack and Finn invited us down for the fire show and even though we felt terrible, we decided that for the sake of a holiday fling, it was totally worth it to see our beaus again.

You know when you imagine what it will be like to get your first ever boyfriend? That was us. Harry and I, snuggled in the sand in the arms of our respective men watching these two young boys, no older than fifteen, do the most incredible fire display. Twizzling sticks of flames into the night sky and blowing fire like dragons for each other to walk through.

'Why do the boys get to play with fire, but the girls have to stick ping pong balls up their fannies?' Harry whispers to me across Jack.

'If we knew, we could help,' I whisper back, shaking my head.

'Shall I get us some beers?' Finn asks as Harry and I look at each other, wincing in pain.

'Go on, you have to, you're on holiday. It'll make you feel better.' Jack nudges Harry.

'Fine, fine.' Harry laughs. 'Hair of the dog and all that. We'll both have one and some crisps please, not pad thai flavour. I need pure salt. I might just eat a handful of sand.'

'I'll help you,' I say, standing up and wiping the sand off my bum and legs. I walk slightly behind Finn for a couple of steps before he takes my hand in his.

'I know it's holiday flings and all that, but I've never seen Jack so chilled with a girl before,' Finn says. 'Normally it's all this bravado shit and trying to act cool.'

'You never know, maybe they'll run off into the sunset together,' I say wistfully.

'You think?' Finn looks at me quizzically.

'No.' I laugh. 'I'm just trying not to be too negative.' I grin. 'Thinking about Buddhism and all that stuff.'

'So, you *do* remember what we were talking about last night?'

'Of course, I remember all of it,' I say, half-flirting, half-trying not to be too cringe as I step closer in the sand and move my lips closer begging to be kissed.

At that exact moment I feel my phone buzz in my pocket. Someone's calling me. Who?

'Sorry, I . . .' I pull away and look at the phone My mum. What does she want? An immediate WhatsApp follows.

Darling! I've been trying to get through to you for days, where have you been?! I know you're all footloose and fancy-free at the moment, but a mother needs to speak to her only daughter! Mike and I are getting married. I know it's not a good way to tell you, but I've been trying to call! It's all happening a bit quickly, next month in fact, can you come back for it? Mike's business has suddenly taken off and it would really help us being married for tax purposes. We've been together for years, so it isn't a big deal. Is it? Be honest. I know it must feel a bit funny to you right now after the divorce and now having to attend your mother's wedding. But let me know if you want to talk it all through. Love you so much darling girl. I hope you're having a fantastic time. You deserve it. Love Mum, big kiss xxx

'Seffy, can you take these beers for me. Seffy? You ok? Everything ok?' Finn's voice is like a faint whisper in my ear.

I feel sick. I can feel Cunty McCunt Face making an appearance.

It could be the hangover or the thought of more beers but it's more than likely the thought of my mother getting married.

My MUM is getting married. I was nothing but the perfect wife, wanting to be the perfect mum but everything conspired against me and now I'm divorced, alone and the love of my life has moved on. And my MOTHER, the definition of a walking disaster, has managed to find ANOTHER man who wants to marry her.

All I want to do is message Luke; he's the only person that would know what to say but he's got a new woman in his life.

How can she manage to make me feel worse from thousands of miles away?

'Sorry, yes of course. Just my mum, you know what mums are like.' I raise my eyebrows and take two of the beers.

'God, yeah, mine drives me crazy.'

'They all do.'

My mother. Married. I want to throw myself into the sea.

I give Harry a beer and fake a smile before snuggling down into Finn, fixing my eyes on the fire show so it looks like I'm enjoying myself.

What is it? I drum my brain for answers.

Why am I so annoyed that my mum is getting married? Is it because when she was married we were a happy family? We all lived in a dream world. We had money. A mum and dad who loved each other. Three bonny children. We went to the cinema and theatres on weekends, Dad played games with us; we laughed and joked, like we were auditioning for an advert with Mr Kipling.

Then it turned sour. I realised marriage doesn't mean for ever, it just means for a bit. I became the mother and lost all of my childhood. My father stole it alongside my happiness.

Oh, the fucking irony. I spent my whole childhood mothering and now that I'm actually ready to be a mother, I'm not. It's like some sick ulterior being took it upon themselves to switch my life around.

It took me ages to find myself again, to find Luke. Then that relationship turned out to be tarnished too. Divorced, like my mother but I won't drink myself into oblivion, like my mother. I thought I'd kind of forgiven her. It wasn't her fault, it was my dad's fault. He left her; he made her drink. Now she gets to have her happiness again after mine was taken away. Is happiness cyclical? Does it have to keep being taken away to be reincarnated? I'm in the gutter and she's like a phoenix rising from the ashes. Why? Is that fair? Shouldn't I be happy for her? What if it all turns out to just be for a bit again and I end up losing my adulthood too, just to be a carer for my drunk mother?

'Seffy?' Harry grabs my arm. 'Jack and I are gonna go. I'll see you back at the room, maybe later or tomorrow morning?' I nod to show I've understood. 'Love you.' And she gives me a little kiss on the head.

'Just us, hey?' Finn says, kissing me on the lips. 'I really want to get back on our conversation from last night. Where were we?'

I don't want to talk; I want to do. I'm suddenly primal.

'It wasn't what we were talking about last night, it was what we were about to do.' I pull him up by his elbow or attempt to. 'Come on, I want to show you something.'

We prance playfully across the beach to a quiet spot I saw earlier near some palm trees. I push him against the trunk of one of them, cast over by shadows, and pull my T-shirt up over my head.

Finn pulls me closer to him, his hands round the back of my waist again. His thumbs gripping my sides, the pressure turning me on even more. His tongue dancing with mine, my blood racing so I can feel the hum in my ears, the beat of our hearts joining in our chests as they reach for each other hungrily.

I plead persuasively, pushing myself up against him. I can feel the bulge in his shorts harden. I pull his T-shirt off and run my hands over his chest. It's not soft and smooth but hard with just enough strands of hair to tangle my fingers in and pull him closer to me.

He pauses and runs his fingers down the nape of my neck, gently round my collarbone before turning the ginger touch to hungry satiation, unbuttoning the front of my shorts and pushing his hand in the gap between my knickers and my skin. I'm already wet, everything about this excites me. I'm in control, I'm having sex for the pure thrill of it, not to create another being. I'm being careless, and I'm half-naked on a beach with a guy who sets my pulse racing.

He takes his hand out and puts his fingers in his mouth before rubbing them on me again. I like this primal instinct. I missed this with Luke. Everything was so regimented by the end. It wasn't his fault; it was all mine.

I unbutton Finn's shorts and pull them off with his boxers, his penis already standing to attention. I hold it in my hands, rubbing it hard before replacing my hands with my mouth, listening to his groans and the lapping of the sea against the shore.

Harry was right, some men do have fantastic penises; this is definitely in my top five, maybe even top two.

Finn gives my hair a little tug before pushing me onto the sand and kneeling on top of me.

It's everything I wanted it to be. Passionate, hardcore fucking. Groaning, hair-tugging. Fingers and thumbs in mouths. Sand-burn on my lower back from his force. I came even before he did. It was all the releases I needed.

We lay back, panting, looking at the stars and listening to the roar of the sea which seemed so quiet moments ago when I was absorbed in everything Finn.

'Fuck, Seffy, that was amazing.'

It's nice for someone to appreciate you. 'Has anyone ever said that you have a top five penis?'

'Fuck off.' He laughs and we lie there, our bodies barely touching but tingling with electrifying satisfaction.

#22 Be footloose and fancy-free at a full-moon party
#23 Act out a scene from *The Beach* with my very own Leonardo DiCaprio

23

We had sex three more times. I relished getting to know the male form again, relinquishing my body to his.

The way he touched me, it released my soul from the jail of my own body. Like I've been holding it captive for so long. That desire of a man wanting me, really wanting me. It's like he craved me, in the way cells need oxygen to breathe. And I wanted him, I felt like I'd die if I didn't have him. Dear god, I can't remember the last time I felt desire! Even with Luke; it became so clinical so quickly for me.

My body's been this broken thing that I walk around in for so long, all the pain and hurt wound up and embedded in my skin, in my entire existence. I dress it up to try and cover the cracks, like gluing up a china doll but when you run your fingers over it you can still feel the ridge of where it was dropped.

Finn made me feel like I lived in my body again. I didn't feel encased in the definition of infertility, I didn't feel like my body wasn't performing properly, or frumpy and bloated from hormone supplements and injections. I wasn't being prodded and preened, my future dictated by diagnosis, people feeling sorry for me.

I allowed him in, and he reignited me. Every touch making my skin tingle and adding life back into me. Like he was my food, water, oxygen, everything.

But we bonded over our past traumas, and I know, in my heart of hearts, that it's no way to meet someone. We swapped Instagram handles because I'm sure in five years, once I've totally forgotten who @legofham88 is, I'll enjoy looking at what he's up to on the other side of that big, blue pond.

Even Harry seemed sad that Jack was leaving and she's never that cut up about boys. It was a nice encounter in our holiday, and such is the circle of life to see what it would actually be like for two best friends to be dating two best friends. It was like I'd been finally living out the plot from Mary-Kate and Ashley.

After Finn left, my thoughts turned to my mother's wedding.

Hey Mum. You just do you and I'll do me. We're never going to really see eye-to-eye. If you think he's 'the one' and all that sentimental-fucked-up-jazz then go ahead. I'm probably not going to make it back in time although not sure why a marriage is suddenly so urgent. Don't worry, I'm not going to hold anything against you or Mike but tax reasons?!?!? Make sure it's legit before you sign on the dotted line. Love S x

She hasn't replied but I wasn't really expecting her to.

Am I a bitch? For not attending my mother's wedding? I spent my whole life looking after her, Chris and Justin. I lost my childhood, the time in your life when you're supposed to be out building mud huts, mixing potions and climbing trees. That time when your parents are supposed to take on the pressure, the worry, plan your meals, your outfits, your weekends. I'm finally having my taster of freedom and she comes along to ruin it again. Her marriage could wait, she could have the courtesy to send save the dates six months in advance like normal people do. I'm not giving everything up again.

I create a WhatsApp group with Justin and Chris. It's not our first WhatsApp group but they aren't very good at replying so I titled this one as URGENT: NEW STEP-DAD ALERT.

Me: *Did Mum message you guys? She's getting married to Mike? WTF. Here we go again.*

Justin: *Yeah, she said. I won't make it back for the wedding it's Carmella's birthday and we don't really have enough money for the flights.*

Chris: *If money's the problem bro, I'll wire you some. Mike's a nice guy, they live together anyway so I don't see the problem?*

Me: *Literally do neither of you care that we're going to be getting a new step-dad?*

Me: *She said it's for tax reasons?????*

Chris: *She's happy with Mike. Whatever marriage is marriage, she's got out of one before it can't be that hard can it. ROFL.*

Justin: *I think it will be nice and she said Merlot will be the ring-bearer.*

Me: *If it ends and she gets like she did before, I'm not being the carer. I did my time.*

Chris: *Stop being so worried about it sis, I'm sure it will be fine. Mike's cool I like him. I'll send you some pics.*

Justin: *Don't worry Seffy, we're adults now, what does it matter? How's Hong Kong?*

Me: *I'm in Thailand now but it's great. Guess I'll call in on the newlyweds when I'm home.*

Justin is right, my baby brother is more attuned to life than me. We are all adults now.

I don't live with my mum anymore; if she's happy then I should be too.

It's been a couple of weeks since we left Ko Pha-Ngan. We've been on beach hikes, jungle explorations, laughing late into the night about nostalgic memories from home, drinking beers, sunbathing, playing cards – all the things I used to do with Luke, but I've been making memories with my best friend instead.

Harry always manages to cheer me up. She knows how to deal with my irks, calls me out when I'm being too caught up in myself and coaxes the fun out of me. If I had to reimagine finding out that my ex-husband has a new girlfriend, I think this would be the best way to get over it. Much better than eating ice-cream and watching movies that I've chosen on purpose to make me cry.

'Would you like a coffee?' I ask Harry as we read our books on the idyllic beach of Koh Samui, the waves slapping at the edge of the sand like a soft percussion.

'Hmmm, no. I don't really fancy a coffee now. Maybe a pineapple juice?' She pulls her sunglasses back and shakes her hair. The sun has bleached it in streaks like the highlights I pay hundreds of pounds for back home. My friend, she really is naturally beautiful. Nature only enhances her beauty – she doesn't need a five-step cleansing routine.

'Coming my lady.' I take a mock bow and walk to the bar.

The pineapple juice is fresh; I watch them chopping and juicing the chunks of fruit. Crushing the succulent yellow squares into liquid sunshine. I rest my elbows on the wooden bar and look out to sea. I really am so lucky to be here. I can't imagine going back to Moira and that grey building in a few weeks.

The barman hands me a rattan tray with our drinks and I quick-step it back across the hot sand to our spot.

'I haven't done a poo in two days; I think that's why I'm feeling sick.' Harry pulls up her kaftan and shows me her belly. 'Look! It's all bloated, it's a full poo baby in there.' She prods it.

'Stop it, that's rank.'

'Do you reckon if I drink loads of fruit juice, I'll be able to go?'

'Maybe. I don't know what the Thai for prune is. I'd probably have a few coffees and smoke some cigarettes if I were you. That will definitely get things moving.'

We sit and continue reading our books, sipping our respective drinks. I can feel the sun beating down on my head, making my hair feel hot. Perspiration building on the back of my neck and my chest, making my skin turn a deeper shade of brown. That gentle percussion of the waves against the sound, the rustle of palm trees, the soft hum of animals and insects and the occasional thud of a coconut dropping to the sand. Pure bliss.

'Seffy?'

'Yes?'

'I was supposed to start my period five days ago and I haven't.'

My heart skips a beat, the waves hitting the sand suddenly sound louder, like it's about to hit a crescendo.

'What do you think that means?' I say, trying to act casual but I know I'm just making myself sound like an imbecile.

'That my moon's in the fourth house? Come on. What do you fucking think!' She pulls her sunglasses off and looks at me dead in the eye. 'I think I might be pregnant.'

I can feel little balls of anxiety and sick bubbling in my stomach and starting to take the journey into my throat. My mouth tastes all sour and metallic. The waves are suddenly crashing around me, the soft hum of insects turning to an irritating buzz that's filling my ears, getting louder and louder.

'Pregnant?' I shout over the noise in my brain.

It's ok, I tell myself. How many times have you or a friend thought they were pregnant and it's turned out to be nothing? It's super common, like it happens allll the time.

'Seffy! Keep your fucking voice down,' Harry snaps. 'I had sex with Jack about two weeks ago and then I was supposed to start my period, but it hasn't arrived.'

Come on, Seffy, say something, act cool, act normal. Your friend, correction, best friend, thinks she's pregnant, be supportive.

'Did you not use protection?' I ask, trying to disguise the croak of my voice.

'I used a condom of course. I'm not on the pill anymore. I was going to get the coil but then I never got round to it, you know, I was busy.' She looks down at her hands, twisting one finger round the other. 'Well, I know I used a condom the second time, after the fire show, or maybe that was the third time, I don't know. But the first couple of times, I can't remember . . . I can't remember.' She bites the bottom of her lip. 'It's all such a blur, with the mushrooms and the drink and the penis covered in glow paint that just kept coming at me.'

She doesn't know! It's like she was actively trying to conceive.

'I think.' *Say it slowly.* 'We should try and find somewhere round here where we can purchase a pregnancy test.'

We hailed a taxi and asked him to take us to a big supermarket. It was said in that grossly ignorant manner that British people use when abroad, expecting everyone to speak English and if they don't it involves hideously over-the-top hand gestures. We played a game of side-street charades where I acted out pushing a trolley and Harry pulled her top out and then pretended to soothe an imaginary baby.

Turns out that the taxi driver's English was much better than our charades and Tesco, or more importantly, Tesco Lotus, is absolutely everywhere.

Walking around the aisles gave me that horrible feeling of déjà vu. But in a weird way, like someone was watching me. I was watching myself from a past life. We weren't stomping through the aisles with the same purpose I did in the Tesco Metro near Luke's and my past abode, we were wandering worriedly, aimlessly. Zig-zagging down every single aisle in the hope that we would imminently come across the Thai equivalent of feminine care due to the fact that we couldn't read any of the handwritten signs.

'Here. They're here,' I say suddenly, stopping in front of a wall of pink, purple and blue packaging.

'I don't know which one to get,' Harry says, looking over-whelmed.

This is my calling, my chance to help.

'I'd probably get a double one, just in case. And digital too, they're the best,' I answer assertively, pulling a pink packet with yellow writing off the shelf. 'If there was ever a Master-mind category in pregnancy tests, I'd be an expert,' I add jovially, masking my discomfort at the situation.

'Thanks, Seffy,' Harry says, trying to force a smile. 'Sorry, if this is . . .'

'Ssssh.' I put my finger to my lips. 'This is about you not me.' We walk to the till to pay for the test and get a taxi back.

'I'm so nervous, Seffy.' Harry looks almost grey as she clutches the test tightly in her palm.

'It's ok, everything will be ok, whatever happens.'

'I don't know what I'll do if it says positive. I suddenly feel so guilty and stupid.'

'It's ok, everything will be fine. It always works out in the end.' Words are falling out of my mouth like someone's planted them there. But not me. I don't think I believe any of what I'm uttering.

'Ok, ok, I'll just do it. I don't know what's got into me, all this procrastinating. Worrying.'

Harry takes the test and goes into the bathroom as I sit on the edge of the bed, looking up at the ceiling, the tiny fan whir-ring breaking the silence. I hear that familiar crunch of the plasticky foil film being unwrapped. A silence as she checks the instructions again. The click of the lid coming off and being placed on the sink. And then the sound of panicked urination. The trickle, stop, trickle, stop to make sure it's on the stick. Then the second click of the lid and the anxious waiting.

My mind hasn't stopped since Harry told me she'd missed her period. My friend, best friend, could be pregnant. I'd be one of those aunties by association, not by blood. Maybe even a godmother if Harry decided to go down that route. Our lives would be swapped. I'd be the reckless one, going away on cool trips, sleeping with random men. She'd be me. Living the life I wanted with Luke. She'd be going to ante-natal classes, hanging out with young mums, going on play dates, having the angst about which school her baby would go to. I'd be the single, happy-go-lucky girl. But I wouldn't be happy. I want my own children, by blood, to be conceived in the good old-fashioned way of a hearty romp. I want to pass on my own genetics. I need them to make me a better person. I need my own children to prove that I can do a better job, be better than my own mother. Harry doesn't need them like I do, they'd just be an accessory.

'Seffy?' Harry breaks the silence. 'Are you still there?'

'Yes,' I call back, willing myself to be having positive thoughts.

'Nothing's happening, it's just blank.'

'That's ok, sometimes it takes a little while.' *That's good*, I think to myself, it would have happened by now if she was pregnant.

'Oh,' Harry says.

'What?' My heart's beating so fast it feels like it's in my lungs.

'Something's happened.'

'What? Harry, what does it say?' I stand up from the bed and feel beads of sweat pour down my back.

'It says . . . Errr. It says I'm pregnant.'

Fuck.

24

After the pregnancy news, we sat in silence for a bit. I had my arm around Harry; my body was physically present, but my mind was far away. It was back in those scenes that I acted out with Luke.

The ones where he'd pull me in close, holding me round my waist, stroking my hair. I'd breathe in his scent of Aqua di Parma, only the base notes left at the end of a long day, warm amber and white moss. I desperately wanted it to hold the same comfort it did at the beginning of the relationship. He'd say he loved me, and mean it, and I would return the comment but be unsure of the meaning and go back to drenching my pillow with my tears.

It was reminding me how hard I tried to get pregnant and how my body failed me miserably every goddamn time. It was reminding me of how I would sit on the toilet, my pyjama shorts round my ankles, or my negligee scrunched up round my abdomen or my pencil skirt unzipped and in a pile on the bathroom floor. It reminded me of how I would sit there, waiting, waiting, for what seemed like an eternity but could only have ever been about three minutes. And the two dreaded words would flash on the screen, 'not pregnant'.

The one time I saw my holy grail, 'pregnant', I was elated. Ecstatic, I couldn't contain myself. I was having a baby, finally, and all the heartache, pregnancy tests, mindless fucking was worth it, for this. A tiny life, part of me and Luke that I can nurture for ever. I waited too long to find out what sharing the news was like because by the time I was ready, the baby was gone.

'How are you feeling?' I ask Harry, wanting to break the silence and knowing that this is the sort of question a best friend would ask.

'I don't know,' Harry replies, glumly. She's been sitting staring at the stick with the two purple lines on it ever since they appeared.

'I'm guessing it's Jack's?' It's essentially rhetorical but I ask it anyway. I'm becoming more and more like Moira by the minute.

'Yes of course! It's Jack's. Australian Jack's who I'm probably never going to see again. This isn't how I imagined getting pregnant.' None of it is very predictable in the end. It wouldn't have mattered how prepared I was for a baby; it was never going to happen. Maybe you were right, Luke, it wasn't the time for us.

'You can always message him; you know, if you felt that was right,' I quickly caveat, not wanting to sound too pushy. 'Being a single mum isn't all that bad; my mum managed.'

'And she became an alcoholic. Anyway, I never said I had a problem with being a single mum.' Harry side-eyes me and then goes back to staring at the stick. She's right, she didn't. I was thinking about myself again. When I imagined having a baby, I imagined it with a partner, in a house with me as director of a top-tier bank. I wouldn't have imagined myself being impregnated on a holiday fling, nor finding out I was infertile, I guess. I should know by now that idealism doesn't work.

'Well.' I ignore the comment about my mum because she's correct. 'We could raise him or her together, like, you know, at one of those female communes.'

'Thanks.' She squeezes my hand. 'It's all such a shock, you know.' To me too. 'I don't think I'm ready to have a baby.'

Maybe this is my calling. I can be like a second mum to this child. I was there at the conception, it's almost like it's my own.

'What if I don't want to keep it?' Harry asks softly.

I hadn't really thought about this option. Being pregnant and not wanting it seems unfathomable to me.

'Wouldn't you feel bad, though, if you didn't keep it? What if you couldn't ever have another one, wouldn't you feel guilty?' I can't stop myself; the filter's broken in my over-active brain. I'm already imagining I am pregnant and not Harry.

Harry bursts into tears. My eyes widen – fuck, I've said too much. I pull her in for a hug. *Don't be a bitch, Seffy. Stop taking out your hurt on Harry. It's not your body. She's not you.*

'I'm sorry,' I say, stroking her hair like she used to do to me when I was crying over my inability to have children. 'I didn't mean to hurt you.' I really don't, even though this whole situation is hurtful for me.

'I know this must be really weird for you. Bring back all sorts of horrible memories, I'm sorry. I didn't mean to ruin our trip like this. You're right about me. I am reckless, stupid. I wish I were more like you sometimes.'

'You don't,' I say, tears pricking in my eyes. 'You really don't.' Rigid, boring, infertile. Who'd want to be me?

'I do.' She nods, wiping her cheeks with her hands. 'I'm not in a relationship, I basically had a one-night stand with a guy I barely knew. Who's going to look after me? Who's going to provide for me? I'm on a Crunchy Nut Cluster salary.' She gives a little snort at her own misfortune. 'And now I'll prob-ably have to stop a little life before it's barely even started due to my own stupidity. Argh, I hate myself.' She punches her stomach.

I pull her hand away.

'Hey, hey! You don't mean that. It's been a massive shock, it's a lot to take in.'

'I do. I either kill off my own genes or have a baby I never wanted and raise it barely hand-to-mouth – we can't all afford to go gallivanting round the world for seven months.' She eye-balls me. Oh no, everything's turning sour again like it always seems to when babies are mentioned near my Satan body. Harry's right, I am fortunate in terms of my finances, but I would give it all up, turn it all in just to be her at this moment in time.

'I promise you, Harry, everything will be ok in the end.' I close my hand on hers, gripping it hard, not quite sure what I'm trying to hold on to. 'Why don't we go on a little walk, grab some food and then come back and watch something totally trashy on Netflix on my phone and snuggle up with some snacks. Sleep on it and then see how you feel tomorrow.' I know I have a natural mother in me somewhere. That's the sort of thing that Luke said to me before I spat it all back in his face.

'Thank you.' The tone in her voice changes back to being soft and grateful. 'Thanks for always looking out for me, even when it's hard. Love you.'

The next morning, Harry wakes up in a seemingly jovial mood.

'I had all sorts of strange dreams last night,' she says, pulling her eye-mask off. I expected her eyes to be red and puffy after her emotions yesterday, but they were bright and alert. 'In one I gave birth on the stage in my old primary school and in another Jack proposed to me on set in front of the cluster-fuckers.' Her eyes look suddenly far away. 'And in another I saw myself pushing the pram round the park with a beautiful little baby girl and I thought maybe this is fate.'

I feel my diaphragm tighten. That's MY image. It should be me walking round the park with a baby in a pram. My friends asking me how I do it. Keep up a successful job, do my make-up, have an amazing relationship with Luke and have such a gorgeous baby.

I'm starting to feel like this whole sabbatical was a waste of time; all the growth I thought I was doing is lying unravelled on the floor. I'm still heartbroken.

'So . . .' She pauses. 'I think I'm going to keep it.' She looks at me, her mouth skewed, like half of it's being weighed down. 'Is that stupid of me? Seffy, you'd tell me if I was, wouldn't you?'

'No, I think it's a wonderful idea.' I smile with my lips, curling them up to make my eyes smile too because that's how you demonstrate you're being genuine. I don't know if I'm happy for Harry. I don't want her to get rid of the baby, but I don't want her to keep it either. I don't want her to be pregnant. My best friend. BEST FRIEND. Is having a baby. The one I thought would be last out of everyone, however malicious those thoughts make me. The one who deep down, when I found out the news about my own fertility, I thought would be there forever without a child so I wouldn't feel as lonely. Rory's having a baby, Harry's having a baby and then me. How do I fit in? Their babies will become more important than our friendship and I will be left with truly nothing.

The rest of the day I felt like there was a tension between us. Something that's not existed before. We read our books on the beach. I drank a coffee and when I offered one to Harry, she replied, 'No thanks, I've been doing some reading and too much caffeine is bad for the baby.' Resting one hand lightly on her invisible stomach.

Every time I look at her I feel the cracks in my heart deepen. I would do anything, ANYTHING to be pregnant and I lost everything because I wasn't.

When we ordered our lunch, Harry checked that the vegetables had been washed and when I asked if she wanted a cocktail, she practically bit my head off about drinking while pregnant.

I tried to be agreeable and nod in all the right places. Find the facts that she said about pregnancy fascinating as if I hadn't spent a year researching every facet of procreation myself. It was fraught to say the least. I've never seen her like this before. It was annoying. I wanted to talk about something, ANYTHING, other than pregnancy. Is that what Luke thought about me?

What I wouldn't do to rewind time and be sharing these life announcements with Luke on the sofa. He'd tell me not to worry and that we would get there. We would have our own moments to share. Instead, I'm stewing in my own thoughts, alone. I can't even share them with Harry.

Harry's behaviour carried on for another day. Cautious. The epitome of being a good mother. Exactly how I would be if God gave me a chance.

But the next day, I knew something was different about her.

In the morning, Harry had not one but TWO caffeinated coffees.

'What about caffeine being bad for the baby?' I ask almost provocatively, like I want an argument.

'Eurgh, I'm allowed the odd one, aren't I?' she replies as if I'm her mother.

At lunchtime she had a cocktail, not a mocktail, a cocktail with a side of two Marlboro lights. I wanted to ask her if she was ok, but she was being the usual Harry, the one that vanished four days ago. I liked her being back. It stopped me feeling like an outsider in my own friendship group.

But when evening arrived, I had to say something.

'Do you really think you should order another bucket? I know it's fine to have the odd drink but two buckets? I'm a bit worried.' I try to say it casually, but I know it's anal Seffy through and through.

'Look.' Harry turns around on her way to the bar, slurring her words slightly, hand on her hip. 'I've had a big shock.

I'm not ready for my life to change. I'll do everything for this baby, but I need a couple of days of fun before I close that door for good, ok? One last hoorah. I've had no time to prepare myself. I've seen it on Instagram. It's all breast pads and grey, sagging maternity bras from now on – I need to give my twenty-nine-year-old body the respect and send-off it deserves.' She grabs her breasts. 'These pert titties will never be the same again – you're lucky, babes.' She goes to grab my breasts, but her comment makes me snap and I slap her hands away. She's just drunk, I tell myself, she doesn't mean to be so insensitive.

Something about 'one last hoorah' doesn't sit right with me. That one drink, one cigarette could damage the baby. Life's so precious, you might only get one chance at it. Why would you want to risk it all for a fleeting good time?

She's been given everything I ever dreamed of and she's ready to throw it in the bin like an empty crisp packet. I'm trying to swallow the negative thoughts, to remember how far I've come. Celine, Tish, Margot, Rita. But the thoughts are coming thick and fast; my brain is riddled with them. Another one floats to the forefront before I've had time to brush away the last one. I'm drowning myself in past trauma.

But I can't say anything; she's going through a lot. It's as much of a shock to Harry as it was to me when I found out that my womb was filled with duds. Allow her to do things her way, *don't be anal* my brain whispers just as *selfish bitch* lands on my tongue. I didn't say it out loud but that's the label that comes to mind.

So, we had one of those nights, exactly like old times. If this was my last night of being free, what would I want to do? I thought to myself. We smoked a twenty pack each, drank drink after drink, laughed about old times and fell into bed about 4.00 a.m. It was exactly what we both needed. I tried to pretend that Harry hadn't just found out she was pregnant, and it worked, for a bit anyway.

It's not just Harry that needs to come to terms with the news; unbeknown to her, it's me as well.

It's one night. People don't know they're pregnant for ages sometimes. One blow-out isn't going to harm a fly.

'Breakfast?' Harry says, pulling her eye-mask off. 'I'm dying.'

'Me too.'

Harry orders two coffees for us, eggs and bacon. It's one of those Thai resorts where they cater through and through for British people. It's welcome when breakfast comes with a side of hanxiety.

'Shall we go somewhere else?' Harry asks, her mouth full. 'I'm getting bored of it here.'

'Yes of course. I was trying to be mindful of how you're feeling but yeah, I like our island routine we've got going but could do with finding my adventurer side again!'

'Thanks, you're a doll.' She smiles, popping a slither of crispy bacon on her tongue. 'Let's do some research on the beach.'

Harry pops a cigarette between her lips. I thought it was 'one last hoorah' not two.

'Don't stare, Seffy, I can feel your judgement boring into my soul. It's one cig, babies survive world wars, it'll be fine.'

I've never felt like this before with Harry, but I feel a tiny bubble of rage pop inside me. It's getting harder and harder to bite my tongue.

By lunchtime, Harry's drunk and the thought of research is well and truly off the to-do list.

She's off laughing with a group of American boys who arrived earlier. Flirting, batting her eyelashes, sweeping the hair off her face. I'm sitting on my sun-lounger, observing, seething.

What's she doing? WHAT THE FUCK IS SHE DOING?

I can't watch her self-destruct anymore; I go back to the room. I want to cry to see if it will make me feel better but I'm too wound up. God, I miss Luke, I miss him so much. I miss what we had. I miss my life before we started trying.

It's me who desperately wanted a baby. ME. Harry never wanted one; she didn't even try and here she is, pregnant. Not a care in the world. Ruining it all. It came so easily for her, and she doesn't care how easily she could destroy it.

I couldn't have a baby and it destroyed me and my marriage. How can she not see that? She should be treating her body like a temple.

It's dark. I must have been asleep for hours. Crunch, click. I can hear someone grappling with the key in the lock. Harry.

Fuck, I'm a bad friend. I shouldn't have left her like that.

She stumbles in the door, giggling to herself.

'Oooop. Sorry, Seffy.' She stinks of spiced rum.

'That's ok, are you ok?' My emotions are so conflicted. I'm angry, upset, but I still care for her. It isn't her fault. It isn't her fault. Maybe I just needed a sleep, a chance to reset, keep the negativity at bay.

'Ok? I'm fucking fantastic.' She falls on the bed trying to untie her sandal.

'You've got sand all over you! Did you fall?' I'm worried about the baby. I'm questioning her own care. I'm exactly like all the people who annoyed me when I was trying – like Diane telling me what I should and shouldn't eat.

'Onto someone's dick!' She cackles loudly, filling the air with wafts of alcohol.

'Oh ok.' I ignore her, thinking it's a joke and untie her other sandal.

'I fucked him, Seffy, and you know I said Jack had a top-five penis? This guy, Horatio or something had the number one. Imagine!' she suddenly shouts. 'Having the number one penis in all the world.'

I stop untying her sandal.

'What the fuck, Harry? Seriously. What the fuck?'

She looks at me, dumbfounded.

'What do you mean, what the fuck?' She uses her hand like a puppet, mimicking me. The rage is back.

'You're pregnant!' That's it, the muzzle's off and my mouth has a mind of its own. 'I don't give a fuck if you wanted it or not. If it was planned or not. You're pregnant. You were right the other night, you are irresponsible. Reckless. You're out drinking, smoking, sleeping with strangers because you're not grown-up enough to get a fucking grip.' Uh-oh. Harry and I never fight. Ever.

'Excuse me?' Harry almost spits the words. 'I'm not grown-up enough? I'm pregnant, Seffy, not you. Ever since I told you I was I could see the hatred and jealously seeping from you like a bad fucking smell. I didn't plan it. I don't plan everything like you. See, good things can happen if you just let go a little, relax. So what if I want to have a few nights of enjoying my life – get over it. It's my body, not yours. I'm the pregnant one.' She taps her belly, smirking. I know she's drunk, she's not this malicious.

'I'm not jealous of you, Harry.' I swallow back the tears that would say otherwise. 'I can't have children; it doesn't matter how carefree I am. I can't have them. I'm at peace with that.' Lie, but what does she care? 'You clearly don't want this baby, so stop pretending. But don't be all upset about it when it doesn't go your way later on. You should be fucking grateful that you're pregnant. Not pissing it all away like you do every good thing. You have no drive, you're lazy at everything you do, that's why you're still on a Crunchy Nut Cluster salary when you're nearly thirty.'

'You're a spiteful bitch,' Harry says. 'I'm going to bed. I don't need to hear your witchy words.'

She pulls the duvet up over her head and I don't hear another sound. She's passed out.

What have I done?

I didn't mean the words I said. I feel so hurt by everything, by everyone. It's like the world's turned against me to conjure up the most hurtful plan it could possibly imagine.

My best friend. My husband. My mum. Does everyone leave me in the end?

Eight Months No Baby

Dear Aphrodite, Venus, I'm sorry it's come to this but go fuck yourselves.

I don't know how I've even managed to write to you this month. In between crying relentlessly, ordering take-away, and conjuring up reasons to fight with my husband, I've barely had time. Oh, and I've been working. Not in the literal sense of the word, but I've been physically present. I've sat at my desk, I've answered phone calls, I've attended meetings – it's not in the job description to be happy about it.

I've spent a great deal of time eyeballing Moira. Watching her every move. It's as if she can sense my unhappiness and is revelling in it, sending me more and more work. The arduous tasks are the only thing making the news more palatable.

I sit watching her, wondering what it's like to be her because that's who I'm going to become. Bitter. Work obsessed. Lonely. The way her eyes dart round a room like a maniac, dissecting people's emotions and then ensuring everyone feels the same with a dart of her poison tongue – miserable.

I'm about to have a breakdown, I'm verging on destructive. I'm channelling all my hatred into my boss because she's the closest person to me right now. Drinking myself into a haze to wake up late enough to avoid the nightmares. Just like my mother. The one person I never wanted to become. I know I'm doing it, I'm on the self-sabotage train. It's what I do when I don't know what to do anymore.

While knowing the whole time that all I wanted my whole life was to have my own family so I could prove to the whole world that I'm nothing like her. That not all genes get passed down and I can be a present, thoughtful and sober mother.

Well, fuck you world, for ruining that.

Here's what happened.

'Hello?'

'Hello, Seffy, it's Dr Cartwright.'

Silence. My heart beating fast, blood rising and falling in my chest, my veins heavy with the increase.

'Seffy?'

'Sorry, yes, I am here.'

'I'm sorry not to be able to give you the "all clear" but we need you to come back in for a few more tests. We need to do a scan on your ovaries and fallopian tubes.'

My heart stops beating.

'What's wrong with me?' The words croak out of my mouth, my lips barely parting. I can barely hear them over my pulsating heart.

'I'm afraid I can't give a diagnosis over the phone, that's why you need to come in. Do you have time today?'

Did you do this, Aphrodite? Make time go slower as some sort of punishment? Because it feels like the longest day. I stare at my screen until I feel my eyes burn. I cry when Moira barks at me even though it's a regular occurrence. I say I have a doctor's appointment to disguise my early finish, but I don't disclose my ailment.

Every second on the tube feels like a lifetime. As I sit in the waiting room, I can feel perspiration collating on my back, my hands so twitchy it's like I have a nicotine habit.

Finally, finally, Dr Cartwright calls me into her office.

I feel like the words are going to explode from my mouth.

'What's wrong with me?' I blurt out, this time panic in my voice. The words loud enough to be heard over my thumping heart.

'Please Seffy, take a seat.' She gestures to the brown boucle chair, and I sit down. 'I can see you're very

distressed.' Understatement. I'm sweating, twitching; I look deranged. 'Remember, the last time you visited, we did that scan?' She makes it sound like I came here on a staycation. 'Well, we found a slight blockage at the end of both your fallopian tubes, and we need to take a further ultrasound to confirm this today.'

'But what does it mean?' This time I beg her to tell me, urgency in my voice.

'It may not mean anything.' How can someone be so blasé? Like it's a fifty-fifty chance but one option is your whole life being over. 'I'll take the ultrasound now and then assess the results.'

I lie back on the bed, my heart racing, my breathing erratic. I can't think clearly because my heart is beating too loudly, interfering with my train of thought.

Dr Cartwright takes some pictures on the ultrasound, then instructs me to get dressed and come back to her desk.

'I'm afraid the ultrasound has confirmed that you have two severely enlarged fallopian tubes, which is known as a hydrosalpinx. Have you experienced any pain in your lower abdomen?'

I sit there in a stunned silence.

'What does that mean?' Enlarged fallopian tubes? Does size matter in this case? I still have no idea what a fucking hydrosalpinx is – speak fucking English to me!

'It's fluid at the end of your fallopian tube. In your case it looks particularly severe, and the blockage is very engorged. Due to the fact that both tubes are affected, it means that a normal pregnancy can't occur in the uterus and there's a high chance of an ectopic pregnancy.'

Her words are whirring round and round my brain.

'But you haven't said I'm infertile. Have you? Have you?' My voice rising an octave, panic bubbling like soup boiling on the stove.

'Infertility,' she pauses like it's the final in a pub quiz, 'it's a hard word to define. There are so many options available nowadays. IVF, I would recommend in your case. The tubes look quite badly damaged and I'm not sure we would be able to operate and open them up successfully without damaging them more.'

The soup's bubbled over.

'IVF?' The words burn my tongue. 'Then I am infertile. That's what infertile people do when they can't have their own children.'

'Infertile is a harsh word. I've never liked it, even in my line of work. You need to explore more options, that's all. Having a family means so many things to so many people.'

'More options?' My voice screeches in a staccato. 'Having a family to me, means getting pregnant through fucking my husband. IVF isn't more options, it's the end of the options. I can't bear children naturally, is that what you're saying? Surely this is the worst-case scenario for anyone who sets foot in your office?' I don't want IVF, I don't want a surrogate, I want to do it all myself.

'Not necessarily. It depends what answers they were searching for, and like I said, you can start your family in multiple ways. IVF is the future for so many couples; it's the option they were searching for years. Have you experienced pain in your lower abdomen? It would be helpful if you could answer, for our notes, as it makes it easier to diagnose future cases.' There really is no emotion in her voice, but after all, this is her job – to ruin people's lives.

'So now I'm a lab rat.' I sob into my hands. 'No, I never experienced pain. I'd still be living my life, none the wiser, if I hadn't tried to have children.'

'I'm sorry it's not the news you were hoping for but it's really not the end of your journey with pregnancy. I suggest *you go home, speak to your husband and let the news sink in. I'll be here if you want to speak in detail about your options.'*

My head is flooded with questions, but I don't feel ready to have them all answered yet.

'But I thought if you were infertile, then you couldn't ovulate. Like, you didn't have any eggs?'

'The female reproductive system is inherently complex and sadly, despite it being crucial to life on earth, hasn't had nearly enough money spent on it, in terms of research or awareness in young people. Hydrosalpinx doesn't stop your ovaries releasing eggs; however it does prevent the sperm and egg from getting together inside the tube due to the blockage.'

'And my miscarriage?' I ask, wondering if there is a tiny bit of hope left. I did get pregnant before, no matter how briefly.

'I'm not sure; stranger things have happened. It could have been an ectopic pregnancy that wasn't diagnosed. I have to be honest with you, Seffy, it would be dangerous for you to try and have a natural pregnancy now without close observation.'

I close my eyes and silently weep. I don't like the answers I'm getting so I think that's enough questions for today.

Luke's already home by the time I return from Dr Cartwright's office. After my appointment, I don't really know what happened. My mind's churning but turning up blank. I wandered the streets for a while. I cried, I sat, I cried some more. I thought about this exact moment. What will I say to Luke? How will he react? When I eventually mustered the courage to make the journey home, it was painful. My chest was all tight, like I was having a heart attack.

I sat on the wall near our flat for a while, giving myself a little pep talk.

Come on, Seffy, it's not your fault. It's just one of those things; if anyone can make infertility work it's you. Luke will be understanding, he is, most of the time. Till death do us part, that's what you said in your vows. You need to give him time to process, you've barely processed it yourself. It will be ok; everything will be ok.

'Darling!' Luke grins as I walk into the kitchen, his arms outstretched. 'I've been calling, was it a late one at work? Moira being a bitch again? I've started the meal, there was a rack of lamb on offer at Marks, bit extravagant for a Wednesday night but oh well!' He stops speaking and looks closer at me. 'Seffy? What's wrong?' By now my blotchy face is in full view, flecks of mascara on my cheeks that I made no effort to wash away. 'Have you been drinking?'

I burst into tears and pull away from him, my head in my hands.

'I've done something. I'm sorry.' My voice is disjointed. 'I should have told you; I should have involved you from the beginning. I don't know what's got into me.'

'What's going on, Seffy? Tell me.' His face looks worried, I can see his eyes flitting from left to right, trying to analyse me, work out what's going on in the split second before I tell him.

'You know I've been worked up about getting pregnant.' He looks at me, confused. 'I know I've been obsessed with it.' I wipe snot away on the back of my hand. 'I just really wanted to have a baby.' I whisper because my tear ducts have somehow managed to block up my voice box too.

'And we will! Darling, come on, whatever this is, it will be ok.' He takes my hand as I pull it away shaking my head.

'Please,' I implore him. 'Just listen to me. The whole waiting to see if it would happen, it's been making me feel really stressed. We did have a baby, you and I.' Luke's face takes on a quizzical expression. 'I was so excited, I was working out the best way to tell you, then I miscarried. I felt so ashamed, I just couldn't tell anyone.' Luke's expression goes from forlorn to angry and then back to sadness again.

'Seffy, we share everything, we talk about everything. That means the good and the bad. All I ever want is for you to be happy. But to not tell me about my own child . . .' His voice echoes round the room, ringing in my ears.

'Please, Luke. Please, I'm sorry. I'm so sorry. Let me finish.' I'm hoping that he can see there's more to this story than what happened a few months ago. I grab his hand, clinging on to his fingers, urging him to stay with me.

'I'm sorry if you felt you couldn't tell me, but it was part of me, too. It's your body, I get that, but the baby is as much mine as yours. I share your sadness, but now I have to do it alone too.' I can't tell if he's angry or sad.

'I know, I know. I'm sorry, I'm so sorry, Luke.' Tears stream down my face. 'Please let me try and explain. I was so worried about everything. I think I was having a breakdown, but I didn't want to burden you with it all, that's why I didn't say. I'd planned this whole baby announcement.' I swallow the words, thinking about my fleeting happiness. 'But by the time I went to surprise you, the baby was already gone, and I felt stupid, oh so stupid. I went to the doctor again, who told me not to worry about it. I went to an ovulation party.' I decided to omit the antenatal class with fake bump. 'I thought the only way to bring me back to reality and stop worrying was to go to a private clinic and have a fertility test.' Luke looks up at me, expectant. I swallow. 'Well, I went last week, and she said she'd call me *back if anything was wrong and she did, and that's where I've been.' I burst into tears again, my diaphragm bumping erratically, hiccupping.*

Luke takes both my hands in his.

'And what was it that she said?' His voice sounds strained, pleading, urgent, like he already knows the answer.

'I have hydrosalpinx.' And then clarify with, 'It means blocked fallopian tubes.' I look at Luke's dumbfounded expression. 'She said the tubes are so damaged that the only way for me, for us, to conceive is through IVF. I'm sorry, I'm sorry I'm so shit. You didn't sign up to this with me.' I cry into his shoulders.

'Darling, it's ok. It's ok.' Luke strokes my hair. 'I love you, I love you. We will get through this, you know we will. So what if we need IVF? We need it. We have money, it will be fine, everything will be fine. I signed up for everything, just like you did with me. The good, the bad. The ugly – all of it, I love you, that's all that matters.'

It's like my ears can't hear him or I'm choosing not to listen. I don't know if Luke feels shocked, if he even cares.

We don't even talk any more about the miscarriage.

Maybe he's trying to make me feel better. Maybe he's glad it isn't him with the dud genes. Maybe it's not a big deal to him, but for me, I feel like I've lost my whole future. It's something I've yearned my whole life for, to be a good mother. I'm failing at the first hurdle – conception. What makes me think I'd be any better at raising a family than my own mother?

This diagnosis. It feels like the end of everything. Like my life is over. I don't care that IVF is an option, I wanted to do it all by myself. And what if that doesn't work?

'What do I say to our families, our friends? Everyone just assumes it's easy to have children, everyone keeps asking when we're going to, what if we can't? What if it doesn't

work? It's embarrassing. I don't want to go round telling everyone about it.'

'Then we don't tell anyone,' Luke says softly, still stroking my hair. 'It's between you and me, it's no one else's business. It's not embarrassing, it's part of life. I love you, ok? I love you, no matter what.'

I want to agree with him. I want Luke's words to make me feel better. I want to take comfort in everything he says. But I can't. Because it's me. It's not him, or us, it's me.

I'm the dud.

Was this the sign I've been asking for, Aphrodite? You don't need to make it any clearer. Thanks.

Seffy

Five Months Until Thirty

25

The next morning, after our fight, things with Harry are different.

I've been awake for hours, staring at the whirring of the fan, counting the knots in the wood on the ceiling.

I hear Harry bang her hand around uselessly on the side table, searching desperately for hydration. I don't move.

She pushes past me as I leave the bathroom, like we're strangers, not best friends of nearly two decades.

'Do you want to get breakfast?' I ask casually, lying back on my bed, but my insides have moulded together and my eyes are closed so I don't have to look at her. Maybe she can't even remember what I said last night.

'Not hungry,' she replies.

'Suit yourself.' I get up from the bed, grab the room key and head to the beach. The quicker I move, the less Harry has to see of my anguish and disappointment.

I don't know how to act in a situation like this. I hate arguing. I know I said some spiteful things but we both did. I shouldn't be made to feel any worse. This is just a knock-back, it will all blow over by tomorrow, even by the end of the day. We've been friends for years; how can a friendship as deep rooted as ours be destroyed by just a few words?

I thought you weren't hungry, I mutter to myself as I see Harry ordering an acai bowl and a juice from the bar. She doesn't look round to see where I am and sits by herself on one of the rattan tables. It's not long before two guys come over and start chatting to her. The slightly shorter guy gives her shoulder a little squeeze and I can only assume he's the lucky owner of the *number one dick in the whole world.*

Harry's acting different to her usual flirtatious self. She doesn't do the hair flick or the knee pat. She doesn't even remove her sunglasses.

Fuck it. This is so stupid.

I close my book and sit up on my sun-lounger, searching for Harry behind my own MI5 dark glasses. Gone. She must be back at the room. I walk quickly across the hot sand and then down the little wooden path to our room, opening the door to Harry sitting on the bed.

'Harry, I . . .' I look around at the sudden cleanliness. Why aren't all her clothes scattered across the floor? Make-up? Toiletries? My eyes settle on her rucksack leaning against her bed. Full. Ready to go.

'I came to say sorry.' The words shake slightly as they tumble out of my mouth. She's leaving me, too. Memories of the shouting, slamming of doors and packed cases from both my childhood and my adulthood flood my mind.

'I'm leaving,' she replies, but she doesn't look up from the floor. The shake in her voice mirrors my own.

'I can see that, but why? I know we both said horrible things to each other but I'm sorry. We still have another week of our holiday together.' The words gush from my mouth. I don't know if I mean them or not, but I don't want to fight.

'I'm having an abortion. I called my mum and told her what I wanted, and she booked me on this evening's flight back to London.'

'An abortion?' I don't think my surprise can hide my judgement. 'What about us looking after the baby together?' The words come out high-pitched, like I'm impersonating someone from a childhood TV show. 'How can you go from wanting a baby to suddenly not?'

'Eurgh, Seffy, give it a rest!' The words land like bullets on my skin. 'That was just a dream of yours. I was entertaining your dream. As if we would look after a baby together. I don't want my life to be like that. I like my life how it is; I'm not ready for a baby. I never was. I wanted an abortion as soon as I found out but then I felt bad for you and what you went through. I thought I could maybe try, see what it feels like to want a baby, but I didn't really. I want to drink, smoke, fuck who I want. I don't want to be sensible or a mother now, I'm not ready. I'll have children if and when I'm ready, when the right person comes along. I don't want your life; I want my own.'

'But it's not my life, it's yours. It will always be your baby.' This is what I wanted, isn't it? For my friend to not be having a baby, for everything to be back to normal again. Two childless women going into their thirties together. 'Abortions are so final, you know. That is a life and none of us can choose how we were brought into the world. I think your baby would be very lucky . . .'

'Shut up!' Harry slams her fist onto the bed. 'Not everything is about you. As soon as I found out I was pregnant, you imagined how your life would change. How you could make *me* being pregnant somehow work for you. I'm not your fucking surrogate.' My mouth falls open. 'You don't need to tell me about abortions and how horrible it is, I fucking know! Do you think this is an easy decision? No. Do you think I wish I could turn back time and make Jack put on a fucking condom? Yes, of course I do. But mistakes happen. Accidents happen. It doesn't make me a horrible person, you don't need to sit there judging me because what's happening to me right now doesn't sit with your morals.'

'I know it's hard.' The words trickle out of my mouth like a whisper.

'You desperately want a baby, I don't. I'm sorry that I can't give you my womb but it's not MY FUCKING FAULT that you can't have children.'

'I just know what it's like to not be able to have children and I want to make sure you know how lucky you are right now.' Surely I'm entitled to my feelings too?

'But that's the whole fucking point, Seffy! I know that being able to bring a life onto this earth is lucky, it's a privilege. But one that I'm not ready to have right now. I'm not infertile. I'm sorry, really sorry that you are and aren't able to have children in the same way I am, but I can't let your genetics rule my life. If I can't have children ever again after this, of course I'll feel guilty, I'll feel terrible. I'll be mourning my whole life, like I guess you are. But I'm prepared for that. I am not ready to have a baby right now. I know I'm not. And I know for that reason that I won't have any regrets about my decision, which is the most important thing.'

'You don't understand what it's like to be given the label "infertile".' My voice shakes with anger this time. 'You can live your life all whimsical and carefree. Fucking guys, having abortions, whatever the fuck you want. It's selfish.'

'Selfish!' Harry almost screams.

'Yes, selfish! People like me would do anything to have our own children, anything. And then people like you have them or the opportunity to have them, dangle it in our faces and then chuck it all away because everything is so easy for you. It's someone's life you're getting rid of, not a fucking chocolate wrapper.'

'You don't get it, Seffy, it's totally ridiculous. You've gone crazy. It's ok for someone to get pregnant and it not be right for them. I've been thinking about everything, what I can offer that child, what kind of mother I'd be and I've come to the conclusion that it isn't right. I'll feel guilty for the rest of my life, and I hope that one day I'll be an excellent mother, but right now this is my decision, my body and it's got nothing to do with you.' She picks up her rucksack and I see her wipe away tears from her cheeks. 'You have this RIDICULOUS idea that you can rewrite your childhood by being this *perfect* mother. You judge everyone around you for not being your idea of perfect, if they don't have the right job, wear the right clothes, say the right thing, that you forget to judge yourself. People get brought into the world in all sorts of ways and they get on with life, they are happy, good people. Take a look at yourself once in a while.'

'You bitch.' It's the only response I can think of. 'I thought we were friends,' I say, my mouth filled with the saltiness of my tears.

'So did I,' Harry says, putting her rucksack on her back. 'Tell me how much I owe for the room, and I'll transfer it.'

'Safe flight,' I stutter as she slams the door behind her.

That's it. The end of our friendship. And just like how the divorce came about with Luke, I don't even know whose fault it was.

What happened? Where did it all go wrong? Is Harry selfish? Am I selfish? I hate her. She belittled my infertility. Who does that? WHO DOES THAT! She brings me down. I was great on my own. I was becoming a new person. Exactly the type of woman I should want to be. Clearly, nothing's going to make me forget my own ailments, but I can learn to accept it, can't I?

I flick back through Harry's and my holiday snaps like I'm grieving a lost love. I hate her, but I miss her at the same time. It's like a tragic break-up. Yet I can't bring myself to throw out everything that reminds me of her because I feel like she will come back in. Unlike Luke. Should I message her? It's too soon. I don't know what to say. I don't want to say sorry. She should be the one apologising.

Maybe Harry is right, I do judge people. And who am I to judge when my life is far from the preened, perfect image I like to portray of myself?

I go on Instagram, looking at my grid. I'm a liar, I'm nothing. This whole journey has been a waste of time. I'm still heartbroken. I'm still lost.

I upload a photo of myself, one of me smiling on the beach in Koh Samui, one Harry took of me. I start typing a caption:

This is me. Infertile. You can't tell who's infertile from their picture, can you? Same as you can't tell if someone's organs are DYING. Why do we make it the norm to ask women if they're pregnant, when they are going to have children, are they trying yet? SOME OF US CAN'T HAVE CHILDREN. I don't want you to feel sorry for me, I want you to understand me. Understand that posting pictures of your children and scan pictures and baby bellies make me feel sad. Really fucking sad. I'm JEALOUS of your lives. I'd swap my Gucci bag for a nappy change and pile of sick any day of the week. So, fuck you world, for making my dream just that, a hopeless dream.

Upload.

That's what I do when I feel like life can't get any worse, I self-sabotage.

The messages start streaming in.

Rory: *Seffy, are you ok????*
Gemma: *Do you want to talk?*
Maria: *Darling, I'm so sorry, I'm always here.*
Pia: *I had no idea, sending you all the love.*

Luke. Fuck it. Unblock.

So, Harry's pregnant, well she's not, she's having an abortion. She KNOWS I want a baby and then she has one and doesn't want it. How is that FAIR? Not that you care, you've got a new girlfriend. I'm sure you'll be swanning round with a baby in your arms in no time. Then it will just be me again, alone. Fuck you. I love you. I think. But fuck you.

Send.

I turn my phone over and cry uncontrollably into my pillow.

I don't even know what to do anymore. How has that one word – infertile – managed to become the be all and end all of my whole life? I'm unable to live mine because I can't harbour another. How is that fair? I blamed myself, I blamed my mother then I put the blame on Luke because it was easier to hate him than love him anymore.

God, I want to be with him. He's everywhere I look, controlling my emotions because our life together is so deeply embedded in my brain.

I so desperately wanted this sabbatical to be more than a physical journey. I wanted it to rebuild my broken heart, show me that there's more to life. Take my mind off Luke. And it was, or I was kidding myself it was because when my worst nightmare happened, I realised that all the growth was a façade.

I cry some more and fall asleep.

I wake up to my phone pinging. Missed WhatsApp calls, Instagram messages – people are worried about me.

Fuck, I've really embarrassed myself.

I delete the post and put some ridiculous transparent story up that my phone had been stolen. Hopefully by the time I return home everyone will have forgotten about my social media outburst.

Oh my God, I messaged Luke.

Fuck.

Fuck.

FUCK.

It's still only on one tick.

Delete.

Block.

I hope Luke didn't see. I imagine him laughing about his 'crazy ex' on the sofa with his new girlfriend before remembering he isn't like that.

Forwarded message
Darlings! It's official, I'm married. Mrs Peters! I'm so sorry you couldn't all make it, but it was a wonderful day. Mike made a glorious speech about you all, I'm sure someone has a recording. We'll have to do a celebration when we're all together again. We're off on honeymoon tomorrow, Mike wanted us to celebrate in true style, like it was our first marriage – we'll be in Anguilla for two weeks. Much love xxx

And then a photo of my mum and Mike; she's in a white crepe suit; she looks glamourous, effortlessly glamorous, she always does. Mike, smart in a navy-blue suit and a lemon-yellow tie. My new dad, I guess. We've got as much genetically in common as any children I'll ever have. Welcome to the fold.

There's something inside me that feels odd. Guilt. But why should I feel guilty about not attending her wedding? She should feel guilty about a whole host of things.

But she's my mum and she's all I have right now.

You look gorgeous Mum, as usual. Hope you had a lovely day, can't wait to see the pictures when I'm back! X

I can't just leave her message without a response. It was her wedding; I should try and do something nice for her when I'm back. This whole thing with Harry, the resurgence of grief that I've had for my old life with Luke, it's made me realise you can't choose family, but you wouldn't want to lose them either.

26

I can't believe I'm here.

It was two days of crying into my sheets and sitting gormlessly on the beach before I could muster the courage to actively move my lethargic body to a new location.

I was scrolling on Facebook, scrolling and scrolling. Looking at nothing, until I saw a friend of a friend had been to a school in Malaysia teaching English as a foreign language. I saw the smiles on the faces of the children in the class and I thought, this is how to make or break me. Be surrounded by children. It's what they do when you face your fear, you know, if you're scared of spiders get in a box with them. If you're terrified of miniature versions of your own species chuck yourself in a classroom.

I found an orphanage in a place called Singburi and here I am.

I don't even know how many days I've been here, but I think I've settled in well. The hard work in the morning ensures I sleep well at night. I go to bed with cement in my hair and under my nails and I don't even bother trying to cleanse it away. It half-reminds me of my work for Moira but I'm desperately trying not to think of my old life.

I help to build a new building for the school in the morning, stirring cement and ferrying materials in wheelbarrows. In the afternoon, I teach English to the children. We sing songs, play games, they give me cuddles and the girls like to plait my hair.

A little boy called Nico – we don't even know if that's his name but that's what the teachers call him – drew me a picture. It was him and a cat and he said, 'family'. It made me cry.

And there's this guy, Will. A teacher. He's been volunteering here for six months. All the children adore him. He lets them hang onto his shorts and T-shirt as he swings them round. They scream and squeal and I can see in their faces and his how much it all means to them. He has sandy-blond tousled hair, all rough around the edges because one of the other volunteers cuts it for him. A smattering of stubble across his cheeks and chin that accentuates his jawline. Blue eyes that sparkle, ones that could take you to all four corners of the earth through a little trust and imagination. Skin golden from the sun, taut across his abs, drops of perspiration dancing in the sunlight on his shoulders.

'Oh, hey.' Will stands up from potting some vegetables in the soil, running his hands through his hair, brushing it out of his eyes. Those eyes, like he's stolen two little pieces of the sky for everyone he meets to fly away in. 'You must be Seffy.' I shake his hand while staring at the way his cheeks fall in on themselves to create two wells of kindness, the shadow of his stubble accentuating each crevice.

That was when I first laid eyes on him, and I still think about that moment even now.

It isn't just his looks that attract me to him, it's his tenderness. It's even the way that he doesn't seem to notice me. He makes me feel good about myself without doing anything. He's not telling me I'm sexy, or he likes my outfit; he's thankful for the work I'm doing which makes me feel better than ever, like my life has meaning again.

'Seffy! Hey!'

I look up from mixing sand and water, wiping my forehead on my arm. Little black bugs and dirt encapsulated in droplets of sweat. Attractive.

'Seffy?' Will's calling my name. 'Thirty more minutes, yeah? Then we should go and sort lunch.'

'See you in thirty!' I want to flutter my eyelashes, but I know I've got cement on them.

I continue mixing sand and water until I feel a warm hand squeeze my shoulder and a waft of hot, male perspiration fills my nostrils.

'Lunch?' His dimples appear and I wish I was having him for lunch. I suddenly feel ridiculously horny. I really hope I'm not about to start my period. It's not even that it's simply a total waste of my body's energy and time because all my eggs are basically coming out that way anyway, I just haven't got to grips with my moon cup yet.

#24 Help build a school in Thailand – me, the girl who NEVER gets her hands dirty
#25 Teach English in an orphanage and cook and clean and play

We stand at the trestle tables while all the children jostle towards us, huge grins on their faces, clutching their plates with both hands.

'Two scoops of vegetable rice each and a spring roll. Fried banana, the ones in the leaves for dessert,' Maggie tells me, passing me a spoon to serve with.

I scoop the rice while Will hands out the spring rolls and fried bananas. Teamwork. We don't have time to talk as there are about eighty hungry children to serve and then ourselves. I scoop and smile, he serves and gives the kids high-fives and affectionate hair ruffles.

I stop and look at him, really look at him. He's so confident in himself, no bravado, or male ultra-ego – secure in his own skin. Comfortable with what he's doing with his life, what his role in the world is.

'Right, shall we grab ourselves some lunch?' Finally, a break. I love it here, I really do, but it's hard work. Especially all that lugging of cement in the mornings but it's helping to burn off my holiday diet of beer and noodles so I can't complain.

We take our portions and sit under a tree in the playground.

'Why do you always eat the fried banana first?' Will asks me.

'It's so delicious,' I say, buttery, hot banana rolling round my mouth. 'Sorry,' I add, gesticulating towards my lips, knowing that speaking with your mouth full is rude. 'And I like it hot, I hate food that's supposed to be hot turning cold.'

'It *is* delicious, isn't it? I tried making it myself once, but the banana turned out all sloppy and not crisp.'

'It wouldn't be the same anyway. There's something about eating hot, fried, fresh banana grown on these trees, out of palm leaves off these exact trees.' I point around at the corresponding foliage.

'True. Why is nothing on holiday or abroad, the same as real life?'

'It's like the world gives you a chance to live in your own fairy tale for a few weeks each year.' And then slaps you in the face with reality – hard. I suddenly think about Moira and shake my head to stop the impending nightmare.

I finish my fried banana and notice that Will has stopped eating his vegetable rice and started eating his fried banana instead.

'Ok, if you could live out a fairy tale in real life, which one would it be?' Will asks me.

I laugh. 'Ok, you need to let me think; I haven't read a fairy tale for years.'

'I can help – you've got your Disney classics, *Beauty and the Beast*, *Cinderella*, *Sleeping Beauty*.' He pauses, '*Snow White*!' he exclaims. 'That was actually one of my favourites – don't tell the lads.' He winks. '*Puss in Boots* or the Grimms' ones: *Rumpelstiltskin, Rapunzel, Hansel and Gretel, Red Riding Hood.*'

'How do you know so many fairy tales?' I find it attractive, and I don't know why. I hear Harry's words in my head – *you have questionable taste in men.*

'I work in a school, not that they can all understand them yet but I'm trying. I act them out to make them laugh.' He grins, flashing his dimples.

'I can't even remember the plots. I used to love the Disney ones when I was younger. My brothers hated me watching them; they liked to watch *Teenage Mutant Ninja Turtles* or *Pinky and the Brain.* So, I used to watch *Sleeping Beauty* and *Cinderella* on the video player at night in my room so I could go to sleep,' I reply, reminiscing how I used to watch them every night until I was about sixteen, waiting for my prince. 'I always loved Belle in *Beauty and the Beast* but I know, in my heart of hearts, I'd probably be too short-sighted to fall in love with a beast.' Harry's words in my head again – *judge yourself for once.*

'That's very honest.' He pauses. 'I'd probably go for *Hansel and Gretel,* because even though it's not meant to be desirable, I've always fancied living in a gingerbread house. Not that it would serve its purpose of a liveable structure very well, but it's every child's dream.' He laughs.

'No, one drop of rain and the whole thing would start to dissolve!' I think about streaming rivers of royal icing and a soggy roof falling in. 'None of the fairy tales are really that nice, are they? They're all a bit dark and scary or something horrible has to happen first before it can turn out good.' I think about it; none of them are all gold glitter and unicorns. It's always an outcast or a dead mother, a wicked witch – all the horrors.

'That's life though, isn't it? Nothing's shiny and perfect all the time and sometimes you need to experience something bad to motivate yourself further.'

'Not all the time. Sometimes things just stay bad.'

'I think you always have the ability to change your life, to be good. In some way or another, if you have enough will-power.' Will finishes his fried banana and goes back to his vegetable rice.

'Not for everyone. Some people might go around waiting for their prince to take them into a new realm, but there really isn't anyone there.'

'You're getting a bit dark now, aren't you?' He nudges me. 'If you're looking for your prince, then you're already halfway there.'

'Halfway to what?' I ask, confused.

'To looking for change, to building a better life. I think the prince is a metaphor for seeing the light of change.'

'But why can't you just have a perfect life?' It must exist for some people, surely.

'What even is perfect? It doesn't exist. The lives you think are perfect won't be for the person that's living them. It's never the case.'

'What, even those people that have everything, the smiling children, gorgeous partner, country house, money?' I think about all those people that fill my Instagram page, the tribe I once thought I was in.

'People always strive for more. They might be unhappy at work, have a gambling addiction, suffer with depression – you can't see what you can't see. Most people don't tell you what's wrong with them, they only tell you the good things about their lives, that's how humanity works.'

'Even you?' I turn and smile.

'Even me.' He rolls his eyes to the sky. 'If you'd seen me before, doing the daily grind in my suit. I had money, friends, I went out on the weekend. But it wasn't me. I wanted something more. I always thought money would make me happy, but it doesn't really. Now, you might think I have nothing, but I probably have more than I ever had. Without going all philosophical on you.' He laughs. 'I feel comfortable, happy, my life has meaning.'

'And what about me? What do you think of me from the outside?' I am interested. I'm not fishing for compliments, I want to know what he sees, really sees when he looks at me.

'I see a woman who's naturally beautiful, intelligent, but it seems like she's lived a life for other people and never really for herself. I see the way you look at the children when they smile at you, it's the same way I do. They've unearthed a happiness that you didn't know you had. And you think it's weird, because how can you have been searching for something you didn't know you were looking for? And then this small person, with no real life-experience yet somehow more than you've ever had, has managed to find it for you.'

Will takes a spoonful of rice and sips his water.

How can he be so spot on? They do make me feel like my life has meaning. It's the emotional release I always imagined I'd have when I gave birth, but I've done nothing of the sort; I'm just out here sharing their life.

I always thought I was this corporate, strait-laced, boring woman but I've started to realise there's more to me.

27

'Seffy, Maggie – we need to get this roof on before the storm sets in. The left side isn't looking as strong as the right, and I'm worried it's not going to hold in substantial wind and rain.' Will looks concerned, anguish in his eyes. 'Have either of you witnessed a storm in the jungle before?'

We both shake our heads.

'Well . . .' Will continues. 'It's rain like you've never seen. All this . . .' he points around him, 'will be like a river. It happens all the time so it's nothing to majorly worry about, I just don't want all our hard work to go to waste.'

We set to work, lugging huge bags of sand from one side to the other, lifting breeze blocks, tiles. There's a group of volunteers from a group called TravelAway and then a group of local Thai men who help us with the structural integrity of the building. But we all pull our weight, equally. No one's job is more superior than the other.

My arms feel like they are about to drop off. I've been holding the left corner of the building up with Maggie while two of the men secure it to the roof. I've realised that I'm mainly a dogsbody in this situation. Clearly, I have no building skills whatsoever, no experience in anything other than tap-tap-tapping away at a laptop all day. But I'm enjoying *trying* to be helpful because it's made me realise how lazy I really am.

I'm exhausted, covered in dirt from head to toe, I smell of stale sweat, my hair's all frizzy, I don't even know where I put my make-up bag because I haven't touched it in weeks, but I'm happy.

I high-five the local builders, who smile encouragingly at us.

I've seen them rebuild the walls I tried my hands at, so I'm pleased to actually be helping them this time, not creating more work.

Suddenly, there are shouts from the builders, and they're pointing at the sky.

'The storm's coming in!' Will shouts. 'We haven't got much time. Seffy, Maggie, you're going to have to get that tarpaulin and help them secure it. And we need bricks, loads of bricks.'

Maggie and I run from left to right, lugging breezeblocks, holding wheelbarrows of cement, pinning tarpaulin. Doing everything we physically can.

My body feels broken; this is real hard work. It's so physically demanding; it's impacting me mentally.

'Fuck, Maggie, I don't think I can do this anymore. My back is killing me, I feel like I've lost both my forearms. My hands.' I look down at them, grazed, my nails all chipped, sores burning on my palms.

'I know, me too. I don't know how everyone's doing it. I'm thinking I might go home; I'm not cut out for this.'

If I go and Maggie goes then who will help Will? We'll be letting everyone down. Will, the children, ourselves. I don't think I could bear to see the dimples in Will's face fade.

'No, you're staying, we're in this together!' I grab both her hands; they feel rough like mine, real workman's hands. 'There's not much longer to go and then think what we will have accomplished.'

We finish the roof, just as the first droplets of rain fall.

'Seffy, you're my fucking rock,' Maggie says, putting her sweaty arm round my shoulders. 'I'd be on the first flight back to Florida if it weren't for you.'

'Seffy, Maggie – I cannot thank you enough!' Will exclaims as we all stand back, admiring our handiwork. 'It means so much to everyone here.'

I always thought my body was broken but it's not. I'm strong. I pushed myself to near breaking-point and I'm still here. Strong as a fucking ox.

I want to see it through. I want to finish the school once the storm's passed.

'Hello, boys and girls.' I wave to the class, pointing at Sajja to indicate 'boys' and Hathai for 'girls'. Both Sajja and Hathai wave back, smiling.

I know you shouldn't have favourites, but they are mine. Hathai loves to paint and I enjoy Sajja's cheeky side.

'Today, we are going to draw ourselves.' Before I even think about it, I draw a stick woman on the board and point to myself. We look nothing like each other: she's been imprisoned by the male psyche for too long, she's only allowed to wear a short, sticky-out cocktail dress and her mid-length hair has to be perfectly coiffed to bounce around her shoulders, like in 1960s *Bewitched*. I wear trousers and my hair is tied up into a bun.

I hand out paper and crayons and the children, aged between six and eight, draw pictures of themselves. It's those deranged Picasso interpretations of faces and bodies again but I understand why parents love them.

I go to the board, holding my piece of chalk.

'Now, we're going to add eyes.' I draw two little dots on the board where my eyes should be, point to my own on my real-life face and repeat, 'eyes'. The children copy and draw two little dots. We go through the details of the face, hair, clothes and finally the surroundings.

'Now, let's try and write our names.'

The children start trying to copy out their own name from the little paper plaque on their desks. It's weird; these children might actually have had two names, but they'd never know. They were all named at the orphanage when they arrived. It's strange to think that there may be a part of your life of which you have no memories, no pictures, no keepsakes. These children technically don't and never will know their own name.

Sajja walks up to my desk and gives me his drawing and clasps his hands together.

'Present,' he says, smiling.

'Thank you,' I reply, feeling a little shiver run down my spine. When you have nothing, like these children, it really means a lot.

A dozen more children follow behind Sajja and leave their drawing on my desk. How could I ever throw these away? I'm going to keep them and when I get a house, I'll frame them and hang them in the hallway.

I hug each of them, and some of them give me a kiss on the cheek. I don't know how I'll ever leave this place. How can I go from one place of work where I get given presents, hugs, kisses and I can see the thanks in their eyes, hear it in the few words they speak, to a grey, soulless office where I get barked at by a deranged hooligan? I loved my job, I felt important, proud of where I'd got to, a woman in a man's world, making it work for her. But I'm not immune to Moira's words. I'd like a nicer boss, wouldn't everyone?

'Shall we play duck, duck, goose?' I ask the children who squeal, push their chairs out from under their desks and jump out of the window onto the field amid the pouring rain.

I'm jittery just thinking about showing the children the new playroom and library once we've finished building it.

'Do you want another beer?' Will asks Maggie and me before going up to the little fridge in the kitchen.

We're all sitting outside in a makeshift seating area, on bamboo seats and colourful mats, listening to the natural music of the jungle mixed in with the beats of commercialisation.

'What do you do, back home?' I ask Maggie as Will takes the tops off the bottles of Asahi. It's odd, one of the first questions you normally ask people is what their job is, but not here. You forget sometimes about your normal life.

'I work in this fintech start-up, it's finance for eco-friendly energy companies. I love it,' she replies.

'That's cool.' Will's eyes widen. 'How did you get the time off?'

'You get unlimited holiday and can work from anywhere sixty days a year, so I'm kind of doing a mixture.'

'Unlimited holiday?' I scoff. Moira would choke on her heavily caffeinated coffee at such absurdity.

'It's weird, once they give you it, you don't really take it. I bet people still have the usual twenty-five to thirty days, give or take. Maybe more if they have a wedding or something.'

'I guess it's that thing, isn't it, once you get the freedom you don't really take it,' Will says, to which Maggie nods in agreement. 'What about you, Seffy?'

'I work in Prime Finance at an investment bank. I barely get any holiday and am often chained to my desk, so the total opposite of you, Maggie!'

'Do you enjoy it?' Will asks me in a way that tells me he already knows my answer.

'Yes and no,' I respond, thinking about it. 'I do enjoy being busy and my work, but I hate my boss, and I hate not having the freedom to do more of what I enjoy.'

'You know nearly everyone hates bankers?' Maggie says, laughing.

'I know.' I laugh back.

'It's all old men in suits making shit loads of cash, isn't it?' Will tilts his head back, grinning, perhaps mocking his own past.

'I mean, you're not wrong about that part,' I say, twinging at the jokes Harry and I used to make about the Jeffs. I wish we were still friends.

'Women can do it too though, clearly,' Maggie says, pointing to me. 'The world's changing, you know.'

'I'm one of the only women in my office and I like that fact. I'm doing my bit for women, being senior in an industry that was previously all men. I mean it basically still is, but you know.'

'I couldn't stand it at my previous work,' Maggie says, her voice suddenly taking on a new tone. 'It was all men there, and everyone got promoted but me, so I moved. A less corporate structure, more freedom, one where you get promoted because of hard work and I love it.'

'I hope you don't hate me because I'm a man,' Will jokes. 'But I get it, it is unfortunately still like that in so many industries. I left my job because I hated the corporate structure, the pressure to be successful. I wanted to do something for me. Now I've left that world, I don't think I could ever go back. I'll probably travel forever.'

'I used to think it was all men working, women leaving to have babies and then staying at home. My mum was sooooooo old-fashioned in her thoughts.' Maggie shakes her head disapprovingly. 'She'd say things like, "you won't be working forever darling, wait till you have kids".'

'Do you want them?' I ask her.

'I don't know. Maybe, one day. I like my career; I love it, in fact. I like my life; I feel like I'm just finding myself. I want to do more things like this, you know.' She waves her hands around where we're sitting. 'And you can't do this when you have children, not for a few years anyway.'

'Do you ever worry it will be too late?'

'Hmmm, yes and no. There are so many options now for women; we're working later and later and that's a good thing! I might decide not to have them, or I could try IVF, surrogacy, adoption. I feel like there doesn't need to be a *timeline* anymore; that way of thinking is just so outdated.' She sips on her beer, totally oblivious to how important her words are to me.

Nine Months No Baby

Dearest Elpis, Goddess of Hope, please can you help me where your ugly sisters can't?

Since I had that conversation with Dr Cartwright, I've felt deflated. Hopeless. Useless. I don't care about anything anymore. Everything is out of my control. My body has failed me. It's broken. I'm broken. I'm nothing. A slug. Not strong enough to even have a backbone.

I want Luke to be my partner; he says we're in it together, but he hasn't been told he's infertile, only me. Why should he have to go through all the treatments, tests, doctor's visits because of me?

He said, 'I can't believe how much you've done without me, I thought we told each other everything?'

'You made me feel like I couldn't tell you,' I replied, even though that's not strictly true. He didn't make me feel like I couldn't tell him, I felt embarrassed too. Cringing at my own worries in case they were unwarranted. Fucking myself over every way I can.

He looked sad when I told him that. Hurt that his wife is getting further and further removed from him but he didn't say anything else.

I don't know if I'm imagining it, but I feel Luke looks at me differently. Like something about me disgusts him. There's nothing sexier than a fertile woman. Luke hasn't said that, of course he hasn't, I know it's in my head. Sometimes, what's omitted says more than the words itself. The way it's just totally normal and fine to ask someone, 'So, when are you having children?' rather than, 'Can you have children?' The way those people who decide to spend their lives without children are silently judged by mothers, fathers, grandmothers, grandfathers as being selfish. No one asks them if it was because they couldn't, or maybe they just didn't want to sacrifice their lives, but no one does them the courtesy of asking.

It's as if everyone around me, people that I know, friends, family, even strangers, suddenly have a vendetta against me. They want to make me hurt. More and more women around me are getting pregnant. The tube is filled with 'Baby on Board' badges like I've accidentally stumbled across some mothers-to-be commuting convention. It's a constant reminder that life's not fair. It's like I'm trapped in the pillory, with baby bonnets and booties being thrown at me. A mockery.

I suddenly feel lonely, too. I don't know who to speak to. I don't know who would understand. I feel so inferior. No one knew how desperately I wanted a baby so how would they know how much this hurts? There are other ways to get pregnant, to have children but it's not the same for me. Luke doesn't seem too bothered. He thinks it will all be fine in the end, which maybe it will, maybe it won't, but it's out of my control.

I put on this mask for outsiders, one that smiles and has perfect hair, perfect make-up. But when I come home and shut the door, I cry. The mask comes off and I'm desperately sad. If I had cancer, people would feel sorry for me, really sorry for me. There would be support groups, counselling sessions, helplines, adverts on television to encourage sympathy. People would understand, they would know the heartache, the trauma, the onset of depression that is associated when you come to terms with something so life changing. They would be supportive, I'd get time off work, be assigned bed rest. Not with infertility.

Dr Cartwright handed me a leaflet and closed the door. I'm alone. More alone than I've ever felt, yet I have people all around me. A husband, even.

Luke researched the best IVF clinic in London and booked it straight away. He's not usually so impulsive but I think he could see from my face that I need it to happen quick. It's the only way I can function. Focus my attention.

I had my consultation, then I waited. The first thing they had to do was suppress my natural menstrual cycle. I've seen enough unwanted blood over the last nine months, so to be honest, it was welcome. I had to inject myself daily for ten days and visit the IVF clinic for vaginal ultrasounds and blood tests.

It's not that Luke and I have secrets or we're prudes, but I prefer him seeing me as this goddess-like woman, one he'll continue to desire, so he'll never leave me like my dad left my mum. I like him not knowing that I have hairy legs or regular bowel movements. The injections must go in my bum. As I lie there on the bed with my dress pulled up over my left bum cheek (we alternate every day because the bruising gets too much), I'm reminded of how little sexuality is left in our relationship.

Usually, I'd be lying there coyly, finger in mouth, aroused for the start of some fantastic romp. Now, I'm lying here, nervous as he asks if I'm ok, 'three, two, one' and he sticks a needle in me as I flinch, lie back on the pillows and cry.

The injections are to encourage my ovaries to produce extra eggs, so I should be grateful. I'm not. My body already feels like a pin cushion; it's not even mine anymore, it's been donated to science without my consent.

I've never had to visit the hospital apart from the odd time I went to A&E because I'd pulled a muscle in my chest at Gym Box but thought I was having a heart attack. I feel like I have a terminal illness, attending these check-ups at the IVF clinic every other day. Clutching my notes, knowing exactly where to walk, where to wait, the names of the receptionists.

'I've got quite a few urgent hospital appointments coming up over the next month,' I explain, slightly on edge, to Moira. There's no way I'm telling her what's going on, she's

not the sympathetic type; she'd probably throw an infertility party.

Her eyes jump over her glasses, and I can see them giving me a dressing-down. A full body search, with them landing on my abdomen.

'Ensure you make up the time,' she replies, her eyes resting back on the screen of her laptop.

'Will do.' I turn to leave her office.

'And where's that pitch for the *JJ* Beam account? I needed that yesterday.'

Fuck, my mind's been elsewhere.

'No problem, I'll have it to you by the end of the day.' I go to the toilet and cry because I know there's no way I'll ever have the pitch deck done, not even if I work through the night.

My emotions are all over the place. One minute I'm feeling ecstatic, thankful to science that I even have the option for IVF, the next I'm banging my fists on the pillow, screaming and sobbing, 'why me?' I've got breakouts all over my chin and my stomach is suddenly so bloated it's a struggle to button my jeans up. The doctor said that would happen, due to the sudden influx of hormones; progesterone makes you bloat, the rise and fall of oestrogen gives you spots and lack of energy. It's ironic that I suddenly look pregnant when I'm very clearly not.

We've stopped having sex, Luke and I. Total abstinence. I'm not really in the mood. I don't know if Luke is or not, but he hasn't pressured me either. I think he's realised that all talk about vaginas, penises and anything sexual is well and truly on the blacklist until we come out the other side. He's probably thankful that the conversation topics have changed.

After the ten days of pricking torment, I take a final medication to mature the eggs. In thirty-six hours, we will finally get to see the fruits of our labour.

I lie on the bed with my legs in stirrups and a blue tent-like cloth between me and my vagina. I look up to the blinding light of the ceiling and say a little prayer to anyone who'll listen.

The doctor touches my hand and injects something into the IV catheter and I'm out.

When I come round, I feel slightly groggy. The doctor explains to Luke that they successfully retrieved fifteen eggs, that these will be fertilised in the lab and then one or two embryos transferred to my uterus in about five days. That's it, back to the unknown. The waiting game. Torture. You're really dragging this out, Aph.

The doctor said it's not supposed to be painful but I'm in agony. I'm constipated, even more bloated, to the point of looking four months pregnant, cramping and spotting all over our new The White Company sheets.

I messaged Moira to tell her there had been some complications at the hospital and I'm having to stay at home. She sent my laptop via courier.

That's what I get. Injections, writhing pain, ovaries the size of meatballs. Luke got given fifteen minutes in a dark room, a couple of screaming college lesbians and a cup.

After four days my phone finally rings with the elusive Unknown Caller, the clinic telling us to come in tomorrow.

That's it, the embryos are placed in my womb, and I'm told to wait two weeks before taking a pregnancy test. Luke squeezes my hand and suggests we go out for a greasy pizza to celebrate but I'd prefer to curl up in bed. Alone.

I told the doctor about the pain I've been experiencing, and she said the fluid in my fallopian tubes was particularly toxic, and everything looked very swollen. She suggested that if this round of IVF isn't successful, they will remove my tubes.

Wow. How to feel even more like a science experiment. All my hope of future natural procreation gone. I know what people would say: but you can still have a surrogate, you can still adopt. You're lucky there are so many options. But I don't want options, I want to have a baby myself. How can you be lucky when it's all going wrong?

I've been treating myself like I'm encased in cotton wool the last two weeks. Knowing that a tiny part of myself and Luke, what I've been yearning for all this time, is garnering the strength it needs in my womb. Come on little baby, grow, grow. I've been eating fresh fruit and vegetables, calcium-rich yoghurt – no caffeine's even passed my lips.

The date's been marked on the calendar with a large X and finally it's arrived. I feel nervous but I shouldn't. Nature's luck has been handed over to science and I should feel positive. Grateful, happy.

I haven't done a pregnancy test for over a month; it almost feels novel. I pull down my pyjama shorts and let them lie in a heap on the bathroom floor. I cock my right leg slightly out to the side of the toilet basin, pull the blue lid off the stick and place it on the windowsill next to me. I hold the stick between my thumb and forefinger and dangle it between my legs. I release and the urine stream splashes into the basin and over the litmus paper. After five seconds I pull the stick out, give it a little shake and watch as my urine seeps up and across the window. The blue lid clicks back into place and I lay it horizontally on the sill. I press start on my three-minute timer, wipe, pull my shorts up and slowly walk to the sink to wash my hands and do a mini-facial to pass the time.

Briiiiiiiiiiiiiiiiiing!

The timer frightens me. I'm all nerves. I close my eyes as I pick up the stick before flashing them open.

Nothing.

Nothing.

I wait another minute.

Nothing.

Then another.

Nothing.

This cannot be true.

I pull out another test from my stash in the wicker basket and repeat the procedure.

Three minutes.

Nothing.

Five minutes.

Nothing.

I feel tears stream down my face.

I hastily unwrap another test.

Luke bangs on the door.

'Seffy?' His voice is worried, pressing, begging me to answer.

'Everything ok in there?' Urgency drips off every word.

'Seffy – let me in.' His voice is sharp yet soft. This isn't a request.

I unlock the door. Luke looks at me, red-faced, blotchy, tears streaming down. He looks at the tests, paper and boxes littering the bathroom floor. It's a massacre of nothingness.

'It hasn't worked,' I sob. 'It hasn't fucking worked.' And I fall in a broken heap on the bathroom floor.

I can't remember what Luke did because all I felt was alone.

So, Elpis, this is why I'm reaching out to you. I have another round scheduled for next month, please give me something to live for. Please give me hope.

Seffy xxx

Four Months Until Thirty

28

The realisation that soon I'll be back on London soil, in my one-bed flat with the teal velvet sofa I bought because Luke never liked it, is setting in. I'll have Moira marking her territory on my entire existence again like a dog pissing round the perimeter of the park.

I came on this trip for a reason, to find out who the real Seffy is. The one hidden under a damaged childhood, the victim of imperfect genetics and personality traits she cannot escape. The bucket list is more like a journey to becoming who I already was. A manifestation of my future.

#26 Stop thinking about myself
#27 Realise there's more to life than an endless strive to perfection

I don't think I've ever tried this hard in my entire life.

I've been waking up at 5.00 a.m. before Maggie and Will and going outside to work with th e builders. They even make me a coffee now.

They do the building, I put breezeblocks in wheelbarrows and do painting. I want to be helpful; I want to achieve something. I'm building something that's for other people, but the accomplishment is for myself. To finish something that I find hard, that I could so easily walk away from is everything for me. It's the final chapter in my sabbatical. It shows me I am not broken.

We thought it would be finished a few days ago, but it's taken longer than expected. I never want to see another paintbrush again.

'Wow, Maggie, that's incredible!' I say as she puts the finishing touches to her mural.

'Thank you! It's nice to make use of my creative side.' She adds another touch of green to the grass and admires her work.

'I'm so excited to unveil this to the children,' Will says, grinning. He's so attractive but I really need to stop basing my life around men.

'I know, I can't wait,' I say, clasping my hands together with glee.

I've become quite pally with a couple of the builders. They laughed at me at first because I definitely came across as a girl who's never really got her hands dirty. I cried when my nail broke, but then I laughed about it afterwards because who wouldn't?

I show interest in their work because I want to make my time useful. I don't want to shoddily place bricks on top of one another just for them to knock it down and rebuild. I don't want to be so set on doing something for myself but just be a total nuisance to them.

Anur, the youngest builder, has been helping me. He showed me how to lay the cement on top of the bricks properly, how to make them even and smooth down the sides. It took me a few tries but now he nods and claps his hands so I'm pretty sure I'm doing it right.

'I think we're done!' Will exclaims, wiping paint off his forehead.

'I think so too,' I say, looking round the building. Something inside me is starting to feel a bit sad. I thought I'd feel better about it.

Anur looks at me and smiles, offering me a Coke and we do a little celebratory cheer.

The building is finished: murals on the walls, colourful paint, seating and toilet area. It's yet to be filled with books and toys but it's perfect.

I sit down, exhausted, dirty and exhilarated. If my body was broken, I'd never have been able to do this. The children spurred me on. They gave me the power, the persuasion to push myself beyond all limits.

All the roles I tell myself I must abide by back home didn't exist. The old Seffy could never have done this.

I made infertility the end of everything, as if it physically smashed my body into smithereens. As if it made me weak, but maybe it has made me stronger. That word took me to the ends of the earth and somehow the kindness of strangers, who don't even know the power of their presence, has brought me back again.

How toxic that I was on this search for a cure. I'm my own person, different to other people. I don't need a cure. I need life.

I want to tell my friends about what I've done. Share my happiness with someone but now I've finished the building, it's probably time for me to go home. I feel so alone again.

I think about how proud Luke would be of me. Harry too.

I can't leave our friendship like this after everything we've been through. I can't walk away from something so good again.

Hey.
Erm, I don't really know what to say and I've never been stuck for words around you.
I'm sorry, so sorry for how I've acted. Are you ok? I'm guessing you've had it by now. I hope you're feeling ok, I've heard it's quite painful too. Can we meet when I get home? I really am sorry, I've been so selfish, thoughtless. I want to explain. It won't come across in the right way over message and you deserve more than a WhatsApp. Love you xxx

As I stand up to speak to Maggie and Will, Anur walks over to me.

'*Kop kun ka*,' I say to him, smiling. That's the only word I know in Thai so I finish it by gesticulating around and putting my hand on my heart. I wonder how he'll interpret the word because he can't possibly know all that I'm thanking him for, much more than teaching me how to lay bricks.

'Thank you, Seffy,' Anur replies and gives me a hug.

I feel my breathing quicken and tears brewing. I taught him how to say 'thank you', and he taught me how to respond in Thai. I don't want to say goodbye to our friendship, I don't want to leave behind my routine or my new friends.

That's what's making me sad, saying goodbye to the one thing I'm actually proud of.

I don't want to go home.

29

Harry was right to tell me to make the most of my travels all those months ago. It's been a week-long Groundhog Day since I returned to London, and I haven't even gone back to work yet.

I've been trying to finish my bucket list, to make my time in the flat at least productive and to prevent the onslaught of anxiety of that first return-to-work day. Finally, I completed my list of ten good books – Tish was right, *The Handmaid's Tale* is an important read albeit fucking terrifying. And I decided to swap out thirty pelvic floors a day because the tightness of my vagina really isn't number one on my priority list right now, and binge-watch the world's greatest movies instead. Sometimes I even eat a pizza and continue my love of iced liquid fat.

When I was travelling, the early-rise, soulless tube journey, mundane chicken salad lunch and black americanos were a distant memory. The old commute almost seemed novel. However, since I returned, it's like those activities were so ingrained in me that my body went on autopilot as soon as I stepped off the plane onto British tarmac.

The sound of the tube doors hissing open, a sort of weird grey carpet laid out before me, welcoming me back into my undistinguished carriage. The worst version of *Cinderella*, the one Disney doesn't want you to watch. There's no Prince Charming waiting for me either, just a load of slugs in suits, some grey, some navy, some pinstripe, reading papers, drinking coffee. Silence. Apart from the rattle of the carriages as the tube hurtles down the track before abruptly coming to a stop; enough for me to slightly stumble in my heels, forgetting to stand legs slightly apart for balance.

I stop by *Notes* coffee on the way in to work, exactly like I did every day, a mere seven months ago. The grinding of coffee fills my nostrils and my ears, the hissing of hot steam, ripping of milk cartons, beeping of payments and the music of the orders – *one double shot Columbian espresso with a soy-milk top, one latte extra shot sugar free syrup, one cappuccino – hold on the chocolate.* And mine – *double shot americano* because, calories. After all the changes I made halfway around the world, it really is like I've never left. Nothing's changed. London's been stuck in a time warp. Life continues, the ratrace never stops, you keep running on that hamster wheel at full pelt because it won't slow down to give you a break. It hasn't stopped and it hasn't changed.

I stand in the atrium of the office. A glass cage, a greenhouse, except we're not plants, we're people. The morning light streams through, but even the sun can't make grey and stainless steel the cacophony of colour I experienced in India.

I take a deep breath, scan my pass and lift number two slides open its doors, welcoming me back to my home with beckoning, metallic arms and a frustrated man who seems to have lost his dry-cleaning – 'Ten shirts, I said TEN shirts and two suits – what am I supposed to wear to the office now . . . JEANS?' Imagine being told to wear a long red dress, a white cap and live in Gilead, I think to myself. Jeans are nice.

I see Moira, hunched over her screens as usual in her own miniature glass cage, like a workplace muzzle to keep us all safe. I raise my hand in a sort of wave, silently saying, *hi, how are you?/it's been a long time/how have things been at work?* but I might as well have been welcoming myself back to the four walls.

A few people look up from their desks, eyes flicking over glasses and screens in my direction, for a second wondering who the new girl is, then remembering I work here.

I was half-expecting someone to pop by my desk and ask me how my trip was, tell me I inspired them to do the same, ask me what Hong Kong, India and Thailand were really like. But I received nothing.

Briiiiiiiiinnggggggggg

My back jerks like I've been electrocuted.

'Hello?' I question my caller. It's rhetorical.

'Nice of you to join us . . . Seff.' Her malice tone making my phone melt into my hand. My confidence dissipating.

'Ha, yeah,' I laugh, even though it's anything but funny.

'We've been busy, really FUCKING busy and I need you to get your head out of the sand and back into the game. Pronto. You got it?'

As if I expected anything less. You know, like a day of leisurely scrolling through the two thousand plus emails I've received while I've been away.

'No problem.' Except it is a problem. 'Anything in particular you'd like me to look at first?' I ask, hoping my fake smile exudes willingness down the phone line – or that she can see it from her office all but two metres away.

'ALL OF IT! I'm very fucking busy, Seff, and I won't be letting anyone else go on a sabbatical for a long fucking time. It's been a fucking shit show, and don't let me get started on Elliot. He's probably splashing round the baby pool right now with his other inept cronies.'

She slams the phone down.

I take a breath and click onto my emails.

Fifty emails in, I realise poor Elliot's been let go. God, he must have really riled Moira. I should be pleased that even though she hasn't asked me about my holiday or made anything about my first morning back pleasurable, I know she values me. Otherwise, I wouldn't be here. From now on, I'll think of every phone call as a big, long snog from the witch herself.

Every so often, my mind takes a trip back to Ko Pha-Ngan, fresh, sweet pineapple juice on the beach, the slapping of waves, the gentle thud of coconuts dropping to the sand, then I hear a *Brinnnnnnnggggggggg* from someone's desk and I'm brought back to a sky-high Canary Wharf office block where fun isn't even a figment of the imagination.

I feel different.

I used to be able to concentrate, and I loved the rat race. Eager to show my worth through staying late and receiving a metaphorical trophy for sending the most emails in a day. Trying to make work my baby because I didn't have an off-spring made of my own flesh and blood. Now, oh I don't know, have I finally realised that there's more to life? There's a whole world out there that likes me for me; it doesn't matter about what is or isn't happening in my womb or what's happened in my past. I made new friends because people liked me.

Harry. Oh, Harry. My best friend in the world and I ruined it all because I was jealous.

I've been thinking about men too.

I'll be back on the dating sites, having fancy dinners in dark, moody west London restaurants and bars, kicking back my stilettos and manoeuvring the slit in my pencil skirt to show the perfect amount of leg. Sucking my straw provocatively, metaphorically writing the invitation back to my flat before I never see them again. Sigh. Dating is such a ball ache. There's no rush; I have all the time in the world.

Moira doesn't speak to me for the rest of the day. Well, not in the usual way you'd expect someone to open their mouth while looking at you, and words come out. She emails constantly as if she's suddenly reticent. It's like she never wants me to reach the bottom of my workload; she sends utterly pointless emails, some with no content, only a title;

YOU NEARLY FINISHED? I CAN'T RUN THIS
ACCOUNT SOLO.
I NEED YOU TO EMAIL CARLOS ABOUT THE HEX
MANDATE
WHERE ARE YOU??? I HAVE A BRIEF THAT NEEDS
BRIEFING!!!

Finally, FINALLY, I can call it a day. Thank the bloody Lord. Right now, there's nothing I want more than to jump into bed with a reduced fat Marks and Spencer's meal for one. I want to think about finishing my bucket list. I don't want to stop my journey simply because I've arrived home.

I say good night to my laptop, allowing it to fall into a welcome slumber, pick up my bag, thankful that there are no stairs to descend and I can be whizzed to ground level like in *Charlie and the Chocolate Factory*. Adults can be children too.

Canary Wharf always looks better in the evening, at dusk – it disguises the grey. The twinkling lights of restaurants, bars and offices make it feel almost festive.

'Seffy?'

The voice startles me. Soft, friendly, but followed by a chaser of nerves.

I turn around.

'Harry?' Why would she be here?

'What the fuck have you been doing up there? I've been freezing my labia off out here; it's almost eight. I thought normal people finish at six?' She grins wildly.

'Ha, you know Moira.' I smile timidly back, not knowing what this is.

'Can we get a drink? I've been meaning to talk to you.'

We walk in silence for a few metres until we reach the nearest bar.

'How did you know I was back?' I ask, hovering my hand over the door handle.

'Instagram, babes – *Ta ra Thailand, hello home* – you really need to think about your cyber security if you don't want people to know your whereabouts.' She's right, she's always right.

I buy us one Pinot and one Corona, to which Harry explains that she would have a turbo (Corona with a shot of vodka) but it's not the time or the place.

We take a sip, softening the tongues, loosening the vowels and consonants before I finally have the courage to pipe up.

'I'm sorry, Harry. I really am. Everything you said to me, you were right you know.'

'No, *I'm* sorry. I didn't want to reply on WhatsApp because it felt off. We were really horrible to each other, and I needed you, I really did.' Tears well in her eyes. How can I have let her go through something like this alone!

I stand up from my seat and rush to hug her. 'I've been so selfish, Harry. All I used to think about was myself and how I was being portrayed, what people thought of me. I never spared a thought for anyone else. How can you have ever been friends with someone like me?'

'I'm not going to lie; I was seriously upset and angry with you, but I understand why you found it so difficult.' Harry fiddles with the label on her bottle. 'You can be VERY judgemental sometimes. I can handle it because I've known you for so long, but you aren't really like that, I know you're not. What I needed was someone to say they'd support me no matter what, just like you wanted Luke to say to you.' It's ironic because I feel like there was nothing Luke could have done at that point; I'd already made my decision.

I swallow hard – she's right. I fight back tears.

'I don't think I ever really understood what it's like to be told you can't have children,' Harry continues, seeing my eyes well. 'I realised when I got home that as much as I wanted you to say you'd support me no matter what, this was probably your nightmare. The day you'd been dreading since finding out your own news and you didn't really know how to act. Maybe you hadn't come to terms with everything just as I couldn't really come to terms with the fact that I wanted an abortion from the moment I found out. But I was lucky, in a way: I had a choice.'

'And I didn't understand how hard it must have been for you to make the decision – you did the right thing you know.' For the first time in a long time, Harry's eyes look all wet and we hold hands across the table. 'I shouldn't lord my opinions or feelings over other people when I really have no under-standing. It was ignorant of me and I'm sorry.' I think about Moira and the type of person she is and how I'd hate for people to think about me like that.

Harry sniffs slightly and wipes her eyes.

'It's weird, you told me about your struggles to get pregnant, but you never *really* told me anything. You didn't tell me how it made you feel, the heartache it caused, how hard it is to deal with.' She pauses, taking a sip of her beer. 'I only have some idea of what you might be going through now because we held a focus group, well, the cluster fuckers did for mums and their breakfast choice for their kids. You know, one of those stupid affairs where we shoehorn all of their answers and come up with the surprising result that our cereal must be best.' She grins, her eyes still slightly damp. I laugh. God, I've missed her. 'And one of the mums went off on a bit of a tangent and started talking about her journey with infertility and afterwards I asked her about it. It was strange; we really hit it off, went for a coffee, and I told her about you, our fight and she made me see what you might be going through.

What she went through. She said it's taken her years to live with it, not come to terms with it, because that's not really what happens. Find new ways to get what you want. I've got her number if you ever feel like talking. Well, she's featuring on this documentary, where they're asking women to talk about their journeys with infertility – they're looking for women between twenty-five and thirty-five.'

'Thanks Harry,' I croak. 'No one's ever spoken to me like that before. Told me what I want to hear, really want to hear. Told me that it's ok not to be ok. That I'm not stupid or a failure for not dealing with it. Thank you.' I squeeze her hand across the table. 'It's not all about me though; you went through an abortion. I'm so sorry. It must have been so difficult; I hope your mum was good to you? I don't want everything to be about me all the time; I don't want you ever to think you can't tell me something for fear of upsetting me. I don't want children or pregnancy or anything like that to be this elephant in the room. It's stupid for it to get between us.' I ignore the comment about the documentary for now; making-up with my best friend is more important to me.

'How do you feel though, Seffy? I know it's really hard. I realise now what you lost. I can understand a fraction of the torment you felt, the worry.'

'I think . . .' I pause. 'I think I need to have more balance in my life. You were right about me wanting to have a perfect life, and I did. But now I've realised, what even is perfect? I don't need to prove people wrong, or my genes wrong or work myself into the ground to have something I never really wanted in the first place. If I do, seriously, really want to have my own family I do have choices, just like you did. Difficult choices but we all have those. I can adopt, I could use a surrogate. But what I don't need to do is rush. I need to stay true to myself now.'

We chat some more. Harry tells me about the harrowing process she went through, but she knows she made the right decision. I know she did too, because there is such a thing as 'not the right time'.

Then Harry says something else.

'I saw that Luke broke up with his girlfriend on Instagram. After speaking to that lady, I thought some closure might do you both good.' She pauses. 'I told him that you were back, well, that you'd been away too, and I told him to email you, old school, because you blocked him on everything else. He seemed really keen to speak to you.'

I thought if I ever heard that Luke wanted to speak to me, see me again, panic would ensue, and I would end up a wreck. But I feel calm, collected, ready.

'You told him I blocked him? Omg Harry, that's so embarrassing.'

'Well, you did. Own it.'

'You're right, as per. Maybe closure's exactly what I need.' I smile back.

And like clockwork, my phone buzzes across the table with one new email in my inbox.

#28 Experience your biggest fear first-hand, come to terms with it, get over it and learn from it

30

You always want to look your best when you meet up with an ex. Not because you necessarily want them back, but because you want them to look at you and think, *fuck, I was lucky*. One time I was playing in my mother's room, dressing up in her clothes and heels and she stormed in and demanded I take off the sheer black tights that made your legs glossy, shading them in all the right places and the patent heels because, *they're the good ones, the ones I wear when I have to see your father*.

It took me ages to get ready. I was up early, mainly because I couldn't sleep. However calm I felt with Harry has totally dissipated now. I washed my hair, put a conditioning mask on, blow-dried it, used my curling tongs to make it fall in effortless waves. I dabbed concealer in all the right places and smoothed foundation over my skin to make it dewy. Light brushings of bronzer to contour my cheekbones and swathes of mascara to coat my lashes allowing them to move in perfect flutters. Finally, a dab of pale rose lipstick to make my lips stand out but not enough so it looks like I've *made an effort*.

I couldn't decide what to wear. I know a tight, bodycon dress and heels would work wonders for the jealousy aspect but I'd look out of place at 11.00 a.m. It could go the wrong way; Luke would think I want him back, which I don't. Do I? I have got butterflies thinking about seeing him again. In the end, I decided on some high-rise Levis, the ones he once said my bum looks good in and a chiffon blouse which could be provocative or smart, depending on angles.

Memories are flooding my consciousness. Memories of us, how we met, our marriage.

Things that I didn't even think were possible to remember. The tiny mole on his left hand, on the crevice between his thumb and forefinger. The way his left eyebrow was never quite aligned with his right when he smiled. The patch of hair above his bellybutton.

His scent.

His taste.

His voice.

His feelings.

His desires.

At one point in life, he was mine. All mine. I knew every inch of him, nothing was left to the imagination. Nothing was unknown between us.

Now it's like someone's taken over his body. I know everything about him visually, physically, but mentally he's a stranger.

Fuck, he's here.

He's looking for me.

He looks anxious. And gorgeous. He must have gone through the same thought process as me when he got dressed this morning. The washed-black straight leg jeans with the distressed knee that I bought him for his birthday, pair of suede camel Chelsea boots and a plain white T-shirt that shows he tried without trying all at the same time.

As I virtually undress him for old times' sake, we lock eyes, and he does the awkward hand-in-the-air-cross-between-a-stop-sign-and-a-hello and walks over. Head down. I look at my phone so I can look up when he's arrived as if we haven't just acknowledged each other a long ten seconds ago.

I'm pretending not to know him, so he feels like he doesn't know me either.

'Hey,' Luke says, smiling, his eyes wrinkling – he's happy to see me. I stand up and he puts an arm in the small of my back to give me a hug. I breathe in the familiar Aqua di Parma smell; the Italian citrus and rosemary top notes tell me he's not long since applied it. 'You look great, caught the sun I see.'

'If you mean I was kissed by the sun, you'd be correct.' I smile back. 'It's . . . err . . . nice to see you too.' We dated, fell in love, he proposed, we got married, we tried and failed to have a family, we divorced, but weirdly it's still nice to see him.

What am I saying? Of course it is. He's a part of my history, my story, he's part of me. My heart's pumping blood around my body in an effort to keep up with the speed of adrenaline being released. I can feel it in my chest, in my lungs, in my breath. He makes me feel woozy, on edge. I want to impress him.

Everything I thought I felt with Finn is amplified a thousand times. I want to kiss Luke, feel his lips on mine. Him to tell me everything's ok. To make me feel comfort in my own body. I want to show him I'm sexy again, confident. That what we once had isn't lost. Wear the remnants of his Aqua di Parma on my own skin.

But instead, I sit here, unknowing, not allowing an emotion to slip onto my face.

Fuck. The message. I really hope he didn't see it.

'I'll get us both a drink.' He gestures towards the empty table. 'We can't do this dry. A Pinot?'

'Yes please.'

Luke walks towards the bar to order our drinks. I'll have a Pinot, he'll have an ale of some sort, probably a Neck Oil. I can taste it on him already, after a night out, bready, malty, toffee sweetness.

What am I going to say? Surely, he'll speak first; he invited me here, he asked for this meet-up. We don't need to have an argument or tread over old ground; we both need closure. Maybe he's got something he needs to get off his chest.

Before I can get too deep into my thoughts, Luke walks back with the drinks and places them on the table before sitting down himself.

'Neck Oil?' I ask, pointing at his beer.

'You know me too well.' He sips his beer. It's ironic because I feel like I don't. Luke certainly doesn't know me right now. He wouldn't recognise me compared to a year ago.

'So . . . this is kind of weird. We're divorced, yet here we are sitting and having a drink together. Shouldn't we be arguing or something?' Luke grins that all-knowing smile. He's right, we can't sit here playing happy families forever.

'We never really argued before, it was only about, well, you know.' I see it flash before my eyes, the screaming, the crying, the hurt. Hour after hour sitting on the cold tiles of the bathroom floor, willing it all to end.

I take a large gulp of wine, cool, fresh, acidic and roll it around my mouth. Emotionless.

'It's nice to see you, Luke, it really is, but why? Why did you want to see me again?' I tilt my head on one side and stare into his eyes the way I used to. I look at his brown eyes and sandy blond hair and wonder how they could ever have belonged to the monster persona I created for him in my head. Did I make it all up? How his eyes sometimes looked like black holes to me, but they were never that, were they?

He swirls the Neck Oil around his mouth.

'I hate this, Seffy, I'm just going to dive straight in.' He takes another long sip, a contrast to what he's just said, like he wishes we could go back to the awkward small talk. 'I hate that we got divorced, I loved you. I think maybe I still do.' I stay silent. It's everything I've ever wanted to hear but I don't know what to say. Is it too broken? Like Harry said. How will I ever know? 'I never wanted the divorce, but you seemed

so set on it and I really didn't know what to do.' I want to
scream at my past self. Why did I walk away from everything
I ever really wanted in a person? But I know why. I was too
hurt, I didn't know what to do, I was scared of failure. I let
everything wind up so tight I had no idea how to untie it.

I never really allowed myself to remember how Luke
looked at me when I told him I wanted it all to end, but I can
see him now. His eyes wet, his head down, his face so filled
with sorrow it was like he'd never see happiness again. And
myself, angry, hurt, upset but so desperate to bring myself
down further I couldn't even deal with happiness anymore.

'Then why didn't you fight for me?' I rasp the words.
Surely he should have come back to me, begging me to try
again, declaring his love for me like he is now? 'What about
your new girlfriend or whoever?' I know they've broken up,
but he doesn't know what I know.

'I see you've still been making regular visits on my profile, even after you blocked me from yours.' His eyes twinkle,
like they do when we have banter. 'We broke up, it was never
really right, she was never you.' I know how he feels, how I felt
with Richard on the plane, with Finn – I was imagining Luke.
'I wanted to fight for you, but I didn't know what to do. I felt
you wanted to be alone, that the best thing for you was to not
be with me. Our relationship was in tatters, and you didn't
seem able or want to rebuild it. There was nothing I could say
anymore, Seffy. I'd told you over and over again how much I
loved you, how much I wanted to help you, how I'd support
you no matter what. But nothing sunk in, it was like you'd
decided to do it all alone, you didn't need me anymore.' He
takes another large gulp of beer. 'But now we've both had
a break, you've been off round the world and if I don't say
something now, then, it really might be gone forever.'

I really wasn't expecting any of this. I thought it was already
gone forever. I can see myself, crying on the bathroom floor,

hearing the taps from Luke on the door but choosing to ignore him. Lying in bed crying into my pillow, feeling Luke's arms curl through mine before I pushed him off. Cooking me meals that I wouldn't eat. Trying to love me so hard while I was desperate to hate him.

'That just seems like such a cop out. I *wanted* to fight for you, but you didn't let me.' It's true, I never really felt like he cared.

'I was a mess; I didn't want to be a failure.' I pause. Why am I acting like the old Seffy again? I need to be honest, like Luke is with me. Stop telling half-truths. Finally, I croak the words. 'I didn't want you to leave me like my dad left my mum, so I did it for you.' I had to hate you first, so I never knew what it felt like for you to hate me.

'I wanted to fight for you, Seffy, believe me. I hadn't really come to terms with your infertility either, but you wouldn't let me. I needed to deal with it in my own way. You were my wife, I was going to have children with you, it would be our family. I would do anything for you; if you didn't want children after it all, then I would have lived with that too.' He looks down at the table. 'I never would have left you; it was stupid of me not to fight for you at the time.'

'Why?' I sip my drink through pursed lips. 'Why didn't you say any of this before?' It's anger, upset, annoyance all rolled into one. How much time we've wasted hating and being upset, mourning our old lives.

'I don't know.' He puts his head in his hands. Those soft yet manly hands. Calluses from the gym, perfectly trimmed fingernails. 'I just don't know.'

'Are you crying?' I ask, reaching out to touch his hand. I'm crying, I know I am. This is what I always wanted, to be loved. To know I'm loved.

'I just don't know what happened between us. How did it all go so wrong? I'm sorry, Seffy. It all seemed so great and then suddenly it went sour. Now you're living your life, getting on with it, going travelling, getting promoted and I'm stuck here, without you. Lonely, divorced. You seem so different in yourself, happier even.'

'Ha, if you think it's all great for me then you'd be mistaken. I'm also lonely, divorced. I have to worry about the conversation I will inevitably have to have with that man I really like, deal with my fucked-up tubes. But no, it's all great for me.' I roll my eyes. 'If you've come back to me because you've not found anything better, then please, walk on.' I don't know why I've suddenly turned on him; maybe it's fear. My fragility coming into full force. How I always act when I'm too scared to let myself be open.

'Seffy.' He places his beer down on the table with force, so a little spray jumps out of the top. 'It's not about that. I've gone over and over this conversation in my head, I would never ask to meet you if I didn't mean it, we've been through way too much. I love you. I still love you. Why did you agree to meet me here today?' I've missed his frankness, the way he, like Harry, tells me everything I don't want to hear. He would never hurt me the way I hurt him. I can remember now how he'd say things and I'd twist them. Change the words in my head, and later his tone until it was everything I didn't want to hear. I'd tell myself he was a monster, a misogynistic pig.

'Honestly?'

'Honestly,' he confirms, looking me straight in the eye.

'I was intrigued to see what you had to say. I do still think about you, miss you, maybe even love you, I don't know. But I came here for closure. I need closure to move on, or at least I think I do.'

'I'm happy to look at all the options you want to. Be as patient as you need. Look at surrogates, adopt, anything. If you still want children?' Luke's hand lays outstretched on the table towards me. However much I tried to hate him I still love him, oh, so very much.

'We're divorced Luke, that chapter has passed. I can't put myself through that with you again.' It's tormenting me. What I've wanted is laid out on a plate for me, ready to devour. I'm scared, oh so scared that the worst time in my life will come back to haunt me again. My brain is toying with me, one minute wanting to push the glasses off the table and fall onto Luke's lips and the next wanting to throw the remnants of wine over him in a bid to act out again so there's no chance of further heartache.

'Seffy, you realise it was you who pushed me away over all those months. You wanted someone to blame, to hate, and that was me. The kindest thing I could do was let you go; I could see how much you were hurting. I tried to speak to you after you said you wanted a divorce, but you wouldn't let me. You changed your number, blocked me on Instagram, Face-book. Never replied to my emails or letters. We are divorced, yes, but we don't have to let some legal title stop us from changing our minds.' He holds my hands in his across the table, I squeeze them before pulling away. 'I feel that you made your diagnosis the end of everything. And now when I look at you, sitting here in front of me, I can see how much you've grown. You look different, like your mental health has transformed your physical health. I know that it must still hurt that you can't have children naturally, but it looks like you've found your zest for life again, like there's more to it. That options do exist.'

'Sorry.' I look down at the floor, and a single tear trickles down my left cheek.

'You don't need to be sorry, Seffy. Life is hard sometimes, none of us know how to deal with it. I'm sorry you felt so alone through it all. I'm sorry that we're sitting here now after all this time apart, not, oh I dunno, having a drink together reminiscing about some loose night out with Harry.' He grins but I can see tears in his eyes.

'But I am sorry. I couldn't deal with it. I wanted to hate someone who wasn't myself, it was easier. I hated myself so much, I needed to blame someone else. I wanted to hate you before you hated me because I just assumed that's what would happen.'

'I'd never hate you,' Luke whispers.

'I went on a self-sabotage mission. I feel I got so caught up in society's stereotypes, I put this ideal family on a golden pedestal. Everything I've ever done has been to fit in, to look good. The diagnosis, the divorce, they forced me to change, try new things and I like this new me. I've achieved so much, tried things I never would have done before. But I do miss us. I miss the safety net of coming home to you, what we had, what we wanted. I do love you, Luke, I know I do. I never stopped. I forced myself to hate you because it was easier than loving and losing you. But I feel like I lost all that once I had that first fertility test.'

'You never lost it,' Luke says softly. 'It's always been there; you're just taking a long time to find it again.' His eyes are twinkling now, his face illuminated by the love I have for him. I remember the way he'd let me cry on his shoulder, the way he'd stroke my hair, kiss my cheeks, wipe away tears. The way I used him like a doormat for my emotions.

'Sometimes I wish we'd never started trying,' I say glumly, looking at the table.

'No, you don't. I'm a strong believer that everything happens for a reason, you know that, even the bad stuff.'

'Everything I've ever done has been to conform. I was so rigid, with all my lists, so habitual. I still wish and pray and have a glimmer of hope that one day I could have my own children naturally. A miracle child that I've heard people talk about, but I'm more accepting of my diagnosis, more willing to adopt or look at surrogates. I was in this orphanage . . .' I smile to myself at the happy memories. 'I think about how

I can still give someone my love, share happiness, I can still be a good mum, just in a different way.'

'You'd be a great mother; I always knew you would.'

'What happens if we try, and it doesn't work, or the same thing happens again? It terrifies me. We've spent the last two years hating on each other, it's been a year apart. How can we go through all of that hate and upset and then waltz back into each other's lives and everything be fine again?'

'If we don't try then we'll never know. We know the worst things about each other now. If we still feel like this after the unimaginable, then surely there's a future?' His brown eyes sparkle, chestnut brown, layers upon layers of emotion.

'This has all come out of the blue for me. You've had time to think about what you were going to say, digest your own feelings. I want you to know that I do care about you, about us, our history but I simply don't know how I truly feel. There's no harm in us meeting again, as friends, but for now, that's it. Friends. I need time.' It's not that I don't want it, us, I mean. But it's too rash to make the decision now.

Luke and I have another drink. I tell him about my bucket list, that I have a new hobby, that I've finally watched the ten cult films he was always raving about. To which he laughs and says there's a lot more than ten cult movies and we agree to maybe watch one together next week.

'Oh, and Seffy?'

'Yes?'

'Did you message me a couple of months ago?'

'No, why?' Fuckkkkk.

'I got a notification from you on my phone but when I clicked on it, there was nothing.'

'Hmmm, weird. Not me. Maybe a ghost of the past.' I wave my hands in the air all woozy, trying to make light of what could have been a highly embarrassing situation.

'Maybe,' he replies in that all-knowing way which means he knows I'm lying.

And then we leave each other.

A simple goodbye hug, but it means so much. It's been so long, so much heartache and all we needed to do was talk.

I've realised that I remembered my time with Luke all wrong. The soft, caring man I fell in love with got replaced with a monster I created in my mind as soon as I realised that having a baby may not be as easy as I'd like. The anger I had growing up, towards my father, my mother, everything, was all pushed on Luke in a mission to make something, someone, to blame when there really was nothing I could do about it.

#29 Realise that your sabbatical did work, and you've managed to reconnect with your mind and body in such a way that maybe you can even reverse time and fall back in love with all that was lost

Ten Months No Baby

Dear whoever is listening, whoever has a heart, whoever has a fucking soul,

I thought last month was bad. I thought that the IVF treatment failing would be the worst thing that ever happened to me. I'm not someone that cries over spilt milk. I'm strong. I'm brave I know that. I've been through my parents' divorce, my dad's affair, my mum's alcohol addiction. I've lost my childhood, I've lost friends, I've lost both my parents through different vices – women and drink.

But out of everything, this is worse. Oh, it's so much worse. I feel as though everything I've ever worked for was for nothing. Everything that I dreamt of, everything that kept me going, like that pot of gold at the end of the rainbow has been set alight and now I'm just standing here, watching it burn.

Harry keeps asking me out for drinks, but I keep declining. I can't even face talking to my best friend right now.

Considering a couple of months ago we were both getting bored of having sex, now I can't remember the last time we had it. I feel disconnected from Luke, but I don't even yearn for the connection. It's not his fault, it's totally and utterly mine, but I hate him. Everything about him is grating on me. The way he takes that piece too much duvet, the way he leaves his toothbrush in the shower caddy and doesn't put it back by the sink, the way he doesn't screw the lid on the milk tight enough. They are small, mundane, pointless things. The things that you let slide when you're married because the insurmountable love you have for one another masks it. But when that love starts to fade, cracks start to appear, and someone decides to rip away the masks.

I don't know why my love has faded for him. He's done nothing but be supportive, but I feel that our marriage is broken. Maybe I'm so scared that he'll hate me, I'm trying to make sure I hate him first.

The days of La Perla lingerie in all the colours of a seductive rainbow are even further than a distant memory. We sleep on opposite sides of the bed and don't meet in the middle for a cuddle. We turn off the lights, lie down and turn over. Luke's snoring irritates me. It stops me from sleeping, that mixed in with the nightmares of the needles, x-rays and phallic metal objects being reluctantly albeit consensually shoved up me from all angles.

It's a horror film and I'm the main character. It's like that dream where you're being chased but you trip, and you're stuck there for eternity.

After the first round of failed IVF, I was distraught. A mess. Luke tried to console me, be the supportive husband but I couldn't breathe for drowning in my own tears. Everything he said was wrong. Why would it work again? How can it be ok? Why would everything turn out well in the end?

I decided not to go with the removal of my tubes and opt for a second round, when again I went through rigorous testing, injections in an arse I used to be proud of but now I feel ashamed of because of the bruising. Doctors measuring my temperature, assessing my egg count, monitoring my bloods while Luke got given a cup, a poorly acted out porn shoot and fifteen minutes of relaxation. He was done in ten. Probably less. He was obviously gagging for the release I no longer give him.

That riled me. He held my hand after the appointment, kissed me and said everything will be ok. I rested my head on his shoulder because I knew it was the right thing to do but I felt angry. Annoyed at everything fuckable apart from me.

We waited again for the all-important call that the egg was ready for reimplantation and then another two weeks of me encasing myself in cotton wool. Nervous to do anything in case it dislodged the egg. Worried that any stress would stress the egg out of my womb. I worked from home for two weeks, although my physical distance from the office didn't prevent Moira from making my once wonderful, joyous home feel as miserable and grey as Canary Wharf. I liked my job but now it feels like an extra thing I must do, something which makes my temperature rise and anxiety riddle my thoughts.

And then it came, the day of the test. I wanted to feel close to Luke again, so I asked him to come into the bathroom with me. To read the results for us both.

There's nothing I want more than for everything to go back to normal, to before we started trying for a baby. Sometimes I wish I hadn't been so impatient and then we could have had a few more years of loving one another.

Pinggggggg

'That's the timer, it's been three minutes. What does it say?' My words uttered in the same rhythm as my heartbeat.

I can tell Luke's nervous; his hands are clammy, shaking as he picks up the test with one hand and holds mine in the other. My eyes are shut. I've still got my knickers round my ankles. It's about as provocative as a nun in a convent.

He takes a deep breath and then stays silent.

I open my eyes.

'What does it say?' Urgency makes the words strain out of my mouth. Begging this nightmare to leave us alone. Let us be happy, please let us be fucking happy.

'I'm so sorry, darling.' I can see tears forming in his eyes. He kneels down and rests his head on my knees. 'I'm so sorry.'

'What does it say!' I know, of course I know, but I need to see the words to be sure.

Luke passes me the stick. The fucking stick that's supposed to bring joy to couples around the world but in my house is cursed.

Not pregnant.

The words ring in my ears. Not pregnant. Not pregnant. NOT PREGNANT.

I punch myself in the stomach.

'You're fucking useless. USELESS!' I screech. I start pummelling with both fists, tears streaming.

Luke grabs my wrists.

'Hey! Hey! Calm down, darling, you need to calm down.'

'Calm down? CALM DOWN? I'm a fucking failure. I'm a fraud. Nothing works. Naturally, unnaturally. I'm a failure.'

'It's a lot to take in, I know it is.' I can see that Luke is trying to stay calm, allowing me to be angry. 'We need to take a break, ok? Maybe we can go on a little holiday somewhere to take our mind off everything that's happened. It's been a long year. Come on, let me put you to bed and I'll make you a tea. Let's watch something super trashy, what's that shit show you like? Real Housewives *or something? Come on, darling. I love you.' He brings me to my feet, pulling my knickers up, escorting me to our room.*

There's nothing for me to say. To Luke, to anyone.

When people go through a major life event, what's the first thing they do? Post it on social media. I don't know why we do it. To tell everyone in one swoop? To boast? For congratulations? To share happiness? For consolation? Because it's not just happy things that people share on social media, it's sad things too. When someone dies, there's often an extremely thoughtful, emotional post to accompany it. Why do we do it? Do we get something out of it? Is it just easier to tell people without really telling anyone?

Because I don't want to tell anyone. I feel embarrassed. Ashamed.

If I scroll through my social media profiles, my life looks perfect. I have friends, a spectacular wedding, a loving husband. I go to fancy bars and restaurants, I have the 'it' handbag, I get my highlights done every six weeks. The sordid news of my infertility wouldn't fit in with my feed. I'm sure people would console me, share their own stories of the struggles of conception through a friend of a friend of a friend, they would try and lift me up. But I don't want that. I don't want anyone to know. The girl from the fairy tale has somehow got mixed up in the wrong narrative and she's now living out a psychological horror.

I can't look on social media anymore, the announcements, the positivity. Scrolling aimlessly through brunches and beaches to suddenly have a child's smiling face come a cropper. It's a stab in the heart. The family holiday snaps, the cute dress-up, the funny videos. I can't. Instead, I sit and stare into space thinking about what's happened and what's going to become of me.

I don't even know how I feel anymore. I'm still Seffy, I have a husband, a nice flat, a good job, friends – nothing, on the surface, is wrong with me. Yet I feel like I'm dying. Part of me has already died. What do I do? Do I persevere with the ongoing anxiety, the needles, the heartache? Or do I accept who I am, what's happened and try to adjust? Can you ever accept the news of infertility? Does it ever get better? I'll be reminded of it every day. Every mother and child, every advert on television, every lost tiny shoe helpfully left on someone's wall on the high street.

People will continue to ask me when I'm having kids until I tell them that I can't. Then they'll ask why. And even when all my family and friends are aware of my non-functioning womb, there'll be the strangers, the friends of friends, work colleagues. The 'have you got children?' comment. The wise, knowing laugh when you reply 'No,' and they respond, 'Good answer, my two little swines drive me wild', as they sip their wine, none the wiser.

It will haunt me forever.

Luke's trying to be sympathetic, be extra nice but it niggles me. He's acting like I've found out some terrible news and it doesn't really affect him. Like my mum's died – he's never really liked her. My infertility doesn't mean I can't have children, it means WE can't have children.

'Darling, I was thinking we could get away for a bit, you know, have a break from it all.'

'It's hard to have a break when it's all you think about,' I say, gormlessly staring at the television.

'That's why we need a break, a fresh start, you know, before we try again.'

I avert my eyes from the screen and look him straight in his. I haven't looked at him, really looked at him for months. I used to think of his eyes as autumnal conkers, deep, chestnut brown. Now they are simply brown.

'A break? Fresh start? What do you think this is, Luke? I am INFERTILE. I can't have babies naturally and it doesn't seem like I can have them through IVF either. That means that none of my genetic material will ever make it into another being.'

He swallows, trying to smile.

'I know it feels like the end of the world now, darling, but it will all work out in the end, it always does.'

'When are you going to get it into your thick skull, Luke? It won't work out, it's the end. There is no natural conception for us. Finito. It's not going to work out how I want it to. There is no silver lining, no happy ending – nothing.' Hate me, hate me. Come on, I know you want to.

Still trying to remain calm, he replies, 'But we can always try again. Maybe we need to relax more. There are more rounds of IVF, even adoption, surrogacy. We can afford it, we're fortunate.'

'Try again? Fortunate? FUCKING FORTUNATE? What? More needles, more tests? It's ok for you. Trying is pretty relaxing. Having a wank in a cup while watching porn isn't exactly an arduous task. It's not working for me. It's hard, it's making me anxious, upset, it's painful, horrifically painful. I don't want to adopt or have someone else carry my baby – I want a normal baby, a normal pregnancy like everyone else. Why can't I have the one thing I want? Why is everything out to get me?'

'So that's it, you're giving up now, are you?' His voice rises. 'On our future?' He's starting to get annoyed with me, I can sense it.

'Giving up?' The words tremble as they hit the air. 'I've been trying EVERYTHING for nearly a year, over a year. EVERYTHING.' I bellow the word, it rings round the room, bouncing off the vases. 'Do you know what it's like to go through rounds of IVF? No. You know absolutely nothing. You haven't cared about having a baby since the beginning. It doesn't bother you because you're fine. Well, it's your problem just as much as it's mine, so let that sink in. You're infertile. How do you feel?'

'But I'm not.'

'Don't be so indignant, Luke. Allow me to be upset, allow me to be angry. You can't fix it, you can't fix me, you have to live with it. We can't have children. WE CAN'T. Not me, US.'

'I know you'll want to try again, you're desperate for children, and I do want them too, I was just trying to be relaxed about it.' He pauses. 'You need to stop shutting me out all the time. It's not all on you, it's on us. You didn't

tell me about the miscarriage, you're saying it's US when it suits you and just you when it doesn't. Make up your mind.'

'Well, it's too late to be relaxed. Yes, I fucking want children, I've always wanted them but now I can't have them so allow me to be upset. Imagine if you were in my shoes and how you'd feel, then maybe you would show me some fucking compassion.'

There we go, my life has become a disaster. I've gone from being admirable to having the least desirable life on earth. Thanks a fucking bunch.

Seffy.

Three Months Until Thirty

31

Luke sent me a message after we met.

I finally unblocked him.

Thanks for agreeing to meet up Seffy. It's been so long. It really is true that you don't know how much you miss something until it's gone. Take care x

There're still no emojis but he did add a kiss. I do miss him; I know I do.

What are you supposed to do when your ex-husband comes back into the frame declaring his love for you? You don't go for a drink with them as a divorcee and come back in a relationship, it's just not normal.

Harry: *So . . . you met Luke . . . what HAPPENED?! What did he SAY?*

Harry: **Voice note left in a growl* Tell meeeeeeeeee . . .*

Me: *He said . . .*

Harry: *What?!*

Me: *Basically, he said he still loved me. And he's sorry.*

Harry: *Sorry for leaving you when you were DIS-TRAUGHT?!*

Me: *Well, like I said in Thailand it was actually my fault.*

Harry: *I mean you basically left your best friend to drown when she was going through one of the hardest periods of her life so I know you can be a bitch.*

Me: **Typing* pause. *Typing**

Harry: *JOKING SEFFY. But you were a bitch. You'll be owing me turbo coronas for eternity.*

Me: *I know, I'm sorry.*

Harry: *I was a bitch too, but you're never wrong, so I do need to revel in your slight comeuppance.*

Harry: *Whatever you decide I think you should at least have sex one more time. Break-up sex is the best. Like I said that time with Rolo . . .*

Me: *STOP!*

Me: *We're already divorced so it would be more like rebound sex.*

Harry: *I mean divorce/rebound sex sounds cosmic to me. Anyway, I know you still love him.*

Me: *Ha. How's that then Mystic Meg?*

Harry: *Do you want me to list the reasons?*

Me: *Go on then . . . you know I love a list ;p*

Harry: *You admitted (finally admitted I might add) that you were a bitch to him, you were upset when you found out he was dating someone else, you still wear the gold bracelet he bought you which you said you were going to sell and buy something he hated, you met up with him again.*

Harry: *And . . .*

Harry: *You two were great together, before all this shit started. It wasn't falling out of love. It was circumstantial. And if you don't at least meet him again, I might start dating him to make you jealous. Now THAT would be fucked up.*

It's not that I don't care for Luke, love him even, I do. But it's been so long, so much has happened, so much has changed. I'm fearful to open that storybook again because I've read it once, I feel like I already know how it ends. What if that book really has no happy ending? But Luke, who knows the knotty, broken state of my fallopian tubes, doesn't seem to care. Kind of like all the people I met on my travels. All those things that defined me for so long don't seem to hold as much weight anymore.

I am more.

I don't know why it took a seven-month trip to Asia, a fight with my best friend, a few days back at work with my nightmare of a boss and a weird reunion with my ex-husband but it has. It's crazy what can be the turning point. I must be thankful to Luke because I think that was the final conversation I needed. The final truth.

Him telling me he wants me back doesn't make dealing with my infertility any easier; it purely makes me realise that it doesn't have to feel like a terminal illness for me. It can be something that I live with, it doesn't need to stop my life, prevent me from living.

Luke knows everything about my journey with infertility, what I wanted, how it hit me, how it made me act, yet he still sees something in me. Being physically pregnant with my own child will be something I, sadly, will never experience. But that doesn't stop me being intelligent, having a great career, thoughtful, generous, determined, anally organised. My infertility doesn't have to change who I am, it doesn't stop me from being any of those things. It did for a while. But however much I wish, more than anything, that my fallopian tubes were as healthy as the virgin Mary's and I wish that it hadn't been me sitting in that room when Dr Cartwright uttered those fateful words, it doesn't have to change my personality, my irritating traits or my fun-loving ones. I don't need a cure. It doesn't need to change all the reasons that people fell in love with me in the first place. I only found out about the state of my tubes nearly two years ago, and it didn't affect any of those things before, so why should it now?

I'm still not a hundred per cent ready to go down to the adoption centre and sign my name on the dotted line but I'm more open to it. That will take time. All the people I've met, those with children, those without, those who had successful IVF, natural conception or even abortions – the steps to procreation are never simple. It's never easy. Not for anyone. Your problems are unique to you. I don't need to compare mine to someone else and feel like mine are worse or I'm stupid for feeling a certain way – everyone's different.

Every day is a bucket list. I'm going to try and not be so rigid, be more spontaneous. I don't think the life I want will abide by society's plan. I don't want to conform; I enjoyed finding parts of me that didn't exist when I was travelling. I want to find out who that Seffy is. Maybe I am supposed to be someone who lives life by lists and plans, or maybe I'm supposed to be all fancy-footed and carefree, like I was when I was a child, before I had to take everyone under my wing.

I should talk to my mum, see what she thinks about it all. We're similar in more ways than I thought. I also had some bad news and went on a self-destructive spiral – who am I to judge anyone?

I don't need to keep my guard up anymore, I'm an adult too. I'm nearly thirty for fuck's sake.

Me: *I hope the wedding went well Mum – the pictures look gorgeous! I'm back in the UK, would love to take you for a celebratory lunch. I've been meaning to tell you something, I don't know why I never told you, I think I felt ashamed. Part of me never wanted to tell you because I always wanted to be this perfect child, perfect specimen of what I thought a woman should be. It was stupid. Luke and I got divorced because I'm infertile, and I didn't know how to deal with it. I don't want to chicken out and not tell you in person, so there I've said it. I will explain. I'm sorry. Love you xxx*

Mum: *[Typing] . . . [typing] . . .*

Me: *[Typing]* . . .
Mum: *Oh darling. I'm so sorry. I wish I'd known. I'm packing a bag as we speak.*

'Darling, oh darling.' My mum rushes through the door with an overnight bag, a bottle of Shloer, chocolates and a pizza on order.

She embraces me, tight. She smells of Chanel No.5 and washing powder. Clean, fresh, like I always thought a mother should. Stroking my hair, wiping my tears, kissing my face.

'Mum, I'm . . . Mum, I'm so sorry . . .' I choke out.

'What for, darling?' She stands back, holding my head between her palms, like she'll never let me go.

'For missing the wedding, for not telling you about the infertility, for . . .'

'Darling, it's ok. It's all going to be ok.'

We sit cuddling on the sofa for a while, with two glasses of red grape Shloer, waiting for our pizza.

'I know we've not always seen eye-to-eye,' Mum says, sipping her drink. 'I was an awful mother. I feel like I mentally abandoned you for so long. You were so strong, looking after Chris and Justin when you were only really a baby yourself. I don't know what happened. I never thought I'd become addicted to alcohol; I really never did.' She looks me in the eye, piercing, meaningful. 'After your father had the affair, I used the bottle as a release, a way to relax me to sleep but it got worse and worse, and I didn't know how to be me without it. I never told you, but your granny, she drank.' She sniffs, thinking about it. 'You know, Seraphina, my princess, you're so strong, much stronger than you think. People might say it should be the other way round, but I idolise you. Everything you've achieved, you're special. Oh, so special.'

'I'm not, Mum, I'm really not. It was so childish of me to miss your wedding. I guess I was worried that it was all happening so quickly and that it could end in, you know, you drinking again.' I swallow. 'And sometimes I just feel so annoyed at the world. I felt like I wanted to have a few months travelling, being free, doing my own thing for once. I was selfish and I'm sorry.'

'Honestly, darling. You don't need to be sorry. I understand. I wish, beyond anything that I could make up those lost years to you. We're more alike than you think – I thought the best thing, for the most part, was to leave you to your own devices. I thought you were happy with Luke. I don't know why but it felt easy to patch things up with Chris and Justin, maybe because they were so young, but with you, it felt different.'

'All I ever needed was my mum.' I whisper the words because they feel so important to me.

'And all I ever needed was you. My daughter, my strong as an ox little girl.'

'What do I do, Mum? I'm infertile. I really want my own children, but I don't know if I ever will be able to have them. And Luke. I—he, messaged me and we met up and he said he still loves me.'

'You know, being a mother, a parent, means so many things. I had you naturally, but I was in fact the worst mother imaginable. I wasn't there for you when you needed me. You were a mother as well as a sister to Chris and Justin. If what you want so desperately is a family, you will have that, and they will mean just as much to you as you do to me and maybe it will be the best thing that's ever happened to you. Life does have a funny way of working sometimes.'

'And Luke? What shall I do about him?'

'You have to do what you think is right, darling. Do you still love him? I can't tell you what to do because I was always taught never to judge someone else's relationship from the outside – you really can never know how the other person is feeling.'

'I think I do love him, but I'm scared. Really scared. I feel embarrassed going back on something, like a divorce that's so final.'

'Don't let fear get in the way of your true emotions. Everyone makes mistakes. Even your father.'

Maybe Mum's right. Motherhood is a rich tapestry of emotions, acts, people – all the things that shape you into the person you are, that keep you growing through grit, determination, passion, love – it's so deep, so powerful, so embedded in our core that it cannot be defined as sperm meets egg, naturally, in a womb and a child is born. Maybe, in some ways, I've been a mother my whole life.

Eleven Months No Baby

Dear no one,

Clearly there's no one watching over me – Aphrodite, Venus, Elpis – where the fuck are you? I'm the project of your dreams. I'm in need of it all – sex, love, beauty, fertility, romance. Instead, I've been watching the world go by like tumbleweed. And NOW, there's not even tumbleweed to roll by because there is literally nothing left.

There was a lot I wanted to say to Luke, the main thing being that I'm sorry. Apologise for the state of my genes, for having such a fucked-up childhood, for pushing him away, that I still loved him. That I just feel so confused and torn with everything. Scared of our future, what will happen, scared of being a failure, scared of being like my mother, that I'm sorry for not telling him about the miscarriage.

But in the end, as usual, I hid my fear, my softer side, my need to be wanted and cared for and walked away.

The irony being that I so desperately seek something to nurture and grow, but in reality, I'm still searching for someone to mother me.

I know I still love Luke. It's hard to stop loving someone but so much has happened, so much has changed. The love might still be there, but where's the passion? We used to be aligned, want the same things, have the same future. Now we can't possibly so I know the love will fade away eventually.

I don't want Luke to leave me for someone else, after our tenth round of IVF, making me feel more broken, less desirable. Like my dad did to my mum. So, it's for the best that this has happened. That I made the decision before anyone else could. He was going to end up hating me anyway, so it's better, much better that I decided to hate him first.

I knew after that argument we were over. Sometimes I wonder if I knew months ago. Maybe it wouldn't have mattered if Luke was the most perfect man to ever walk this earth. After that meeting with Dr Cartwright, maybe everything was destined to fail.

He'll find someone else, move on, get married, have babies, naturally. Be happy and thankful that we didn't work out.

What I will do though, that's still up for discussion.

I need to hunt out someone who is happy to live their life childless. I'm sure there are benefits to not having children, but I'm not aware of them yet.

I haven't even told my mum. Not about the break-up, not about the infertility. The only person that knows is Harry.

Maybe Luke was right, maybe I am obsessed with being pregnant. I don't know if infertility is one of those things that gets better with time because I haven't had enough of it yet.

This was our last conversation. The last one where things could have taken a different path. From now on, I guess we'll speak through the medium of email and lawyers.

'*Come on, Seffy, you have to come out of this hole at some point. It's hard for me too, I hate seeing you like this,*' *Luke says to me as, again, I sit gormlessly watching TV. Still working from home. No shower, greasy hair, another takeaway. I don't look myself; I don't behave like myself; I don't feel myself.*

'*It's not a hole, Luke.*' *I hiss the words. '*I'm depressed; my whole life has fallen apart around me.*' He simply doesn't get it. Ignorant male. I think. I don't even know why but I'm starting to blame everything, hate everyone.*

'*I know it seems the end of the world right now, but it really isn't. We still have each other.*' *He says the words, but I know he doesn't mean them. He's bored of this now. Bored of me. Bored of the depression, lack of sex, lack of cooking and cleaning. He wants his perfectly preened 1950s house-wife back who gives blowjobs on demand.*

'We have each other for now but when you come to the realisation that there really is no light at the end of the tunnel, you'll run faster than you can imagine. What's your mum going to say? She won't want you to stay married to me, no one will.'

'It's not all about having children, Seffy. I married you before children, I wanted to be with you. Not the future children we don't yet have.'

'So, you don't want them then?' I knew it. I knew he didn't care.

'Of course I do.' He takes my hand in his.

'What are you going to do then? I can't have them. You'll have an affair with some busty fertile blonde who sends your sperm into a procreation oblivion.'

'Seffy, whatever I say is wrong. It's like you actively want me to hate you. I want children, I don't want them. I don't know what to say anymore. I feel like I don't know you. Ever since that first month we were trying for a baby we've been distant. I'm sure if we ended up not having children it would be different, not what I had planned, what you had planned, but I'm sure we could deal with it.'

'So, you'd spend the rest of your life just dealing with me?'

'That's not what I'm saying.' I can sense the frustration. 'You're twisting everything. Admit it, you became obsessed with getting pregnant, even to the point of going a little crazy. I was and am a pawn in your journey to having a baby. It's what you want, when you want it, how you want it and if I don't oblige then somehow, I'm being difficult. All I ever wanted is you, everything else is background noise but you're not happy with how I feel.'

'I'm not crazy, Luke. Don't you know the first rule? Don't call a "crazy" person crazy. So what if I am obsessed with getting pregnant. You don't understand me.' I can feel that familiar rage bubbling.

'Yes, you're right, at this point I don't understand you – fake antenatal classes, ovulation ceremonies, hiding a miscarriage. This isn't you. Every time I question any of this behaviour, you lash out at me and now I feel just as lost as you.' His eyes glare; they're not even brown anymore, just black holes of empty darkness. 'You never even let me grieve for the loss of our child. You just told me, mixed in with other things and I was just supposed to get on with it. What's happened, don't you love me anymore?'

'Mixed in with OTHER things? You make it sound like baking a cake. Those OTHER things were my infertility diagnosis.' Everything is so bitter between us. I can't acknowledge his statement about loving him because I don't even know what love is.

'You don't think I care. That was my child too, Seffy. Just because it wasn't my body doesn't mean that I feel any less attached to it. We're both grieving and it's pushing us apart.'

'But it's not your diagnosis, it's mine. I've thought about having a family my entire life and now my dream's been crushed. No one else's dream, mine.' My emotions are whirling round my brain – anger, upset, jealousy. I don't even know who or what they're aimed at anymore.

'I think you need help – we both do. At dealing with this situation before it gets out of control.'

'I don't need anyone, Luke, I just need time by myself to work through it.'

'But the problem won't go away, it never will. It will always be the elephant in the room. You'll always think I have a problem with you because we can't have a baby.'

'Do you have a problem?'

'No.'

'It will always be an obstacle but that's what you've signed up for.'

'No, I didn't sign up for this. Neither of us did. You need to get out of this mindset that being pregnant and having children is how you'll make amends for your past.'

'What do you mean?' I say curtly.

'I know you want to have children to prove something. To prove that you'll be a better mother than your own, to give them the childhood you dreamed of. It's admirable, wonderful, but you don't need to prove anything. You're your own person, Seffy.'

You're right. Annoyingly. There are a lot of things I've never come to terms with. This is the icing on the cake.

'You're telling me that in ten years when we go to christenings, birthday parties and all of our friends' children are running around, you won't feel something, have regrets about us, our life?'

'I don't think it will come to that.'

'We are there, Luke! That is our life! Can't you see? You don't understand the life you've signed up for, that's why you don't understand me.'

'Right, Seffy, this has to stop. All of it has to stop. It's ruining us. I'm going to go to my mum's for a few days and then I think we should go away for a weekend, relax, talk and make a plan, ok?'

'It's already done.'

'What do you mean, "it's done"?' He juts his chin out in that infuriating way he does when he's annoyed and confused at the same time.

'I mean, I can't do this.' I hesitate ever so briefly, not enough time to think even though that's what the situation warrants. 'I want a divorce.'

And that's how it happens. It doesn't have to be adultery or fighting, it can just be two people with different genetics. One person who's had enough and knows the end will be inevitable at some point – why not cut the cord before it becomes too painful?

It's just a word. Divorce. It's just a word. I said it but I could have come back from it. I could have said it was just an 'in the moment' thing. I didn't mean it. I'm not myself. I'm upset. Luke was right, we should have gone on a break. He was still willing to make it work; give our family another go. But I didn't. I chose to act upon my word.

And now I'm back to square one. Before we tried for a baby. Before the wedding. Before we met. Sitting on my bed, alone. Waiting for my period to start. Waiting for the cycle to begin again.

Waiting. To see if I can come to terms with everything I've lost.

Seffy.

Thirty, finally

32

People always say that therapy makes you see clearly again. They're right. It's like I've been walking round with my head stuck in a fish tank with algae and water scum smeared all over the sides.

So, this happened.

I look at the piece of paper on the desk in front of me, folded in three. I take it in my right hand, trembling slightly, stand and use my left hand to adjust my pencil skirt.

I do the walk across the bumpy, grey carpet tiles and knock on the outside of the cage, hoping the brute stays chained, muzzled too.

Nothing. I'd say she's been tranquillised, but I can see and hear the clack of her claws furiously typing.

Knock, knock.

'Can't you see I'm busy?' Moira snaps, eyes fixed on the screen. 'Email like a normal person – it's less invasive.'

I'd like to disagree – receiving ten curt emails in capitals interferes with my day much more. I wouldn't normally, but . . .

'I only sit a few metres from your desk. A few years ago people didn't have emails or mobiles, it must have made work much more enjoyable. You know work when at work, live while you're at home.' I tilt my head to the left and smile.

Moira stops typing and looks up from her desk; someone's unbuckled her muzzle.

'You've not gone nuts on me again have you, Seff? I only said yes to that HIGHLY RIDICULOUS sabbatical of yours to stop you having a mental breakdown – you know most people wouldn't have had a desk to come back to.' Her eyes bulge slightly and flick back to her screen.

'It's a real shame; sabbaticals would probably do a lot of people the world of good.'

'Spit it out, whatever you need. I'm busy, really fucking busy and I don't have time for silly mind games.'

I take a deep breath and momentarily close my eyes.

'I'm sorry to have to do this to you, Moira, but I'm resigning.' I reveal the folded piece of paper in my hand.

I wait for the barrage of abuse, hoping those chains are strong. I hold my breath.

She looks at me for a mere second.

'I don't have time for this crap. That's for HR, thanks for your time.' She waves her hand to gesture me to leave the office. I see her look back at her screen but there's something off about her eyes.

'You know there's more to life than work and being mean to people.' I pause because I don't know what makes Moira so difficult. What's going on behind the glare and the words. 'If you ever want to go for a drink, it would be nice to get to know you on a deeper level than your Linked-In bio.'

Not long after I've been to HR, a security man, dressed in a smart black suit and tie, appears behind my desk.

'Sorry, ma'am, you need to pack your things, hand in your pass and leave.'

'I'm all packed.' I point to the box on my desk. 'But I just need a minute if that's ok?'

'Your access to the system has already been revoked,' the security man says, slightly smirking, as if I needed thirty minutes to download all the top-secret figures and client names.

'I know. I've worked here for seven years; I just need a minute.'

The man stays standing behind me, but I assume his lack of response means I'm allowed to sit here for a couple more minutes.

It's the good thing about working in a bank; when you resign, you must leave immediately. But I get a solid three months of full pay which is perfect. They call it gardening leave. I guess some of my green-fingered colleagues would be using the time to relax, trim their bushes and spawn some seeds but I won't be taking up a horticultural pastime.

I've realised what I'm missing in my life is balance. I loved my job, kind of, but Moira, she isn't the boss for me. I don't want to work till 10.00 every night to get a promotion; there's more to life.

I like routine, structure, but before I left I felt rootless. I loved travelling around, meeting people, but that's also not made for me. I feel like I understand what life's about now. I have roots. I want a sense of community, a role in life, I want to give back because that makes me feel good. Why can't I have all of that in a job too?

I'm using my gardening leave to find a new career; I still want to work in finance but maybe for a sustainable bank or a charity. I'm excited about this new chapter.

'Harry . . .' I say tenderly. 'You know I hate surprises.' I'm blindfolded because Harry likes to make everything dramatic. Her hand is clammy from excitement.

'That's something boring people say, and I know you're not boring.' She squeezes my hand tight. 'Oh my God, I'm so excited! I've always wanted to plan something for someone. You're thirty, bloody thirty, Seffy, how cool is that?'

It's a strange sensation walking with a blindfold on, putting all your trust into someone, but Harry's right, I am enjoying it. Someone has planned something for me, and I don't feel on edge about it or that I need to take the reins, be an over-bearing micro-manager; I'm relishing in it.

'I know, thirty, ey. Who would have thought it?' I stop walking.

'Come onnnnnn.' Harry pulls at my hand. 'What are you doing?'

'Can we pause for a second?'

Harry sighs exasperatedly. 'What? You can't look at the scenery because it's a surprise and you're blindfolded.'

'Thank you, Sherlock.' I snigger. 'Before I get too drunk or whatever, I just want to say thank you. You really are so special to me, Harry, a true best friend. I wouldn't be here if it weren't for you. Everything good that's happened to me in the last year has been down to you pushing me – you really are one in a million and don't let anyone tell you otherwise. My only wish is that I can be just as good a friend to you.'

Harry pulls me in and kisses me on the face.

'I love you, Seffy. And you're right, my thirtieth better be a fucking baller, I'm telling you.' And she laughs, sprinkling the earth with her sunshine.

We walk for a couple more minutes.

'Ok, ready?' Harry asks me and I can feel her pushing a door open.

'Ready,' I reply back.

'Now,' Harry whispers.

I remove my blindfold.

'SURPRIIIIISE!' everyone shrieks in front of me, pulling party poppers.

I look around. It's The Flying Elephant bar, designed by Diya Preet, reminding me of the festival in Jaipur with Belle. I told Luke I wanted to come here a few weeks back. All my friends, here for me.

'My photos!' I exclaim, looking at three boards filled with snaps from my travels.

'It was Luke's idea, he helped me with the organising,' Harry says in my ear as I see him standing at the front of the crowd, smiling, his love for me spread across his gorgeous face, his eyes like deep, chestnut conkers again. 'And your mum. Just wait till you see the photos she found of you. I'd say somewhere between the Michelin man and Wednesday from the Addams family.'

'I had a very desirable look, I'm telling you.' I nudge her jovially.

Luke comes over and kisses me gently on the cheek.

'Happy birthday, darling.' I kiss him back. 'You look so beautiful. If only I could still call you my wife.'

'It's all just titles – maybe we can go to the hotel in Jaipur second time round.' I grin.

'No, you've already been there. Let's write a new story.' He kisses me again.

'I can't believe you printed all my photos!' I say to him, walking over to have a closer look.

'I wanted to, it's part of your journey to thirty and they're really good.'

'I mean, they're not that good.' I laugh, looking at the blur from the lens on one of the photos. 'But I like them. It's nice having a hobby; it gives me something to focus on.'

'I can't wait to see the pictures from Route 66.'

'Route 66?' I question him.

'It was always your dream, wasn't it? To drive around America with nothing but a camera and good conversation.' His eyes flash with excitement as he hands me an envelope. 'Happy birthday, Seffy. We fly tomorrow. I thought it would be a nice trip before your new job starts. And . . .' He pauses. 'It takes us through Vegas . . . . so.' He winks as I narrow my eyes.

'Luke!' I grab his cheeks and kiss him, hard. It's passionate, without seduction, it's everything, it's the old us. 'Thank you, thank you, thank you!'

We tried to take things slow, Luke and I, after our first meeting but the feelings were too strong. There was too much history to pretend we barely knew each other or to simply be friends. Part of me is scared that something might go wrong again but I can't live in fear or not follow my dreams on the off chance. No one's judging me for getting back with Luke; I think everyone's keen for the Coates wedding round two.

Luke leaves me to catch up with everyone else.

'Mum! The photos, where did you find them?' I laugh, hugging her.

'How could I have got rid of them? You looked just like me when you were younger.' I see a tear forming in her right eye.

'What's wrong, Mum?'

'My princess, darling baby girl. Thirty! Who would have thought that I'd have a thirty-year-old daughter? You're so grown-up and I'm so proud of you.'

'Age, it's just a number, Mum.' I grin back. 'I'm so glad that you're here, it wouldn't be a party without you.'

'I made you a cake too – lemon drizzle, your favourite. At least, it used to be.'

We have these occasional awkward moments because you can't go back to the past, but you can at least try and make up for lost time.

'I still love it.'

'There's someone else here to see you too.' Mum points to her left, beckoning him over.

My father.

I messaged him after the first conversation with Mum. I realised everyone makes mistakes in life and you can't hang it over them for eternity. I'd like to have my dad walk me down the aisle second time round, do everything properly for the right reasons.

We met and went for a drink in my local pub a couple of weeks ago. He had the same eyes as I've seen in photos, crinkling when he smiles, showing the creases on his face, but he looks older, much older. Time hasn't been as kind to him as it has to my mother.

We're trying to start again. We share the same humour and a love for organisation. I never realised he was as regimented as me but why would I? He told me he'd come to my birthday, but I never imagined him actually being here.

My mother and my father and me, all in the same room. Happy.

Harry bustles in front of me.

'Here, open this.' It's a card and inside in her scratchy scrawl, identical to Quentin Blake's drawings, is my bucket list.

#1 Read ten good books

#2 Watch ten cult movies

#3 Eat in front of someone and be filmed

#4 Go on a seven-month sabbatical

#5 Be spontaneous EVERY DAY

#6 Sleep with random men and DON'T WORRY ABOUT ANYTHING OTHER THAN STIS!!!!!!!

#7 Seffy's version of the mile-high club

#8 Stop restricting myself with my own sexuality

#9 Get a tattoo while drunk and abroad

#10 Attend a self-defence class and for apparently no reason, verbally abuse a mother of two

#11 Skinny dipping with friends on a public beach in BROAD DAYLIGHT

#12 Find yourself with Buddha

#13 Stop feeling guilty and be grateful

#14 Start a hobby – I think mine's photography?

#15 Ride an elephant (with non-blood child)

#16 Dance and don't be afraid to be part of something

#17 Embrace your own life through learning from others

#18 Clear out digital wardrobe through major social media detox

#19 Get high with strangers – mushrooms at the Mahal

#20 Eat crickets for a midnight snack

#21 Get kicked out of a live sex show while sticking up for women's rights

#22 Be footloose and fancy-free at a full-moon party

#23 Act out a scene from *The Beach* with my very own Leonardo DiCaprio

#24 Help build a school in Thailand – me, the girl who NEVER gets her hands dirty

#25 Teach English in an orphanage and cook and clean and play

#26 Stop thinking about myself

#27 Realise there's more to life than an endless strive to perfection

#28 Experience your biggest fear first-hand, come to terms with it, get over it and learn from it

#29 Realise that your sabbatical did work, and you've managed to reconnect with your mind and body in such a way that maybe you can even reverse time and fall back in love with all that was lost

#30 . . .

'Number thirty, it's blank. I should have finished it.' I suddenly feel disappointed at my inability to complete a task – you can try but you really can't change genetics; part of me will always love a list. But with all the recent changes in my life, I kind of forgot about my bucket list.

'I know.' Her face morphs into that mischievous grin.

'What now? Not more croissant fetishes?'

'Not quite.' She hands me a microphone.

'Harry, noooo,' I beg.

'Sing in front of a crowd. It was on your original bucket list – so here you go, your wish is my command, Aladdin.' She bows, turns and shouts to the crowd. 'You'd be hard pushed not to know about Seffy's bucket list but unusually she's started a list and has failed to complete it!' The crowd boo and hiss jokingly, egged on by Harry – she loves the limelight. 'Not to worry – the list will be saved! Born at 11.59 p.m. we still have a few hours to complete it, so . . . !' She waves her hands round as if she's in the circus. 'Tonight, Seffy is going to perform her inaugural performance of "Stop" by the five spiciest girls on the planet.' She pulls out a short black wig from behind her back and puts it on my head. 'Remember, you always wanted to be Posh Spice, and I was Ginger.' She puts a red wig on her own head.

The music blasts from the speakers, and Harry and I sing in unison. We know all the words and that's it, my thirty under thirty bucket list completed. It seems appropriate that I get to finish it in front of all my friends and family, the people who really got me to where I am today. A shared moment of happiness that I will treasure forever.

I take a step back from the crowd to write my final line on my bucket list:

#30 Sing in front of a crowd

I pause and add one more because, it's only true Seffy style to go above and beyond a list:

#31 Live life without a list

I look around at everyone cheering us on, joining in, dancing. I already have a family, maybe not the most conventional in the world but family all the same. I don't need to prove anything to anyone. No one loves me any less or thinks differently of me simply because my genetic make-up may not be how we all expected.

What I do know is that I have a lot of love to give, and I will eventually find the best way to share it.

Living life is all about balance. Things go wrong, things go right but in the end it's all an equilibrium. There is no 'perfect' life in terms of having it all, but you eventually find your own perfect.

I'm excited about my thirties. Ageing, I've come to realise, is a privilege. My best years are yet to come. You're supposed to live life, that's what it's here for.

Dear Seraphina,
Please find your reference from PP LEWES attached.
I wish you all the best at Louvres, although I hope you realise that there is no money in sustainable finance. The world will give up on green energy soon enough, mark my words.

I'm not happy about it but if you change your mind, you can have your director position back; we moved James over from EFX and he's only gone on a bloody sabbatical.

Regards,
Moira

Acknowledgements

I would like to thank my friends, family and the following people: Hayley Steed and Elinor Davies at Madeleine Milburn for helping make my rambles eloquent. My editors, Bea Fitzgerald and Amy Batley, for ensuring I always get the right balance between sensitivity and wit, and being a huge support to me through the writing and publishing process. Thank you to everyone who read my first novel, *Love, Loss and Little White Lies*, and spurred me on to write this one. For all your support, reviews, kind words and ideas – it makes everything worth it.

I would also like to thank all the people, friends, family, NCT class members, strangers who shared their own stories about having families and what motherhood means to them. This book would be nothing without you.

Finally, thank you to my two children Archie and Raffy, for keeping to your nap times so I can find time to write! And of course, my husband for always being by my side.